Dear Cedric...

BASED ON A TRUE STORY OF WWII

by Patricia Mashiter Cooper

Published by:

FriesenPress

Suite 300 – 852 Fort Street

Victoria, BC, Canada V8W 1H8

www.friesenpress.com

Distributed to the trade by The Ingram Book Company

Dedicated to my precious family.

Also dedicated to the memory of Audrey Joan Baker and to the memory of Richard Robertson and the millions of child casualties of World War II.

Author's Note

In 1939, when World War II broke out a massive evacuation plan sprang into action. Almost immediately 1.5 million children, including mothers and babies, and the disabled were sent to any corner of the country, or the world, where they would be safe. In the ensuing months, tens of thousands of children ranging in age from three to teens, were shipped abroad to Canada, Australia, America, South Africa. Likewise, hundreds of thousands were squirrelled away to what were considered "safe" havens within the United Kingdom. By 1940, more that 3 million children had been evacuated. This exodus was not limited to individual kiddies and their siblings but included those bastions of learning, public schools, which were uprooted and shifted lock, stock and text book to country mansions, hotels and estates that were buried deep in the countryside. Smaller preparatory schools also packed up their Beacon Readers and scurried away to find country houses large enough to accommodate their needs. In total, 827,000 children and their teachers were evacuated. For those parents who could afford it, a hundred guineas or so would buy a year of safety for their child, and peace of mind whilst they went off to defend their country.

I was one of those fortunate children, although I would question the word 'fortunate.' In 1940, when Churchill warned that the invasion of England was a possibility, my parents decided to send me away to a place where safety went hand-in-hand with a comprehensive preparatory education. With a trunk-load of clothes and the required bedding, I was (for the want of a better word) dumped into the capable hands of Miss Audrey Joan Baker, principal of Normanhurst, her private preparatory school, which she had relocated to a manor house in Shropshire, close to the Welsh border and where the war seemed a million miles away.

I was six-years-old at the time and wasn't reunited with my parents until I was eleven. There were occasional visits from my mother; summoned when I either ran away, or was seriously ill. Memories of those years, although fractured chronologically, remain vivid in my mind to this day. As I wrote them down, other memories surfaced and were reinforced when I revisited Normanhurst fifty years later and discovered that time had not distorted, nor falsified the experiences of those five years; borne out when I accurately identified a squeaky floor board and a fish-shaped gouge in the wainscotting. My research also focussed on the woman who shaped those childhood years, and to whom–in retrospect–I owe far more than I ever could have envisaged at the time.

Audrey Joan Baker was a woman born before her time. A Classical degree from Oxford, and a London Teacher's Diploma, she was primarily an educator, but she also had the wisdom and compassion to mentor and shape the futures of her charges in a unique fashion. Sadly, as a child, I never appreciated her fully. It was only when, as an adult and a mother, my memories harked back to those childhood years of WWII, that I recognised the teachings and principles she instilled into me, and which undoubtedly sparked my love of the classics and literature.

I was in touch with a member of Joan Baker's family, and she graciously read and approved my manuscript. Both she and the then owners of the Manor House, gave me permission to use original photos taken during the era of which I write; I was thrilled to identify myself and some friends on a couple of them.

"Dear Cedric..." is based on recollections of my time at Normanhurst and the mandatory letters home, which my mother kept. I say "based" because, although some of the characters (including Miss Baker) are truly chronicled with love and respect, other players are, for obvious reasons, composite characters, but all carry an element of true anecdote. Some names have been changed, including Cedric, in order to protect his family history, but the antics and adventures we all got up to, were very real–as were the inescapable angst and tragedies of war.

I would like, briefly, to mention those who contributed to my journey with Cedric.

My sincere thanks to Tony and Jayne Cant, owners of Eardington Manor, for their generosity and hospitality when I visited in 2004. They let me roam around and revisit the only home I'd known during the war years. I was delighted that the 'child-height' coat rack was still there—in the side entrance hall. I am particularly grateful for the vintage photographs they gave me, and for allowing me to take the "now" photos.

Thank you to Mary Collings who also provided photographs, and gave the manuscript her seal of approval.

A big thank you to Barrie and Elizabeth Davis, without whom I would never have rediscovered Normanhurst.

My profound thanks to my lifelong friend, Antony Neales who granted me *carte blanche* in my weaving of his character through the fabric that was Normanhurst. He also insisted that I chronicle the role Edward Bear played in the "Night Ops" adventure.

Sincere thanks go to my dear friend and mentor, the late Iris Gower, and who, along with Peter Snadden (a Scot!) provided me with the correct spelling of the Welsh phrases.

Thank you to my on-line literary friends from *The Blank Page* (they know who they are) whose critiques and encouragement were invaluable.

And finally, my deepest thanks to my family who gave me the incentive to start on this project and the support and encouragement to see it through and, if they look hard, my grandchildren will find themselves at Normanhurst.

Prologue

April, 2001

How could I have forgotten the daffodils? I had remembered so much, and yet I'd forgotten the daffodils.

And there were hundreds of them, everywhere. Not just bouncing in the town flowerbeds and neat gardens, but growing wild in the hedgerows, and creating golden borders along the roadside. Wordsworth's golden hosts. Fifty years ago, there must have been daffodils but I don't remember seeing any. Just cabbages. Rows and rows of dull green, wartime cabbages.

It was the first time I'd been back to Shropshire since 1946. I was visiting friends who lived about a half-hour's drive from Eardington, a tiny village with roots in the iron age, and where Normanhurst, a preparatory boarding school, had been relocated at the outbreak of World War II. My family had been evacuated to the very heart of Wales, but as Ann-the-Bank's Da had said,

"There aren't many schools in Wales. Mostly sheep."

So Ann had been shipped off to Normanhurst and I begged my father to send me there too. I missed my friend. I might not have been so quick to beg, had I foreseen it would turn into a five-year exile from my family.

I phoned Ant. "I'm going to find Normanhurst."

"Brilliant," he replied. "Let me know what you find."

Crossing the river Severn from the east, we drove through Bridgnorth Low Town and up the hill. It was market day and High Town was bustling. Mingling with the busyness, I felt caught in a time warp. The black and white buildings hadn't changed; the pubs, the cafés, the shops, were all still there. But the people had changed. Smiles and jolly greetings had replaced the thin, tired war-time faces. I wandered around with my camera, snapping indiscriminately. Now I wonder...?

"Is the cinema still here?" I asked a passer-by.

"Right down there." She pointed down Whitburn Street.

And there it was, the old Majestic Cinema. Grubby paint and all. Another photograph. Another memory.

Driving out of Bridgnorth, my heart skipped a few beats. Would we find Normanhurst? Would it have changed? Did disappointment lie ahead? For an instant, I wanted to turn around and go home. But I'd come 4,000 miles for this day. The moment passed.

Up another hill, I saw the familiar sandstone cliffs cradling the fields where I'd hidden after the murder. A mile farther on, neat houses lined the outskirts of the village of Eardington. Then, right on cue, I saw the tall sandstone brick walls of the kitchen garden. "There it is," I shouted. "There's Normanhurst."

My friend parked the car, then grabbed my hand. "Come on," she said. "Let's go in."

The tall wrought iron gates were open, and I stepped—almost reverently—between the grey stone pillars, up the gravel driveway to the white columned porch . It was just as I remembered.

Chapter 1

September, 1940

It was an afternoon in September 1940, when my father drove his old Wolseley Wasp through tall wrought iron gates set between stone pillars, a crouching lion topping each. On one pillar was a notice which read:

NORMANHURST
Preparatory School for Boys and Girls
Day and Boarding Pupils Accepted
Owner and Principal: Miss A.J. Baker, B.A. (hons), Oxon.
London Teacher's Diploma

On the other pillar were two red and white notices, one said:

Caution: Children at Play

the other,

Private: Trespassers will be Prosecuted

I felt a small tingle of excitement. Did Piglet's grandfather live here too?

My father, a staunch Oxonian, remarked that it was fortunate Miss Baker had been to Oxford.

Oak, chestnut and elm trees bordered a gravel driveway leading to a magnificent mansion, set in a curved lake of green lawns. To me, it looked like part of Buckingham Palace. My father stopped the car in front of a white columned entrance.

While he hauled my trunk out of the boot, I jumped down from my perch on the back seat and out of the car. I had to see the garden that I would be playing in. To the left of the house, was a thick shrubbery of yew and holly. On the lawns to the right, there were two tennis courts and beyond them, orderly paths bordered beds of brilliant late summer flowers set against a brick wall of soft red sandstone, that was at least twice as tall as my father. Flat against the wall, fruit trees grew—apples, pears and quince; just like the ones in my grandmother's garden. Arched openings in the wall framed a kitchen garden, where I could see a man hoeing between rows of vegetables. Towards the back of the house, I caught a glimpse of more flowers set around a white garden seat. It reminded me of a special place in the gardens of our home in Worcestershire, where we lived before the war sent us to Wales. I wondered if someone would sit on the seat and read to me, like Mummy used to on golden summer afternoons, before the war took our home away.

"Georgian, and exquisite." My mother shaded her eyes as she gazed at the creamy-white building. Three storeys high, tall-windowed, with a shallow sloping roof. Red brick chimneys stood tall against a cloudless blue sky. Two long stone steps fronted the entrance leading to double front doors.

When I caught sight of the doors, I backed away. They were terrifying. Painted black half-way up to where crimson glass bordered a hundred small leaded panes, each reflecting bright, dancing colours. Randomly set amongst them, were whirlpools of dark glass—eyes that stared right through me.

Then the eyes disappeared and everything changed as the doors swung open and a young and pretty lady came out to meet us. She was shorter than my mother and seemed to bounce rather than walk. Brown curls bounced above dark eyebrows and even the bobbles on her yellow and green striped jumper, bounced as she came down the steps. A wide smile made her eyes crinkle at the corners.

"Miss Baker?" My father moved forward and shook her hand.

After greeting my parents, she bent down and took my hand. She welcomed me to Normanhurst and then, in reply to an urgent whisper from my mother said, "Of course Edward Bear is welcome. About a dozen of his relatives live here already. Do come in. You must have tea before your journey back to Wales."

She led the way into a bright, comfortable room to the right of the front door. I soon learned that this was Miss Baker's study. Tea was laid on a small round table in front of deep arm chairs and a sofa in brown leather. There were paste sandwiches, home made scones with strawberry jam, and a cherry cake. My father ate a lot, my mother fiddled with a scone, and I remembered my manners and only ate what was offered to me.

During tea, Miss Baker told my parents that Normanhurst provided a full preparatory curriculum. She also said that were bathed on Wednesdays and on Saturdays, when our hair was washed ready for Church. She said my bowels would be watched, we got three meals a day, and all children were required to write to their parents every Sunday afternoon.

"We keep chickens," she said. "And have a very productive kitchen garden. Did you remember to bring Patricia's ration book and Identity Card?"

My mother and father stayed just long enough to sign some important papers that gave Miss Baker 'charge over me.' It was a long drive back to Wales and it was getting late. Blackout came with the sunset.

My father leaned down and kissed me on both cheeks, his mustache somewhere between scratchy and tickly. His hazel eyes gazed into mine. "Chin up," he said. "Remember, this is *your* war effort. We all have to make sacrifices in wartime and yours is having to leave home and live at Normanhurst. You are also here because it is a very safe place. You will soon settle down. I expect you to learn a lot and do as you are told."

He hesitated for a moment and then swept me up into his arms. He hugged me and whispered in my ear, "Be good, my little treasure. I will come and get you as soon as the war is over. It won't be long."

He set me back on my feet and it was Mummy's turn. Crouching down, she took me in her arms. The familiar scent of lavender water mixed with Pears soap enveloped me and I clung to her. Her cheek pressed against mine and I could feel a tear between them; I didn't know whether it was mine or hers. "Goodbye, my darling baby. Be good. I'll write to you every week. I promise."

My father put a hand on her shoulder. "Come, my dear. It's time to leave."

As the Wolseley disappeared down the driveway in a cloud of red dust kicked up from the Shropshire sandstone gravel, I got a terrible sinking feeling in my tummy; I didn't really want to be here. As the awful feeling around my middle got worse, I wondered if perhaps someone was already watching my bowels.

Miss Baker picked up my little suitcase and the bundle of required bedding my father had placed in the hall. Facing the great front doors from the inside, the eyes still stared, as if challenging my right to be there. Eyes that could look both ways? Eyes that would be watching me. I shivered. I took a step towards the doors. I wanted to go outside. I wanted to run down the driveway and catch up with my parents before they left. I wanted Mummy to take me on her lap and hold me close where I would be safe. I didn't want to be left with this strange lady, however smiley and bouncy.

"Come now, Patricia. Your parents have a long way to drive. Someone will carry your trunk up to your room later."

I started to cry.

"Crying won't help, Patricia."

Miss Baker looked down at me. She seemed, at that moment, to be very tall. "You have to remember you are a very lucky little girl. Your parents are paying for you to be at Normanhurst, where you'll get a good start to your education. Just think," she continued, "how many children are living in London and Birmingham, where their homes and schools are being bombed. They are not so lucky."

I wanted to tell her there weren't any bombs in the Welsh valley, only sheep. But I didn't. I looked at my shoes so she wouldn't see my tears.

The suitcase and the bundle bumped to the floor again, and Miss Audrey-Joan Baker knelt in front of me.

"Patricia, I want you to be happy here. This is a very happy place and I promise that in addition to learning your lessons, you'll have lots of fun. We try to be a family instead of a school. I know you are only six years' old and that's young to be away from your parents and friends, but you'll soon make new friends. You know, there are children here even younger than you." A small shadow moved behind her. Her left hand reached out and a black and white kitten appeared in front of me.

"This is Tristan," she said. "He has a sister called Iseult. I am sure they'll be happy to be your friends. That is, if you like cats!" She smiled and tickled Tristan behind his ears. I noticed that her hands were broad, her fingers short. Not like Mummy's soft hands and long fingers with their pretty rings.

I nodded. Miss Baker seemed friendly, but what about the other people here? I could hear distant chattering and laughter, but they were all strangers, except for Ann-the-Bank.

"The cats like the girls but they usually run away from the boys." Miss Baker leaned closer and whispered in my ear so Tristan wouldn't hear. Her breath was warm and smelled of the strawberry jam we'd had for tea. "I think the boys sometimes pull their tails."

I nodded again. Tears had gathered under my chin, I rubbed them away with my fist. "Can I see Ann-the-Bank?" I asked.

"Ann-the-Bank? Oh! You mean Ann Jones, your friend from Wales. Of course. I've put you in the same dormitory. So dry your eyes and wipe your nose and we'll find her. You know Patricia, we all have to learn that there is no place for unnecessary tears in wartime."

I pulled a hanky from my knicker-leg and wiped my eyes and blew my nose. I didn't want Ann-the-Bank to see I'd been crying. I felt a gentle hand on my shoulder and Miss Baker turned me away from the massive front door with its scary eyes.

"Follow me, Patricia."

Picking up my luggage, she led me towards a flight of stairs that stretched up as far as I could see and disappeared into darkness. "Come and see where you'll be sleeping and meet Ann and your other dormitory friends," she said brightly." Then you can tell your parents all about it in the letter you'll write to them next Sunday."

I didn't answer her. Everywhere seemed so dark. I glanced over my shoulder. The eyes were following me upstairs.

"This isn't a bit like home."

"Patricia, when I speak to you, you answer 'Yes, Miss Baker.'"

"Yes, Miss Baker."

Clutching Edward Bear, I climbed the stairs behind Miss Baker. I thought about Mummy and Daddy and how they had hugged and kissed me. I wanted them to come back. And in that awful moment I realised they really were gone. Getting farther and farther away–all the way to Wales, to the funny little house where, because of the war, we were forced to live. And I thought of Dilly and how she'd hugged me when I left. She'd run all the way up the road after the car, waving her handkerchief while I knelt, gazing out of the back window, waving, waving...until the car turned a corner and she was gone.

"What was I going to do without Dilly to look after me? Who was going to bath me and tie my hair ribbons?

"And was my father really going to fight in the War?

"And who was going to read to me at bedtime?

"And nobody had said when I would see them again."

I was freezing cold in bed that night. Through the thin, hard mattress I could feel the iron mesh bed and I longed for my feather bed and teddy-bear hot water bottle. Even the familiar blankets and eiderdown from home didn't help. I drew them over my head and, as the tears trickled down my face to dampen the pillow, I realised I'd made a very big mistake when I had begged my father to send me to Normanhurst.

Chapter 2

When Can I Come Home?

Mummy is reading my favourite Rupert Bear story. Snuggled in the nest of her lap, I feel warm and safe. I am at home. I am loved.

A loud and terrible clanging broke my perfect dream. Someone was poking me and pulling at my eiderdown under which I lay in a cosy ball.

"Wake up! Wake up! It's time to get up. That's the getting-up bell." Ann-the-Bank pulled at the covers around my face. I opened my eyes to see what was going on. Not much. Just the blurry outline of a large lady framed in a pale patch of doorway. Now the bell was clanging inside the dormitory and there was no chance of anyone still being asleep.

"Come along, all you lazy bones! Jump to it. Up you get. All of you. Including the new child."

The bell was dumped on the end of my bed, just missing my toes, and the large lady unlocked the blackout shutters and swung them back. Early morning sunshine flooded the room. Satisfied everyone was awake, she marched out to clang her bell in the other dormitories.

"Who was *that*?" I asked.

Ann-the-Bank's pink flannelette nightgown lay in a rumpled heap on the floor and she was already half-way wriggled into her vest,

Liberty-bodice and knickers. I looked around at the other four girls who shared the dormitory. Wendy, Gillian and Annabel were almost dressed. Only Jennifer still sat cross-legged on her bed talking to her teddy-bear.

"That's Mrs. B. She's Miss Audrey-Joan's mother. She sees to our welfare. C'mon. Get up. We can't be late for breakfast."

"Miss Audrey-Joan?"

"That's what *we* call Miss Baker, silly. Now GET UP!"

I scrambled out of bed and pulled on the clothes I'd hung through the foot rail of the iron bedstead the night before. I dived under the bed, my knees bouncing hard on the wooden floor and groped for my shoes and socks, which I'd stuffed into the toes.

"Don't forget your tie," Ann reminded me as she helped me with the buttons on the back of my green and white check overall. "Can you tie it yourself?"

I slipped the tie over my head and pulled the knot into place; just as Dilly had shown me. Ann's face was hidden as she pulled on her jumper, so she missed my little trick. "Yes, of course I can. But I can't do my hair. Dilly always ties my hair ribbon."

"Can't you brush it yourself?" Ann-the-Bank was getting cross. "We have to get down to breakfast."

"Of course I can brush it."

"Then brush it and use a Kirby Grip. You *do* have Kirby Grips, I suppose?"

Last night I had jammed all my things into two small drawers of the chest which Ann and were to share. I grabbed a card of Kirby Grips from the top drawer, pulled one off and shoved it in my hair.

"That'll do. Now for goodness sakes, COME ON. And don't forget your gas mask." Ann grabbed my hand and dragged me out of our attic dormitory, to race at top speed along the corridor. We hadn't reached the first flight of stairs before we came to a slithering halt. A mountain in a flowered pinafore and plimsolls was blocking our way. Mrs. Baker.

"And may I inquire whether our faces have seen soap and water this morning?"

Ann-the-Bank answered in a flash. "Yes, Mrs. Baker."

She lied. *"Ann-the-Bank actually told a lie."*

"And our new child? Patricia?"

Ann's fingernails dug deep into my palm. I nodded and looked down at my shoes.

"Hmph. Let me see." Mrs. Baker's finger lifted my chin. I looked straight into a pair of terrifying dark grey eyes. "Hmph. Very well, off you go."

We ran down the two flights of back stairs, our feet clattering on the grey painted wood, gas mask boxes bouncing on our backs. We finally slid to a stop in the corridor outside the kitchen door. Ann pulled me in behind the last child waiting in a line against the wall. "The queue for breakfast. Follow me and do what I do."

First we took a thick white crockery bowl from a pile that looked as though it would topple over. The queue moved slowly towards a huge Aga cooker. Following Ann-the-Bank's example, I held my bowl out and a strange lady plonked a ladle-full of stiff and steaming porridge into it. Moving on to an outsize wooden kitchen table, I recognised Miss Baker. She smiled at me as she poured a moat of milk around the hill of porridge. "Good morning, Patricia. I hope you slept well. Just follow Ann. She will show you what to do."

"Yes, Miss Baker. Thank-you, Miss Baker."

Ann tossed her head, again indicating I should follow her. She led me into a wood-panelled room where three long tables covered with shiny yellow oilcloth, were lined up side by side. There was just enough room to squeeze between the benches set around them. One table was already full of chattering children. Ann pulled at my jumper and pointed to the one closest to the door. I sat down and looked around.

Bright sunlight streamed in through two big windows, their hinged blackout shutters folded back against the wall. Outside, was a small lawn with bare patches. Beyond, I could see a dark shrubbery. Against the opposite wall from the windows, stood an enormous three-shelved metal trolley on wheels. On the top level, was a tray crammed with cups of the same thick china as the porridge bowls. The middle tier had four rows of labelled jam-jars. Next to the jam-jars, four rows of butter-crocks, also labelled, contained a small square of bright yellow margarine and an even smaller square of pale butter. On the bottom tier were six big plates of thickly sliced bread.

"Get your sugar jar." Ann seemed to enjoy telling me what to do. I found a dark-brown glass jar with a metal screw top; my name written in spidery capitals on the label. It was half-full of sugar.

"That's your whole ration for the week," she told me. "So make it last or you'll be eating porridge with no sugar on Friday. We get new rations on Saturdays."

Today was Monday.

"The same goes for your butter ration. Four ounces of marg and two ounces of butter for the whole week. And we get that," Ann jerked her head at the dry bread, "twice a day. Breakfast and tea."

I didn't know what two or four ounces meant and I later found out that neither did Ann—even though she was six-and-a-half and had been at boarding school for six months. It was just the size of our butter and margarine rations and had nothing to do with Arithmetic.

"Why did you make me hurry so much to get down for breakfast?" I asked.

"Because if you don't get the porridge off the top of the pot, you get the burned stuff at the bottom. The boys are usually the last down anyway, so they get the burned stuff. Besides, then we get to eat our breakfast first and get into the loo queue first, which is good because the lavvies aren't so smelly."

I couldn't think of an answer to that so I ate my porridge, which was stiff and horrible. The tables were filling up fast. I looked around. So many strange faces turning round to stare at me, then turning away to whisper amongst themselves.

Ann noticed me watching them. "Don't worry. It's only 'cause you're new. They're waiting for you to cry."

"Cry? Why?"

"Cry for your mummy, silly. That's what a lot of them do. Cry 'cause they're homesick and want their mummies and daddies. Then the others start teasing. *'Cry a baby cry! Put your finger in your eye! Cry baby cry!'* But crying just makes them tease you more. So don't you dare cry."

"I won't." I certainly didn't want to be teased. Last night, I'd cried under the bedclothes before I went to sleep but it hadn't done any good. Mummy and Daddy didn't come back."

A small skinny boy with red hair and a red nose, was busy stuffing his porridge into his overall pocket. I nudged Ann. "Who's that, and what's he doing?"

"Who? Where?"

I knew it was rude to point. "That boy with red hair. At the next table."

Ann sniffed. "Oh that's Rowley Smythe. He's always stuffing his food in his pockets and then he puts it down the loo afterwards. Nobody tells on him because if he's made to eat it, he usually sicks it up into his bowl again and that's *so* disgusting. Never, never sit next to Rowley Smythe. Unless you want him to sick-up on you."

I noticed that the children sitting next to Rowley Smythe were huddled close together on the bench leaving a wide space between them and him. Rowley was at the end, next to the wall.

"Does he sick-up everything?"

"Only white food. His pockets are always full of porridge, potatoes and rice pudding. You have to stay far away from him because his pockets stink so bad."

Rowley Smythe saw me looking at him. He crossed his eyes and stuck his tongue out. I quickly got back to my porridge.

The room was strangely quiet; just the clatter of spoons scraping on porridge bowls. And, all the time, Rowley Smythe was stuffing his overall pockets. One overflowed and globs of porridge dripped onto the floor. He looked around to see if anyone had noticed. My eyes were back on my porridge just in time.

"Eat up, eat up!" Mrs. Baker arrived in the room carrying a huge red enamel teapot. She held it over the tray of cups and, without pausing, poured a continuous stream of tea, slopping from one cup to another, right through to the last one. She brought the tray to the table and under her watchful eyes, we carefully passed the cups of greyish brown tea down the table; taking great care not to spill any. The milk must have been in the cups before she poured the tea.

"Who wants saccharine?" Mrs. B plonked a small bowl full of little white pills on the table. I knew what saccharine was. My parents always put it in their tea so their sugar ration could be used for other things. But I'd never tasted it.

Ann nudged me. "Go on, take one. It'll save your sugar."

I dropped the tiny pellet into my tea. It popped to the surface where it fizzled and spread into a blob of white foam. A spoon was passed around. I stirred my tea and drank it down. The sweetness had a bitter taste which I didn't like. I made a face.

"You'll get used to it," A girl with long black plaits smiled at me across the table. "You have to get used to it. It's war time. Are you the new girl that came last night?"

I nodded.

"What's your name?"

"Patricia."

"I'm Wanda. You'll be all right. Just don't let the boys bully you. But if they do...don't let them make you cry."

"Thank you very much." I decided to keep well away from the boys.

After the porridge, tea, and two pieces of bread with a scrape of our precious margarine, topped with a smear of Marmite from the big jar Mrs. B passed around, we collected our dishes and carried them out to the back kitchen—all grey stone and red tiles. A tired looking woman, whose wispy, grey hair and red chapped hands matched her surroundings, stood at a stone sink under the window. She nodded at me as I placed my bowl, cup and plate on the pile to the right of the sink.

"You new?"

I nodded again.

She smiled and flicked a strand of hair from her eyes with the back of a soapy hand. "Knife and spoon in the wire basket, if you please."

As I stood on tiptoe to do as she asked, she looked down at me. "You're a young 'un, aren't you? How old are you? Six?"

"Yes."

"Well at least you ate your breakfast up which is more than I can say for that new laddie. Looks like he's been cryin' all night."

"There's another new child?"

The tired looking lady bobbed her head towards a thin, brown-haired boy standing by the back door. "That's 'im. That's young master Cedric, and he's mopin' after 'is mum."

She called to the boy, "Off you goes my laddie. Boys' lavvy is outside and across the yard. You'd better hurry, or you'll be last."

The boy called Cedric used both hands to tug open the brass-knobbed back door leading to the outside yard. I could see he was going to cry again.

The woman turned back to me. "You'll soon get used to it, my flower. It ain't that bad: It's all what you makes of it. You accepts it or you don't. As for him," she jerked her head towards the back door, "he won't make it unless he cheers up. Now run along to the loo queue and get done. The bell goes for lessons in half-an-hour."

My lavatory performance was inspected by Mrs. B and noted with a large tick against my name on the bathroom register sheet. Another tick confirmed my teeth had been brushed. Back in the dormitory, I made my bed to Ann-the-Bank's instructions so, when the big bell clanged again, I was ready for my first day at Normanhurst Preparatory School.

"Maybe the war will be over tomorrow and I can go home."

Chapter 3

A Clean Sheet

'A noun is the name of a person, a place or a thing.
Archibald, Caroline, London, bird, wing.'

My first lesson with Miss Audrey-Joan Baker, B.A. (Hons) was English Grammar.

"Good morning, children."

"Good morning, Miss Baker."

She moved to the blackboard, picked up a piece of white chalk from the shelf on the wooden easel, and started writing. Her long back teacher's gown flowed almost to the floor and the crisp, white sleeves of her shirt showed below the long slitted armholes. She turned to face the class. "First, I want you to copy the date off the blackboard into your exercise books. You will always date your work at the top, right hand corner. Then, open your Grammar Primer and look at the first lesson."

My hand hovered over the shiny red cover of a brand new exercise book. I opened it to the first gleaming white page. I had never had a book to write in before. Mummy, who had taught me to read and write and Daddy who had taught me Arithmetic, always gave me just plain, single sheets of paper on which to write my lessons. This was different. This was a whole book full of new, clean white pages with pale blue lines and a fine, double red-lined margin exactly one inch from the inside edge.

"And I have to write in this? Suppose I make a mistake?" I didn't want to spoil such a beautiful book. I sat and stared it at.

There was a clatter of pencil cases being opened. I unzipped my brown leather pencil case, decorated with oak leaves and acorns, and with the words *'The Value of Education is the Knowledge of its Worth. Anon.'* embossed in gold. I chose a red wooden pen with a shiny new nib, to match the book. I looked around. Everyone had their heads bent over their exercise books. Ann-the-Bank was sitting next to me, her tongue waving and wagging in concentration, and her pen scratching as she carefully formed her letters. I stared at the blank white page, my fingers clutching the pen.

We all had a copy of *Archibald and Caroline: Introduction to English Grammar, Book I* on our desks. It was the story of two kittens named Archibald and Caroline. Each page had a different picture. Underneath each picture was a sentence, and under each sentence was an exercise. Miss Audrey-Joan looked up and down the rows of desks. I knew she was going to pick one of us. I slid lower into my seat. "Arabella, will you please read the sentence under the first picture."

A girl, two desks away to my left, stood up. She tossed her long blonde plaits over her shoulders. They reached right down to her bottom, almost to the hem of her very short pleated kilt. Before reading, she looked around as if to make sure we were all watching her. "Archibald and Caroline are kittens."

"Helen, will you please read the next line."

"Write down all the nouns you can find in the sentence." Helen kept her eyes on her book, read quickly, then sat down again with a thump. She looked a lot nicer than Arabella Long Plaits.

"Now children, I want you to write the answer in your exercise books." Miss Audrey-Joan walked up and down the aisles between our desks, bending to look at each child's page as she passed. She arrived at my side.

"Patricia, you haven't written a thing. Do you understand the exercise?"

"Yes, Miss Baker."

"You haven't even written the date."

"No, Miss Baker."

"Do you have a pen? And is there ink in your inkwell?"

"Yes, Miss Baker."

"Then get on with it, child."

"Yes, Miss Baker." I dipped my pen in the inkwell and moved my hand to hover over the right hand corner of the top line.

Miss Audrey-Joan sighed as she squatted down beside me. Her face was on a level with mine and her black gown billowed out, dusting the floor around her. She lowered her voice almost to a whisper, "I know you are a new child, but I also know you can read and write. Can you tell me what is wrong?"

"I-I don't want to make a mistake. It-it's so *clean*. I don't want to spoil it."

I could see she was surprised. She looked at me for a long time before answering. I wriggled in my chair. "You won't make a mistake, Patricia. Look." She took a pencil from my case and made a tiny dot in the centre of the top line. "If you start right *there*, you'll have plenty of room for the date." She made another dot, two lines down at the ruled margin. "If you start at *this* dot and write your answers with a comma in between each noun, it will look quite perfect."

She got up and walked briskly to the front of the class. Looking straight at me, Miss Audrey-Joan announced, "Children, you have five more minutes to finish writing your answers."

I drew the open exercise book closer to my chest and, starting at Miss Audrey-Joan's centre dot on the top line, I wrote slowly and neatly: *Monday, September 3rd, 1940.*

It was cosy in the Kindergarten room. It wasn't only for the Kindergarten children. Ann-the-Bank and I were in Form One. The room was a long, prefabricated building set at the end of a cinder path, its back to the high holly hedge that separated the school grounds from the main Bridgnorth Road. Four wooden screens stood end-to-end from the front to the back wall, dividing it to make one small and one larger room. Our form was in the smaller one. A big black stove was set against the back wall. It was not lit as the warm September sun shone through big windows built into the front and sides of the building. Even the double, dark green entrance doors had window panes in the top half. The only sounds in the room were the ticking of a big wall clock and the scratching of pens on paper. A shaft of sunlight lit up my page as I started to carefully write the name 'Caroline'. Capital 'C', little 'a'... I heard the big boy in front of me jabbing his pen nib into the inkwell.

Suddenly, the back of his chair tilted and violently knocked the front of my desk. At the same time, the boy half turned and a spray of ink flew through the air. It landed on my face, my overall, all over my hands and—horror of horrors—over my beautiful new exercise book. This invasion of my desk had jolted my own hand, and the 'r' that I was forming ended up as a big black blob. I screamed and then—realising what had happened—burst into tears.

Miss Audrey-Joan, who'd been writing the next sentence on the blackboard, spun around to face the class. "Just what is going on? Great heavens, Patricia. What's the matter now?"

I pointed to the boy in front of me. "He-he knocked my d-desk and s-sus-sprayed me with ink. And-and he m-made me make a b-b-blot." Now I was sobbing. "And I want to g-go home. I want my Mummy."

The whole class giggled and snickered, except Ann-the-Bank who folded her arms across the desk and buried her face in them. The tips of her ears were red.

Miss Audrey-Joan marched down the aisle to our desks. She looked at me, at my book and then at the boy. His pale, almost white, hair was cut short and he had a really strange nose, the tip of which turned up so far I could see the grubbies hiding up it. His pale blue eyes were tiny and very close together under almost white eyebrows. He looked at me and grinned. "She did it herself. She messed up her book."

I gulped back my sobs. "I did *not*. He b-banged my desk and m-made me blot."

Miss Audrey-Joan glanced at me and then at the boy. "And what, Giles Farmer, is all that ink doing on your fingers?"

"So that's his name. Giles Farmer. Got a face like a farmer's pig too."

I sniffed and swallowed. Miss Audrey-Joan gave me a look that said *"Blow your nose, child."* I fumbled up my knicker-leg for my handkerchief.

Giles Farmer started to go pink. It spread all around the back of his neck right up his ears. Just like a pig. A big pink pig with a snout. He half turned to look at me and licked his lips. "I dropped my pen, Miss Baker."

"Hmph. Go and stand in the corner for the rest of the lesson. Facing the wall." She turned back to me, "Patricia, you'd better go and get cleaned up. Run to the house and find Mrs. Baker."

Tears still streaming down my face, I slid from my chair and, without looking at anyone, scrambled for the door. Everyone was watching me. It took both hands to turn the big brass knob on the door and both hands to push it shut from the outside.

I found Mrs. B in the back kitchen, picking out the eyes and the black spots from a heap of potatoes. Sighing, she put down the small knife and dried her hands on her apron; her eyes inspecting me from top to bottom. Muttering to herself, she scrubbed the ink from my face and hands, and reached in a cupboard to find me a clean overall. "It's lucky I keep plenty of spares. Put this on and I'll soak your dirty one in salt to draw out the ink." Spatters of ink had also soaked into the collar points of my new white Vyella blouse. "Stop blubbering, Patricia. Go and change into a clean blouse and I will soak this one too. If the salt doesn't work I'll try some of that new-fangled ink eradicator. If it works on paper, it may work on your collar."

Twenty minutes later, cleaned up, tears wiped and nose blown, I walked slowly back down the cinder path to the Kindergarten room. I arrived just as Mrs. B clanged the bell. The double-doors burst open and the children rushed out for the 'elevenses' break. Ann-the-Bank came over to me but all the others just looked me up and down and then turned their backs on both of us. They stood in little huddles, the boys separate from the girls. I turned to Ann.

"Why are they turning their backs to me?"

"'Cos they don't like you."

"Why?"

"'Cos you told on Giles."

"Well, he did it."

"I know. But you're not supposed to split on him."

"Poof. I don't care. He shouldn't have done it." I turned my back on them and went around the corner of the building, out of their way.

Then the chanting started. *"Tell tale tit, your tongue will split. And all the little puppy dogs will get a little bit. Tell tale tit, your tongue will split. Yah, yah, yah."*

I looked at Ann and the back of my nose started to prickle again. Tears swilled into my eyes so I couldn't see properly.

"Don't start crying, Pat. Please don't start up again. You'll only make things worse."

"I don't care. I w-want to g-go home. I want m-my mummy."

The chanting changed. *"Cry baby, cry. Put your finger in your eye. Cry, baby cry."*

I squatted down, put my head on my knees, and sobbed. I wished I could just disappear. I wanted to go home to Wales. I wanted my mummy and my daddy.

A cloud of black gown covered me. Strong arms lifted me up and I was carried away up the cinder path, across the lawn and into the yard to the back kitchen door. Miss Audrey-Joan carried me through to the front kitchen and sat me down on a chair at the table. Mrs. B hurried in.

"Now what's happened to her?" Her eyes examined me for blood and bruises—or more ink.

Miss Audrey-Joan was fussing under her breath. "This has to stop. It happens to all the new children. However hard they try, however quiet they are. Unfortunately, it's the quiet ones that get picked on."

A glass of milk and two *petit-beurre* biscuits, the ones with little nobbles all around, appeared on the table in front of me. But I didn't move. My hands were twisting a soggy hanky into knots and my chin was sunk on my chest. I was desperately unhappy. I hated boarding school.

A chair scraped on the red tiled floor and Miss Audrey-Joan sat down beside me, a steaming cup of tea in front of her. "Now, Patricia. We have to talk sensibly about this."

I sniffed, chin still stuck in my chest.

"Here, child. Look at me." A finger prodded me under my chin and I looked up into Miss Audrey-Joan's face. Her eyes looked kind. "My dear, you know you can't go home. That's the first thing you have to get used to. It's only natural you want your mother and father because you've never been away from home before. I know you're only six years old, but you've been put in my...in *our* care until the war is over. But it won't be for long. The war will only last a few months."

I sniffed again.

"Drink your milk and eat your biscuits."

I picked up a biscuit and bit a nobble off one corner.

"I know Giles Farmer flicked his pen at you. He must have heard you saying that you were worried about spoiling your page and decided he would do it for you. I'm truly sorry it happened."

I remembered the spoilt new book and the tears started again.

"Now, now, Patricia. Don't start crying again. And don't worry about your book. It will be replaced. Just this once."

Miss Audrey-Joan put one arm around me and with her free hand, picked up her tea. I decided to eat my biscuits and drink the milk. "That's better. Now the next lesson is Arithmetic and there will be a new book for that too. But you're allowed to do Arithmetic in pencil, so there won't be any accidents with that, will there?"

"No, Miss Baker."

"Do you like Arithmetic?"

"No, Miss Baker."

Miss Audrey-Joan grinned. "Neither do I. But we have to learn Arithmetic, and we have to be good at it. You must work equally hard at all your lessons, even the ones you don't like. Besides, your father is a Mathematics teacher, is he not?"

I nodded, my mouth full of biscuit.

"Then it's important you please him by working hard at his subject."

Mrs. Baker turned from the stove where she had saucepans bubbling. They smelled good. I hoped she was cooking our dinner. "Patricia will also have to learn to stand up to the teasing," she said.

Miss Audrey-Joan nodded. "Stand up to them, my dear, and they will soon stop. But if you keep crying for your mother, they will taunt you all the more. If you stand up for yourself they'll soon leave you alone."

"Bullies," muttered Mrs. B. "Big bullies, some of those boys. Especially that Giles Farmer."

"I know. This school-yard teasing is getting to be too much." Miss Audrey-Joan frowned and a brown curl flopped on her forehead. "But apart from punishing him, there's nothing much else I can do. He seems to enjoy picking on the smaller ones."

"They should give him a taste of his own medicine, Joan. Teach them to fight back."

"This is supposed to be a school for little ladies and gentlemen. Not a hoard of pugilists."

"Hmmph," was all Mrs. B said to *that*.

Miss Audrey-Joan stood up, and pushed her chair under the table. "It's time for the end of break bell. You'd better run along if you have finished your elevenses. And remember, Patricia. Try to ignore the spiteful comments. The more they make you cry, the more you'll get teased."

"Yes, Miss Baker."

I walked slowly back down the cinder path to the Kindergarten room and the Arithmetic lesson. Giles Farmer had been made to sit at a desk at the side of the room, away from the rest of us. Another new exercise book, this time with a green cover and a label that said 'Arithmetic' was on my desk. Inside the pages were covered with little blank squares. The primer was titled *Simple Arithmetic*. I looked around. Ann-the-Bank smiled, then hurriedly looked away. The girl behind me muttered "favourite" under her breath. I didn't turn around. Arabella-Long-Plaits stuck her tongue out at me. I watched Miss Audrey-Joan. She was busy writing on the blackboard, her back to the class. So I stuck my tongue out and waggled it at Long-Plaits. At that very moment, Miss Audrey-Joan turned back to face us. I think she saw. I held my breath. She spoke. "Now, class. Open your primers at Chapter One." I thought I saw a corner of her mouth twitch, but I couldn't be certain.

The next day, I found a brand new red-covered English exercise book on my desk. The spoiled one had disappeared. Giles Farmer was seated far away where he couldn't harm me, or anyone else in the class. Miss Audrey-Joan picked up a pile of new, brown-covered exercise books and, walking between the rows of desks, handed one to each of us. When she got to my desk, she took one from the bottom of the pile and placed it in front of me. The label said in large letters *For Scribbling and Notes.* I opened it up and on first page was written in Miss Audrey-Joan's handwriting,

"Sticks and stones may break my bones, Words will never hurt me."

I slammed it shut.

Picking up my pen, I opened the shiny red cover of my new English exercise book and, starting in the middle of the top line, carefully wrote: Tuesday, September 4th, 1940.

Sunday, 9th September, 1940
Dear Mummy and Daddy,
I don't like it here. When can I come home?
Your loving daughter, Patricia.

Sunday 9th September, 1940
Dear Mummy and Daddy
Mrs. Baker says I like it here. When can I come home?
Your loving daughter, Patricia
P.S. Mrs. Baker reads our letters.
P.P.S. I miss Dilly.

Chapter 4

Cedric

Sunday 16th September, 1940
Dear Mummy and Daddy,
You asked me to tell you about the teachers.
Miss Baker is clever she is a B.A. (hons). She teaches us everything except Geography and Arithmetic. She says she is looking forward to introducing us to the Classics. Who are the Classics?
We sometimes call her Miss Audrey-Joan so as not to muddle her with Mrs. Baker.
Mrs. Baker is Miss Audrey-Joan's mother. She cooks our meals and knits socks for soldiers. She is a good knitter.
Mrs. Tommy teaches geography because she lived in India. She has a little girl called Jane. Jane doesn't sleep in the dormitories, she sleeps with her mother, she's only three.
Mr. Baker is here too. He is Miss Audrey-Joan's father. He doesn't teach or cook. He unblocks the boys' lavatory.
Please can you send me some chocolate.

Your hungry daughter,
Patricia

Sunday, 23rd September, 1940
Dear Mummy and Daddy
Thank you for the chocolate. Mrs. Baker gives me one piece
after tea.
You said that Dilly wants me to write her a long letter and
tell her my daily doings. I would like to write to Dilly.
Is it the end of term yet?
Love from,
Patricia

It was break time and Ann-the-Bank, Wanda Reynolds and I were playing hopscotch on the cement patch below the front steps of the Kindergarten room. We could hear some boys chanting round behind the building where a narrow path ran between it and a high holly hedge.

"Cry baby cry. Put your finger in your eye. Cry baby cry."

I knew they were teasing Cedric Robinson. He was a new boy at school the very same day I was a new girl. Cedric was very quiet and never joined in anything, not even a game of hopscotch or squares. He always stood apart and alone; but he watched us play. He hardly ever spoke, except when a teacher asked him a question during lessons. Sometimes, when he thought no one was watching, he sucked his thumb. He always sat at the back of our class.

One end of the Kindergarten room was for the babies' class. They were mostly about four years old and didn't know anything. They were learning their ABC's and how to count. At the other end of the room was the class for the rest of us younger ones, who could read, write and do sums. Most of us were five- or six-years old. Miss Audrey-Joan said that if we worked really hard this first term and learned some Latin and French, then, after the Christmas holidays, we would probably move into classrooms in the big house where the older children had their lessons.

The chanting got louder. Then we saw Miss Audrey-Joan marching down the cinder path, her black gown flying out behind her. She had the 'someone's going to get into serious trouble' look on her face. Running to keep up was a new teacher, Mrs Riley, who had very short legs and a big bosom. Red in the face and puffing, she almost bumped into Miss Audrey-Joan who had hauled up short of our hopscotch squares. Miss Audrey-Joan cocked her head to one side, then strode around the back of the Kindergarten room. Immediately, the chanting stopped and there was silence.

Then I heard her voice booming at the boys. Miss Audrey-Joan always boomed when the boys were doing something they shouldn't. I crept towards the corner of the building to hear what she was saying. "You are a pair of nasty, spiteful little boys. You are behaving like ignorant guttersnipes instead of pupils of Normanhurst School. Consequently, you will be sent to Coventry for the rest of the day. You will sit in the babies' class, one in each corner, facing the wall. When lessons are over you will spend the rest of the day in your dormitory. And with no tea. The next time I find you bullying someone, you will be caned. NOW GET OUT OF MY SIGHT."

Moments later the two boys, one of whom was Giles Farmer, stumbled into the Kindergarten room. We could see them standing inside the door; their heads down. Cedric had disappeared.

I heard Miss Audrey-Joan talking to Mrs Riley, then she marched back up the gravel path and back into the big house. Ann, Wanda and I crouched on the steps with our ears close to the door. It wasn't hard to hear what was going on. Mrs Riley was almost shouting.

"Now, you disgusting boys, take a stool and sit, one in each corner at the babies' end, and face the wall. And you WILL stop this bullying and become exemplary pupils of Normanhurst School from now on. You disturbed Miss Baker's elevenses; she could hear you all the way from her study. NOW MARCH!"

I knew break time would soon be over because we'd already played two games of hopscotch before all this had happened. I told the others I was going to the loo before lessons started again. I took my favourite short cut. Run between the trees, across the driveway, jump over the narrow flower border and across the little side lawn with the bare patches, to the children's entrance. The cloak room, shoe lockers and the downstairs loo were all just inside. Under the back stairs there were more coat hooks and lockers where the smaller children—who were short enough to fit without banging their heads—hung their coats and changed their shoes. Right in the farthest corner under the stairs, I could hear sobbing.

"Cedric," I called softly. "Cedric, is that you? It's only me, Patricia. I won't tease you. I want to be your friend. Please come out."

"I want to go home. I want my Mummy. I don't like it here." Cedric's words were very muffled because he was hiding behind the coats.

"I know. I don't like it here either. But I have to stay. My Daddy says so. He's away in the war."

"So's mine," Cedric was hiccupping between his words, but he wasn't crying so hard.

"My Daddy's away, but I want to stay with my mummy and my baby sister."

"Where's that?"

"Birmingham."

"You can't go back there. Birmingham gets bombed by the Jerries. We lived near there and had to leave, 'cos it was too dangerous to stay."

"But my mummy and sister are still there."

"They'll move," I said.

"I haven't got any friends here."

"I told you, I'll be your friend."

"Your Ann-the-Bank's friend. Besides you're a girl."

"What does that matter? You've got a little sister and I bet you play with her. Lots of us all play together. And you can too."

Cedric was out from behind the coats now. His tear-streaked face was red and blotchy.

"You'd better wash your face in cold water," I told him. "Then it won't show you've been crying."

"How d'you know that?"

"Before the war, when I was only four, I had to have my photo taken. On the way I fell down and hurt my knee. Look, I have the scar—right here." I pointed to a little white pucker on my knee. "Anyway, I cried a lot because it hurt, but I couldn't have my photo taken with my eyes all red. There was a pump in the market square in the town where we lived, and Dilly—she looked after me before the war and now she stays with my mummy to help out. Well, Dilly took all our hankies and wetted them under the pump. Then she made me hold them on my eyes while she carried me all the way to the photograph shop. When we got there, my eyes weren't red any more. So come on. I've got a clean hanky, and there's a pump at the back kitchen sink."

While Cedric pumped, I held the hanky under the cold water. It was just about ready, all cold and wet, when Mrs. B's voice from behind us made us jump. "And what do you two think you are doing here?"

"Oh, Mrs. Baker. Cedric's eyes are all red because the boys were teasing him and I'm making them better for him."

"Hrrumph." Mrs. B always said 'Hrrumph' when we tried to explain something.

"Well," she said. "You had better hurry back to lessons or you'll be standing in the corner for the rest of the morning and that'll make more tears. For both of you," she added.

Cedric and I got out of her way and I pulled him into the bigger girls' cloakroom which was a real room, not just coat-hooks and lockers under the stairs. "Do you want to be proper friends?" I asked him. "Friends that don't tell tales on each other? Friends for ever?"

"Yes." Cedric was looking much better and his big brown eyes stared straight into mine.

"Cross-your-heart-and-hope-to-die-friends-for-ever?"

"Cross-my-heart-and-hope-to-die-friends-for-ever."

"All right then. Come here and I'll show you something—but first I've got to make sure Mrs. B has gone."

I slipped off my leather-soled shoes and crept across the grey flag-stones into the back kitchen again. I saw Mrs. B making her way across the yard towards the kitchen garden. Good. She was going to check on Mr. B. That would give me the time I needed.

Back in the cloakroom, I dragged a box over to a high counter, that ran the length of one wall. Above the counter were cupboards. I climbed up onto the counter and opened one. "I think this used to be the but-ler's pantry when it was someone's home," I explained. "We have one like this in our home in Worcestershire. The one the government took to use for war offices."

"What are you looking for?" Cedric strained his head back, trying to see into the cupboard.

"Secret. A very big secret. And you're not to tell."

"I won't."

"Here. Look." From the cupboard, I took down a jar of jam. It was about half full. I removed the lid, stuck my fingers in and scooped some jam into my mouth. I held the pot out to Cedric. "Take some."

Cedric shifted from one leg to the other. He looked a bit scared.

"You have to take some," I ordered him. "You have to take some and then you can't tell."

"I wouldn't tell."

"You might. Don't you like jam?"

"Yes.

"Then take some, quick. Before we get caught."

Cedric hesitated, then dug his fingers into the jam and scooped some into his mouth. I quickly screwed on the lid and put the jar back in the cupboard. Just as I was sliding off the counter onto the box, I thought I heard footsteps. "Get the box back," I whispered. "Quick."

But nobody was there. I slipped my feet into my shoes, went into the lavvy and pulled the chain. Then I grabbed Cedric's hand and dragged him out of the house. We ran like the wind back to the Kindergarten room. We were both out of breath when we got there but Cedric was grinning. At the door he said, "We're going to be friends for ever and ever. I know we are."

"Well, just until the war's over and we leave here. You'll go back to Birmingham and I'll go back to Wales."

"No," said Cedric, firmly. His eyes stared hard into mine. He had soft, silky brown hair cut in a fringe across his forehead, almost touching his eyebrows. "No!" His eyes flashed, caught in the sunlight. "It'll be forever, and ever. You'll see."

Then he turned and darted ahead of me into the Kindergarten room.

"Where have you been?" Mrs Riley asked.

"I had to go to the lavatory."

"Well get to your desk, Patricia. It'll be your turn next. I hope you know your six-times table."

"Yes, Mrs. Riley."

Sunday, 23rd September, 1940
Dear Mummy and Daddy
We have a new boy called Cedric and I have made him my friend because he is homesick.
Please (can) may I have some more chocolate. I've only got 4 squares left. Mrs. Baker said I counted wrong but I don't think so.
It will be half-term soon. Does that mean I can come home?
With love from your homesick daughter
Patricia

Sunday, 30th September, 1940
Dear Mummy and Daddy
Thank you for the chocolate.
I had to write "please MAY I have some more chocolate" 100 times. Mrs. Baker says it's the only way to teach me.
With love from your VERY homesick daughter,
Patricia

Chapter 5

Roman Legionaries

'Mensa, mensa, mensam, mensae, mensae, mensa.
Mensae, mensae, mansas, mansarum, mensis, mensis.'

Over and over again, we chanted our Latin declensions and verb conjugations, and learned them by heart. For the life of me, I couldn't understand how a table could be a person, or so many different people. *"A table is a THING. Four legs and a top."*

Miss Audrey-Joan always made us laugh when she declined what she called personal pronouns. *"Ego...me...mei"*...and when she came to *'mihi,'* she wrinkled up her nose and breathed in as she said *"mihi,"* so it sounded like a big snort. She liked it when we laughed, and told us we would probably remember it for the rest of our lives, because we'd remember how she snorted.

Miss Audrey-Joan told us she was a classicist and she was going to make jolly sure that by the time we were ready to go on to big school, we would have a solid grounding in Classics and Literature. She started off by giving us all Latin names. When it was my turn she told me that I had a very impressive name already; Patricia was a very noble name in Latin. "However," she said, "just for fun, we'll call you Portia."

It didn't sound much like fun to me but it was better than Hortensia—the name she'd given Arabella Bosworthy—which made Bossy Bella pout. So that *was* fun.

After a few lessons, we started to read stories in Latin about the Roman Legions and how they fought great battles all over Gaul, then came to Britain and lived in places like Londinium. When we had breaks, and outside before tea, we played at being conquering Romans and, with foot soldiers and cavalry, fought great battles against the Celts and the Gauls.

Children who had skipping ropes were soldiers; those who didn't were horses. The soldier wound the rope around the back of the horse's neck, criss-crossed its chest and back under its arms. The soldier held the two handles and galloped his horse madly over lawns and pathways, playing at being the conquerors or, sometimes, the conquered. Because I didn't have a skipping rope, I had to be a horse, which I didn't like. Occasionally, I borrowed a skipping rope and made Cedric my horse, but the owner always came and gave me a slap or a pinch, and demanded it back. Then I had to go back to being Alex Gilbert's horse.

A massive weeping ash at the end of the lawn, formed a domed area; a perfect Roman Forum. Here we became gladiators fighting lions–and each other. Miss Audrey-Joan also brought the adventures of Odysseus to life, and we switched to fighting monsters, such as the Minotaur and Cyclops. Ann-the-Bank, who hated running around and fighting battles, was happy to perch on a branch of the ash tree and knit; the patient Penelope creating Odysseus's shroud.

A few days later, after dinner, Miss Audrey-Joan called me into her study. She didn't look very pleased with me. "I hear you are taking other peoples' property, Patricia."

"No I'm not, Miss Baker."

Miss Baker made her eyebrows disappear under her curly fringe and puckered up her lips. It was a while before she asked me another question.

"I was told you have been taking other children's skipping ropes."

"Oh no. I'm not taking them. I'm just borrowing them."

"Hmm. Borrowing, Patricia? Without asking?"

"Well, they weren't there to ask. Anyway, they weren't using them. So I borrowed them to play Roman Cavalry horses. But I always put them back...except when they came and got them first. Which they did mostly."

Miss Baker sighed. "Borrowing...or taking...without asking the owner's permission is very close to stealing you know."

"Oh, no. I wasn't stealing them. They got them back."

There was another long silence from Miss Baker—then, "Well, Patricia, I'm not too happy about this turn of events. However, I'll give you the benefit of the doubt. THIS TIME. But if I find you taking things again—or borrowing—without asking permission, the punishment will be severe. Very severe. Do you understand?"

"Yes, Miss Baker."

Cedric, Ann-the-Bank and I were huddled together on the steps of the children's entrance. The wind was chilly and snatched up dead leaves from the chestnuts and sycamores, and whirled them around us. They settled on the bushes, on the flower beds and in little heaps against the wall that separated the garden from the stable yards.

"What do you think the 'benefit of the doubt' means?" I asked.

Cedric sighed and shoved his hands deeper into his pockets; he'd lost his gloves. "I dunno. Though I heard my mummy say that we would benefit a lot if we went to America or Canada."

Ann's nose was pink from the cold wind and she sniffed as she reached up her knicker leg for her hanky. "My Da says he gets a lot of doubters in the bank where he works. He says they're mostly liars as well."

None of that helped. And I didn't like the sound of the liar bit.

There wasn't much else to say or do, except wait for the tea bell. So we just sat there, shivering, watching the crackly dry leaves sweep the summer dust from the garden path.

Sunday, 6th October, 1940
Dear Mater and Pater

We are learning Latin now. We all have Latin names. I am called Portia. I don't know why.

Please ~~can~~ I have a skipping rope. I don't like being a horse. Miss Baker made the red line through 'can' and I have to write this again. Please may I have a skipping rope? Then I won't have to borrow someone else's.

Love from Patricia

Sunday, 13th October, 1940

Dear Mummy and Daddy,

Thank you for the skipping rope. Now when we play horses, I don't have to be the horse. I made Cedric my horse and he has to wear my rope and go where I say.

Please (can) may I have some more chocolate. This evening, we are going to listen to Princess Elizabeth talk to children on the wireless.

Next week is half-term. Does that mean I (can) may come home?

With love from,

Patricia

Sunday, 20th October, 1940

Dear Mummy and Daddy

Thank you for the chocolate.

I had to write "please may I have some more chocolate" another 100 times. Mrs. Baker says I have to learn it, OR ELSE. I think she means I (can't) mayn't ask for any more chocolate. We listened to Princess Elizabeth talk to us on the wireless. She said that all children at home are full of cheerfulness and courage. And she said that in the end all will be well.

I'm sad that I mayn't come home for half-term. Ann-the-Bank is sad that she mayn't come home too. So is Cedric. We are all sad, even though Princess Elizabeth said we are all cheerful.

Love from your sad daughter,

Patricia

P.S. I lost my skipping rope.

Chapter 6

Half Term

Mrs. Baker bustled around the house shutting windows against a blustery wind that was blowing dead leaves and old summer dust onto our beds and the floor. Half-term and autumn had arrived together.

Half-term was the eagerly anticipated break when we could go home for a long weekend. There were twelve of us who couldn't go home. The dailies were never there on the weekends anyway, and the weeklies stayed at school during the week and went home every Friday. Most of us were full boarders because it was not safe to stay where we lived. Some didn't even have a home any more because it had been bombed. Then there was Ann-the-Bank who lived in Wales, and me who had been evacuated to Wales, where there were no evacuation schools, only sheep. Our mothers were still there, but we were told it was too far to go just for a long weekend.

"Besides," my mother had written to Miss Baker. "Patricia is just getting used to being at boarding school and with her father now away in the War, I think it would be too unsettling for her to come home for only a few days."

As I stood in front of her desk, Miss Baker read most of what my mother had written out loud, but I knew there were bits I didn't get to hear because, when she stopped reading out loud, her eyes kept going from side to side over the familiar blue writing paper. She made little *hm-hm* noises as she read to herself.

I could feel the prickling in the back of my nose. I didn't want Miss Audrey-Joan to see tears in my eyes, so I stared at my shoes. But she must have known that anyway because in an instant she was kneeling down beside me with her finger under my chin so I was looking straight into her face. "Come on, little one," she said. "You're really doing quite well you know. You're getting used to being at Normanhurst, and you're making new friends. Apart from the time and attention you lavish on the cats, you've been helping Cedric feel less homesick, and you and Ann are good company for each other."

"Yes Miss Baker."

"Besides, we have lots of things planned for half term. There will no lessons, only fun and games, I promise. And I've found an exciting book to read to you all before you go to bed. It'll be a holiday here too."

Then Miss Baker gave me a quick hug and told me to run along. To what or where I was supposed to run along, I wasn't sure, but she was so nice I just said, "Yes, Miss Baker," and left. Outside her study door, I turned to take the big brass door knob—that was just about level with my chest—in both hands. Before I shut the door, I could see Miss Baker moving slowly back to the big leather chair behind her desk. She was shaking her head and looked sad. I closed the door quietly; I hoped it wasn't me that was making her sad.

And now, to celebrate half-term there was going to be, according to Mr. B, a 'mother and father of a storm.' As he was closing the big wooden shutters across the windows and latching them in place with iron bars, we could hear him forecasting all sorts of exciting happenings that would come with the storm. "Shouldn't wonder if it takes down some of the dead tree branches. And of course, the fruit will be whipped off the trees in the orchard."

We were in the middle of tea when the lights went out. There were squeaks, squeals, yells and giggles as our group of twelve groped in the dark to finish scrambled eggs and baked beans on toast. Someone knocked over their milk mug and others shrieked as the cold liquid dripped onto their bare legs. Suddenly, there was an almighty yell from Cedric. "Stop it! Stop taking my tea!"

That horrible pig and bully, Giles Farmer, had reached across the table and grabbed a handful of Cedric's tea. At the very moment he scooped up the food, Mrs. B came into the dining room, followed by Miss Audrey-Joan and Mrs. Tommy, each carrying an old-fashioned oil lamp.

We all gasped in horror at the sight of Cedric's beans and scrambled egg spilled across the table, and of Giles Farmer stuffing a handful into his mouth. With a thump that made the flame flicker madly inside its glass funnel, Mrs. B banged her lamp down on the end of the table. She marched around to where Giles was sitting. Grabbing him by the back of his shirt collar, she heaved him out of his seat and dragged him to the far corner of the dining room. Pushing him sharply away from her, he stumbled and landed with his nose against the angled corner. "Stay there and don't you dare even twitch a muscle, *Mister* Farmer. You will stand there until I say you may move."

Mrs. B, now very red in the face, came back to the table. Cedric was sobbing and I had my arm around him trying to comfort him. I felt sorry for him–he was always getting bullied and picked on. Besides, I felt especially responsible for Cedric after Miss Audrey-Joan had said I was helping him get over being homesick.

"Don't cry Cedric," said Mrs. B. I'll get you some more tea." With her hand, she swept the spilled food back onto the plate and left the room. Nobody spoke. The only sound in the room was Cedric sobbing, but no-one teased him, or told him to stop being a cry-baby. Miss Audrey-Joan and Mrs. Tommy had followed Mrs. B. In the corner, Giles Farmer sniffed and wiped his piggy-nose on the sleeve of his green school pullover.

It only took a few minutes for Mrs. B to come back with a fresh plate of scrambled egg and beans. But this time the toast was cut into eight little triangles and arranged around the edge of the plate. And there was REAL BUTTER on the toast. Not the usual dry toast, not even a scrape of the disgusting bright-yellow wartime margarine, but soft, golden pools of real butter that were slowly melting into the fresh hot toast.

We all stared at it. Nobody said a word.

I nudged Cedric. "Go on. Eat it. Eat it while it's hot and melty."

Cedric looked around. Everyone nodded. Somehow, it seemed right that he should have such a treat. "I can't eat all this. I'd already eaten half of my first tea."

So Cedric carefully spread two of the toast triangles with scrambled egg and topped them with a tiny heap of beans. One he put on my plate, the other he gave to Alex Gilbert who sat on the other side of him. Ann-the-Bank was on the other side of me, so I cut the triangle exactly in two, counted out the beans, and gave her one half. Alex did the same for his neighbour. Then more triangles went to the children sitting opposite, and at the end of the table. Still silent, everyone took their small bite of golden buttered toast and passed a piece on, until all had a share.

Cedric still had two triangles of toast left. To a chorus of "thank you, Cedric" he ate the rest of his beans and egg and then, with a toast triangle in each hand, sat back in his chair and bit into them. Ever so slowly, he licked the butter off his lips. Then he smiled.

And while the storm battered and banged at the tightly shuttered windows, we sat cosily in the glow of the oil lamps, licking the golden butter off our fingers, and remembering the nursery teas of the days before the war.

An hour later, the storm was still rattling the windows behind the shutters and the lights were still out, but eleven of us were sitting in front of a crackling log fire in Miss Audrey-Joan's study. The twelfth child—Giles Farmer—remained standing in his dark corner of the dining room.

In a worn brown-leather arm-chair, Miss Audrey-Joan sat on one side of the fire, a bright oil lamp beside her so she could see to read. Mrs. B sat on the other side, her feet on a tapestry footstool, and by the light of another lamp darned our socks where they had worn into holes. As I sat on the warm patterned hearthrug, in the golden glow of oil lamps and flickering firelight–and listened to the adventures of Mowgli and Shere Khan, I thought that perhaps half term could turn out to be quite fun–even though I was not going home to see my mother and Dilly in Wales.

Next morning, Mrs. B opened the shutters to a pale morning sun. Bits of twigs and leaves littered the lawns and pathways and an enormous branch from one of the big oaks had fallen, completely blocking the driveway. Pieces of red clay from a shattered chimney pot lay scattered in front of the columned porch.

While Mrs. B was pouring our tea at breakfast, she told us two things. First, that Giles Farmer had been sent to Coventry for the whole weekend and ABSOLUTELY NO-ONE was to talk to him. "His punishment will be given in front of everyone on Tuesday, when school starts again after half term," she announced.

We all knew what *that* meant. We looked at each other in silence and wriggled uncomfortably in our seats. Except for being expelled, a caning in front of the whole school was the most horrendous and direful punishment anyone could have.

"The other thing," Mrs. B went on quickly, "is that the wind last night blew down an apple tree in the orchard and after breakfast we're all going out to collect the windfalls."

Breakfast, bed-making and lavatory duties over, the twelve of us–dressed in Welly boots and our oldest clothes–trooped out to the orchard. We were excited and looking forward to a day of running around instead of lessons. A strong, warm breeze buffeted our chests and blew our hair 'all ways for ninepence,' as Dilly used to say. The only one who wasn't laughing was Giles Farmer, who trailed way behind us in the deepest Coventry. Cedric, who was walking between Ann-the-Bank and me, kept glancing over his shoulder at the big bully.

"Don't worry Cedric," I said. "He won't hurt you. He won't even come near you. Ever."

Cedric said nothing and started skipping along, enjoying the fun. As we caught sight of the apple tree that had been uprooted by the storm, we all leaped around in excitement. It was terrible to see the great tree stretched out the ground, like a huge fallen giant. The gigantic roots at the foot even towered above Mr. B, and there was a deep hole where they had been torn from the ground. The most incredible sight though, was a wicked looking black gash right down the centre of the trunk where the lightning had struck. The branches were still laden with rosy apples, although dozens littered the ground where they'd been blown or knocked off. Mr. B had two wheelbarrows full of willow baskets for us to collect the apples in. We children had to pick up the ones on the ground while Mr. and Mrs. B, Miss Audrey-Joan and Mrs. Tommy picked the ones off the tree. We were longing to explore the tree, so when most of the apples had been collected, we had a stupendous time climbing all over it, swinging from its branches and examining the great cleft where the lightning had struck. Then Miss Audrey-Joan made up a great game where we were Robin Hood and his Merry Men and we lived in the trees, ate apples, and chased each other with sticks for swords. Cedric was Robin Hood, which made him very happy. Alex Gilbert was Little John, and I was Will Scarlett because I was wearing a red jumper. Ann-the-Bank hated climbing trees and wanted to be Maid Marian but soon got bored because she had to sit on an old tree-stump all alone, pre-tending to be imprisoned in Nottingham Castle. She kept asking Robin Hood to rescue her but Cedric was too busy hiding in the branches of the apple tree and shooting arrows at all who passed by. Then David McArthur got poked in the eye so we had to put down our sticks.

At the end of the day, we traipsed back into the house where a won-derful smell of baking met us at the kitchen door. From the apples we had collected, Mrs. B and Mrs. Tommy had made some fat and juicy pies, which we ate—with lots of thick yellow custard—for tea. Later, Miss Audrey-Joan read more of *The Jungle Book* while we sat in front of the fire in her study, and Giles Farmer sat in his Coventry corner.

After that, half-term seemed to fly by. In no time at all it was Tuesday. At morning assembly on Tuesday, after the prayers and the hymn, Miss Audrey-Joan gave us a very serious lecture.

She told us that, in wartime, there were hundreds and thousands of starving children in Europe where food was very hard to come by. That anyone should steal someone else's food was the most heinous of crimes and would not be tolerated. She said that Giles Farmer had violated the good name of Normanhurst School, and indeed of Britain, by stealing food. He would be punished.

We all had to watch while Giles Farmer, his trousers and under-drawers down around his ankles, was told to lean over the back of a chair. Then he was caned on his bare bottom. We stared, horrified, as great red marks appeared each time the cane smashed down. One- two-three-four-five – six strokes. Giles was screaming and blubbering and some of the younger children were crying too. Cedric covered his face with his hands and wouldn't look. I could see his shoulders shaking.

"THAT," thundered Miss Audrey-Joan, "is the punishment for stealing food. Food is rationed and we all have equal shares. Anyone found steal-ing food from now on, will not only get the cane, but will be expelled from Normanhurst. It must never, never happen again."

We filed out of the assembly room in silence and went to our class-rooms. At break time, Cedric came up to me and whispered in my ear. "I have to talk to you. It's very important."

We went into the shrubbery where nobody could hear.

Cedric looked at me very solemnly, his brown eyes red and watery. "I've been thinking. I don't think we should steal any more jam."

I thought for a moment about what had happened to Giles Farmer. "P'r'aps you're right."

So we didn't.

Sunday, 27th October, 1940
Dear Mummy and Daddy,
We had a nice half term. There was a big storm and the lights went out and an apple tree fell down when it was struck by lightning. We had apple pie for tea.
Please send me two large pots of your home-made jam. Any sort will do.
With love from
Patricia.

Sunday, 27th October, 1940
Dear Dilly,

I'm glad that you want me to write to you. I miss you very much. But I'm happy that you are staying to look after Mummy while Daddy is away fighting the Germans.

It's half-term now and there are twelve of us who can't go home but we are not having lessons. It's supposed to be like a real holiday but we are still at school.

After church today, we went out to play our Robin Hood game, but it started to rain, so we have to occupy ourselves indoors. Mrs. Baker said I could write to you.

I remember when you told me that you were an orphan. Now I know what it's like to be an orphan. There is no mother and father, and we have to live in a strange place with lots of other children we don't know. Except Ann-the-Bank. We have beds next to each other. Sometimes when it is really cold and everyone is asleep, we both climb into one bed to get warm and whisper about home. Just like I used to climb into your bed and you told me stories about when you were a little girl in the orphanage.

I have a new friend, his name is Cedric and is a New Child. I found him hiding behind the coat racks and he was crying for his mummy. I told him I couldn't be his mummy but I would be his best friend and we'd be like brother and sister. Cedric is very nice and has good ideas for games. Not all the children are nice. Giles Farmer is a terrible bully. And the worst girl in the school is Arabella Bosworthy. She is spiteful. We call her Bossy Bella.

I'm going to fold this letter and send it with my Sunday letter to Mummy and Daddy. Just in case they didn't know about you telling me stories in bed, I will glue the edges together and write 'private' on the outside.

I miss you doing my hair. And scrubbing my back. We only have two baths a week. There are four bathrooms and two children in each bath at a time. The girls have the front bathrooms and the boys are at the back. We are allowed five inches of warm water in each bath. When our hair is washed on Saturdays, Mrs. Baker pours a bucket of water over our

*heads to rinse out the soap and then we dry it in front of the
fireplace. I'm going to grow my hair long and then I will get
more time at the fireplace.*
Please write back and tell me YOUR daily doings.
With lots of love from
Patty

Chapter 7

Ghosts and Guy Fawkes

Sunday, 3rd November, 1940
Dear Mummy and Daddy.
Mr. Baker is building a straw man for Guy Fawkes tomorrow.
He says we can't have any fireworks because of the blackout.
Mrs. Baker says we can have a bonfire before dark and roast
chestnuts and potatoes. We are lucky to have a chestnut tree
in the garden and we collected three big baskets full.
Miss Baker says we can play ghosts in the garden when it is
dark to make up for not having fireworks.
Love from
Patricia XXX

There was a space between the rubbish dump and the orchard,
where Mr. B burned stuff. All the rubbish that couldn't be used either
in the compost, or put in the village pig-food bin, was sorted out and
burned. The Saturday before Guy Fawkes Day, dressed in our play

clothes and Wellies, we collected all the dead wood from the orchard and Mr. B piled it up in his rubbish-burning pit. By the time it was finished, there was a tower was as tall as Mr. B.

The only thing I remembered about Guy Fawkes night at our big home before the War, was burning my hand on a sparkler that my father was twirling. My mother told me I was fascinated by the shower of bright stars that whirled and danced from his hands. When the last spark flew and died, I grabbed the glowing little stick and was burned. Since then, because of the war, fireworks have been forbidden. Bonfires and rockets after dark would make easy targets for enemy bombers.

"But we can have an afternoon bonfire," Miss Audrey-Joan promised us. "And we'll roast chestnuts and potatoes. After tea we'll have some fun and play 'ghosts.'"

We had already played 'ghosts' a few days before, on Hallowe'en. It wasn't a very complicated game. All we did was run around in the half-dark, and scare each other. We hid behind trees and, with blood curdling yells, jumped out at whoever passed. Mrs. Tommy and Mrs Riley dressed up in white sheets and scared us all to death by flitting around the gardens, then jumping out at us when we least expected it. Miss Audrey-Joan, dressed up as a witch and, astride Mr. B's hazel switch-broom, she galloped amongst us, cackling and shrieking. We chased, raced, screamed and shrieked at every shadow, until we ended up rolling on the lawn and gasping for breath. When Miss Audrey-Joan thought we'd had enough, we traipsed back into the house, for milk and biscuits. Then we scurried off to bed as fast as we could, Miss Audrey-Joan's reminder ringing in our ears to get tucked into bed and off to sleep before the *real* witches and spirits of Hallowe'en came a-hunting and a-haunting.

We'd had such fun that we begged and pleaded for more games of 'ghosts.' So the promise of after-dark ghostly fun on Guy Fawkes night, more than made up for not having fireworks.

Ann-the-Bank, Cedric and I, gulped down our dinner, as fast as we could. Saturday dinner was usually a sausage each with vegetables and gravy. Today, the sausage came with stewed tomatoes and mashed potatoes, followed by semolina pudding with a dollop of red sticky jam in the middle. As usual, Mrs. B hovered over us to make sure we minded our manners.

Rowley Smythe was slapping a mound of pink mush with his fork. Mrs. B had mashed all his tomatoes and potato together. She was standing watching him–her hands on her hips. "*Mister* Smythe. We *will* eat our dinner up today. There are starving children in Europe who would give their eye teeth for what you are playing with on your plate. You will stay here until that plate is scraped clean, like the other children's. *And I am watching your pockets, Mister Smythe.*"

Rowley was obviously hungry. He'd wolfed down his sausage in two bites. He glowered at everyone from under his pale carrot-coloured eyebrows, while making swirly patterns in the mush with his fork.

But we didn't have time to be bothered with Rowley Smythe battling with Mrs. B over his dinner. We had plans to go and find Mr. B, who was making a guy for the bonfire. As soon as our spoons had scraped up the last smear of the gluey semolina pudding, our hands were waving in the air, requesting to be excused from the table. If Mrs. B deemed that we had earned our dismissal by behaving like ladies and gentlemen and finishing every morsel on our plates, we were free to go. She nodded at Cedric, Ann-the-Bank and me so we left—not forgetting to take our plates, cups and utensils into the back kitchen for the washing up gang. Glancing over my shoulder as I left the room, I saw Mrs. B, fists leaning on the table, towering over Rowley Smythe who was making minute dents in his pink mashed potatoes.

We ran Mr. B to earth in the stables. He was heaving the guy onto a wheelbarrow. We shrieked with laughter at his funny creation. Mr. B had stuffed a dusty old sack with rags and burnable rubbish mixed with straw. By tying some garden twine in the right places, he'd formed a head and a bulky body. Attached to the body, was a very tattered pair of trousers—also stuffed—tucked into a pair of ancient and leaky Wellies. The body was wearing a red jumper, so full of holes and rips that even Mrs. B couldn't unpick it to knit up again, and an old scarf that had been a moth's dinner, was tied around its neck. Two cardboard milk bottle tops served as eyes, two slices of turnip formed a perfect mouth, and a long withered carrot stuck out through a hole cut in the centre of the hessian face. To top it off, the guy was wearing a tin hat.

"Don't worry," said Mr. B when he saw Cedric eyeing the tin hat. "That's just for show. I'll take it off before the bonfire can get at it."

After Mr. B had settled the guy into the wheelbarrow, he produced an old Ovaltine tin with a slit in its top. It rattled as he shook it. "C'mon, now. Penny for the guy. Give us a penny for the guy."

"Why a penny for the guy? He's already got all he needs." Ann-the-Bank was always so logical, when it came to money matters.

"Well now, kiddies. I thought we might collect a few pennies to send to some of those poor children who have been bombed out of their homes."

"I don't know that I have a penny," Cedric was fishing in his pockets.

We didn't keep money on us anyway. Miss Audrey-Joan had a 'Pocket Money Bank' where she kept any money our parents sent us. It was supposed to be spent on toothpaste, any medicines we might need, and the offering plate at church."Can we get some pennies out of our Pocket Money Bank," I asked.

"Well," Mr. B replied. "You'd better go and find Miss Audrey-Joan and see if she can help you there. And we'll pass the collecting tin around when we light the bonfire."

"Can I do that?" asked Cedric.

"What? Light the bonfire?"

"No. Collect the pennies."

"Of course you can, Cedric. That would be a nice gesture."

"What's a gesture?" I asked, as we scuried off to find Miss Audrey-Joan.

"I dunno." Cedric shrugged.

"Prob'ly just a nice thing to do." Ann-the-Bank usually came up with some idea for words we didn't know. She didn't know them herself. But sometimes they sounded right.

We found Miss Audrey-Joan in her study. We tiptoed across the blue patterned Persian rug in the hall and scratched on her door. Entry into Miss Audrey-Joan's study was by invitation only and then it was mostly when we were in trouble. However, she'd promised us more story readings by her fire when the wet and wintry weather stopped us going outside to play.

She was expecting us. Smiling, she beckoned us to come in and we saw she had the shoe box where she kept our pocket money envelopes, ready on her desk. They were individually named on the front and on the back, an account of our in's and out's.

"How much would you like to give?" She asked, her eyes darting at each of us in turn.

I nudged Ann, "Your Da's a bank manager. You should know."

"Is it like Church?" Cedric asked. We were always given a penny from our envelopes on Sundays to put in the collection plate.

"Well now, Cedric, I suppose it is. Something like that. Many boys and girls live in cities that have been bombed, and didn't have the opportunity to be evacuated. Some of those who stayed have lost their homes, and some have even lost their families.

"They're orphans?" I asked

"They could be."

"Dilly's an orphan."

"Is she now. Then you know that means these boys and girls have no parents."

"I think we should give two pennies," said Cedric. "One for orphan girls and one for orphan boys."

So that was settled, and we went back to find Mr. B; our pennies for the bombed orphan children, jangling in our pockets.

To our surprise, the mothers belonging to the dailies and weeklies turned up for the bonfire. Mr. B had built a chestnut-roasting grill out of bricks and an old oven rack. Worrying that she didn't have enough for everybody, Mrs. B hurried away for more potatoes to bake in the ashes. She needn't have worried, there was plenty of everything. Mr. B had set the Guy–without the tin hat–on top of the bonfire and while we hopped and danced from one foot to another in excitement, he set light to the massive pile. Cedric ran around shaking the Ovaltine tin. The mothers who were there didn't just give pennies, for I saw a lot of stubby three-penny bits go in the tin, and the occasional glint of a silver sixpence.

Miss Audrey-Joan and her helpers were kept busy making sure we didn't get too near the fire, or burn our hands or mouths on hot chestnuts and potatoes. Even Giles Farmer behaved himself because his mother was there. Arabella Bosworthy's mother was there too. She was wearing a fur coat, just like the one my Aunt Mathilda wears. She also had long scarlet-painted fingernails. I thought it odd that, while her mother wore long red claws on the ends of her fingers, Bossy Bella bit her nails 'til they bled.

By sunset, all the potatoes and chestnuts had been eaten and Mr. B threw water on the bonfire to make sure it was out by blackout time. Then we showed the dailies and their mothers how we played ghosts. It was stupendous fun. All the mothers joined in and made good ghost shrieks. Ann, Cedric and I wore our pillow cases over our heads. We'd cut holes for eyes and another for the mouth. We scared everybody by jumping out from behind trees and bushes.

"Whatever will your mothers say?" Mrs. B was shocked when she saw what we'd done. But Miss Audrey-Joan laughed and said that she'd probably done the same thing when she was our age.

When the dailies and their mothers had gone home, Mrs. B and Miss Audrey-Joan scrubbed the bonfire ash from our faces, hands and knees until we were clean and ready for bed. With my pillow case back on its pillow, I fell asleep quickly. But I remember that, for a long time afterwards, my pillow smelled of smoky roast chestnuts and, every other week 'til the end of the war, Ann-the-Bank and I slept on pillow cases with three little holes.

Chapter 8

We Go to Church Every Sunday

Apart from it being the right and proper thing to do, it was listed in the school curriculum. It was called Divinity if you belonged to the Church of England–Religious Instruction if you were a Catholic. Most of us were Church of England, except for three brothers, Jeremy, Jonathan, and James aged seven, eight and nine, who were Catholics. Then there was Ann-the-Bank. Ann was a Welsh Baptist and proud of it.

Divinity had three distinct routines for our development as good and devout Christians. Every day, we had Morning Assembly and Prayers when we would sing a hymn and pray for those in peril on the sea, in the air and in the trenches. We would pray for those who'd been bombed out of their homes, and for the souls of those who'd been blown to bits when their homes were hit. We also prayed for ourselves mostly, I remember, that the Lord was our Shepherd, that we should be humble and meek–for the meek inherit the earth– and that we should be charitable towards our friends, neighbours and teachers. The Catholic boys were weeklies so didn't go with us to church on Sundays, but they were obliged to attend Morning Assembly. They didn't have to join in the prayers unless they wanted to—which they didn't, or sing the hymns—which they did. Ann-the-Bank attended, for two reasons: one was that the alternative was learning passages from the Bible by heart; which was what Welsh Baptists were supposed to do. And the other was that she was afraid she might miss something. So she prayed and sang in the right places and throughout the whole assembly, wore an expression of total martyrdom. She might as well have been Joan-of-Arc.

Once a week, we had a Divinity class which all attended, Catholic, Anglican and Welsh Baptist. For Divinity class, Miss Audrey-Joan read stories from the Bible appropriate to the particular time of year, or event; like Christmas, Easter and Whitsuntide. If it was raining stair-rods outside, she read us the story of Noah's Ark; she said the rain made it more believable. Once, when she read the story of Samson and Delilah, all the girls had their eyes fixed on Giles Farmer, each concentrating on a plan to bring the bully down by cutting off his straggly, greasy hair. Our Divinity lesson was usually on a Friday just before dinner, which was always fish pie. This was fine by me because I loved fish pie. It was hot and filling, full of potatoes and onions and had a crispy, golden crust.

Then there were Sundays. On Sundays we didn't play games. Instead, we all dressed in our Sunday-best uniforms and walked in crocodile, to church. Along with her Sunday hat, Ann donned her Welsh Baptist persona, and marched beside me, her eyes cast heavenwards–Joan-of-Arc bound for the stake.

Miss Audrey-Joan Baker, B.A. (Hons.) knew her Christian duty towards her charges, and abided by it. However, she applied the same unique method and style to the development of our souls, as she did to educating our minds; she made it as much fun as possible.

Part of this fun was not going to the same church every week. Sometimes we went to the Eardington village church, which was around the corner from the Dog and Cock pub and opposite the post office. Sometimes, when the weather was good, we marched three miles to the parish church of St. Leonards in Bridgnorth. And sometimes, when it was hot and sunny, we went to the parish church in Quatt, which was perched high on a sandstone bluff on the opposite bank of the River Severn.

At breakfast on this particular Sunday, Miss Audrey-Joan told us we were having an Indian Summer, which was unusual for November. Also, she'd heard from Constable Penny, that the river was still low enough for us to cross one last time before winter set in. We would go to church in Quatt.

To go to church in Quatt was the best Sunday adventure. Even though the objective was boring, it was well worth it. We lined up two-by-two and walked through the school gates into the world outside. We crossed the main road and into a lane leading to the railway line. In a tiny cottage next to a level crossing, lived a short, fat man with his short, round wife, who were in charge of the crossing gates. We called them Mr. Tweedledum and Mrs Tweedledee. Although the white-painted railway gates were usually open for us, the cheery couple would run out to greet us; smiling and waving us on.

"Off to church be ye all? Well that's nice. Take care not to fall in the river, or ye'll get your pretty uniforms wet. And please be so kind as to say a prayer for us railway folk." Then they would run back into their cottage, laughing and waving. "Nice kiddies," we could hear them say. "Such nice, well-behaved kiddies."

We would wave back and as we turned another corner in the lane, we would shout, "See you on the way back!"

Another half-mile or so brought us to the River Severn. By that time, the lane had turned into a muddy pathway. Mrs. B would huff and puff and tell us not to get our good shoes muddy, and to "Keep in line now. Remember, you are Normanhurst children, not guttersnipes." And all the while, she would be hanging onto her second best navy-blue straw hat with a bunch of white silk daisies on the brim.

At this point, there was a fairly shallow ford where it was possible to cross the river when it was at a normal level; which it was for most of the summer and into the autumn. In the spring, however, the river rose and often burst its banks and flooded the surrounding fields. In Bridgnorth Low Town, an old stone wall displayed dozens of metal plaques, each recording the date and height to which the River Severn rose in that particular year. Some plaques were level with second storey windows in nearby houses. When the river was in flood, the ferry boat would be turned upside down on high stilts, for no-one would risk taking it across the fast currents and treacherous swirls of muddy water.

On the river bank, in a miniature stone tower, hung a big iron bell; it's purpose to summon the ferryman from his cottage, high on the opposite cliff. Mrs. B yanked on the rope and the loud clanging echoed and bounced across the bright dancing water. Someone came out of the cottage and climbed down steps cut into the cliff to a wooden landing stage. We watched as the ferry boat came across to pick us up. A tall, thin woman stood in the stern and poled the vessel upstream a little way to avoid two big rocks, then turned and came slowly down with the current and across towards us. Her husband was really the ferryman but, since he'd joined a Royal Navy warship on the high seas, she had taken over.

"Just wait a minute, nippers," she called out as we jostled to be the first in the boat. "Wait until I get her beached and tied up, before you get in. And no jumping, please. I don't want to have to patch any more holes in her." She winked at Miss Audrey-Joan, who grinned back.

The ferryboat made two trips across the river to get us all to the other side. We loved it. Especially when we were right out in the middle of the river and we could see such a long way up- and down-stream. It was then I noticed Cedric. He wasn't enjoying it at all. He sat between Ann-the-Bank and me and for the whole trip across he had his eyes shut, and his knuckles were white as he clutched the rough board of the seat. I nudged him with my elbow. "Cedric, what's the matter?" He didn't answer, just bowed his head on his chest. This was odd behaviour for Cedric, who usually enjoyed the river outing.

"Cedric. Say something. Tell me what's wrong." He still said nothing. I nudged him again.

His bowed head twisted sideways towards me. His eyes were still screwed up and shut. He was not crying, but his feet and legs were trembling. "I–don't–like–the–water."

Bossy Bella, who was sitting opposite him, kicked him on the shin. "He's just a cry-baby and a scaredy-cat."

"Leave him alone, Arabella Bosworthy. You shouldn't be spiteful on a Sunday."

I spoke just loud enough for Mrs. B to hear and at her sharp look Bossy Bella turned her head away and started chewing on her nails, pretending nothing had happened.

When we reached the other side, the ferryboat lady lifted Cedric and swung him way over our heads and onto the little plank dock. Then she turned back and helped the rest of us scramble out. We climbed the steep cliff steps cut into the sandy rock, up into the churchyard, where Mrs. B and Miss Audrey-Joan inspected us for any mud, burrs, or river water that we might have collected on the way. With a reminder that we were now entering the House of God, so Speak-at-your-Peril-and-Behave-like-Ladies-and-Gentlemen, we dutifully bowed our heads and entered into the chill of the ancient stone church.

Apart from a lot of kneeling for prayers, and the endless sitting while the vicar preached his sermon, we all quite enjoyed going to Quatt church. The Vicar had white hair and twinkly blue eyes and always appeared to be enjoying himself. And he always spoke some special words just for us. He told us that, in this time of strife between nations and although we were separated from our parents, we should be Thankful for the Small Mercies that God grants us. And one Small Mercy he could offer us was that he'd decided that next Lent—which was a long way off anyway and the war might be over by then—we would not be asked to give up our sweet ration. Instead we should give more of our free time to learning how to knit. Then we could spend Lent knitting socks and scarves for our brave soldiers, sailors and airmen.

Now *that* Small Mercy, I could easily handle. Knitting–poof! That was the easy part. Dilly had already taught me to knit, and if that was all I had to do to avoid sacrificing my chocolate ration during Lent…well.

I started thinking about Small Mercies and decided that the best Small Mercy I could come up with at this moment, was the fact that Arabella Bosworthy was a daily. This meant we didn't have to put up with her at night or on weekends. However, this particular Sunday, Bossy Bella and her brother D'arcy had joined us for church. Some of us challenged them when they turned up at school on Sunday morning.

"What are you doing here? You're s'posed to go to church with your mother."

"Well, we're here because our mother is too busy to take us to church. So there."

"More like your mother doesn't want to take you. She's prob'ly doing something better."

Arabella was always bragging how her mother entertained at the weekend. She did something called a 'Let's Get Together for a Pink Gin Sometime.' This happened to be one of those Sundays when Arabella and D'arcy Bosworthy's mother was 'Getting Together with a Pink Gin.' So for the rest of the Vicar's sermon, I thought about how we could make our return trip on the ferry more interesting.

Sunday, 10th November, 1940

Dear Mummy and Daddy

Mr. Baker found my skipping rope in the boys' lavatory. Cedric took it and hid it because he didn't want to be my horse.

Mrs. Baker smacked Cedric. Cedric is still my friend.

I am a Roman Cavalry Soldier so I have to have a horse. Rowley Smythe is my horse. It's nice that I have a horse. What is not so nice is that Rowley smells like one. We are learning about the Romans in Londinium.

Love from,

Patricia

P.S. Please give the enclosed letter to Dilly.

Sunday, 10th November, 1940

Dear Dilly:

We went to church in Quatt Village this morning. We had to cross the river Severn in boats like the Romans did when they conquered the Vigornians. On the way back, we pretended we were Roman soldiers in their triremes going to battle. We thought the horses shouldn't be in the boat. So Arabella Bosworthy pushed her horse out of the boat. Mrs. Baker was so cross. She put on a face that would rupture custard and said it was fortunate for us that it happened on the way back, and not before we went to church. She also said that Arabella

Bosworthy would be severely punished. So that made up for her being so spiteful to Cedric.

Mrs. Baker told us to be Vikings from now on. Vikings didn't have horses. They went in ships and didn't push each other into the water.

Arabella Bosworthy says I have to give her the chocolate I promised her for pushing her horse into the river. Please will you ask Mummy to send me some.

With love from

Patty

Monday, 11th November, 1940

Dear Daddy,

We had another Sunday today and as it's a Special Day to remember soldiers and sailors, I have to write a letter to you because you are a soldier.

We had a special service at the village church and there were lots of flowers. We were given red poppies to wear and we had to stand in silence for two whole minutes. Some ladies were crying. I'm not sure why.

We are not allowed to play today. It is too sad a day. Mrs. Baker started reading A Tale of Two Cities *and told us that we should not be sitting around with idle hands. She is going to teach us to knit because there is a war on. I told her Dilly had already taught me how to knit. She said that was good as it meant she had one less child to struggle with. If I knit a scarf for a soldier, will you get it?*

Will you come home from the war soon?

Love from your daughter,

Patricia

Chapter 9

Nativity Play

Sunday, 17th November, 1940
Dear Mummy,
I am enclosing a birthday card for you that I made myself. I also have a brooch that I made for you but Mrs. Baker says it will be squashed in the post so I will save it until the war is over.
Mrs. Baker says Christmas is six weeks away and then we get to go home if our parents can take us. Please, please, PLEASE may I come home for Christmas
We are doing a nativity play. I have to be the Virgin Mary.
Mr. Baker calls me Pat-a-cake, Mrs. Tommy calls me Patty and Mrs. Baker mostly calls me Pat. Only Miss Audrey-Joan calls me Patricia. In Latin I am Portia and in French I am Paulette. Which am I?
Your loving daughter, P.

Wednesday, 21st November, 1940
Dearest Pooh-bear! (Which is what I like to call you!)
Thank you so much for the lovely birthday card. I look forward to seeing the brooch you made for me.
I thought it would be nice for you to come home for Christmas. Aunt Mathilda is bringing your cousins, Rachel and Rupert from Colwyn Bay so we can all have Christmas together. Of course Dilly will be here to help out.
Daddy and I are pleased to hear that you have settled down nicely in the three months you have been away.
I have written to Miss Baker. She will see that you are put on a train in Bridgnorth. We will meet you at this end.
I hope your Nativity Play goes off successfully. I am sure you will make a good Virgin Mary.
With lots of love from,
Mummy.

Sunday, 24th November, 1940
Dear Mummy and Daddy,
Thank you for letting me come home for Christmas, it makes me very happy. Mr. Baker says he will put me on the train and I will have a label on me like a piece of luggage and the guard will put me off at the right station in Wales.
I am looking forward to seeing everybody. Will Daddy come home for Christmas?
With love from
your excited daughter,
Patricia (Pooh-bear)

Sunday, 1st December, 1940
Dear Mummy and Daddy,
Thank you for the ribbons and the picture of the Virgin Mary. She doesn't look like me.

We all found white caterpillars in our porridge yesterday. We had to pick them out and then eat the porridge. Judy Ross, Miles Meredith and Cedric were sick on the floor.

Mrs. Baker caught Rowley Smythe stuffing his porridge into his pocket. She took his trousers down and smacked his bottom with a ruler. We all watched. Rowley got red marks on his bottom.

With love from

Patricia

Sunday, 8th December, 1940

Dear Mummy and Daddy,

We are practising for the Nativity play. Mr. Baker is building the scenery.

I asked Mrs. Baker why I have to be the Virgin Mary because I don't look like her in the picture you sent me. Mrs. Baker says it's because I am the only girl who can carry a tune. I didn't know I could carry a tune. I'm not very sure what it means to carry a tune.

We are knitting socks for soldiers. The boys are knitting scarves so they don't have to turn a heel. Mrs. Baker says she doesn't have the patience to teach them.

Love from

Patricia

Sunday, 15th December, 1940

Dear Mummy and Daddy:

We are doing the Nativity play on Friday. I have to wear a blue scarf on my head but it keeps slipping off. Mrs. Baker says I have difficult hair.

This is the last letter I have to write before I come home for Christmas. May I have a blue scarf and a music book for Christmas?

Mrs. Baker says if I have learned nothing else I have learned
to write 'may' instead of 'can' in the proper places.
Seven children have to stay for Christmas. My friend Cedric is
one of them.
You didn't tell me if Daddy will come home for Christmas.
Love from your happy daughter,
Patricia-Pooh-Bear.

The Saturday before the Nativity Play, Mr. B hauled a huge trunk filled with dress-up stuff from the cellar. Miss Audrey-Joan said that some of it had been there since she and her sister, Miss Margaret, were little girls. The trunk was full of treasures. There were flapper dresses from the twenties, crinolines and corsets, bonnets and beads, crowns and tiaras. We had such fun choosing the costumes for the Nativity Play. Velvet robes transformed Alex Gilbert, Dudley Armstrong and Andrew Simon into three Kings, complete with golden crowns and jewelled caskets. Soft brown woolen monks' habits, tea towels and a band of rope for the proper headdresses, and behold!—we had two poor shepherds to watch over their flocks. A flowing white robe and floor-length cardboard wings, touched up with gold tinsel, turned Arabella Bosworthy into the Angel Gabriel. It must have pleased her because she was nice to everyone for the whole week. Cedric in striped pyjama trousers, a white shirt belted with rope, and a striped towel draped over his head, became Joseph. Mrs. Tommy let me wear a heavenly blue silk sari she'd brought from India, and with a cushion tied around my tummy (for I was great with child) and I leaned on Cedric's arm.

The only unhappy person was Ann-the-Bank, who didn't want to be in the Nativity play because she didn't like singing in front of people. When she saw us all dressed up and having fun, she disappeared upstairs. Mrs. B found her on her bed, sobbing. She wanted to dress up. So Miss Audrey-Joan wrapped her in a white sheepskin rug, painted her nose black, and put some little ears on a piece of elastic around her head. "There now, Ann. You are a little Welsh sheep and all you have to say is 'baa.'"

So Ann snuggled into the sheepskin and sat cross-legged beside the shepherds. In the end, she had the most to say in the whole play, because she never stopped 'baaing' from the opening carol to the final curtain.

The Nativity Play was performed in the dining hall, because it was the biggest room. Miss Audrey-Joan said it had possibly been a ballroom in olden days. Mr. B who's very clever at building things, built Bethlehem at one end. Centre stage was a peak-roofed stable thatched with straw. From the stables, he brought in a wooden feed trough, for the manger. Scattered all around were bundles of hay and dried wild flowers. Hanging from the ceiling, over the stable, was the shining star of Bethlehem. Mr. B fixed up a bicycle lamp behind it so it lit up to look heavenly. To one side of the stage, pieces of green carpet and rocks from the garden, made the shepherds' field, and on the other side, a plywood board with a hinged door front, looked just like the picture of the inn in our Christmas storybook. A china doll, wrapped in strips of sacking, was laid in the manger. The cats were quite happy to lie around in the hay being themselves. The smallest children were wrapped in rugs and given painted cardboard animal faces. They huddled down on the hay, moo-ing, grunting or squeaking.

The whole play fell somewhere between an operetta and a carol service. Miss Audrey-Joan had composed singing lines and speaking lines. Leaning heavily on Cedric's arm as we travelled to Bethlehem, I had to sing some solos; as did Cedric who had a high and perfectly pitched soprano voice. Miss Audrey-Joan pounded the piano and led the carol singing. *We Three Kings of Orient Are* was a great success, as was *Away in a Manger* with three of the little animals each singing a verse. But nobody heard *While Shepherds Watched*; it was drowned out by 'baas' from the Welsh sheep. Arabella Bosworthy glided onto the stage but only managed to say "Hail Mary" before a wing fell off and she tripped over it. Pink-faced and angry, she picked herself up and started again, but she forgot the bit about being 'highly favoured amongst women.' After four more 'Hail Mary's,' she burst into tears and ran off the stage. So we finished without her. The play ended with the whole cast–except Arabella–singing *Adeste Fideles* which we'd learned by heart in our Latin lessons. On the very last note, the lights were dimmed and the Star of Bethlehem shone brightly down on Baby Jesus in the manger. Mr. B let go a net he'd attached to the ceiling and tiny pieces of white paper floated down on the stable roof. Everyone ooh'd and ahh'd and clapped.

There were only a few days of school left before we broke up for the holidays and I would be going home to Wales.

"Perhaps the war would end at Christmas. After all, wasn't that what the angels sang about? 'Peace on Earth?'

"Then I wouldn't have to come back to Normanhurst."

Chapter 10

Home for Christmas

Sunday, 15th December, 1940
Dear Mummy,
On Wednesday, Mr. B is going to put Ann-the-Bank and me
on the train for Wales. I wonder if you will get me before
this letter.
Will Daddy be home for Christmas?
With love from your excited daughter
Patricia

The Sunday before I went home to Wales for Christmas, there was a candlelight Carol Service at the Village Church. In the deep, hard wooden pew, Cedric and I sat one each side of Miss Audrey-Joan. Ann-the-Bank, on my other side, kept kicking me because she was jealous of me sitting next to Miss Audrey-Joan, so I pinched her arm hard enough to make her yelp. Mrs. B grabbed Ann and made her sit at the far end of the pew in front of her. For the rest of the service Ann sat wearing her

Welsh Baptist Martyr look, her eyes fixed on the roof rafters, and her hands in a prayer clasp on her chest.

"I think I'll call her Ann-of-Arc instead of Ann-the-Bank."

While Miss Audrey read one of the lessons, I looked at Cedric. His eyes were sparkling bright in the candlelight—as though he had tears in them. Outside, after the service, I asked him,"Cedric, what was wrong in church. Were you so sad because you couldn't go home for Christmas?"

He was trying to dislodge a small stone from the frozen ground with the toe of his shoe. "Yes," he said, "but there was something more than that. I just felt very sad. I don't know why." He finally loosened the stone, picked it up and put it in his pocket. "C'mon. Race you to the church gate."

And off we went, racing, chasing, and laughing, the red winter sun sinking behind the leafless elms.

The next two days flew by. Last minute presents to be made: a book mark for my mother, a painted beechmast brooch for Aunt Mathilda, a little acorn-man brooch for Dilly, and a pair of acorn cuff links for my father. We painted Christmas cards with sprigs of holly, Christmas trees, and robins with red breasts, in as many different variations as we could crib off each other.

Our trunks appeared in our dormitories. Mrs. B and Mrs. Tommy came and helped us cram in everything we needed, including what we'd grown out of, and taking care not to squash the precious home-made gifts.

Finally Wednesday came. As I came down the stairs, ready for Mr. B to take us to the station, I found Cedric sitting on the bottom step. "Merry Christmas," he said, handing me a small package. "But take it with you. You mustn't open it 'til Christmas Day. Promise?"

"Thank you Cedric. And I promise I'll save it 'til Christmas Day. My present to you is under the Christmas Tree. I told Miss Audrey-Joan and she said she'll make sure you find it on Christmas morning."

"That's all right then. G'bye. See you next year!" He grinned and took off, leaping up the stairs two at a time without even looking over his shoulder.

I yelled after him, "See you next year, Cedric."

I looked at the little package–brown paper (the stamps still on it) from a parcel his mother had sent, pulled into a little sack and tied at the top with a bow of red wool. Then Mrs. B called me so I put it in my coat pocket and, gas mask bouncing on my back, ran out the front door.

Mr. B was in the float, Ann-the-Bank was sitting on one of the side benches. Our trunks, locked and roped, were on the floor. Mr. B took Dobbin's reins, " C'mon Lady Patricia. Your carriage awaits. We don't want to miss the train for that unpronounceable place in Wales."

I shook hands with Miss Audrey-Joan and Mrs. B. Mrs. Tommy gave me a hug and hung a luggage label around my neck. On it, printed in large black letters, was my name and the words:

"Passenger to
Llanwyrted Wells, Breconshire, Wales.
To Be Met."

Ann had a similar label.

"Now you don't take those labels off for anything. Do you under-stand?" Mrs. B was fussing around us, making sure the labels were set just right and the straps of our gas masks wouldn't cover them up. She gave us each a brown paper parcel with a string handle that she looped over our wrists.

"This is your food for the journey. Try not to eat it too soon–or all at once. You'll be on the train for a long time, and Lord only knows how long you'll have to wait to get your connections."

Lifting me up, she settled me on the seat by Ann, and wrapped a tartan rug around our knees. She gave our scarves an extra twist around our necks, made sure our gloves were pulled up over our wrists, and checked our gas masks. "Off you go now, you two. Have a lovely Christmas."

They all waved good bye as we set off down the driveway, their cries of 'Merry Christmas,' and 'see you next year' getting fainter and fainter. I looked back. I thought I saw Cedric standing at one of the top windows. I waved just in case it was him.

Dobbin started off at a brisk trot and in no time at all–or so it seemed–we were in Bridgnorth. Divided into Low Town and High Town, a cable railway joined the two levels for anyone who didn't want to walk up the steep hill. High Town is way, way up, perched on the cliff above Low Town, which is down by the river. Dobbin pulled us up into High Town and along to the station.

Mr. B bought tickets and took us to find the stationmaster. "These young ladies are going to Wales. I'll put them on the train, but I need you to make sure the guard keeps an eye on them."

The stationmaster took a big gold watch from his waistcoat pocket and flicked the cover open. "Well now," he said. "Their train will be here in about ten minutes. Platform One. Get them settled in a non-smoker. The guard will look after them, but they'll have to change at Craven Arms, and then again at Builth. But with those big labels around their necks, I'm sure they'll be just fine."

Apart from a big number '1', there were only three other signs on the platform. One said 'Ticket Office,' another read 'Stationmaster,' and the third, 'Waiting Rooms and WC.' All the other signs, including the name 'Bridgnorth' had been painted over in black.

"So if the Germans land, they won't know where they are," Mr. B explained.

A few minutes later, we saw a plume of smoke along the line and watched as the engine puffed into the station. It was filthy and dripping with water, and when it came clanging and squeaking to a halt, clouds of steam whooshed from somewhere underneath it. Behind the coal tender, were a half-dozen carriages criss-crossed with dirty sooty streaks. Two were a yellowy-cream on the top, and chocolate brown on the bottom half; the letters 'GWR' just visible through the grime. The rest were an equally dirty maroon, with 'LMS' painted on their sides.

Mr. B found the guard and, after talking to him about Ann and me, settled us in the compartment next to the guard's van. "Now remember, girls. You're going a long way on your own, but lots of kiddies do it in wartime. You'll be quite safe, I promise. You've got your picnic and a book to read. Try to sleep if you can. And the lavvy is next door when you need it."

He looked at us both without saying anything, then suddenly he hugged us, one in each arm. Just as suddenly, he let us go and pulled a handful of sweets from his pocket which he divided between us. He wished us 'Merry Christmas' and was gone. We hung out of the window and waved as he went along the platform to where he'd hitched Dobbin. At the end of the platform he turned and waved again. Then, with a noisy gush of hot smelly steam, the engine jerked, the carriages rattled, and we were off. We heaved on the wide leather strap to pull the window up; we both knew that if we didn't, the compartment would soon be full of flying ash and grit from the engine. Since the war began and petrol had been rationed, we'd often travelled by train and once, a cinder had blown in my eye; I remembered the pain.

It was a long journey. We enjoyed it to begin with. Using our mittens to rub a clear space on the steamed up windows, we excitedly pointed out the little houses, farms and fields as the train raced by. Apart from convoys of army lorries and tanks on some of the roads, it didn't look as though there was a war on. Often we saw people, boys on bikes and mothers with prams, waiting by level-crossing gates for our train to flash by. We waved and they waved back.

When the guard put us off at Craven Arms, the stationmaster told us to go in and sit by the fire in the waiting room. "You've over an hour to wait, young ladies. You'd best be taking forty winks. The time will pass quicker."

Ann and I sat on the hard benches in front of the tiny fire. It smoked a bit, but was warmer than outside. Our picnics had long gone: two Spam sandwiches, a wrinkled apple and a piece of Mrs. Tommy's bread pudding. I was just wishing for a drink when the porter came in with two steaming mugs. "Here, nippers. My mate just made a pot o' tea. Thought you might like some. Sorry, it's tinned milk though. Cows am short changin' us these days, unless 'tis that Lord Woolton wot's taking all the milk." He handed us the hot tea, which tasted heavenly. As he went out, I heard him say to his mate, "Get more nippers with luggage labels around their necks these days than we do bloody parcels. Cryin' shame if you ask me."

We'd barely finished the tea when our connecting train arrived. Smaller and even dirtier than the first one, its cold compartments smelled of stale smoke and wet clothes. But we didn't care; we were excited to be that much nearer home. The deeper we travelled into Wales, the more it looked like nothing ever happened there. Sheep dotted the hills, which were patchworked with grey screes of tumbled rock, the brown of last summer's heather, and the green gorse bushes.

Another wait at Builth Wells for the local puffer—as my father called it—to Llanwyrted Wells. When it came, it was even smaller and smellier than the last one, with no corridor or loo, but we didn't mind. About twenty minutes, the guard had said, and we would be home. But it seemed to take forever. We stopped at every little village platform–the names all painted over in black–where passengers either got on or off. All we could hear was the banging of carriage doors and cheery shouts of '*Nos da!*' and '*Shw mai!*' and '*Nadolid Llawen!*'–'Merry Christmas!' before the little 'puffer' jerked and rattled on to the next station.

Finally, at one stop, the guard came along the platform and banged on the window. "Next station is yours, young ladies. You'll soon be with your Mams. I'll get your trunks ready."

Ann and I looked at each other in silence; our eyes shining with excitement.

At the next stop, I practically fell off the train into Mummy's and Dilly's arms, and hung on as though I never wanted to let go.

Ann's Mam was there too. Ann burst into tears when she saw her.

When my mother finally untangled herself from my clutches, she held me at arm's length and looked me up and down. "Goodness me! I think you've grown an inch."

Dilly laughed, "More than that, I wouldn't wonder. I'm off to find a porter for her trunk."

It was then I noticed that my father wasn't there. "Where's Daddy? Is he at home?"

My mother knelt down–her face level with mine. "I'm sorry, my darling, but Daddy won't be home for Christmas."

Chapter 11

Christmas, 1940

Cledwyn-the-Car had his Alvis Atlantic waiting to take us home. To save Cledwyn's petrol ration, Ann-the-Bank and her Mam squeezed in with us. They sat in the front, Ann chattering away nineteen-to-the-dozen. I sat on Mummy's lap in the back, with Dilly beside us. But I couldn't think of anything to say. The excitement of coming home for Christmas had vanished with the news that my daddy wouldn't be with us. Mummy hugged me tightly and Dilly held my hand. They asked me questions about the journey, and about school. I think I answered, but I don't remember what I said. Anyway, Ann was talking enough for both of us and she chirpily replied to everyone's questions, even Cledwyn's.

I shivered, the car was cold. My mother wrapped a Welsh wool rug around me, but my feet were numb. "We'll soon be home," she said, gathering the folds of the rug a little tighter. "Then we'll get you some hot soup. Dilly made it especially for you."

I nodded in the dark, but I felt the familiar prickling at the back of my nose.

"Why isn't Daddy coming home? Where is he? Where is the war? And why doesn't it stop for Christmas?" I sniffed back my tears, and leaned closer to Mummy. She didn't say anything. Neither did Dilly.

But she was right about one thing. A few minutes later we were home.

After Cledwyn-the-Car had pulled my trunk into the tiny stone hallway, and Ann and her Mam were home next door, and the front door closed, it was strangely silent. Dilly had disappeared into the kitchen, and Mummy was helping me out of my outdoor clothes. She took the label from around my neck, and hung it on a peg, along with my gas mask. I stood still, taking in the familiar smells and sights of home. The comforting scent of Mummy's lavender water. The loud, slow tick of the Grandfather clock at the end of the hall. The watercolour of Lake Windermere, where my grandfather had a big old house. The smell of food coming from the kitchen, where I could hear Dilly humming to herself and the clattering of plates as she set the table. Home!

Mummy took my hand. "Come along, Pooh-Bear. Let's go into the kitchen and see what Dilly has for tea."

That was strange. I didn't remember eating in the kitchen; ever. We always ate in the dining room. But I didn't question it. The kitchen was warm and cosy, the oil lamps were lit and there were three steaming bowls of soup on the table.

"You're very quiet, young lady." Dilly tucked a napkin under my chin. "Left your tongue at school, have you then, *bach*?"

"I think she's just tired." Mummy smoothed my straggling hair back from my face. "It was a long journey. She'll be her old self after a good sleep."

Later, scrubbed and soaped clean in a tin tub by the kitchen fire–"the upstairs bathroom is too cold"–Mummy had said and after Dilly had rubbed my hair dry and dressed me in warm pyjamas, Mummy carried me upstairs to listen to my prayers and tuck me in. When I was snuggled down in the huge feather bed with Edward Bear, and a towel-wrapped stone hot-water-bottle at my feet, she leaned over to kiss me goodnight.

"I know you're disappointed that Daddy isn't coming home for Christmas. I'm disappointed too. But there's a war on and the sacrifices we make come in many different disguises. However, we *do* have something to look forward to."

I turned my head on the pillow and saw she was smiling. "Daddy will talk to us on the telephone. He's not fighting overseas. He's working hard at training young men to be soldiers, here, in England. He's promised to telephone us on Christmas Eve. Besides, your Aunt Mathilda, Rupert and Rachel will be here the day after tomorrow and that will make Christmas very jolly. Aunt Laura and Uncle Fred will be here too. So there'll be a houseful. Just like old times...well almost."

Mummy picked up the oil lamp. "Do I have to be in the dark?" I asked.

"No. Of course not. Dilly found a battery for your night-light. See? Owl is right here." From the bedside table, she picked up the familiar white glass owl, who'd lived in my bedroom ever since I could remember, and switched it on. It shed a soft glow throughout the room.

Through the half-open door, I could see my Mummy's shadow against the wall as she carried the oil lamp down the landing. "Good night, Pooh-bear," she called out as she went downstairs. "*Nos da.* Sleep tight, don't let the bed-bugs bite!"

I looked Owl. I was really, really home. Normanhurst was a very long train journey away.

"And so was Cedric."

In Wales, especially in the middle of winter, a feather bed is the warmest and cosiest place to be. It's also very hard to get out of. The more so, when Jack Frost has crept up in the night and painted the windows with magical fern and snowflake patterns, and when you poke your nose out from under the covers, you can see your breath steaming. I could see all this because Dilly must have taken the blackout down and switched Owl off while I was still sleeping. It was light outside, and I could hear her raking the kitchen fire into a blaze, after it had been banked down all night.

I inched out of my feather nest and looked over the side. It was a long way to the floor, but my bedroom slippers were there and, on the end of the bed, my red dressing gown. I was awake and hungry, so there was nothing else but to brave the cold floor.

Sliding down from the high, old-fashioned bed, I scooped up my slippers and dressing gown and ran into Mummy's room. She was sitting up in bed, wearing a pink woolly bedjacket, looking pretty and perfect. She had a writing pad on her knees and her blue Swan fountain pen in her hand. I leaped into the bed beside her and under the covers.

"Oooh. Get away from me you little imp. Your feet are cold."

"What are you doing?"

"I'm writing to your Father. I write to him every day."

"You don't write to me every day."

"I write to you twice a week, which I think is enough. If you had letters to read every day, you would never have time for lessons."

"Are you getting up?"

"When I've finished. Why don't you take your clothes downstairs and Dilly will let you dress by the kitchen fire. It's warm there."

Mummy was right. The kitchen was warm, the kettle was singing on the hob and Dilly was humming along with the wireless. It was a nice song about bluebirds and white cliffs.

Dilly was my pet name for Dilys, and she was my favourite person in the whole wide world. Dilly helped with the cleaning and the cooking. She looked after me, she looked after Mummy and she helped in the garden. She called herself a 'general factotum' and said it was what she liked to do best. Before the war, and before we had to evacuate to Wales, we lived in a very big house and we had a lot of people to look after us. But they were all gone now. Gone was our cook, the maids, the gardener and the charlady. Gone was my nanny. The men were gone to fight and the women to join the ATS, the WRNS, the Land Army, or the Nursing Corps to do their bit for Britain. But Dilly stayed. She was 18 and an orphan. She had nowhere to go and she loved me and my mother dearly. So here she was, 'buried in Welsh Wales' as Mummy would say. Dilly was our rock.

"Well, now, *bach*. How about a piece of bacon and an egg for breakfast? Better than wormy porridge, I'll be bound."

Bacon! I hadn't had bacon in a long while. And it smelled so good. At Normanhurst, bacon and egg with fried bread, had only been in my dreams.

"By the way, Patty. I don't suppose Mrs. Baker gave you your ration book to bring home, did she?"

"She gave me an envelope to give to Mummy. It's in my gas mask box, for safety."

"Well, I hope that's what's in the envelope. Rationing is bad. Each person gets only one egg a week now. And the dried ones are horrible."

"Then whose egg is this?"

"Oh, don't worry. I've been making friends with the farmers here, and we've been collecting a few extra goodies for Christmas."

There was a knock at the back door and John-the-Post came in, stamping his feet and blowing on his hands. "*Shw mae*. Good morning. And here's the little one, home for Christmas. Welcome *bach*?"

I sat and sorted through a pile of Christmas cards and letters, while John-the-Post and Dilly had a cup of tea and chatted. I put aside an envelope addressed to Mummy in Daddy's familiar tiny scribble.

When Mummy came down to breakfast, John-the-Post left. I sat and watched while she opened her cards and letters. She didn't eat bacon and egg–just a piece of toast.

"It was nice to be home. No lesson bells."

The next two days were full of busyness. We went shopping in the village, which was at the bottom of a steep hill (our house was at the top). We bought our meat and grocery rations for the week; Dilly had saved some points for a few extras. Mrs. B had sent ration points for two weeks, so that helped too. Our last stop was to see Bronwen at the village sweet shop. As the door bell jangled, her short round form bustled out from her back room. "My, my. If it isn't our little school-girl back from England. And I do believe you've grown, *bach*. It must be all those chocolate bars your Mam sends you."

I leaned my chin on the counter and smiled. It was good to hear her soft, lilting Welsh voice again.

After she had packed up our purchases, she came round from behind the counter and, leaning down, slipped something into my pocket. "*Nalodid Llawen*. A little treat for Christmas, *Cariad*."

"Thank you very much, Bronwen. *Diolch yn fawr.* And Merry Christmas to you." She hugged me. She smelled of chocolate, aniseed and toffee all mixed up together.

The next day, Dilly took me out to a farmer who had some Christmas trees. He cut one for us and John-the-Post turned up to help drag it back to the house. It was a steep hill to climb and we were all puffed, red-cheeked and hungry when we got home.

"We'll decorate it when your aunt and cousins get here," Mummy decided. So we left the little tree leaning against the coal shed out in the cold.

The day before Christmas Eve, my aunt and cousins arrived, their noses pink and sniffy from the cold journey. While Cledwyn-the-Car unloaded trunks and boxes, bundles and bags, they squeezed into the tiny hallway, all talking at once. I was so excited that all I could do was hop from one foot to another.

"Patty," Aunt Mathilda said, "show Rachel the bedroom you're sharing."

"Sharing?" Rachel squealed. "I'm not sharing! I want my *own* room. I have my own room at home."

"Well, you will be sharing a room here," Aunt Mathilda told her. "You'll also be sharing a bed. A nice big double-bed with a feather mattress."

Rachel's horror was obvious. Tossing her mop of golden curls–of which I was very envious–she stamped her foot and started whining at my aunt. "I don't *want* to share a bed. I don't *want* to share a room. I want my *own* room."

Rachel was a whiner. She whined when she had to get up and she whined when she had to go to bed. She whined if she lost at Snakes and Ladders. She whined about everything.

"That will do, Rachel. You WILL share a bedroom, and a bed, with Patty."

At my aunt's tone of voice, Rupert, who was only three, started to wail. Rupert was a wailer. He wailed when he was hungry. He wailed when he couldn't get his own way. He wailed even louder when Rachel pinched him. And I didn't like him very much because he also had a lot of golden curls. Far too many for a boy, was my opinion.

"Oh, dear, oh, dear." My mother was not used to whining and wailing children. I neither whined nor wailed for the simple reason there was no one there to hear me if I did. I didn't have a brother to pinch and I didn't have a sister who bullied me. I had a bedroom of my own, although sometimes, when it was very dark and lonely, I wished I could share it with someone. I was not sure that I understood why my cousins were so miserable. I soon found out.

"They're tired," explained my aunt."It's been a long journey. And I think Rupert's had a little accident in his trousers."

"Oh dear, oh dear." Mummy *really* didn't know what to do. "Dilly," she called, "Dilly, we need you."

Dilly immediately sorted everything. With flaming and uncontrollable curly red hair falling onto thin shoulders, laughing grey eyes and hands that were scarlet and chilblained with constant housework, she went to work on Rupert, Rachel and my aunt. Swiftly sticking a dolly mixture into each of their mouths, she scooped up Rupert, grabbed Rachel by the hand and calling to me over her shoulder to follow, the hallway was instantly quiet and orderly; except for my mother and Aunt Mathilda standing amongst all the luggage.

"I'll bring you ladies some tea in five minutes," Dilly said.

Suiting actions to words, she sat us down at the kitchen table, dumped a big black iron kettle on the hob, then disappeared with Rupert into the back kitchen to clean him up.

From that moment, it seemed that Dilly waved a magic wand and Christmas 1940, silently and vividly, took it's place amongst my childhood memories.

In the middle of the afternoon on Christmas Eve, Aunt Mathilda produced a big cardboard box tied up with string. Rachel, Rupert and I sat wriggling impatiently while Dilly carefully untied the string, wound it around her fingers and stowed it away in her pocket. Then we all watched while Aunt Mathilda unpacked the family Christmas tree decorations.

When she had reached the bottom of the box, she took out a magnificent tree stand that looked like polished silver. Dilly brought in the tree and helped my aunt fix it into the stand. We all spent the rest of the afternoon decorating it; us children doing the bottom branches and the grown-ups the higher ones.

When the final trail of tinsel had been set in place, Aunt Mathilda pressed a button on the stand. Slowly, the tree started to revolve. She pressed another button and it played Christmas Carols; the tinkling sounded like an old music-box. Whether it ran by clockwork, battery, or a crank, I don't know. But I do remember being transfixed by the sight of this little fir tree, the tinsel and ornaments glinting and glittering in the firelight and in the pale glow of the December sun that streamed though the window. The star of Bethlehem, caught in each rotation, twinkled at us from ceiling height.

No one spoke, everyone watched.

When Dilly called us for tea, none of us wanted to leave the tree. So she laid a cloth on the hearthrug, brought in a long toasting fork and toasted tea-cakes by the fire for us children. Mummy and Aunt Mathilda sat in the kitchen to have their tea. "They're making Christmas plans," Dilly told us.

When tea was cleared away, the carols were turned off although the tree still revolved. "It is time," Mummy said, "to sing our own carols."

She played the piano and we all sang. Rupert lay and banged his heels on the hearthrug but nobody took any notice of him. We just went on singing–everybody choosing their favourites. As Mummy said, "We have time to sing them all."

We were only half-way through the carol book, when we were interrupted by a loud knocking at the front door.

When Dilly opened the door, she screamed. Then Mummy went to see what was happening and she screamed. Then I ran out and screamed the loudest.

Cledwyn-the-Car was hauling a brown suitcase and an army haversack into the hall. Behind him, stood the tall figure of my father. My mother and I grabbed him. He hugged us both at the same time. When he kissed me, I felt scratchy cold icicles on his mustache. Finally we let him go so he could take off his coat and boots.

"Just pulled a few strings and managed a forty-eight-hour." He smiled so sweetly at my mother as he shrugged off gas mask, great coat and boots, gloves and scarf. "But at least I'm here for Christmas with my little treasure." He leant down and scooped me up in one arm–the other tightly around my mother's waist. "With both my treasures."

Mummy's face was pink and smiling, and her dark eyes sparkled in the lamplight.

"Christmas in Wales was going to be perfect after all."

Christmas Day started early, with bulging stockings at the foot of our beds that had mysteriously arrived during the night. No tangerines this wartime Christmas. I found a few nuts and a bright new shilling in the toe, a twist of dolly mixtures, ribbons for my hair, woolly mittens for my hands, and a tiny handkerchief with my name embroidered in the corner. And, treasure indeed, a pretty blue beaded necklace.

The house was bustling and busy, everyone hugging and 'Merry Christmassing.' By the time we'd breakfasted, it was time to get dressed in our Sunday best—my father in his Major's uniform–and go to Church for the Christmas service. Aunt Laura and Uncle Fred were also at church, so we all walked home together. We found Dilly putting the finishing touches to the Christmas dinner.

From who-knows-which farmer friend, she had acquired a goose. Roasted and bursting at the seams with stuffing, everyone ooh'd and aah'd as she set it on the dining-room table. All the trimmings were there, including a bowl of my favourite bread sauce, and potatoes roasted to a deep, crisp brown. Aunt Mathilda had donated a Christmas pudding, hoarded from before the war and we all eagerly hunted for the silver favours and threepenny bits. Rachel got the bachelor's button–which she didn't like–so she started whining. She stopped complaining when Daddy offered her his threepenny bit in exchange for the button. Mummy said something about "You'd better not take the bachelor's button too seriously while you are away, or there could be dire consequences." But she was laughing while she said it; Daddy laughed too, and kissed her in front of us all. We were all very merry Christmassy, and ate too much. Dilly had made crackers from an old magazine. With pin holes poked around the centre they were guaranteed to pull apart. Each one contained a boiled sweet and a paper hat. Then my father opened a bottle of port, Uncle Fred lit his pipe, and the familiar fragrance of his special 'Heather Mixture' tobacco filled the room.

As it was Christmas, we all helped Dilly with the washing up. Even Daddy and Uncle Fred helped, although Aunt Laura said they were worse than useless with a dish towel. This sent Rachel and I into fits of giggles. We children rushed around to help as we knew that, once the dishes were done, it would be present time.

There was a pile of gaily wrapped and decorated presents under the tree. They weren't wrapped in the pre-war bright shiny paper and ribbons, but in ordinary paper, painted and decorated with dried flowers, and holly sprigs. Before breakfast, while the grown-ups were at early morning Communion, I had crept down and put my little packages there, including the one from Cedric which I stashed at the back where it wouldn't be noticed.

My father handed out the presents. I got a *First Steps in Music* book and a cuddly doll made from one of my mother's old brown woollen stockings. Two more packages contained books: an Enid Blyton adventure from Aunt Mathilda and the latest Arthur Ransome from Mummy. She'd also knitted me a new jumper, which was the same colour as the blue scarf I'd asked for. Writing paper and envelopes from Aunt Laura, a five-shilling book token from Uncle Fred, and the promised fountain pen from my father, completed my pile of presents, or so I thought.

Dilly said, "Wait a minute." She disappeared into the dark hallway. I held my breath. Moments later she was back carrying a big square newspaper parcel. Inside I found a dolls' house made from a wooden box she'd begged from Albert-the-greengrocer. Painted a very bright pink (I learned later it was the only colour she could find), it had windows framed with little net curtains, a front door with a shiny Zip Fastener tag for a knocker, and a shoe-button door knob. In every room, Dilly had placed furniture which she had fashioned from empty matchboxes, twigs and conkers. Perfect. And sitting on one of the conker and twig chairs, was the tiniest teddy bear I'd ever seen. He was wearing a striped knitted jumper, red shorts and he had twinkling blue glass eyes.

"His name is Blue-eyes," I announced unnecessarily.

Another constant companion, he lived in my pocket for years–actually, until I was sixteen–after he'd been promoted from companion to mascot.

He helped me through exams, tennis matches, school plays and concerts, until one day he disappeared. Where he went, I'll never know. He just vanished. But I still miss him.

Still more surprises. Daddy cleared the clutter of presents and paper from his lap and left the room. I heard him open the back door and go outside to the shed. A couple of bumps and bangs and he was back, standing in the doorway; he was hiding something behind him. He beckoned me to him, then stepped aside revealing a spanking new, bright shiny bicycle. I had *never, ever* had a bicycle before.

"How in heaven's name did you manage to find that? In wartime?" Mummy was looking at it suspiciously. "A bicycle of all things. Oh my!"

I didn't bother listening to anything else Mummy said. With one hand supporting the bike, Daddy lifted me onto the saddle. Shiny chrome handlebars with a bell, the rest was painted maroon red, except for the saddle which was black. It even had a tiny maroon luggage grid on the back.

"Can I ride it? Oh please, Daddy. Can I ride it? Oh...*may* I ride it?"

"Well, suppose I take you out tomorrow and help you? We'll use Mummy's camera to take a photo."

"But what is she going to do with it?" Mummy was still bewildered at my present. "She can't ride it in the winter, and it looks a little big for her."

"I telephoned Miss Baker," Daddy replied, "and she says a lot of the older children have bicycles, and so I think it can go back to school with her. Miss Baker will decide when she's ready to ride it. I happened to come across it, and bought it." He paused. "A sort of a spur-of-the-moment impulse. Children's bikes are almost impossible to find now."

At that moment, I couldn't be bothered to listen to Mummy's "Oh dear's," and "She'll fall off and hurt herself's." I just wanted to touch it, hold the handlebars and ring the wee bell. Then a ruckus started as Rachel and Rupert realised that I'd got a bicycle and they hadn't. Both wailing and whining that they wanted bikes. But I didn't care. I followed Daddy outside again and watched as he carefully put it back in the shed.

I flung my arms around him. "Thank you, Daddy. Oh thank you a hundred times. I love my bicycle."

"There, there," he replied. "I'm glad you like it. And don't worry. Mummy will soon get used to it. Happy Christmas, my darling."

"Happy Christmas, Daddy."

I felt something soft on face and looked up. Gently and slowly, as if they didn't really mean to, snow flakes came floating down to make my Christmas perfect.

The rest of Christmas day was spent playing our favourite party games. Charades, Passing-the-Ring, Blind Man's Bluff and Pass-the-Parcel, which was great fun. Then Dilly put out cold ham and goose, trifle, Christmas cake and mince pies for supper and soon after that, it was time for us children to go to bed. The time had come for the grown-ups to sit quietly, have their Christmas ports, brandies and sherries, talk about the War and remember Christmasses of long ago. I know, because when Rachel was asleep, I crept downstairs to listen. Dilly was sitting with them, saying nothing; just gazing into the fire and scratching at her chilblains. When my feet got cold, I went back up to bed.

Sometime in the night I awoke again and remembered Cedric's present–it was still under the tree. I slid down from the high bed and pattered across the floor. The cold sent me back for my slippers. I knew everyone was in bed, as I could hear snores coming from Aunt Mathilda's room. I could hear Mummy and Daddy talking quietly to each other, but I was certain they wouldn't hear me. I crept downstairs.

I reached under the tree for Cedric's present. Embers were still glowing in the fireplace, and there were some scraps of wrapping paper and a small log on the hearth, so I pulled the fireguard back and threw them on the coals to make a blaze. Just enough to see.

I undid the red woollen bow and opened the little sack. Inside was a necklace Cedric had made from three oak-apples which had holes bored right through them. *"He must have got Mr. B to do that."* He'd painted designs on them. On the centre one, he'd painted my name, 'Pat.' They were threaded on a piece of black velvet ribbon.

"Oh Cedric. It's beautiful. But where did you get the ribbon?" I sat and looked at it for a while, wondering what Cedric had done this Christmas Day.

There were soft footsteps behind me. I jumped up. It was Dilly. "It's all right, *cariad*. I heard a little noise and thought 'twas a mouse come to find Christmas crumbs. Now what have you got there?"

I showed her.

"My, my. Isn't that just handsome. And he made it, you say?'

I nodded.

"Well, now, he must like you an awful lot to make you such a pretty present."

"He's my special friend. Ann-the-Bank is my special friend, but Cedric is too. A sort of different special."

"Well, now, boys *are* a different sort. And Cedric must be very special, for most little boys I know are made of slugs and snails and puppy-dog's tails."

I giggled, "Even Rupert?"

"Oh, *that* one," was all Dilly said.

"But not Cedric."

"No," said Dilly. "Definitely not Cedric." She turned the necklace over in her hands, examining the painting, while I told her all about Cedric.

"And would you be thinking of a-marrying young Master Cedric when you grow up?"

"Of course," I answered. "Of course I will."

"Well now, on that happy note, I think we should go back to bed, don't you?"

Dilly carried me back up stairs and tucked me into bed beside Rachel, who was fast asleep. She put Cedric's present under my pillow. "There, me darlin'. Now you'll dream of your true love. But," she bent low to whisper in my ear, "I'm thinking you'd better not tell your Mum and Dad about your wedding plans for young Cedric. Wait 'til you're a bit older. After all, you're mum's had enough shocks for one day with that fancy bike. We'll keep it a secret, just between you and me, *bach*."

I must have fallen asleep before she left the room, for I don't remember anything else.

There were good things and bad things about Boxing Day. The good things were that you got to play with all your new toys, and eat any sweets and nuts still lying around. The bad things were the fights with the cousins over who played with what. And–worst of all–the bread-and-butter letters.

After breakfast, us children had to sit at the dining-room table and write thank-you notes to everyone who had sent presents, hope they'd had a merry Christmas and to wish them a Happy New Year. This took all morning and was very boring. The only good thing about it was that I got to use my new fountain pen. Anyway, they all got written and Mummy—who had been writing her own bread-and-butter letters—enclosed mine with hers and that was done for another year; at any rate, until my birthday.

There was one that went in its own envelope, which Mummy properly addressed and stamped. And she didn't even read it to check my spelling.

Boxing Day, 1940
Dear Cedric,
Thank you very much for the lovely neckliss. I will keep it forever.
I hope you had a nice Christmas with Miss Audrey-Joan, and everyone.
My daddy gave me a maroon bicycle and I am bringing it to school
With love from your special friend,
Pat

The very best thing about that particular Boxing Day was that, after lunch, Daddy got out my brand new shiny bicycle and propped it up against the wall at the back of the house. He lifted me onto it. Luckily, Mummy had a film in her Brownie Box camera and snapped a picture of me on my bicycle. When it was developed, it looked just as though I was riding it.

After tea, came the worst time of that Boxing Day in Wales. Daddy had to go back to his regiment. Dressed as a soldier again, muffled up in his great coat, and with his gasmask over his shoulder, he was kissing me goodbye. Then Cledwyn-the-Car came and Daddy was gone.

Rachel and Rupert ran noisily back to their toys, Aunt Mathilda helped Dilly clear away the tea things. Mummy and I were left standing in the hall.

"Come," she said, taking my hand. "Let's start reading one of your new books. The Arthur Ransome would be nice I think."

The day after Boxing Day Mummy was very quiet. Rachel and I went next door to see Ann-the-Bank, and help her play with her Christmas presents. While we were there, it started to snow and it never stopped for a week. 1940 turned out to be one of the worst winters in living memory, or so John-the-Post said.

"Soon the post won't be getting through," he said, stamping the snow off his feet as he came in for his morning tea with Dilly. "But I see there's one here for you today, *bach*."

Dilly smiled as he handed me the envelope. I recognised the writing and ran upstairs to read it:

> *Dec 27, 1940*
> *Dear Pat,*
> *Thank you for the car. It was clevver of you to make it out of a matchbox and bits of stuf. I had a decent Xmas, all the teechers were nice and frendly.*
> *See you next year – ha ha.*
> *Luv from your frend Cedric*

Still more snow fell. As John-the-Post had predicted, our little Welsh valley village was soon isolated from the outside world, and the great adventure began. Christmas was long over, and we celebrated the New Year of 1941 with just my aunt and cousins as Uncle Fred and Aunt Laura were snowed in. It seemed as though Daddy had been gone forever. Twelfth night came and the Christmas tree was taken down, the decorations carefully packed away. The tree, along with the holly and mistletoe, were now dried and withered skeletons; useful only as kindling.

And still it snowed. One day we woke up to find the snow was up over the back door, almost up to the bedroom windows, and John-the-Post had to dig us out .

"After all," he said, winking at Dilly, "I'm not getting any letters to deliver, so I might as well do something useful."

The pipes froze and Dilly had to melt snow in a bucket on the stove so that we could have water. But a full bucket of snow only melted down to about three inches of water. So we all helped and crammed snow into every pot, saucepan and dish-pan that we could find. We melted enough to drink and to make tea and to cook with, but none of us could have a bath.

"Just enough for a lick and a promise." Dilly had a special saying for everything.

"A promise for what?"

"A promise to wash better next time," she explained.

"What if there's still no water?"

"Well then, make it a promise to do a really good job when there *is* enough to have a bath. And that means behind the ears and between the toes."

The next day–more trouble. Mummy and Aunt Mathilda tried to walk down to the village to shop for food. On the way, Mummy slipped and broke her wrist and two workmen had to carry her back. It took hours for the doctor to tramp through the snow to set it and when he did, she fainted, which frightened me.

So I got a longer Christmas holiday than I expected. It was three weeks before the trains were running to take Ann-the-Bank and me back to Normanhurst. But the day finally came when Cledwyn-the-Car put chains on the Alvis and drove us all to the station. Dilly had packed my trunk and tied a big label around my neck. My bicycle got its own label and was put in the van with the luggage. The guard was a nice man and said he would look after us and make sure we got the right connection. As ice still made the pavements slippery, John-the-Post offered to send a telegram from the Post Office ("I have to go there anyway," he pointed out) to Mrs. Baker, giving our arrival time in Bridgnorth. Mrs. B sent one back saying that Mr. Baker would meet us.

Christmas 1940 was the last one I spent with my family until after the war.

I will never forget it.

Chapter 12

Goodbye Wales

Ann-the-Bank sat in the corner of the compartment bawling. Tears were dripping from the corners of her tightly shut eyes, and her nose was running. I felt like crying, but I'd promised Mummy I wouldn't. So I couldn't.

I stood with the side of my face against the cold, steamy window peering back along the railway embankment. The line had curved and I could see the guard's van and beyond it; Llanwyrted Wells' tiny station getting smaller and smaller in the distance. Soon all I could see were the mountains that sheltered our valley. I gazed at them for as long as I could see them, knowing that below them was the little grey pebble-cast house with the bow windows and green painted front door. And inside would be Mummy and Dilly, Aunt Mathilda and my cousins, all cozy around the fire. I hated that Rachel would have the big, warm feather bed all to herself–*my bed*. The only comforting thought was that, as most of the railway lines were now clear of snow, they would be returning to Colwyn Bay the next day.

Another curve in the railway line and now even the mountains were out of sight. And Ann-the-Bank was still bawling–loudly. I sat down beside her and put my arm around her shoulders. Her mouth opened wider and she cried even louder. The front of her green woolly scarf was damp with tears and snot. "C'mon Annie. Please don't cry any more. You'll only make yourself be sick. And blow your nose, you look disgusting."

She looked at me through red, watery eyes.

"Your nose is all swollen," I told her. "You don't look pretty at all."

That helped a bit. Ann liked to think she was pretty. Straight fair hair, blue eyes (now red) and a rather silly little nose. She was always telling everybody that her mam said she was going to be a beauty when she grew up.

"Look in the mirror above the seat. You're all blotchy."

She climbed up and looked in the mirror. For a while she stared at herself, an occasional sob jerking her shoulders.

"I d-d-don't want to go back t-to s-school. I want to stay with my Mam."

"I want to stay too," I said. "But my Daddy says I have to get a good education. And I won't get it if I don't go to boarding school."

"That's what my Da says." Ann had more or less stopped crying now. I fished in my pocket and took out some Dolly Mixtures. I picked out three of my least favourite flavours and handed them to her. "Here. Have these and cheer up."

She examined them, "How did you know these are my favourites?"

I didn't answer. Instead, I said, "My Daddy says we have to make sacrifices for the war effort. And our contribution to the war effort is going to boarding school in a safe place. So we have to be brave, like the soldiers."

Ann chewed on her Dolly Mixtures. She leaned her head against the window, looking at snowy Wales rushing b;y.

"We'll be in Builth soon, and we have to change trains," I told her. "You'd better clean your face."

"What with?" Ann looked around helplessly.

We were in a non-corridor carriage, so there was no lavvy and no water.

"Use your hanky with some spit."

"Ick," was all she said, but she dried her eyes and blew her nose. Just in time, for the train was slowing down and whistling as it approached the station.

We had to wait half-an-hour for our connecting train, and a raw wind was blowing around the platform, that froze our ears and noses. We went into the waiting room which, although out of the wind, was also freezing cold. Long-dead ashes were in the fireplace and the room felt damp and miserable. A sad looking lady sat with a sleeping toddler on her lap; her open coat wrapped around him to keep him warm. In another corner, two old men were chattering away in Welsh, pausing occasionally to wipe away a dewdrop from their noses with the back of a mittened hand. A Welsh Collie lay across both their feet, his long tan and white fur obviously keeping their feet warm. I watched the dog and it returned my gaze, eyebrows twitching at every movement.

Suddenly, the outside door was pushed open and a group of soldiers in battledress came in, bringing with them a gust of the cold, damp wind. They threw their kit bags on the floor and sat beside Ann and me. One pulled out a packet of Woodbines, scraped a match and lit it. Another looked at his watch. "Ten minutes to go," he said. "That's if the bloody thing's on time."

I tugged at Ann's sleeve and pulled her towards me. "C'mon," I whispered in her ear. "We'd better go to the lavvy in case it isn't a corridor train."

Mummy had given me some pennies for the loos but Ann didn't have any. When I'd done, I held the door open so she could go in and pee for the same penny.

The train was on time and the guard put us in the carriage next to his van. It was the only carriage with a corridor. He put us in a non-smoking compartment which we had to ourselves. The short train was full of soldiers, crowding in friendly huddles in the smoking compartments. When the train was well on its way, Ann and I crept down the corridor, past the next compartment where the two old Welshmen sat– their feet warm and snug under the dog– to look at the soldiers. They were smoking, laughing and playing cards. One of them saw us peeking and opened the sliding compartment door. "Hey, nippers. Where are you off to?"

We were too shy to answer. He looked at the labels around our necks and shook his head. "Poor little nippers. Being sent away to evac school then?"

We nodded.

He dug in his pocket and brought out a Mars Bar. "Here! Have this one on me."

I thanked him politely and we turned to go.

"Hey. Hang on a tick." The other soldiers all gave us something. Toffees, chocolate bars, and little packets of biscuits. One of the soldiers reached in his kit bag and pulled out a tin of humbugs. He turned to me. "Your daddy in the Army then, nipper?"

"Yes, Sir."

"Where's he stationed?"

"I-I don't know for sure. But he gave me a bike for Christmas."

"Did he now?" The soldier smiled at me. "Here, take the whole tin. Take it back to school with you."

"Thank you, Sir."

"What's your name? And how old are you?"

"Patricia Mashiter. And this is my friend, Ann-the-Bank...um...Ann Jones. And we're six."

"Well, Miss Mashiter, if I ever run into your daddy, I'll be sure to tell him he's got a plucky daughter."

"Thank you, Sir."

Ann and I scuttled back to our compartment. I laid out all the treasures on the seat.

"What've we got?" Ann put out her hands to scoop up some loot.

"Hey. Keep off! You didn't even talk to them. You just hid behind me."

One look at her face and I knew I'd have trouble. Ann-the-Bank in a temper tantrum, was a fearsome event. So I gave her one of the chocolate bars, and a few toffees.

"But the tin of humbugs is mine," I told her. I stood on the seat and took down from the luggage rack, the covered willow basket, that Dilly had packed with food for the journey. Ann had food too, but hers was in a paper bag. Keeping out the Mars Bar, I stowed the rest of the sweets in the basket and shoved the peg through the loop to fasten the lid.

Without warning, there was a squeal of brakes and the train 'back-chuffed' as Dilly called it, and slowed down. A few more yards and it clanked and creaked to a halt. I don't know how long we were stuck there. It seemed like forever. At first we ran from side to side and into the corridor, to look out of the windows. One of the soldiers came into the corridor, opened the small sliding window at the top and stuck his head out. "Can't see a bloody thing," he said and went back into his compartment, full of smoke and laughter.

Ann and I ate some of our picnic. I had Spam and Marmite sandwiches, some Christmas cake, and an apple. I swapped half a sandwich for one of Ann's sausage rolls. Dilly had put a small Thermos of tea in the basket and I carefully poured some into the cup-lid.

The train never moved.

We were both tired of looking out of the window and wondering what had happened. Ann was looking gloomy again.

"Want me to read to you?" I asked her. "I've got the new Arthur Ransome in the basket."

"All right."

So I read three whole pages of *Swallowdale* out loud. By that time the windows were all fogged up and ice patterns had formed on them. I shivered.

"I'm cold," said Ann.

"So'm I."

It was bitterly cold. With the engine stopped, there was no heat getting through to the carriages. I curled and up sat on my feet to try and warm them. Ann started to cry again. I felt the prickling start in the back of my nose. I sniffed. I couldn't help it. The tears just started. I brushed them away with my sleeve. It was too cold to take my glove off and search for my hanky.

When the guard came along to our compartment, we were both huddled together, trying to keep each other warm, and not even bothering to wipe up the tears. He was carrying a bucket of coal.

"Hey, hey, now. What's to-do? Come with me, me darlin's." He put down his bucket, grabbed my basket from the rack with one hand, and me with the other. "Get your gas masks and follow me," he said to Ann.

The connecting door to the guard's van was open, and glory be! the van was warm. A pot belly stove was anchored to the floor, the stove-pipe behind it curved up and disappeared through the roof. A wooden chair and some boxes were semi-circled around the stove.

"Just a tick now, littl'uns, while I get me coal." The guard went back for his bucket, locking the connecting door behind him on his return. He fed his stove with the coal which, as he told us, he'd "borrowed from the engine."

"Trouble with this 'ere war, nothin's the same. No decent rolling stock and only old engines to pull carriages. That's why, when they stops, the 'eat goes. Get warm, nippers, we'll be here for another half-hour or so." With that, he settled himself in his chair.

"Why are we stopped?" I asked.

"Ruddy engine's broke. It's like I said. Give us nothing but old junk on secondary lines. Got ter wait fer 'nother puffin' billy."

Ann and I sat on the boxes in front of the stove–warm again. An oil lamp swung overhead, even though it was the middle of the day, the van was dark.

It was ages before we heard and felt the bumps, jerks and grinds of the replacement engine. After telling us to stay put and not touch any-thing the guard disappeared. He didn't have to worry about that. We were quite happy—just being warm. I watched the oil lamp swing and sway above my head. As it swung, its glow lit up the gleaming maroon and shiny chrome of my new bicycle. I began to get excited, *"What would Cedric say when he saw it?"* I realised that, although I would miss Mummy and Daddy, going back to school wasn't the worst thing that could happen. I wondered why Ann was so unhappy about it.

More noisy yanks and tugs and then, with a lurch, the new engine gave a hoot and some chuffs, and we were moving again. The outside door swung open and the guard jumped in, bringing with him a rush of cold, frosty air.

"There we go, nippers. We're on our way. We've lost two hours, but as you had a three-hour wait at Craven Arms, you should make your connection. You'd better stay here with me 'til we get there, and I'll make sure you don't miss it."

Which we didn't, because that train was late too. On the last lap of our journey from Craven Arms to Bridgnorth, we wiped the steam away from the window with our mittens, and watched as we passed little villages and flashed over level crossings. The Welsh mountains, had long since disappeared, but I recognised the round hump of the Wrekin and a little later, the dark winter waters of the River Severn. Thick snow lay everywhere, and the last glow of the pale mid-winter sun, turned the landscape golden, patterning it with long black shadows of skeleton trees. Then the guard came and pulled all the blackout blinds down, and we were left in the dim glow of a single hissing gas-lamp high up in the ceiling. I couldn't even see to read.

It was pitch dark when we got to Bridgnorth and I was worried that Mr. B wouldn't be there. But he was; stamping his feet on the cold platform, his breath in clouds around his head. He swung us up, one in each arm. "Hey! I thought I'd lost a couple of little Welsh lambs. But here you are, safe and sound."

It felt good to see him again. He heaved our luggage into the float. When he came to my bicycle, his eyes widened. "My, my," he said. "Now isn't *that* a posh looking bike."

It was a snail's pace drive back to Normanhurst. The headlamps on the float were hooded and half painted-out with black, so they would cast only a very dull glow on the road directly in front of us. All traffic had the same blacked-out lights so no enemy planes could spot them.

Ann curled up under the rug and went to sleep, but I sat up front with Mr. B–which Mrs. B would never have allowed; I promised I wouldn't tell her. Mr. B asked me all about my Christmas.

"My daddy gave me that bike for Christmas."

"It's a beauty, Pat-a-cake. I'll make a special rack in the barn and hang it up until Spring."

This made me happy as all the other bikes were thrown higgledy piggledy in the bike shed, and I didn't want mine to get scratched. "Is Cedric there?" I asked.

"Where? At school, you mean?" Mr. B chuckled. "Of course he is. And he's been a proper mope all the while you were away. But don't tell him I said so. But he was happy to get your letter. *And* he's allowed to stay up 'til you get back."

I smiled in the dark.

Cedric was waiting. And so was Miss Audrey-Joan. And Tristan. And everyone.

Just for a moment, it felt almost like coming home.

Chapter 13

A Winter's Tale

Ann-the-Bank was so sound asleep when we arrived at Normanhurst, she didn't even wake when Mr. B carried her up to our dormitory and Mrs. B put her to bed. I was wide awake and enjoyed the hug that Miss Audrey-Joan gave me as she lifted me down from the float. She cupped her warm hands over my ears. "My goodness, child, you're freezing. Come inside and we'll get you a hot drink."

Moments later I was in the familiar front kitchen, enjoying the warmth from the Aga. Miss Audrey-Joan helped me out of my outdoor clothes and shoes and then pulled a small foot-stool close to the stove. "Sit there and get warm while I make some hot chocolate. But first I have to get someone who has been waiting for you. Two someones actually."

I put my cold feet against the base of the stove, where I knew it would be warm but not burning hot. It wasn't long before Miss Audrey-Joan was back, followed by Cedric who was carrying Tristan. He put Tristan on my lap then sat on a chair beside the kitchen table, looking down at his feet, which he swung back and forth. Miss Baker busied herself making the cocoa.

Cedric looked up and grinned. "Tristan slept on *my* bed while you were away."

I thought about that for a minute. Tristan opened one eye and looked at me. He started to wash behind his ears. "That's all right. I told him to."

Miss Audrey-Joan laughed. "I think Cedric should adopt Iseult, then you'll both have a cat to sleep with."

Iseult must have heard her name, because she strolled into the kitchen. Miss Audrey-Joan scooped her up and put her on Cedric's lap. "Now you two, you have quarter-of-an-hour to drink your cocoa and exchange news. Then it's off to bed." She looked at me, probably noticing my bedraggled hair with its trailing ribbon, and the dirt smudges on my face I'd forgotten to wipe off with spit. "Patricia is dog-tired. You have the whole winter ahead to talk."

We sat, silent, just grinning at each other. When we did speak, it was both at once, and we both started to say the same thing.

"Thank you for the present."

"Did you get my letter?"

We began to giggle. Then I showed Cedric the three little round knobs of his oakapple necklace under the ribbed collar of my jumper. He didn't say anything, but he looked pleased and the tips of his ears turned pink. He dug in his pocket and took out the the little car I'd made from a wooden matchbox, and drove it along the edge of the kitchen table and around his mug. "You had a long holiday. You were s'posed to come back a fortnight ago."

"I know. We got snowed in. We couldn't even get out of the door. And then, when my Mummy did get out, she fell and broke her wrist."

"That's jolly bad luck."

"Yes. But it's her left wrist, so she can still write to me."

"Miss Audrey-Joan and Mr. and Mrs. B were jolly nice to me at Christmas. They even gave me presents." He paused, and continued to zoom his car around on the table. "But it wasn't the same."

He stopped zooming and swivelled his bottom around on the chair until he was sitting sideways and looking straight at me. He drew his heels up onto the seat and hugged his knees. "I'm really glad you're back," he said, smiling.

We drank our cocoa and I put the mug down on the floor beside me. I felt the warm safety of the familiar kitchen steal over me, and hugged the soft furry lump that was Tristan.

I don't even remember Miss Audrey-Joan picking me up and putting me to bed. But the next day, Cedric told me she had done so after I'd fallen asleep with my head on Tristan's back.

I hated the winters at school. Especially that first one. Endless cold, raw days and freezing nights. We got up in the dark and by the end of lessons, it was dark again. Sometime during breakfast, Mrs. B would come and open up the wooden blackout shutters in the dining hall but we couldn't even see outside; the windows were covered with the thick patterns Jack Frost had painted during the night. Although the stoves and fireplaces were kept going during the day, the heat never reached the backs of the rooms. We huddled as close to the stoves as possible, but if we were in the back row during lessons, we could barely hold a pencil our fingers were so cold. And I don't remember having warm feet the whole winter.

The dormitories were the worst. In the morning, there were little patches of ice on the blankets where our breath had frozen. Jack Frost had even crept inside and the walls beside the windows, sparkled with frost diamonds. With no heating in the dormitories, our breath looked like little puffs of steam in the dim light of the one lightbulb hanging from the ceiling. Dressing and undressing became a race, not against each other, but against the cold. Twice-weekly bath nights were the best as our bodies, especially our toes, were warmed from the water and when we were dry, we hurriedly pulled on thick woolly bedsocks to keep the heat in. I wrote letters home complaining of the cold, and asking for my feather mattress and stone hot-water-bottle.

Sunday, 13th January, 1941
Dear Mummy and Daddy
Ann-the-Bank and I arrived safely back at school. The engine broke down so we were very late.

Thank you for my Christmas presents. Mrs. Baker says that she hopes the fountain pen will improve my writing. She is going to teach me to play the piano because I have the music book. Miss Baker has a grand piano in the drawing room. There are photos on it and one shows Miss Audrey in some robes like Daddy wears when he is a teacher and not a soldier. Mr. Baker says she is wearing her Oxford glad-rags.

I told Mrs. Baker I didn't want to come back. It's too cold at night and there is no fire the dormitory, and the beds are cold too.

Please will you send me some thicker bedsocks and a hot-water-bottle.

Mrs. Baker doesn't read my letters any more as she says I have settled down.

With love from,

Patricia

Sunday, 20th January, 1941

Dear Mummy and Daddy,

It snowed again last night and Mr. Baker and Miss Audrey-Joan took us sledding. It was fun but my feet were cold.

May I have some more warm clothes and a feather bed. It's very cold here.

Your freezing daughter,

Patricia

The sledding *was* fun. If there had been a heavy snow fall and it was a bright sunny day, Miss Audrey-Joan would announce at assembly there would be no lessons that afternoon and we would all go tobogganing. So, with permission from Farmer Bourne, we trudged up the lane to a grand slope in one of his fields. We dragged with us, an assortment of sleds, tin trays from the back kitchen, and any old smooth piece of wood we found in the barn. We built humps and bumps and went flying down the hill to land in the snow drifts piled against the bottom hedge. The duck pond by the lane was frozen solid, so we slithered around on it, squealing when we fell on the hard ice. The boys made long slides;

then they would take a run across the snowy field, leap the bank and slide right across the pond from one side to the other. Miss Audrey-Joan brought skates with her, and we watched her twirling and whirling on the ice. And when she did jumps and twists, we all clapped madly and thought of writing to ask our parents to send us skates.

And still more snow fell. We built snow-men, igloos and snow-castles. We had snowball fights, and contests to see who could roll the biggest snowball. We ate the snow, we rolled in it, we laid in it and swished our arms up and down to make angel wings. When we'd had enough and were soaked through to our knickers, we went indoors, tracking the snow into the back kitchen. This made Mrs. B "tsk tsk" and ask who did we think was going to wipe up the puddles. And she would grumble how there was not enough room on the clothes-racks to dry all our coats, mittens, scarves and hats, least of all our knickers. Then we would rush to help hang our stuff on the long double clothes-racks, which she hauled up to the ceiling and criss-crossed the holding ropes around the wall cleats. Then, for all her grumbling, she would give us steaming mugs of cocoa and pieces of bread pudding. The cocoa was dark, grainy, and bitter with saccharine, but it warmed our tummies and it *did* taste chocolatey.

A few days later, I got a large, odd-shaped parcel from Wales addressed in Dilly's round handwriting. Inside was a big bundle of newspapers and I wondered why on earth Dilly was sending me news-papers? I dug deeper and found, sandwiched between the paper, a rubber hot-water-bottle, a pair of thick bright red bedsocks and a letter from Dilly.

17th January, 1941.

My dear Patty,

Your Mummy and I went to a village "Bring and Buy" run by the W.I. We found these lovely thick bedsocks and the hot water bottle for you. It seems that the government issued hot-water-bottles to the Cottage Hospital, but they sent one case too many by mistake. So they donated the extras to the sale. Wasn't that lucky for you?

The newspapers are for your bed. John-the-Post says that if you put sheets of newspaper between your blanket and eider-down, it will act as insulation and keep you much warmer on freezing winter nights. John has been collecting them and there are enough for you to share with Ann and your Prince Charming, Master Cedric!

Your Auntie Mathilda is sending some of Rachel's winter clothes that she has grown out of and I will post them on to you as soon as they get here.

Your mother's arm is getting better and the plaster-cast will come off soon.

With good wishes,

Yrs. Respectfully,

Dilly

P.S. John-the-Post says that you must not wriggle around in bed too much, or the teachers will hear your papers rustling.

26th January, 1941

Dear Dilly,

Thank you for sending the parcel of newspapers and the bedsocks and hot-water-bottle. I shared the papers with Ann and Cedric. Cedric was happy because he is very cold in bed. He said boys don't wear bedsocks unless they are sissys. Ann thought the newspapers were silly but when I told her that John-the-Post sent them, she changed her mind.

It is still cold here and it's hard to hold a pencil, specially in the early morning. Everywhere is frozen, even the jugs of milk for our porridge. I think winter is going to last forever.

Please say diolch yn fawr to John-the-Post for the newspa-pers. Ann and Cedric say thank you too.

With love from,

Patty XXX

9th February, 1941

Dear Mummy and Daddy,

Thank you for sending Rachel's jumpers and her old coat. I'm glad she grew out of them. I wear socks over my stockings now to keep my feet a bit warmer.
Everything is frozen here. I am too. I would like to come home again now, please. Is Daddy still in the war or does it stop when it gets too cold? And does he have a hot water bottle and newspapers to keep him warm?
With love from your ice-maiden daughter,
Patricia

The bitter weather went on for weeks. We hardly went outside at all, except for a quick run when the snow was so frozen it wouldn't make us wet. Mrs. B complained that she couldn't keep up with the wet clothes, and everyone was getting coughs and colds. So we stayed indoors, huddled around the stoves and hearths to keep warm. After school, in the long, dark evenings, we drew our chairs in a semi circle around the fire and, while Miss Audrey-Joan read us wonderful adventure stories, we knitted socks and scarves to keep soldiers and sailors warm. When it was time for bed, I ran up the icy stairs to an even icier dormitory, burrowed under my newspaper covers, hugged the lukewarm hot-water-bottle and remembered Christmas.

And sometimes I cried.

Chapter 14

Shipwrecks and Worms

Easter came and went. The only difference was we had to go to church more, and we didn't have so many lesson days. None of the full boarders went home for the week's holiday, but, by now, most of us had got used to being at Normanhurst instead of with our families. Of course, the best part about Easter was that the winter was over. Daffodils, bluebells and primroses bloomed and nodded in the wind under the tall elm and oak trees and the orchard was full of fruit blossom. Mr. B spent all his days behind the high walls of the kitchen garden. Mrs. B said there was lots of work to be done: sowing vegetable seeds and planting potatoes to feed–as she put it–"forty ever-open doors." I thought it was funny to call anybody's mouth an open door, but we always scraped our plates clean and finished every crumb of bread that was put out for us. Except Rowley Smythe of course, who stuffed most of his food in his pockets and emptied it down the loo afterwards. He was always getting caught and then he had to either stand in a corner for hours, or get a caning, or go to bed straight after tea. Mrs. B would shove spoonfuls of *Extract of Malt with Cod-Liver-Oil* down him to make up for his not eating. We all got a spoonful of something too. My favourites were *Radio Malt*, or *Virol*, but I hated the one with Cod-liver-oil.

My mother sent me an Easter parcel with some green knitted knee socks, and two Liberty bodices. Because of the war, there were no Easter eggs, so she sent a jar of orange marmalade instead. After Easter, we all settled down again to lessons and looked forward to summer which, Mrs. B said, was just around the corner.

Well, it was a jolly long corner.

Another wet Saturday turned breakfast into a gloomy affair. The only game left to play was to pick out the little white worms from our porridge. Whoever had the most won, and could choose which game to play at breaktime. The next step was to try and poke some of them back to life so we could race them across the breakfast table. That they were dead–after all they'd been boiled, and probably singed, in the porridge pot–didn't enter into the equation. Easter had just passed and with the story of the Resurrection still fresh in our minds, there was always the chance of a miracle. Besides, there was a war on and miracles always happened during a war. Only last week, Janey Summers got a letter from her mother telling how her Auntie Gladys survived for a whole day under a heap of rubble after a German bomb hit her house. She hadn't gone to a shelter because the cat was having kittens under her Uncle Arthur's grand piano and Auntie Gladys wanted to stay with them. And there it was, in Janey's mother's own handwriting, for all to read:

"It is a miracle your Auntie Gladys was alive and well and without a scratch, when the ARP dug her out the next day. Dirty she was, and cursing Hitler and the Jerries a blue streak, but whole and unhurt. She was still crouching under the remains of the grand piano and clutching a cardboard box containing Clementine the cat and four kittens. And just after they dug her out and put her on a stretcher, didn't the King and Queen themselves come by. Walking all through the dust and rubble, they were. They stopped to talk to Auntie Gladys and Auntie Gladys was ever so embarrassed because

she'd wet her knickers, but the kindly ARP warden put a blanket over her so that Their Majesties wouldn't notice. Queen Elizabeth, God bless her, admired the kittens and then took Auntie Gladys's hand in hers and agreed it was a miracle she was alive and unhurt."

Janey's mother's letter had been passed around the whole school at break time and we all read it. Of course, Giles Farmer just laughed, crumpled it up and threw it back at Janey who burst into tears when it landed in a mud-puddle. But Cedric picked it up before the ink started to run. He cleaned it with his handkerchief and when we came back into class, we all helped to smooth it out and put it between two pieces of blotting-paper to dry. By lunch time it was almost as good as new, except for a few wrinkles, and the only part where the ink had run was the row of X's across the bottom of the last page.

There were, however, no miracles for the porridge worms. They lay, round and fat and dead on the oilcloth table cover, refusing to move. We concentrated hard on them, waiting for the slightest twitch. No one spoke.

It was Arabella Bosworthy who broke the silence. "Boys have worms stuck on to the bottom of their tummies."

If she was looking for the attention of the whole dining-room, she got it.

Arabella Bosworthy, who was really a day-pupil, should have been at home but her mother had to go and stay with Arabella's aunty who was having a baby. So Arabella and her brother, D'Arcy, were boarders for two weeks.

"Don't be silly," said Ann-the-Bank.

Most of the children giggled, Giles Farmer snorted so loud that a gob of snot blew out of his nose, and Rowley Smythe dropped some of the porridge he was stuffing into his pockets, on the floor.

I looked at Cedric. He put his head down and wriggled in his chair. "Worms?" I said. "Don't be daft."

"Soppy date," said Ann-the-Bank.

"'S'true," said Arabella. "'Cos D'Arcy's got one. I've seen it lots of times." She yelled as D'Arcy reached out a foot under the table and kicked her shin.

That brought Miss Audrey-Joan into the dining room. "What's all the noise about? Arabella, what's wrong?"

"Fains you tell," hissed D'Arcy under his breath. Miss Audrey-Joan didn't hear him, but Arabella did.

We all looked at her. "Nothing, Miss Baker." Arabella bent her head towards her porridge.

We expected Miss Audrey-Joan to pursue her inquiry into what had been going on, but her attention was caught by the little rows of worms in front of each bowl. "Good grief. Don't tell me the porridge was wormy again?"

We all answered, in chorus. "Yes, Miss Baker."

"Pass up your bowls, children. You don't have to eat any more. I've made toast this morning for a treat, and I'll find you all an extra apple too."

Miss Audrey-Joan stayed with us while we spread our toast with small scrapings of our margarine ration and, for those who had it, a dollop of jam. A jar of Marmite was on the table for anyone who wanted it. Good toast was a treat, because we usually had it when the bread was really stale and Mrs. B had to toast it to cover up the little green mould spots. Miss Audrey-Joan drew up a chair at the end of the table and sat with us, her hands cradling an enormous blue-and-white striped cup. She usually joined us at Saturday breakfast, to talk about what she had planned for the day. "I know you are all gloomy that it's raining and you can't go out, but we will have some good games inside. What shall it be?"

"Sardines."

"Hide and seek."

"Ghosts."

"Robin Hood." That was Cedric's choice.

But the loudest shout was, "Shipwreck. Shipwreck. Please. Shipwreck."

"No," said Cedric. "No. Not shipwreck. I don't like shipwreck. I want to play Robin Hood."

We were all surprised at this outburst from him. After all, shipwreck was one of our favourite games, and I'd never heard Cedric say he didn't like it.

"I'm sorry Cedric," said Miss Audrey-Joan. "But shipwreck seems to be the popular vote. And besides, Robin Hood is hard to play indoors."

By this time, Cedric was really wriggling uncomfortably in his chair. He bent his head as though embarrassed by drawing attention to himself, but I could see a glint of tears in his eyes.

"Maybe, if the rain stops, we can play Robin Hood this afternoon?" I looked at Miss Audrey-Joan.

"Of course," she said.

And so that was that. After we'd finished our dormitory and bathroom duties we would play shipwreck. As for Arabella Bosworthy's remark about boys having worms coming out of their tummies–that was just too silly to bother about any more.

We played shipwreck in the Kindergarten room, which could be set up as a gymnasium. Miss Audrey-Joan and Mr. B moved the desks against the walls. Everything to do with lessons was put away: books, the mechanical pencil sharpener, the twin globes of the world and the moon, and all the little jars and boxes that were scattered around. Then two pairs of thick ropes were let down from the ceiling, the wooden, leather-padded gym horse and springboard were pulled out and long, wooden gym benches were angled to make a maze of balancing beams that zig-zagged across the floor; some with metal hooks were attached half way up the wall bars to make slopes. When finished, the kindergarten room looked like a topsy-turvy obstacle course. We changed into plimsolls, and put on our house colour bands; blue for the Normans and yellow for the Saxons. The girls tucked their skirts in their knickers and the boys rolled up their sleeves. We were ready.

The rules of Shipwreck were simple. You had to keep going around the room without setting a foot on the floor. We climbed from desk to bench, up the sloping benches to wall bars, working our way along the wall sideways, then catching a rope to swing over or onto another desk. Teams worked together, sending a rope back, or lending a helping hand to a team-mate. Anyone who put a foot on the floor, was out. You were in the ocean–and drowned. Drowned children had to sit on the floor against the end wall. Miss Audrey-Joan and Mr. B were referees and made sure we didn't fall off a wall bar, or miss our landing when leaping from the springboard to the horse. They were also there to make sure no one tried to trip or shove a member of the opposite team off balance. The boys often tried to nudge the girls, although they had to be pretty sneaky about it because if they got caught, their side lost ten points.

We'd been playing for quite a long time, when I realised Cedric was missing. He and Ann and I were all Saxons and usually helped each other. "Where's Cedric?" I asked Ann.

"Dunno. Haven't seen him. P'raps he's out already."

Out—meaning he'd fallen off into the ocean and was drowned. But he wasn't sitting against the end wall.

I grabbed a rope and launched into my favourite swing. From the wall bars, clear across half the room to land on the soft leather-topped, gym horse. Mr. B was standing by to catch me. I loved this bit; I felt as though I were flying. Halfway through my swing I looked up and saw Cedric. He'd climbed to the very top of a rope and was hunched on a cross-beam in the peaked ceiling. His arms were around an upright strut and he wasn't moving.

"Hey, Cedric!" I yelled.

He didn't answer. By that time I'd landed on the gym horse, a steady-ing arm from Mr. B around my middle. I whispered to Mr. B, "I don't think Cedric's feeling very well. He's up in the ceiling."

Mr. B glanced up, then went to talk to Miss Audrey-Joan. She blew her whistle and announced a half-time rest. Cedric still sat up in the ceiling, shaking his head when told to come down. So Mr. B fetched a ladder and climbed up to him. It took a while for Mr. B to persuade Cedric to come to him; but finally he did and when they reached the floor, we could all see that Cedric was as white as a piece of paper and shaking all over. He said he felt sick so Miss Audrey-Joan took him to Mrs. B, who was in the house cooking dinner.

We played shipwreck until the dinner bell rang, but Cedric didn't come back. After dinner I went to look for him. I found him huddled down in bed. I could see he wasn't asleep, so I pulled back the covers.

His face wasn't white any more, but flushed pink and he was sweaty. "What's the matter? Are you sick?"

I'd never noticed before how big Cedric's eyes were. Big, brown eyes. They were usually covered by a long fringe of silky hair, almost the same colour as his eyes, but now his hair was sticking up, damp with sweat.

"You'll get into trouble," he mumbled. "You're not allowed in the boys' dormy."

"I don't care. No one will know I'm here. The rain's stopped and we're going to play outside this afternoon anyway. Aren't you coming? We're playing Robin Hood, just for you."

"No. Mrs. B says I have to rest this afternoon."

"Cedric, what happened? You usually like to play shipwreck. Did you climb up too high and get dizzy?" I was trying to think of the right question to ask him, because I didn't want him to think I was calling him a sissy, or a fraidy-cat; which was what some of the others were saying.

"I...I had a dream."

"A dream?" I asked. "When? At the top of the rope?"

"No, silly dope. The other night. I dreamed..."

"Dreamed what?"

"That I was in a real shipwreck. And I drowned."

"Silly-billy! That was just a dream. 'Cos you weren't and you didn't."

"I know. But I can't forget the dream. It was so real. The water was very cold, I could feel it. And I was going down, right under the water. I was hanging on to the ship but the ship was going down too. And..."

"And? Go on."

Cedric began to cry. He turned over and buried his head in the pillow.

I didn't know what to do. So I laid my head down beside his on the pillow, and put my arm across his shoulders and hugged him to me. "Cedric. Don't cry. It was only a dream. Tell me what happened."

It took a minute or two before his sobs got quieter. I groped under his pillow and found a hanky; we all kept hankies under our pillows. I pushed it under his cheek. He grabbed it, wiped his eyes and blew his nose, then turned to face me. Our heads were very close on the pillow and I could feel his breath on my face. He was breathing quickly; occasionally giving a hiccuppy sob.

"Tell me what you saw," I said.

"I...I called out to my mummy but she wasn't there. Then I looked for her in the water and she floated by me and her mouth was open. I thought she was calling me but there was no sound. Then my Daddy swam up to me and told me she was dead. Drowned. Then my daddy picked me up off the ship and swam down...a very long way down...to the bottom of the sea and laid me on a rock. Then he swam away and left me. And he never came back. And...and then I woke up."

"That was a nasty nightmare. But it had nothing to do with us playing shipwreck."

"Yes it did. Every time someone talks about playing shipwreck, I remember the dream. And it doesn't go away. I remember every little bit. Even the fishes that were swimming around me at the bottom of the sea."

"That would be fun. Like Tom and the Waterbabies."

"No. It wasn't like that at all. Tom was happy. I was sad."

"So why did you get stuck on top of the beam? Why didn't you come down?" I asked.

"I climbed up and it was like we were playing in a dream. I felt dizzy and you all looked like tiny people far, far away. And I wasn't part of you. I was somewhere else."

I didn't know what to say to that. Cedric lay there, so I stayed with him and watched his big brown eyes. He began to blink and his eyelids dropped. Then, instantly, he was asleep. One second he was awake, and the next second he was fast asleep.

I watched him for a while. Tiny tears sparkled on his long eyelashes, like dewdrops on a spider's web. One tear trickled out of the corner of his eye and slid down his cheek. I caught it on my finger.

After a while, I crept away and left him sleeping. I hoped he wouldn't have any more bad dreams about shipwrecks.

"Where've you been?" Ann-the-Bank was waiting for me at the bottom of the back stairs. She was dressed in her Mackintosh and welly-boots.

"I went to see if Cedric was all right. He's sleeping."

"You were in his dormy?" Ann squeaked. "You can't go in the boys' dormy."

"Oh do be quiet," I looked around to see if anyone was listening. Luckily we were alone. "What does it matter, anyway. He was crying, and sad. Really Ann, sometimes you're such a twit."

Ann sniffed. "Well I was waiting for you. Arabella Bosworthy wants us to go behind the Kindergarten room. She's going to show us D'Arcy's worm."

"D'Arcy's WHAT?"

"D'Arcy's worm. You remember what she said at breakfast—that D'Arcy has a worm hanging out the bottom of his tummy."

"Piffle. That's a load of codswallop."

"What if it isn't? Have you ever seen boys undressed?"

"Well…not really. Only when they have their bottoms smacked."

"And then they are bending over a chair, right?" Ann was getting squeaky again.

"Shhh. Don't talk so loud."

Ann put her mouth close to my ear. "You—never—see—their—fronts."

I thought about that. She was right. "No. But…"

"Well put your outdoor things on. And we'll go and see if it's true." Ann still liked telling me what to do. Outside, Ann took me by the hand and started dragging me towards the Kindergarten room. As I ran, I was thinking hard.

I was an only child and so was Ann-the-Bank. We didn't have brothers. I had boy cousins, but I'd never seen them without their clothes. I remember watching Aunt Mathilda bath Rupert on the kitchen table in front of the fire. I was four then and only just tall enough to peek over the table. All I remembered seeing, was a round pink bottom and fat little baby legs as she scooped him out of the wash tub and wrapped him in a cocoon of white fluffy towels. And when my cousins came to Wales last Christmas, Rupert was always bathed and put to bed first, then Rachel and I shared a bath; just like the girls do here.

I was thinking so hard, I wasn't paying attention to where we were. Without warning, Ann skidded to a dead stop and I bumped into her, nearly knocking the breath out of both of us

"S-sorry. Wh-what's the matter?"

She didn't have to answer.

We'd reached the back left-hand corner of the Kindergarten room, where a narrow path ran between the back of the building and the holly hedge. Trouble blocked our way. Arabella Bosworthy, legs planted firmly apart, hands on hips, stood guard. "You have to promise to pay." Her shrill voice was demanding and it was obvious we had no choice. This was her game and her rules. There wasn't even an opportunity to "fains" payment, because you couldn't "fains" anything you didn't know about.

"Pay for what?" I still had the choice of turning away and leaving her standing there.

Ann dug me in the ribs with her elbow. "How much?"

It was obvious Ann-the-Bank wanted to see Arabella prove that boys have worms hanging out of the bottom of their tummies.

"You have to pay me a bar of chocolate and pay the boys one sweet each. Or they won't show you their worms."

"A whole bar of chocolate?" Never. "That's ridiculous," I said. 'Ridiculous' was one of Mummy's favourite words and I rather liked it. Anyway, it had the desired effect.

Arabella tapped one foot on the ground and frowned at me. I stared back at her. She knew she would never get a whole bar of chocolate out of me. She also knew I didn't really believe her anyway. Ann-the-Bank said nothing and moved behind me. She could never stand up to Bossy Bella. Besides, she knew that neither of us had a whole chocolate bar between us.

"Oh all right," said Arabella. "Two pieces of chocolate for me and one sweet for each of the boys. That's from each of you." She was in one of her bossiest moods.

I was surprised she'd come down to two pieces instead of a whole bar. "How many boys?" I asked.

"Three."

"Oh all right." Ann and I crossed-our-hearts, hoped-to-die and promised to pay the price.

Satisfied, Arabella Bosworthy nodded. "Both of you grab the biggest and prickliest holly leaf you can find, and follow me."

Armed with large prickly holly leaves, we followed Bossy Bella along the narrow path between the back of the Kindergarten room and the hedge to see what was going to be worth two pieces of chocolate and three sweets each.

It turned out Arabella was right. Dilly always told me that little boys were made of slugs and snails, and puppy dogs' tails. But she forgot to tell me about the worms.

Arabella had three boys, David Thorne, Rowley Smythe and Sammy White lined up in front of the holly hedge. There was a ledge on the chimney-stack where we often sat in winter because it was warmed by the stove.

"Where's D'Arcy then?" I asked. "I thought you were going to show us D'Arcy's worm."

Arabella shrugged. "He wouldn't come. Said he would tell our Mother if I made him do it. But he won't tell. I've seen to that," she added. By the expression on her face, I knew she had threatened D'Arcy with all kinds of torture if he should even *think* of telling.

So Ann and I squeezed together on the ledge to watch while Arabella told the boys to take their trousers down. And their underknickers. They said they would if we each gave them some of our sweet ration. I still wasn't too happy about that, but Bossy Bella said, "Of course."

And so we saw their worms. They weren't very nice, and they were all different shapes and sizes.

David Thorne's worm was small and fat. Rowley Smythe's worm was very thin and bright pink–just like Rowley is very thin and has a bright pink nose.

And Sammy White's worm was really long and had a funny purple blob on the end. Arabella Bosworthy poked it with a stick. It moved and grew a bit.

Then Rowley Smythe piddled out of his worm and we all yelled at him that he was disgusting. But he just grinned and wiggled it at us.

That was when we all three decided we'd seen enough. We showed the boys the holly leaves we'd picked and told them that if they breathed a word, we'd use the prickles on their ears. Then we left the boys to get dressed and ran back to the house. I was surprised to find

Cedric sitting on the children's entrance steps. "I thought you didn't feel well and were sleeping."

"When I woke up I felt better...so I came to find you."

Cedric asked me where I'd been and I told him it was none of his business. He told me he'd found us and spied on us, and insisted I give him my sweet ration or he would tell.

So now I had to find two sweet rations for one day.

I cornered Molly McTavish in the girls' lavvy and told her that I saw her stealing a piece of bread from the kitchen and that I would tell. She was really frightened and told me she would give me two sweet rations if I didn't tell on her. I told her that it had to be two pieces of good chocolate or humbugs, but no dolly mixtures as they were too small and didn't count.

When we lined up for our sweet ration after tea, Molly gave me two humbugs and a piece of Fry's Chocolate Peppermint Cream. I gave one humbug to Cedric and one humbug to David Thorne and ate the peppermint cream. I gave Rowley and Sammy old and sticky boiled sweets that had stuck to the bottom of my tin,. I persuaded Ann to lend me two pieces of chocolate until I got some more from home, which I gave to Arabella Bosworthy.

When all was said and done, Ann-the-Bank and I agreed that it hadn't been worth sacrificing our sweet ration.

Sunday, 26th May, 1941.
Dear Mummy and Daddy,
Thank you for the ribbons and the chocolate. The chocolate came just in time as I had run out. It was very kind of Daddy to send some too.
We learned about worms this week. I think they are a bit nasty.
Your loving daughter
Patricia

Chapter 15

Thatcher's Woods

The first Monday in June, was a holiday. We all knew the day before had been Whit Sunday, because there had been a lot of talk in church about tongues of fire and we'd sung happy hymns. We also knew the Monday after Whit Sunday was a Bank Holiday. Ann-the-Bank had told us all about it and how her Da's bank would be closed so everyone could go on a picnic. She was also complaining loudly, that she would miss it because Wales was too far away to go for a picnic. I told her that, since her Da was away fighting the war, he wouldn't go on a picnic anyway, and probably no-one else would either. In wartime, picnics just didn't happen. Besides we'd had a sort of a holiday on May Day. Mr. B had put up a maypole on the front lawn and all the girls made flower crowns from dandelions, daisies and buttercups and everyone danced around the maypole. Then it started to rain, so Miss Audrey-Joan said we would have our May Day holiday on another day when the weather was warm and sunny.

"No-one has said anything about a holiday," I told Ann. "Besides, there's a war on. We don't have holidays when there's a war on."

"We had Easter." Ann-the-Bank was beginning to whine.

"That was different. We had to go to church a lot. We'd know if today is a holiday, 'cos we'd've sung about it in Church. So there!"

I hated being wrong about things. But when I found out that Ann-the-Bank was right this time, I didn't mind so much.

At breakfast, Miss Audrey-Joan came into the dining hall. It wasn't even a Saturday, but she was wearing trousers and carrying her blue-and-white striped teacup. Cedric, Ann-the-Bank and I looked at each other. Something stupendous *was* going to happen today. It always did when Miss Audrey-Joan wore trousers, and if she brought her teacup into the dining hall, it was even more stupendous because it meant she was going to sit down and tell us something special.

Sunlight poured through the tall windows and bounced off our porridge spoons. There was no wind stirring the branches of the dense yew trees that reached over the high stone boundary wall; above them, the sky was a deep summer blue.

"It's a wonderful day, children. And I have a big surprise for you. Today is Whit Monday and a Bank Holiday, so there will be no lessons. On Friday, I sent a notice to the dailies' parents. So they'll stay home today."

Ann-the-Bank gave me her '*see-I-told-you-so*' look.

Miss Audrey-Joan sipped on her tea while we all hurrah'd. She held up her hand. "There's more."

"More? What more could there be?"

"It's such a lovely day, I thought we would pack a picnic and spend the day in Thatcher's Woods."

Ann-the-Bank gave Cedric and me another very important look. By this time we were all jumping up and down and squealing; whatever remained of our breakfasts forgotten in our excitement.

A Bank Holiday picnic! Whizzo!

Bedroom and bathroom chores were completed in record time. Nobody came to check if we'd made our beds properly or our pyjamas were folded and placed under our pillows. We changed into our Saturday play clothes, only pausing long enough to decide what to take with us. What *does* one take on a picnic to Thatcher's Woods? As this was my first summer here, I'd never been on a picnic. Ann was the only one in the whole dormy who had been here last summer so we all crowded around her, asking questions.

She said she hadn't taken anything with her last year, except a toy rabbit because she thought it would like the outing. She told us that one of the boys threw it in the stream and Mr. B had to rescue it and it's never been the same because, after it had dried, all the stuffing had gone lumpy. We decided not to take any toys with us.

"What else?" we asked.

"We took bathing-costumes. Because we paddled in the stream."

Nobody had a bathing-costume.

Ann-the-Bank showed off her bathing-costume, and rolled it up in her towel like a sausage. The rest of us decided not to take anything at all.

Miss Audrey-Joan had told us to assemble in the stable–yard when she rang the bell, but we were all there, waiting and chattering excitedly long before. Some of the boys had bent pins stuck into their shirt pockets and carried long sticks with a pieces of string tied on the ends for fishing. Jeremy Whiting had a toy yacht tucked under his arm. Mr. B harnessed up old Dobbin and backed him between the shafts of the grey wooden cart that Mrs. B called a float. I went up to him. "May I stroke Dobbin?"

"Of course you may. He's an old softie and likes his nose scratched."

I wasn't sure about scratching his nose because, as I reached up, Dobbin snickered and drew back his lips displaying huge yellow teeth. So I combed his shaggy mane with my fingers and patted his chestnut brown neck. "I'd like to ride a horse."

"Would you now, young lady? Well, maybe next year when you've grown a bit. You'd have to ride Dolly as Dobbin's too big and hefty."

Besides Dobbin, there were three more horses in the stables. Dolly, who was a quiet pony for the children to ride. Paddy, who was taller and skinnier than Dolly and a bit frisky. Then there was Bondy, a tall bay who belonged to Miss Audrey-Joan's sister, Miss Margaret.

Finally, Mrs. B and Miss Audrey-Joan appeared carrying a big wicker picnic basket between them. It seemed to take forever to get all the baskets and packages and Mrs. B onto the float, along with very young ones, including Little Elaine—who wore a big boot on one foot with iron rods up either side of her leg.

When all was ready, the big stable–yard gates were swung open. With Mr. B in the driver's seat and Mrs. B beside him, Dobbin pulled the float out into the lane. The rest of us gathered in little groups to walk the half-mile or so up the lane to Thatcher's Woods. Miss Audrey-Joan, Mrs. Tommy and Mrs. Riley were walking with us.

I called to Ann-the-Bank and Cedric. "C'mon. Quick. We can walk with Miss Audrey-Joan. Bags-I walk next to her." I sped off as fast as I could to get beside her before anyone else.

"Bags-I the other side." I could hear Cedric running close behind. Ann, who had been looking the other way, missed her chance.

We were clamouring to know what adventures awaited us in Thatcher's woods.

"What are we going to do there?"

"Can we climb the trees?"

"Can we paddle? *May* we paddle?"

Miss Audrey-Joan smiled her holiday smile and took my hand. I noticed she took Cedric's too. Ann-the-Bank had caught up and was walking beside me. She said nothing but sniffed a lot.

"Well," said Miss Audrey-Joan. "There are lots of things to do in Thatcher's Woods. We can explore, play games, and paddle. And yes, you may climb trees so long as a grown-up is supervising."

"Can we play Robin Hood?" I knew Cedric would ask that question, but I didn't mind because it would be the real thing; Thatcher's Woods would become Sherwood Forest.

"That's a great idea, Cedric." Miss Audrey-Joan swung his hand high in the air and back down. "We'll play Robin Hood and his Merry Men as soon as we find a good place to picnic."

The lane, bordered by hazel and hawthorn in full bloom, curved gently uphill. The float's wheels kept to the well-worn cart tracks running either side of a strip of grass dotted with clover and chamo-mile daisies. We soon came to the five-barred gate by Farmer Bourne's duck pond where Miss Audrey-Joan had skated last winter. Today, it was busy with ducks and dabchicks, all up-tailed in the shallow brown water. When we passed his farmyard, Farmer Bourne waved and called "hello" to us. He was busy harnessing a pair of giant shire horses to a cart, that a Land Army girl was loading up with buckets and sacks. Next to the farmyard, was the whitewashed cowshed and its manure pile; we all pinched our noses. *"Pheweeeee. What a stink!"*

Not much further. We could see the grist mill and hear the wild roar of the mill-race as it turned the huge wheel, then gushed into the deep, dark mill-pond. From there, the mill-stream slowed down and ran under an old stone bridge, which marked the boundary to Thatcher's Woods.

"Can we play Pooh Sticks on the bridge?"

"NO." Cedric yelled at my suggestion and tugged at Miss Audrey-Joan's hand. Then he went red and looked down at his shoes. "I-I mean...well, you said we could play Robin Hood. And-and I don't like that water. It's too deep and too...too *loud.*"

Ann and I stared at Cedric. He *never* asserted himself like that. *Ever.* Miss Audrey-Joan looked surprised too. "That's all right Cedric. This isn't a good place for us to stop anyway." She turned to me. "The stream runs right through the woods where there's an excellent footbridge for playing Pooh Sticks. Besides, you can find more sticks in the woods than you can here."

Turning back she called, "Come along, children. Let's find a good picnic spot."

Where the lane ended, an ancient cart track took over. Miss Audrey-Joan said that traces of Norman charcoal burners' huts had been found in Thatcher's Woods and that thousands of years ago, there had been an Iron Age settlement close by. The deeply rutted trail wound through tall oak, elm and beech trees. Not far down, it stopped at a shallow stream, that gurgled and splashed its way through the woods before winding down the hill, past Normanhurst, and emptying into the River Severn. Hundreds of years ago, flat stepping stones had been placed across the stream to join the track on the other side. It was only a few inches deep so Mr. B drove Dobbin and the float right across, which made the little ones squeal with excitement. A few yards up-stream was a wooden footbridge that had been built about 50 years ago; so Mr. B told us. It had a rail either side and was a perfect Pooh Sticks bridge.

But that would be later. We gathered around Miss Audrey-Joan and the other teachers while they sorted us out according to what we wanted to do. The bigger boys wanted to try fishing, so they went off up-stream with Mr. B. The little ones stayed with Mrs. Riley to play Hide and Seek, and the rest of us found a good spot in the woods to play Robin Hood. Cedric was Robin Hood because he'd asked first, and I was Maid Marian because he said so; which I didn't mind. Ann-the-Bank minded very much so to make her feel better, she was given the part of a damsel in distress whom Robin Hood had to rescue. With her pout and her pale yellow plaits, she looked the part as she sat on a log that was supposed to be Nottingham Gaol.

Everyone else got to play a part: Miss Audrey-Joan said she wanted to be Friar Tuck, Andrew Simon and Declan Campbell were Will Scarlet and Alan-a-Dale, and Nathan Robbins was the Sheriff of Nottingham. Whoever was left were Merrie Men, Knights and Vassals. Rowley Smythe was a vassal. We had a wonderful time. Miss Audrey-Joan let us climb trees and hide in the branches, so when the Sheriff with his Knights and Vassals rode underneath, the Merrie Men pelted them with leaves and twigs from above. We were having such a good time, we forgot to rescue the Damsel in Distress. We only remembered her when it was time to stop for our picnic lunch, and we'd all gathered around the big hamper full of food and drink.

So Friar Tuck went off to rescue the Damsel in Distress.

But Ann was so angry she sent Cedric and me to Coventry, along with all the other Merrie Men. It turned out she ate her picnic lunch in silence anyway; she was in such a pout, nobody wanted to speak to her.

Lunch was delicious. There were ham sandwiches and cheese sandwiches, some of them had Marmite or chutney spread on the ham or cheese. There were apples and biscuits, and two roasting pans full of Mrs. Tommy's best bread pudding, which was cut into wedges and handed out. There was orangeade, made out of the bright orange sticky stuff that came from the government, and sweetened with a little sugar and a lot of saccharine; I knew that because I'd once seen Mrs. B make some. Jugs of milk covered with muslin doilies to keep the flies out, had been set in the stream to keep cool, and squash and cider bottles had been filled with water so we didn't have to drink stream water. We were given permission to go to the loo behind the trees–girls on one side of the stream, boys on the other.

I traded my apple, which had a worm in it, for Rowley Smythe's piece of bread pudding. I held the apple with the worm-hole downwards so he wouldn't see it, but he didn't even look at the apple before biting into it. I hurried off to find Cedric before Rowley found the worm in his mouth.

"Want to play Pooh Sticks now?"

"All right."

The old wooden-planked footbridge was high enough that even when the stream was in full spate during the spring floods, people could walk across and not get their feet wet. It was quite wide and had two rails either side, set close enough together to prevent a child slipping through. Perfect for playing Pooh Sticks.

Cedric's sticks kept winning at first. Then I noticed there were some leaves caught in fast current on one side of the stream. So I moved towards it and on the word "go" from Cedric, dropped my stick. Racing to the other side of the bridge I jumped up on the lower rail to watch it come through. It was way ahead of Cedric's.

"How did that happen then?" he yelled from the other end of the bridge.

"Come and see."

I pointed to where the little current swirled around up-stream and then shot a leaf out and made it sail faster towards the bridge. "It's like a little whirlpool in there."

Cedric came closer to my territory to throw his sticks in. It got exciting because the races were so close, we couldn't guess whose stick would appear from under the bridge first. Then Cedric's stick rammed mine, and they both came through together.

"Pax," said Cedric. I've run out of sticks. We've got to find some more."

As we turned to hunt for more sticks, I saw a movement amongst the reeds. "Hey. Look. A big fish." I lay full length on the bridge and eased my head under the bottom rail. I grabbed Cedric's leg. "Get down here and take a look."

Cedric lay down beside me and I pointed to a deep part of the stream ahead of us. "There's nothing there," he said.

"No wait. Wait and look properly."

Then we saw them. Dark shadows weaving in and out of the tall green weeds that grew up from the stream bed. Fish!

What Cedric did next frightened me. He scrambled to his feet. I thought he was going to run from the bridge, but he squatted beside me, hid his face in his hands and started to sob.

"Cedric? Cedric, what's the matter?" I looked around to see if any of the other children were close by, but we were alone. Most of them were paddling in the stream near the stepping stones, shrieking with laughter and having fun.

Cedric's shoulders were heaving as he sobbed. I put my arm around him. "What frightened you?" I turned back to look at the stream again.

"Did he see a monster? Or a bogey man? There were a lot of bogey men around, 'specially in war time."

"Did you see a bogey man?"

Cedric shook his head. He fumbled for his hanky and blew his nose, then scrubbed at his eyes. "It was that really bad dream I had. About the water."

"What about the dream?"

"Remember when I told you I saw my mummy f-floating in the water, with her mouth open. And then my Daddy came and carried me down to the bottom of the sea and left me on the rock all alone. It was dark. Just like that stream.

Cedric shivered in the bright afternoon sun. He hugged his knees and dropped his head on them. As I leaned closer to hear what he was saying, his soft brown hair brushed my arm. It felt like feathers. "Can you remember what happened after that?" I asked.

"Some great big fishes came swimming through the seaweed and made a circle around me. They started nudging me with their noses."

"With their noses? Fishes don't have noses."

"These did. Giant blue fishes with long pointy noses."

"Did they bite?"

"No. They didn't bite. But..."

I waited. "Cedric? Tell me what they did."

I waited some more. Then Cedric slowly raised his head and turned to me. His face was very pale. "They...they...um . . .they *talked.*"

"*Talked?* Fish don't talk."

"These fishes did. They were talking about me."

I thought for a moment. I thought Cedric was being really silly. But then, dreams can be silly, so I asked him, "What did they say about you?"

His buried his head on his knees again, and rocked gently from side to side. I knew he didn't want to tell me.

"Cedric, tell me. What did the fishes say?"

Cedric sighed. I didn't dare speak. After some long minutes, he leaped to his feet so suddenly it made me jump. He stood in front of me; his hands were clenched so tight by his sides, I could see his knuckles turn from pink to white. Tears streamed down his cheeks.

"THEY SAID I WAS DEAD! DROWNED! DEAD!"

He turned and raced off the bridge and before I could scramble to my feet, he'd disappeared. I could hear him crashing through the tall undergrowth. I followed him because I thought he just wanted to get away from the water, and he would stop for me to catch up. But I could hear he was getting further and further away. He wasn't going to stop. Now what was I going to do? I stopped running and listened carefully. He'd gone. I was out of breath. I needed to think–think what to do. I sat on a log and the sun felt warm on my bare arms and legs. I could hear the shouts and splashes of the little children playing in the stream, but no sound from the direction in which Cedric had fled.

"Perhaps I should go and find Miss Audrey-Joan. I don't want to be a tell-tale-tit, but Cedric may be lost, or perhaps he's fallen down and that's why I can't hear him any more."

I scrubbed at the soft moss under my feet with the toes of my plimsolls. Then I heard a noise that I thought was Cedric coming back. But it came from the opposite direction from where Cedric had run away.

"Run away? Oh Lordy, Lordy, I hope he hasn't run away."

More cracking of twigs under the feet of the person coming through the woods towards me. Heavy footsteps. A grown-up. I thought about getting up and running the way Cedric had gone, but by then it was too late. Brushing leaves from her hair, Miss Audrey-Joan stood in front of me. "Patricia? What are you doing here? I thought you were playing

Pooh Sticks and then I noticed there was no-one on the footbridge. You shouldn't come into the woods by yourself, you might get lost."

I didn't answer, just hung my head and went on scuffing at the soft mound of moss and last year's pine-needles.

Miss Audrey-Joan sat down beside me on the log. "Is something wrong? Have you and Cedric had a quarrel? Can you tell me about it?"

Somehow, she seemed different today. In school she was more strict, demanding answers. She would never have said, "Can you tell me about it?" More likely she would have said, "Tell me immediately what you have done."

I looked up at her. She was smiling. "Come, Pat. This is a holiday. We're having a picnic. This is not a time for long faces and doldrums. Tell me, where's Cedric?"

I took a deep breath, but didn't know what to say.

"What were you about to say, Pat? Come on, you can tell me. I won't bite!" Miss Audrey-Joan grinned at me.

"If somebody has done something, but didn't say I wasn't to tell, would that be telling?" I asked.

Miss Audrey-Joan looked puzzled. "That sounds like a riddle." I didn't say any more, so she went on, "Do you mean that Cedric has done something, but you don't want him to think you are a tell-tale?"

I nodded.

"Well, it depends." Then she paused and looked hard at me. "If...if something has, or may have happened to Cedric, that distresses you, and you think he may be troubled rather than *in* trouble, then it would be proper for his best friend to come to his aid. Does that clear the way for you to tell me?"

I nodded again.

"Then why don't you tell me? Cedric's not hurt is he?"

"I...I don't know. He could be. But he's very upset."

"Oh dear. I think you had better tell me everything. And I'll never tell Cedric that you told me. "Cross-my-heart-and-hope-to-die. How's that?"

Miss Audrey-Joan hardly ever called me 'Pat.' She seemed more like a friend–especially with the 'cross-her-heart-and-hope-to-die bit.' I decided to tell her what had happened.

So I told her how we were playing Pooh Sticks and how Cedric told me about his dream when the big fishes frightened him. I told her about the other nightmare and how it kept coming back and frightening him. When I'd told her everything, I pointed in the direction where Cedric had gone running. "And he was crying. Crying buckets," I finished.

Miss Audrey-Joan took my hand. "Come. We will go and find him together." She looked at the dense underbrush with its stinging nettles, tall thistles and bracken blocking the direction in which Cedric had gone. She turned back the way we'd come. "I have an idea."

She led me back to our picnic spot. Mrs. B was sitting against a tree, fanning herself with her hat. She looked hot. Everyone else was either playing in the stream, or playing Hide-and-Seek with Mrs. Tommy. Mr. B was still up-stream with the boys and their fishing poles.

Miss Audrey-Joan called to Mrs. B. "Tell Dad I'm taking Dobbin for a short walk. Pat and I are going on a mission."

Mrs. B stopped fanning herself and looked at us. "Are you sure you can manage? There's no saddle, Dobbin's in harness."

"We'll be fine. His blanket will be enough. We're only going for a gentle walk, not trying to run in the Grand National. Besides, Pat is wanting to ride anyway. This will probably either kill or cure the ambition."

"I've ridden before," I told her. My Daddy taught me on a Shetland pony before the war when I was very little. And once, in Wales, he borrowed a pony for me."

"Well, that settles that then." Miss Audrey-Joan threw a blanket over Dobbin's back and lifted me up. "Throw your leg over and hang onto his mane. I'll be right up behind you in two shakes."

She unclipped the long driving reins from Dobbin's bridle leaving a short riding rein in place. Then, in one light bound she was up, sitting behind me on Dobbin's broad back. With her hands forward on either side of me, she gripped the reins and clicked at Dobbin. I could feel the great lumbering horse-shoulders move under me as we set off to find Cedric. We passed Ann-the-Bank, who was squatting on her heels searching for hopscotch stones. As Miss Audrey-Joan urged Dobbin across the stream, she stood up and, with dripping hands on her hips, glared at me. Seeing that she'd sent us all to Coventry for forgetting the Damsel in Distress, I had no trouble ignoring her.

As we rode through Thatcher's Woods on the back of Old Dobbin, I couldn't have been happier. Then I remembered how Cedric was so upset about the fishes, and I didn't feel so happy. We rode along, looking left and right. It didn't take long to find him; he popped up, like a bunny, right in front of us. But when he saw who it was, he hung his head.

He told me later that he'd heard the old horse clip-clopping through the woods, so he came out from where he'd been lying under tree, to see who was coming.

"It could have been a gypsy caravan, Cedric. And they could've stolen you away. Gypsies steal children."

Cedric just shrugged as if he wouldn't have minded being stolen by gypsies.

Miss Audrey-Joan slid down from Dobbin's back and then lifted me down. "Stay here with Dobbin for a few minutes while Cedric and I take a little walk. Maybe you could find some flowers to press."

We were making little blotting paper presses in Art. With mine, I intended to make an album of pressed flowers for my mother.

Miss Audrey-Joan tethered Dobbin to a small birch sapling, and took Cedric's hand. They walked away down a small animal-path between the trees. They were gone for a long time. I had collected a big bunch wild flowers before I heard crashing footsteps, and Miss Audrey-Joan came galloping out of the trees with Cedric bouncing up and down on her back. I sighed with relief. *Everything must be all right if Miss Audrey-Joan is giving Cedric a piggy-back ride.*

They were both laughing and when they reached me; Miss Audrey-Joan tripped accidentally-on-purpose and together they went rolling over and over on the ground. Still laughing they got up, brushing leaves and pine needles from their clothes and hair.

"Come, children," said Miss Audrey-Joan. "Let's get the two of you up on Dobbin and we'll go back for the rest of our picnic. I think we'd all enjoy a cold drink."

She hoisted Cedric and me up on Dobbin's back, then climbed up behind us. Cedric was the middle of the sandwich. He put his arms around my waist and Miss Audrey-Joan's arms encircled both of us as she guided Dobbin back to the stream. We were half-way back to the picnic stop when we passed a glade, and saw a giant rock within a circle of trees. Something caught Miss Audrey-Joan's eye as she made Dobbin stop. "Children, I think there's magic here."

She caught us as we slid off Dobbin's back but we stood and watched as she walked towards the rock. She bent down, looked at something on the ground, and then slowly walked around the rock.

"What is it, Miss Baker? What have you found?"

"I thought as much." She beckoned to us. "Come. Come."

As we approached the centre of the glade, she called, "Mind you don't tread on it."

"On what?"

"The ring. It's a fairy ring. Look." She pointed to a ring of toadstools growing around the rock. There was just enough room for us to stand between the toadstools and the rock.

"Come. Cedric, Pat. Let's join hands around the rock."

We stretched and just managed to join hands around the big grey rock which glinted where the sunlight caught embedded grains of shiny quartz.

"Now," said Miss Audrey-Joan. "Make a wish. It must be a good wish and not a wish to harm someone. But don't say it out loud, or it won't be granted. Let's be very quiet. Eyes tight shut, hold hands and wish."

Which we did.

Then all three of us tiptoed out of the fairy ring to where Dobbin was patiently waiting. Miss Baker swung me up. Just before she swung Cedric up to join me I heard her whisper to him, "Nothing can harm you now, Cedric. You've been inside a magic fairy ring. The fairies will protect you."

Abruptly, he broke away from her and ran back to the rock. He leaned his forehead against it, his arms stretching out and around it, as though he wanted to hug it. Miss Audrey-Joan put her hands on my shoulders and we stood, watching and waiting. Then Cedric turned and, stepping carefully over the fairy toadstools, walked slowly away from the magic glade. I couldn't tell what he was thinking; he looked neither happy nor sad. And he was silent as Miss Audrey-Joan lifted him up to join me on Dobbin's back.

Over the next four summers, we often went for picnics in Thatchers Woods.

But I will never forget that first one.

And I will never forget the promise—that the Fairy Ring's magic would protect Cedric.

8th June, 1941.
Dear Mummy and Daddy,
We all went for a picnic in Thatchers Woods last Monday. We played Pooh Sticks and I went for a ride on Dobbin.
Please may I have a bathing-costume for my birthday.
In twelve days I will be seven. Will you be here for my birthday?
With love from,
Patricia

Chapter 16

Camelot

We never played Robin Hood again. I don't remember why except that, on the Saturday after the picnic in Thatcher's Woods when I suggested it, Cedric said he didn't want to. "Let's think of another game."

"What sort of game?"

We were sitting on the steps of the children's entrance at the side of the house. It was a favourite play area, especially for the girls. Sheltered by the high wall separating the stable-yard from the garden on one side, the house behind us, and the thick yew trees against the boundary walls, it was a warm and quiet place to play. Below the steps, a broad path led to a wooden door, which was the entrance to the stable-yard. The smooth grey-painted door was perfect for playing Ten's and we could always find an old tennis ball from somewhere. Equally important, was the path. Scraped smooth and dusted with loving care, it was the ultimate summer hopscotch pad. Ann-the-Bank and Hilary Cooper were on hands and knees picking off the odd leaf and bits of grit that had collected overnight.

"Well..." Cedric was leaning forward and poking at some ants that were scurrying in and out of the cracks in the step. One was trying to pull what looked like a grain of rice, twice as big as himself, through a very small hole—big enough for the ant, but not his breakfast.

"Well, what?" I asked.

"Well, you know we're learning about King Arthur and the Knights of the Round Table." Cedric tried to help the ant by pushing its breakfast into the crack. "I thought we could play at King Arthur and His Knights. They had excellent battles. Fought dragons and stuff."

"That was St. George who killed dragons."

"King Arthur did too, in the Welsh hills. *You* should know. You live in Wales."

He was right. There had been a lot of dragons in Wales.

Ann-the-Bank got up, lifted her kilt and dusted her hands on her knickers. "What's in Wales?"

"Dragons," I said.

"'S'true," said Ann. "My da's seen one."

"You're fibbing," I said. "There're no dragons left. King Arthur and St. George killed them all."

"Nope. My Da's seen one. It was late one Saturday night. At least, that's what he told my Mam and me."

"And what did your Mam say?"

"She said that all he'd seen was the fiery sparks of the last train from Llandovery."

"See! I told you it wasn't a dragon."

Ann-the-Bank came up the steps and shoved her face close to mine. "And I tell you that's what my Da saw. And that finishes it, Patricia Mashiter. If my Da says he saw a dragon, then he saw a dragon."

"Well that settles it," said Cedric. "There are dragons out there so we can go slay them. We can be King Arthur and his gallant knights rescuing damsels in distress from dragons. C'mon."

"Where?"

Cedric moved down to the second step and peered at the ants. "Look! That ant has found another hole. One that's big enough to pull his breakfast through."

He was right. The ant was disappearing through a hole at the other end of the step. Two more ants had joined him and were helping push his booty through the small opening. Then they were gone.

"Cedric, where are we going to play King Arthur?"

"The sunken garden, of course. The rockery can be King Arthur's castle."

And that's how we happened to spend the summer in Camelot.

On the right side of the house, between the boys' outside lavvy and the walled kitchen garden, was a sunken garden. It was an excellent place to act out whatever adventures we were creating at the time. It had, in turn, been Nottingham Castle, a sailing ship and a circus ring. At each side of the formal front gardens, neat gravel paths edged with low boxwood hedges, bordered deep flower beds set against the kitchen garden wall; all of which framed velvety green lawns that swept around the front of the house and clear down to the creeper-covered wall bordering the main road from Eardington to Bridgnorth. On the lawn to the right of the house, a tennis court was marked out; behind it, a long pergola arch led to the sunken garden. Covered in summer with climbing roses and honeysuckle vines it was, for us, a magic tunnel to another world. At the end of the pergola, a flight of steps led into the sunken garden itself. Here, around a circle of lawn, more boxwood hedges formed a miniature maze. But the most stupendous feature of the whole garden, wasn't sunk at all. In its very centre, a pyramid-shaped rockery soared skywards. The rocks were chunky enough to climb on—right to the very top. In between the rocks were spongy cushions of heather, aubretia and tiny pink thrift. At the summit of the pyramid was a fountainhead. The metal, ancient and speckled with ver-digris, stuck up like a flagpole on top of a castle, or a masthead of some ancient sailing ship. That summer it was King Arthur's Royal Standard, complete with dragons, flapping above Camelot.

All summer long, we were King Arthur and His Knights of the Round Table. We took turns at being King Arthur, Guinevere, Sir Lancelot, Galahad and Merlin. Sometimes I was Guinevere to Cedric's King Arthur, and other times we were Merlin and Morgan le Fay. We rescued damsels in distress, vanquished dragons, and quested for the Holy Grail. Out came the skipping ropes again, and Vassals became horses on which we galloped into every corner of the Summer Kingdom. Armed with lances and wearing our pillowcases for cloaks, we competed in jousting tournaments on the tennis court. On Saturdays, Miss Audrey-Joan pulled out the dressing-up chests and with golden circlets on our heads and jewelled swords in our belts, we held court in Camelot. Normans fought Saxons and all enemies were vanquished, whoever they were.

Then one terrible day, Declan Campbell, who was Mordred at the time, scaled the walls of Camelot and struck Arthur with his sword. "You're dead, King Arthur. You're no longer King. I am King."

Cedric dutifully slithered down the rockery and lay on the deep green grass. "I die," he cried. "I die for the love of my Queen."

Then the tea bell rang and we all rushed to wash our hands and be first into the dining hall to bag the best seats. As I ran through the halls and clattered up the back stairs, I could still hear King Arthur's words ringing in my ears. "I die for the love of my Queen."

"Dear Cedric..."

Since Cedric couldn't be King Arthur any more, because Mordred had killed him and it was Declan's turn, he decided he would become Merlin–permanently.

He was pacing up and down a small landing halfway up the back stairs. Arms folded and head bowed, he was practising being Merlin. He said, "Merlin was magic you know."

I sat on the stairs watching him. Tristan was on my lap chewing at one of the buttons on my cardigan. "He lived in a cave," I said. "A magic cave. So we'll have to find a cave."

Cedric stopped his pacing and looked out of the tall window that overlooked the stable-yard. "It's still raining so we can't go and look now. Anyway, the bell will go for lessons any minute."

"If you're Merlin, then I'm going to be Morgan Le Fay," I said. "She was magic too."

"Jolly good. You can cook the magic potions."

I wasn't too sure about the cooking part, although the mixing would be fun." We'll have to find a magic lair first."

Cedric turned away from the window and came to where I was sitting. "I know where there's a magic lair."

I stared at him. "Where? In the stable-yard?"

"No. It's a secret place I found, and no-one else knows about it."

I thought about that for a minute. It couldn't be the Rabbit Hole because everybody knew about the Anderson shelter buried between the barn and the rubbish dump. Besides, it was out of bounds except when the village "Wailing Winnie" practised its warning and we all had to pretend there were enemy planes coming to bomb us.

The bell rang for afternoon lessons.

"Tell me, Cedric. Tell me where it is."

"That cat's almost bitten your button right off."

I pushed Tristan off my lap and stood up. "Tell me where your magic lair is. Please, Cedric."

He grinned. "After lessons if it's stopped raining, I'll show it to you. But I fains you tell anybody. Nobody must know. And especially not Ann-the-Bank."

Ann was not very good at keeping secrets.

"All right. But..."

"C'mon, we'll be late for lessons."

Cedric leaped down the stairs two at a time. I ran down after him. I wished I could leap two stairs at a time. He looked as though he were flying. I wished I could fly—like Peter Pan."

"Drat Cedric. Drat the school bell. Now I'd have to wait until after lessons to find out where his secret place is."

Arabella Bosworthy was blocking the way into the classroom. Hands on hips and feet apart, I couldn't get by her. She must have let Cedric in because I could see over her shoulder that he was at his desk. The lid was up and he'd buried his head inside, pretending not to see what was going on.

"Bossy Bella. Now what did SHE want?"

"Let me by, Arabella Bosworthy."

She stuck her face two inches from mine. I could see an evil glint in her eyes. "So, Patricia Mashiter. What were you and Cedric Robinson having secrets about on the stairs, then?"

"Secrets? We weren't talking secrets."

"Cross-your-heart-and-hope-to-die? With a wooden stake in your heart?" Bossy Bella had a fascination for witches and vampires and all things nasty.

I was saved from answering. In a swirl of black teacher's gown, her soft-soled shoes making no sound, Miss Audrey-Joan came round the corner. Arabella jumped back.

"Now children, why aren't you in your seats? You're wasting good story-telling time."

Friday afternoon was always the best afternoon of the whole week. In fine weather, we would play games, go for a nature ramble, or help in the kitchen gardens. When it rained, Miss Audrey-Joan read to us and sometimes, we would act the stories. Friday afternoons also finished early, so the dailies and weeklies had plenty of time to get ready before their parents came to pick them up. Us boarders were left to play amongst ourselves and do pretty much what we wanted, except climb trees.

At half-past three, Mrs. B rang the bell. And another weekend had begun.

Cedric grabbed my arm, and we both dodged Bossy Bella. She was a daily anyway, so we wouldn't see her until Monday morning. "C'mon, Patty. I've got something to show you."

"I've got to change my shoes first." In summertime we often wore our indoor shoes, or our plimsolls, outside.

"Why?"

I sat down on the shoe lockers and wedged my foot over my knee. The soles of my shoes had worn into holes, right under the balls of my big toes. "Look, they're right through. And the gravel hurts my feet."

Cedric examined them. "That happened to mine. Mrs. B cut some cardboard and fitted it inside my shoes 'til my mummy sent me new ones. She'll do that to yours if you ask her."

I wore my Welly-boots with thick socks inside them–it had been raining, so there would be puddles to splash in.

Cedric put his Wellies on too. "We're going to the orchard anyway," he explained.

So this secret place was in the orchard? Now it was my turn to get impatient. "Then let's go. Before Ann or anyone else sees us." I started down the stone-flagged passage leading to the children's entrance. Cedric grabbed my arm. "Not that way," he hissed. "Too many people."

That was true. Mothers were hurrying the dailies and week-lies into their shoes and coats and packing up what they needed for the weekend.

Cedric pulled me towards the back kitchen door that led into the part of the yard by the storage outhouses, the old wash house, and the girls' outside lavvy. "There's no one there right now," he said. "We can get out without being seen."

Minutes later we were running along the path to the orchard, past the kitchen garden wall on the right, the Rabbit Hole and rubbish dump on the left. As soon as we'd climbed over the five-barred gate, Cedric ran off in front, heading towards the far corner of the orchard, where boundary hedges separated Normanhurst from Farmer Bourne's prop-erty and the main Bridgnorth Road.

When I caught up with him, Cedric was standing, hands on hips and staring at a tangle of brambles and spiky hawthorn that towered above us. Underneath, thistles and nettles warned us that this was *not* a friendly place to play. Beyond the brambles, where the two hedges met, was a twisted old crabapple tree.

I stared at Cedric. *"He must have gone off his rocker."*

"And this is supposed to be your secret place? Merlin's lair?"

Cedric turned to me and grinned. He pointed to a broad-trunked old quince tree. "Stand over against that tree. Hide your eyes and count to fifty."

"Now you want to play Hide-and-Seek?"

"Sort of. Go on, shut your eyes and count."

There was nothing better to do anyway, so I played along with Cedric's little game. "All right. I'll do it. But I fains you run away and leave me here."

"I won't." Honour-bound not to peek, I leaned against the trunk of the quince tree and counted to fifty–quickly. "Fifty," I yelled, as I turned around. "I'm coming."

Cedric had disappeared. I looked behind a couple of trees. No Cedric. I walked around the mass of tangled brambles, carefully avoiding nettles that came up to my waist, and thistles that were even taller. I walked all the way around it–twice. Still no Cedric.

Then I heard him call, "Do you give up?" His voice was so close that I jumped.

"Cedric? Yes...yes. I give up." I was tired of his silly game. I wanted see his secret place.

"Go and hide your eyes again."

I stamped my foot. My Welly-boot squelched in the wet grass. "I will *not*, Cedric Robinson. You come out. RIGHT NOW."

"Well, I fains you tell anyone where this is."

"You already fainsed me on that. Besides, you know I won't."

"Cross-your-heart-and-hope-to-die?"

"Yes." I wet my finger, made an X over my heart and hoped to die.

There was a scuffling, and I saw the brambles swaying. Then, from the far left side of the thicket where it melded into Farmer Bourne's hedge, Cedric appeared. He was on hands and knees; a leaf was caught in his hair. He was wet from wriggling through the damp undergrowth.

"Where on earth...?"

He stood up, grinning. "C'mon, I'll show you." He crouched down again on a small rabbit path that ended against a curtain of tall grass. I dropped down on hands and knees behind him. Cedric parted the tall grasses and inched forward. "Follow me and hold the grass back like I do." I followed Cedric, squeezing through a small tunnel in the grass and scrambled to my feet the other side. I couldn't believe my eyes. This was the most perfect secret lair I'd ever seen; Cedric's secret place and he'd shared it with me. I would never, ever tell anyone where this was.

"Gosh, Cedric. This is perfect."

It was a miniature glade. No long grass under the old crab-apple tree, just soft cushiony moss between knotty roots that formed interesting shapes and hollows–one even making a perfect seat with a back. I immediately sat in it and looked around. Above, in the old tree, chattering birds hopped from branch to branch. On the high tangle of brambles, green blackberries were already forming, and across one corner a small ditch-stream gurgled; fed from a spring that trickled from nowhere in particular.

"Merlin's Lair! Cedric, this is stupendous."

Cedric was grinning and jigging up and down with excitement. "There's something else I have to show you." He knelt down by the roots of the tree. "There's a secret hiding place here. Come and see."

Sure enough, there was a hole leading deep down into the roots of the tree.

"Put your arm down the hole."

It was a miniature cave. But it didn't go on for ever. I could feel its soft, sandy back. On one side I could feel a tiny hole that went further down, and on the other side...? "There's something there," I said.

"I know. Bring it out."

I pulled out a blue and gold patterned tin with the words, 'Blackcurrent, and Glycerine Throat Lozenges.' I shook it. It rattled. "There's something in there."

"Open it."

Inside was a farthing.

"That's my treasure chest," Cedric explained. "I found that farthing. As I get more treasure, I'll put it in the chest. No one will ever find it there."

"That's brilliant. May I put a treasure chest down there too?"

"Of course. But we have to collect stuff for you to brew my potions and magic spells."

So we lay there, planning what spells and potions to concoct for the benefit of everyone (mostly) and the downfall of some (Bossy Bella) until the tea bell went.

After tea, Cedric told everyone that he was now Merlin and I was Morgan Le Fay for the whole summer. And he fainsed anyone to challenge us. Nobody seemed to mind, as they all wanted to be King Arthur, or a Knight, or a damsel to be rescued from dragons. And nobody minded when Merlin and Morgan le Fay disappeared to their secret lair, so long as they brought back magic potions. Only Ann-the-Bank asked where the secret lair was and when we told her it was by the orchard, she screwed up her nose and said that it must be in the rubbish dump and that *she* wasn't going to go there for *anything*. Not even for a potion to make her hair curl.

So the secret lair remained a secret for the next five years. And no-one else knew about it, ever. Well, almost no-one.

Only when Cedric was gone and I knew that he would never come back, did I share it with one other person.

But that wouldn't be for years and, anyway, Cedric told me I could.

Sunday, June 15th, 1940
Dear Mummy and Daddy,
I hope you are well.
I have holes in my shoes. I am enclosing an outline of my foot that Mrs. B drew on a piece of paper so you can get me a new pair if you have enough coupons. Mr. B put some cardboard inside over the holes but it makes them too tight and my toes hurt.
We are learning about King Arthur and the Knights of the Round Table.
Will you be coming to see me on my birthday? In 5 days I will be seven.
Your loving daughter,
 Patricia

Chapter 17

"Happy Birthday"

Birthdays at Normanhurst, were special. After assembly, Miss Audrey-Joan would announce the Birthday Child's name. Everyone would sing, "Happy Birthday" and "For he's (or she's) a Jolly Good Fellow." But most important of all, it was a rule that no-one could be mean or spiteful to a birthday child.

One special treat for the birthday child was that they were allowed to choose the whole day's meals. Days before, in Miss Audrey-Joan's study and with Mrs. B making notes, we made our choices. Of course, we couldn't ask for anything that wasn't a regular school meal, but we could have our favourite breakfast, dinner and tea.

However, the very best thing of all, was that instead of the last lesson of the day, there would be a birthday party. This made the birthday child the most popular girl, or boy, in the school. The birthday child chose the games, which we played either inside or outdoors according to the weather. We were a princess (or prince) for a day.

My birthday was in midsummer which—I thought—was the best time of the whole year. I'd chosen Spam fritters for breakfast (I knew better than to ask for bacon)—this made Rowley Smythe my slave for the day, sausages and mash with gravy for dinner, with treacle tart for pudding, and cheese pie for tea. Mrs. B wrote all this down and looked at me over her spectacles. "Well, Miss Patricia. Have you forgotten there's a war on and treacle is hard to find?"

"Oh Mrs. B. You have big tins of treacle hidden away in the pantry."

"It isn't just the treacle, Miss. It's the lard and flour to make the pastry. But we'll see what we can do. However, I can guarantee you'll all be eating Woolton Pie and porridge for the rest of the week."

Miss Audrey-Joan winked at me, so I knew that Mrs. B's grumbling was just for show. I'd once heard her say to Mrs. Tommy that it was a good job they'd had the foresight to stock up on supplies before rationing started. But she often muttered about how the war had better not last too long, or they would be running out of things.

The day I turned seven was hot and sunny. The Spam fritters were delicious–and there wasn't a bowl of porridge in sight. During breakfast, little birthday cards and notes piled up in front of my place. As usual, Ann-the-Bank was sitting on one side of me, Cedric on the other.

"Is your Mummy coming, then?" Ann mumbled through a mouthful of fritter.

"I dunno. I asked her, but I haven't heard yet. I 'spect she will."

"S'long way from Wales, just for your birthday. That's what my Mam said when it was *my* birthday."

I hadn't really thought about it much. I'd taken for granted that my mother would be here, bringing presents and a birthday cake. Before the war, we always went to Dudley Zoo on my birthday and afterwards my aunts and cousins would come for a strawberries and cream picnic in the Randan Woods.

"Of course she's coming," I said. But deep down, I wondered if Ann was right about it being too far. All morning, I couldn't concentrate on my lessons and kept looking out the window to see if Mummy was walking up the driveway. It wasn't until dinner and I was eating my last mouthful of treacle tart, that Miss Audrey-Joan came into the dining hall and beckoned to me.

"Mummy?" I scrambled down so fast, that my chair fell over backwards. I didn't bother to pick it up, but rushed out after Miss Audrey-Joan.

"Is Mummy here?" I clattered after her as she went towards her study. At the doorway she turned. "She's on the telephone. She wants to talk to you."

I picked up the phone. She sounded very far away and the telephone was crackling.

"Happy Birthday, Pooh Bear!"

"Mummy? Where are you? Are you here?"

"No, my darling. I'm in Wales. But I am calling you to wish you a Happy Birthday from Daddy and me, and Dilly."

All I heard was, "*No,*" and "*I'm in Wales.*" I started to cry.

"Patty, don't cry. Listen to me."

I was sobbing now. "B-but it's my b-birthday."

"Patty, listen to me. The pips will go any minute and I have something important to tell you."

Miss Audrey-Joan knelt down beside me, put a hand under my chin, and turned my face towards her. "Pat. Listen to your mother."

So I listened.

"Patty. I'm so sorry to miss your birthday but I have a big surprise for you."

I said nothing.

"How would you like to come home for the summer holidays? Daddy has a whole week's leave."

I nodded at the phone.

"Patty? Are you there?"

"Answer her," Miss Audrey-Joan whispered in my ear.

"Yes," I whispered. "Yes, please."

Then, pip-pip-pip, and the telephone was silent, except for the crackling. I handed the receiver back to Miss Audrey-Joan. Leading me to her big leather armchair, she sat down, took me on her lap and, with her own hanky, wiped away my tears.

"I know it's disappointing not to see your mother on your birthday. But, you know, the other children are the same. You're a boarder here for the duration of the war because, like the other boarders, you can't live with your parents. Their mothers also live far away, or in a town where it's dangerous because of the air raids—and their fathers, too, are away fighting in the war. But, do you know how lucky you are to be going home for the summer holidays? Just imagine. Going to Wales for a whole six weeks."

"When will that be?" I didn't know anything about school summer holidays.

"It's in about a month's time."

Then I understood what my mother had said. "And my daddy will be there too?"

"So I believe, for a whole week."

I sniffed. Then I smiled. Things weren't quite so bad after all.

Miss Baker put me down from her lap. "A big parcel came for you this morning. You can open it after school."

"Is it a birthday parcel?"

"I'm sure it is. Now, run along to afternoon lessons. It will soon be party time."

As Friday was a short afternoon anyway, there was only an hour of lessons. So when Mrs. B clanged the bell at two o'clock, everyone hip-hip-hurrahed me. Even Bossy Bella came up and handed me an envelope. Inside was a card with a picture of fairies with pink wings, dancing around a small hedgehog holding a toadstool with a candle stuck in it. On the card was written *"Happy Birthday to Arabella from Aunty Mary and Uncle Stan."* The words, 'Arabella,' 'Aunty Mary and Uncle Stan.' had been crossed out, and it now read, *"Happy Birthday to Pat Mashiter from Arabella Bosworthy."* In the bottom of the envelope were two red jelly babies.

"Thank you, Arabella. Red ones are my favourites."

I was sitting on the back stairs chewing on one of the jelly babies, when Miss Audrey-Joan found me and handed me a pile of envelopes and a big brown-paper parcel. I dashed upstairs to my dormy, where I tore the paper off; remembering to put the string aside for Mrs. B. All sorts of birthday treasures were inside. Books, sweets and chocolate. Also a very small bathing costume–all in little puffy elastic squares. When I pulled it on, the puffy squares stretched out to fit me. Dilly sent me a pretty card and a small china Bambi. She had written on the card that Bambi had luminous paint on him and would glow in the dark. She must have been thinking how I missed my owl nightlight. Inside the envelopes were cards with book-tokens or postal-orders pinned to them, from my aunts.

I'd just finished opening everything, when Ann-the-Bank came stamping up the stairs. "Pat. C'mon. Your party's started." Without waiting for an answer, she stamped back down the stairs. I was close behind her.

For the rest of the afternoon, we played Sardines, Hide-and-Seek and Tag. We were allowed to climb trees, and play in the barn. Later, Miss Audrey-Joan played records on the gramophone for country dancing, and Mrs. B brought out jugs of saccharine-sweetened orangeade to quench our thirsts.

At teatime, there was one final birthday surprise. After the cheese pie, Mrs. B carried in a tray of teacups filled with red, orange or green jelly, each topped with a dollop of custard. Behind her, Miss Audrey-Joan carried in a chocolate sponge cake, topped with seven candles, and placed it in front of me. Mrs. Tommy always made a cake for a birthday party, but they weren't always chocolate. Because of rationing, the cake was small but there was enough for everyone to have a mouthful. I'd never had a birthday like this before. It was stupendous fun, especially as everyone was nice to me for the whole day.

When it was time for bed, and the midsummer evening sun was still bright through the thin curtains, I read until Mrs. B crept in to pull down the blackout blinds. It was then, in the pitch dark, that I discovered that the little Bambi really did glow. I fell asleep day-dreaming of all the wonderful things that would happen during the summer holidays in Wales—when Daddy would be home.

I'd never seen Cedric so excited. It was Saturday, the day after my birthday, and after breakfast Miss Audrey-Joan had summoned him to her study. Ann-the-Bank and I had just finished making our beds and were getting ready to play outside, when we heard him calling us. We ran and met him half-way down the back stairs.

"I'm leaving," he yelled. "I'm going home. I'm going home."

Ann and I sat on the stairs and watched him leaping around.

"What do you mean, leaving?" I asked. "Is the war over? Are we all going home?"

"Well, we're both going home for the summer," said Ann. "I s'pose Cedric is too now."

Which was good news, because ever since we'd told him we were both going home to Wales for the summer, Cedric had been down in the dumps. No wonder he was excited.

"But your home's in Birmingham. And it's dangerous there with the bombing, and all."

"No, no, no," said Cedric. "I'm not going to Birmingham."

"Where are you going then?" I asked.

"To America. We're all going to America."

"Who's going to America?"

"My mummy, my auntie and my baby sister. We're all going to America 'til the war's over."

Ann and I looked at each other. "Why," I asked, "are you going to America?"

"Where's America anyway?" Ann asked.

"Let's look on the map," I suggested.

A large map of the world hung on the dining-hall wall. It was all rolled up like a blind, a little chain hanging from it. I climbed on a chair, pulled the chain and fastened it to an upside-down hook in the wall. The others climbed up and we traced our fingers all over the world to find the word 'America'.

"There 'tis," Cedric jabbed at it with his forefinger. "There's America."

"And here's England," I put my finger in the middle of the little pink bit that was Great Britain. "It's a jolly long way to America."

"That it is," said Miss Audrey-Joan, who had come to see what we were up to.

"How far is it to America?" We all asked.

"Well, between three and four thousand miles, depending upon where Cedric will be landing in America. And all that blue in between is the Atlantic Ocean. You'll be going on a big ship, Cedric, right across the Atlantic."

Cedric was silent for quite a while. Then he asked, very quietly, "Will it be a really *big* ship?"

"Of course," said Miss Audrey-Joan. "It will be enormous. And you'll have your own bed to sleep in, and there'll be a dining-room much bigger than this one. You'll play lots of games on deck and have a wonderful time."

"Like a house?" asked Cedric.

"Yes, Cedric. Just like an enormous house. Except it has engines to push it through the water. You will be living in a house on the ocean."

That sounded pretty terrific to me and when we went outside to play, Ann-the-Bank and I talked about how lucky Cedric was to be going on such a marvellous adventure.

But Cedric didn't say much about it at all.

Sunday, 22nd June, 1941.
Dear Mummy and Daddy,
Thank you for the parcel and all my birthday presents. I have written a hundred letters to thank everybody for sending me money and book-tokens. I was sad you were not here for my birthday.
I am very happy that I can come home to Wales for the summer holidays. I am specially glad that Daddy will be home too.
I am bringing my bicycle and Ann-the-Bank on the train with me.
My friend Cedric is going to America, but not for long as he is coming back after the war which will be over soon.
With love from
Patricia (aged 7)
P.S. Please give the enclosed letter to Dilly. It is to thank her for Bambi.

Chapter 18

Summer in Wales, 1941

The last days of the Summer term flew by. There was a sports day, when the mothers of the dailies and weeklies came to watch and cheer us on. We had jumping competitions, and races: relay, spoon and potato, three-legged, sack, and plain running. The Normans and Saxons battled it out in rounders and cricket matches, the older children played in a tennis tournament. The Saxons won four trophies, the Normans only won two, so we were very proud at being the best. Cedric and I won the three-legged race, but as we'd been practising for a week, we knew we would. The sun shone hot and bright every day, and Mrs. B said she hadn't known such a good summer for ages. On the last Saturday morning, Mr. B dragged out our trunks and everyone who was going home, packed up their stuff. After dinner, Cedric grabbed my arm and pulled me into the space under the back stairs where the smallest children hung their coats.

"We have to go to Merlin's lair. To get my treasure tin."

"Are you going to take it to America with you?"

"Of course. C'mon."

Cedric had collected more treasures for his Blackcurrant and Glycerine lozenge tin. An empty snail-shell, two pink and four white pebbles–one with a glittering gold thread through it, and more coins.

"Where *do* you find all that money? I never see money on the ground."

"I always look down when I'm walking. People often drop small coins, like the farthings and the tiddleys."

"What's that one?" I pointed to a dirty old coin. "I've never seen one like that before."

"I dug it up in the kitchen garden when we were helping Mr. B in the spring. I showed it to him and he said it looked like a Roman coin. He says he finds lots of them."

Cedric put his hand down the hole again. "I've got to get my Allie."

Cedric's Allie was the champion marble in the whole school. Other children had often tried to steal it, or bully him into giving it up. So he kept it hidden in the lair.

"Owee. Ow. Noooo."

"What's the matter?"

"I dropped it and it rolled further down the hole, I can't reach it."

"Let me try." I reached down the hole for the Allie, but my arm wasn't long enough either. Cedric was near to tears.

"Don't cry, Cedric. It'll stay there and when you come back from America, you can come and get it. Your arm might have grown by then."

More prodding and grabbing, only sent the marble further down the hole. Finally, Cedric gave up and admitted it was lost. "But not for ever," he said. "If you get it out, you can send it to me in America."

"Do you want me to write to you?"

"Of course. And I'll write back and tell you all about America."

"That would be nice," I said. "But the war will be over soon and you'll be back."

Cedric nodded. "Yes, I'll be back soon."

Cedric left before I did. Early the next morning, his mother came in a car to get him. She put all his stuff into the boot, while he jumped around waving his arms in the air and shouting. "I'm going to America! I'm going to America!"

We all came out to wave goodbye. Some of us ran down the driveway after the car. I ran the farthest–as far as the big gates. I could see Cedric still bouncing on the seat and waving. Then the car drove through the gates, turned left onto the Bridgnorth road, and Cedric was gone. I'd never seen him so happy.

Ann-the-Bank yelled at me from the porch steps. "C'mon, we've got to finish packing."

I ran back into the house, thinking that by this time tomorrow I would be on my way to Wales. And I jumped around and waved my arms. Just like Cedric.

That summer in Wales was magical. Every day was hot and sunny. When Daddy came on a week's leave, we went trekking up the mountains and picnicked by the streams that tumbled down them. We spent long afternoons by the river that rolled and rippled through the valley. Daddy took me into the water and carried me over the fast moving shallows, swinging me high above his head, then bringing me down so my feet skimmed through the white rushing rapids. I would scream and lock my legs around his waist. Sometimes, he waded into the deeper parts and swam while I clung to his furry chest. After, he would drop me on the grass under the shade trees, and tickle me until I begged for mercy. Then Dilly would rescue me, dry me and take me for a long walk, leaving Mummy and Daddy sitting under the trees to talk.

His leave was over on August 11th. On the 10th, he had a telephone call. His face looked grim as he turned to my mother, "Well, I got my leave in just in time. It seems the balloon is about to go up."

I didn't understand any of it, but when Daddy left he hugged me so tight I could scarcely breathe. I stayed with Dilly while my mother went to the station with him. When she came back, I could tell she'd been crying.

There was another whole month of holidays. The weather stayed hot, and I remember running barefoot out onto the black roadway once to meet John-the-Post, and the hot, melted tar stuck to my feet. He picked me up and delivered me back with the letters.

I learned to ride my bicycle, and I rode around the garden paths for hours on end. I went with Dilly and Mummy for walks along the river-banks and we played Pooh Sticks on the bridge by the woolen mill. We hiked up the mountains, and played Hide-and-Seek in bracken that was taller than I was, and searched for early bilberries. There was a lot of talk about the 'Battle of Britain,'—which I didn't understand, and grumbling about the new sweet rationing—which I did. That I would get less chocolate than ever, cast an even darker cloud over the misery I was already feeling–that in a few days, I would be back at boarding school.

Finally, the dreaded day arrived, and I had to say goodbye to everyone: Aunt Laura and Uncle Fred, John-the-Post, Bronwen-the-Sweets, and all the other friends Mummy and Dilly had made during the past two years. Cledwyn-the-Car loaded up my trunk and my bicycle. Ann-the-Bank who, with her mam had spent the summer at her Aunty's in Aberystwyth, had her stuff loaded up too and we all went to the station together. In no time at all, the train came in and, once more, I had to say goodbye to Mummy and to Dilly. It seemed to get worse each time.

I hung out of the carriage door window, waving to Dilly and Mummy who were standing at the very end of the platform. I waved until the railway line curved away through the valley and they were out of sight. I pulled my head in from the window and sat down with Ann who, as usual, was crying noisily in the corner.

I wanted to cry too, but I'd promised Mummy I would be brave. Had I known how long it would be before I saw her again, I don't think I would have been so brave.

Especially if I'd I known I would never, ever see Dilly again.

Especially if I'd known I would never go back to Wales. Ever.

Normanhurst children 1940. Patricia is fourth from
the right and Ann-the-Bank is on her right.

The glass 'eyes' in the front door - outside and inside, May 2001

Left: Summer in Wales with my father. Right: A photo taken by my mother in Cornwall, August 1939, just before WWII broke out. My father is on the left, one of my aunts in the centre and Dilly and me on the right.

Left: my soldier father in 1941, and my mother in her Sunday silks, 1939. Right: Patricia perched on her Christmas 1940 bicycle.

Playing in the fountain in the sunken garden.

Dobbin and friends on the way to Thatcher's Woods.

The way to Thatcher's Woods, 2001.

The stable-yards showing the path to the orchard, 2004. The long window on the right is where Patricia saw 'murder most foul.

**Normanhurst showing the gates to the stable-yard and to the right,
the yew tree and Patricia's escape route after the murder.**

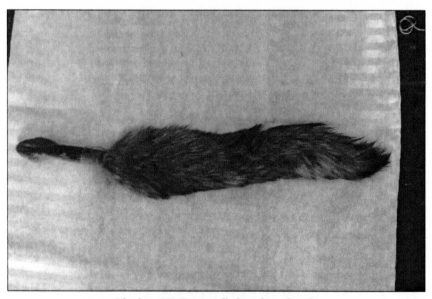

The late Mr. Reynard's brush and pad.

The Manor House, Erdington, 2004. The 'side garden' is on the left and on the right of the house is a glimpse of the kitchen garden wall, where the children lined up for the first photograp.

Normanhurst School, 1945. The author is at the top left (half of her face showing) next to the tall boy at the end.

Chapter 19

New Beginnings

The minute we arrived back at Normanhurst, I knew I didn't want to be there. So many new faces. Chatter, clamour and crying. Pushing and pinching, shoving and slapping. Boys bullying. Girls being spiteful.

And no Cedric.

Hard beds, wormy porridge, and cold classrooms. Queues for food, for the loo, and for a sweet ration that was down to about one a day.

And no Cedric.

I hated it.

I wanted to go home.

> *Sunday, 14th September, 1941*
> *Dear Mummy and Daddy,*
> *I don't like it here. Please come and take me back to Wales.*
> *Your unhappy daughter,*
> *Patricia*
>
> *Sunday, 21st September, 1941*

Dear Mummy and Daddy,
I hate it here. When can I come home?
Your very, very unhappy daughter
Patricia

Sunday, 28th September, 1941.
Dear Daddy
I'm very sorry I tried to run away and that Mummy had to
come up all the way from Wales because I was so naughty.
I understand that I have to stay here because of the war.
I also understand that you and Mummy should not have
to worry about me because you have enough worries of
your own.
I promise I will try harder to like it here.
Your repentant daughter,
Patricia

Everything about that Autumn term was the same as the year before: Guy Fawkes, half-term and the Nativity Play. Except that Cedric wasn't there to be Joseph. Andrew Simon, who had the best singing voice of anybody in the whole school, was Joseph and I had to be Mary again.

Then, on top of everything else, I couldn't go home for Christmas. Ann-the-Bank did, but I had to stay. Mummy went to my grandfather's house in the Lake District for Christmas. She wrote that it was a long and difficult journey, and Bridgnorth was too far away for her to come and get me. I cried a lot about that, but Miss Audrey-Joan promised me that Christmas would be fun at school. No lessons and lots of play-time. But I knew it wouldn't be the same.

Just before Christmas, I got a letter from Cedric.

3rd Dec, 1941.
Dear Pat,
I haven't gone to America yet. Mummy and I have been living
with my Aunty cos we had to wait until they got my Aunty's
new baby. But it's here now and we are going to America in a

fortnight. We are sailing on a very big ship just like Miss A-J told me.
See you after the war and Merry Christmas.
Luv from your friend forever,
Cedric
P.S. Did you find my Allie?

7th December, 1941.
Dear Cedric,
Thank you for your letter. And a Merry Christmas to you too.
I can't go home for Christmas as Mummy is going too far away. But she isn't going to America.
I hope you will write to me from America.
With love from your friend,
Patty
P.S. I didn't find your Allie, my arms aren't long enough yet.

Sunday, 4th January, 1942
Dear Mummy and Daddy,
Mrs. Baker told us today that Cedric's ship got sunk by the Germans. The vicar came in and said some prayers and told us to knit more socks for sailors.
I told Mrs. Baker that I forgive Cedric for putting my skipping rope down the boys' lavvy. She said that's best.
Has Daddy gone back to the war? Will he be going on a ship? Has he forgiven me for running away and making him worry?
I really miss Cedric. He was my friend.
Your lonely daughter,
Patricia

The following Saturday, was a bright, crisp day. No snow had fallen yet, and by afternoon the frost had disappeared from the lawns. A yellow wintry sun made the tree branches look like spider's legs against the pale blue sky. I was sitting on the dry moss in Merlin's lair and thinking about Cedric. Was he really dead? The Germans might have sunk his ship, but he could be swimming around in the ocean. I'd seen dead mice that Tristan had caught, but they were chewed, not drowned. Miss Audrey-Joan said that Cedric was drowned, but how did they know? He could be holding his breath underwater and a mermaid could find him and take him to a safe place. Tom was supposed to have drowned, but he lived with the water babies and was quite all right, and very happy.

I put my arm down the hole to see if I could reach Cedric's Allie. I could feel it with the end of a twig, but I couldn't scrape it back up the hole. I leaned against the trunk of the crab-apple tree and wondered what to do next. Dry stalks of summer flowers and grasses bent their heads, leaves had fallen from the hawthorne and bramble bushes. The nettles had lost their sting.

"Cedric will come back. I know he will. A mermaid will help him swim back."

Then I remembered how he didn't like deep, dark water. I put my head on my knees and cried. But not for long. I heard Miss Audrey-Joan calling me, "Patrishaaaaa. Where aaare you?"

"Oh dear. P'raps she thinks I've run away again."

Although I hadn't gone far down the Bridgnorth Road when Mr. B caught up to me, it had been far enough for me to get the cane across my bottom. I wriggled, remembering. Then Miss Audrey-Joan sent for Mummy. She was *very* angry with me. It was nice to see her, but I don't think she thought it was nice to see me. However, before she went back to Wales, she forgave me and gave me a hug. But she said I didn't deserve any extra chocolate.

I climbed up to a low branch of the crab-apple tree that Cedric and I always used for a lookout. I could see Miss Audrey-Joan–far away, down beyond the Rabbit Hole. It would be a catastrophe if she were to find Merlin's lair, so I quickly crawled back down the tunnel entrance and, dodging behind the thick brown tree trunks, made my way to the apple tree that had been uprooted in the storm last year. Under the enormous upended roots was a shallow sandy hole where it was fun to sit and play in the summer time. I sat in the hole, my back against the hard, spiky roots and waited for Miss Audrey-Joan to find me.

Which she did. She didn't ask what I was doing there, but sat down in the hole beside me, picked up a twig and drew a noughts and crosses grid in the sand. After two games, she said, "Remember how we played Robin Hood on this tree?"

I nodded.

"And Cedric was Robin Hood, wasn't he?"

I nodded and sniffed.

"That was fun, wasn't it?"

I nodded again.

"We have to remember the best things about Cedric. How you used to play with him. The things he said, and how you were such a good friend to him. You were, you know. A very good friend who helped make him feel less homesick."

Miss Audrey-Joan made another noughts and crosses grid. I won this time. "Where is Cedric?" I asked. "Is he at the bottom of the sea? With the water babies and the mermaids?"

"I don't think so. I'm sure he's in Heaven."

"Where's that?"

"It's hard to say. Perhaps it's where Cedric liked to be the most. And now he's there. His mummy, his little sister, and his aunty and baby cousin are all with him. He's not alone; he has friends there too."

I thought of the hymn we often sang at Prayers, *"There's a friend for little children, above the bright blue sky."* I looked up. Well the sky was blue all right. A faint shadow of the moon hung–far away, dipping below the hedge on the other side of the orchard. "Is Heaven on the moon, Miss Baker?"

She laughed. "I don't think so. It's surely in a better place than the moon. After all, some say the moon is made of green cheese."

I shivered. The short mid-winter day was nearly over.

"Come, Pat. It's time to go indoors. We've been sitting long enough. Let's go and make a cup of tea? And Tristan's been looking for you."

Miss Audrey-Joan helped me up, brushed the sand from my coat bottom and led me by the hand back to the warm kitchen. Tristan rubbed up against me, weaving figures of eight around my legs. Tea smelled good. It was Cedric's favourite–toasted cheese with baked beans.

Chapter 20

The Measles

Tuesday, 17th February, 1942
Dear Mummy and Daddy,
It isn't Sunday today but I have to write an extra letter to you for Mrs. B. You have to telephone her and tell her if I have had the measles. Everyone except me, Rowley Smythe, Miranda Tredinnick and Ann-the-Bank has the measles. There are no lessons and Mrs. B says she is run off her feet looking after so many sick children.
Have I had the measles? If I haven't had the measles Mrs. B says I can't go to church because they are spreadable.
I want to talk to you when you telephone.
Love from
Patricia

Thursday, 19th February, 1942.
Dear Mummy,
It was nice talking to you on the telephone. It was very crackly.

Mrs. B says it's a pity I haven't had the measles and that I will probably start sickening soon. What does sickening feel like? Miranda, Ann-the-Bank and I are playing nurses. Rowley Smythe had to be the patient because we all wanted to be nurses. Rowley wanted to be the doctor and make us be the patients. But Miranda said that when boys want to play doctor they pull your knickers down. Not even Doctor Mole does that, so why should Rowley. I asked Miranda how she knew that. She told me she has a brother who always does that to the girls. But he is 12 now and away in big school. The next day Rowley got the measles so we had nobody to nurse. With love from your bored daughter,
Patricia

Sunday, 22nd February, 1942
Dear Mummy and Daddy,
I am having the measles tomorrow. I couldn't eat my dinner today so Mrs. B says I am sickening and will have the measles by tomorrow.
You don't have to send me chocolate, I don't feel like any.
With love from your sickening daughter,
Patricia.

I didn't like the measles. Mrs. B put me in a tiny room by myself where it was all dark and quiet. She put cold wet towels all over me for days. I didn't like that and I definitely didn't like that tiny room. There were hundreds of animals on the wallpaper that kept getting bigger and bigger and crowding down on my bed. Then they started jumping on me and smothering me.

But all that changed when Cedric came to talk to me. I wasn't a bit surprised to see him. When he came, the wallpaper animals stopped jumping on me and stayed on the walls. Cedric told me he was living in another place now where there were real animals, not just on the wallpaper, and where there were real flowers that bloom for ever.

I asked him if he was really dead and he said it depended on what you call dead. He said he was with his mummy and his sister. His auntie and her new baby are there too, but his daddy was still fighting in the war. Then he told me that his daddy will be with them very soon and they will all be a family again.

As we talked, Cedric sat on the end of my bed, just about where my toes were, but I couldn't feel anything. Although it was dark, I could see him perfectly–as though he was sitting in a patch of sunlight.

"I'm happy that you are still my friend and I can still talk to you–even though you're supposed to be dead. Shall I still write to you?"

"Of course," said Cedric.

"Where do I send the letters? 'Cos you aren't in America. Do you have an address in Heaven?"

"I don't think so. Just leave them anywhere. I'll find them."

"Where's Heaven then? Miss Audrey-Joan doesn't know, I asked her."

"Anywhere you want it to be," Cedric replied.

"May I come with you and see your garden?" I asked.

"Not right now. It's not the right time. You have to stay here and grow your own garden. And I came to tell you that you have to get better."

Then something odd happened. Cedric floated away, above my bed and his voice became very soft–just a faint whispering in my head. He whispered that I would start getting better tomorrow and the wallpaper animals won't jump on me any more. Then I fell asleep and when I woke up, Cedric was gone.

The next morning, when Mrs. B came in to take my temperature and bring me a drink of water, I told her that Cedric wasn't dead, and that he'd been to see me and told me I was going to be better tomorrow—which was really today. Mrs. B's face turned quite pale. Her hand shook and some of the water spilled on my bed and onto the floor. But she didn't say anything. I decided I'd better not to tell her that Cedric said I could write to him.

Soon after Mrs. B left the room, old Doctor Mole came in. He didn't ask me about Cedric's visit but said I'd turned the corner—whatever that meant.

It was strange that Mrs. B had told me I was going to get sick the next day, and Cedric had told me I was going to get better the next day.

All I needed to do was turn a corner. I don't remember a corner, and certainly don't remember turning one.

That afternoon, Mrs. B told me I could get up and leave my tiny dark sick room with its animal wallpaper. She said I didn't have to write any letters, or do lessons for a while; just concentrate on getting better and not tax myself unduly. The tax bit confused me because the last time I remembered learning about taxes was in the Nativity play when Joseph took Mary to Bethlehem to be taxed. And she was great with child; I was only great with measles.

There was a special room at Normanhurst called the sick room. Not my tiny sick room in the attic, but a bright and sunny room with a window that overlooked the gardens. The window sill was a wide, white-painted bench covered with old cushions, so the sick child could lie on the cushions and look out the window. It was a cozy room over the kitchens and the heat from the Aga stove warmed the floor. There were two beds, a fireplace with deep cupboards on either side, and a wall-full of books. And, oh joy! The cupboards were crammed with toys and treasures, games and jigsaw puzzles, that Miss Audrey-Joan and her sister, Miss Margaret, had collected when they were little. I wasn't alone either. Ann-the-Bank had been badly measled too, so we were to stay together in the special sick room until we were better.

The measles made Ann-the-Bank look pale all over. Her pale straight hair was done in two skinny plaits that started just below her ears, and stuck out above her shoulders. Big, pale grey eyes were dark hollows in her thin pale face. Her pale arms and legs stuck out of a washed-out pink winceyette nightdress and dressing gown. The only thing about Ann-the-Bank that wasn't pale was her nose, which was bright red. She sniffed a lot. I called her Ann-the-Bank because before the war, her daddy was the manager of the only bank in the Welsh village where we'd lived. In Wales, everybody is called by their first name followed by what they do. There is Bert-the-Baker, Arthur-the-Fish, Thomas-the-Pub, Cledwyn-the-Car and, of course, John-the-Post; then there was Dafydd-the-Drip. I asked her what Dafydd-the-Drip did. Ann-the-Bank said she didn't think he did anything.

The next day, we were having a good time diving for treasure in the toy cupboards when Mrs. B came in and told Ann that her mam had come to take her home to recuperate. That was nice for Ann-the-Bank and when she'd gone I had the toys all to myself. I wondered whether 'to recuperate' meant she wouldn't sniff anymore when she came back.

I wondered if my mummy would come and take me home to recuperate too. I asked Mrs. B and she said she'd talked to my mother but, with my father away in the war and as it was such a long way, she thought I'd be better off staying where I was. "Besides, your mother is very busy with the war effort, Patricia. But she promised to telephone to see how you are and, when she does, you may speak with her for one minute. Or a least until the pips go," Mrs. B added brightly.

When Old Doctor Mole came again, I asked him how long I would have to stay in the sick room.

"Well, Patty, you've been a very sick little girl. Your measles were much worse than most. You will have to recuperate for about four weeks. But," he added cheerfully, "as soon as the weather warms up, you may go outside and get some spring sunshine and fresh air."

After he left, I climbed up on to the window-seat and looked out. Black clouds were chasing each other across a grey sky. Wild winds bent the bare branches of the trees, and blew little birds all over the place. Patches of snow lay on the lawns and flower beds, and hard raindrops pattered against the window. I wondered if Cedric was enjoying his flower garden, and if the sun was shining in Heaven.

Mr. B came in and found me gazing at the wet and wintry garden. "Well, Pat-a-cake," he said. "I thought you might like a fire to cheer you up."

He soon had a fire crackling in the tiny grate and logs piled inside the fire guard. "Now don't you go touching this. Mrs. Baker or I will keep the fire built up. Can't spare coal because the ration is nearly all gone, but thank the Lord we've plenty of wood from last year's downed trees. I hear you've been real poorly."

"Yes. But Old Doctor Mole says I can go out when the weather warms up."

"Tell you what. Spring is just around the corner. When it arrives, you can come out to my greenhouse and help me sow seeds. We'll soon get some colour back in your cheeks."

"There was that corner again."

"May I write letters out there too?" I asked.

"Bless your heart, of course you can. You can read, help me in the garden, write, do whatever you want. And we'll brew up some tea in my shed and have story-telling time too," he added.

That night, I didn't miss Ann-the-Bank so much. I thought of all the adventures I was going to have with Mr. B in the kitchen garden and the greenhouse. I dreamed of Cedric. He was happy and smiling, and told me he was looking forward to hearing about my garden.

"I think I will start writing to Cedric tomorrow. I could ask him what seeds to plant."

Chapter 21

Suitable Weather

In Spring 1942, my daily life at Normanhurst changed. After the measles, with Ann-the-Bank recuperating in Wales and Cedric gone, I had to find other things to do.

I liked being with the grownups. The kitchen, with the comforting Aga stove, was my favourite place. Nobody seemed to mind me being there–so long as I was quiet and not in the way. I spent hours sitting with Tristan in a little nook at the side of the warm ovens, watching the bustle of cooking and listening to the grownups discussing the war. When I was there alone, I would read or knit.

I'd learned plain knitting in the nursery, before the war. I remember a pair of red celluloid needles, a ball of bright green wool and my struggles to keep the same number of stitches in each row. However hard I tried, I was much better at dropping stitches than knitting them. Eventually, it was Dilly who had the patience to help me persevere and finally knit a whole ten rows without dropping one stitch. Mrs. B insisted that we all knit for the forces, and those who didn't know how, including the boys, had to learn. In needlework and music appreciation classes, and during story-telling time, we knitted either socks or scarves. On weekends, we were allowed to knit for ourselves. I was knitting a striped scarf from tiny scraps of wool I begged, or stole; mostly leftovers from Mrs. B's or Mrs. Tommy's unpicking and re-knitting of jumpers. These scraps I knotted together to make a small ball. My scarf was already three inches long but, if I didn't get more wool from somewhere, it would never fit me and I would have to give it to Edward Bear.

One rainy afternoon, when a chill wind howled around the house, I crept down from the sick room to the kitchen. I was surprised to find a three-legged stool, topped with a bright patchwork cushion had mysteriously appeared in my little corner.

March 22nd, 1942
Dear Mummy and Daddy:
I'm sorry that you don't think I'm well enough to come home for Easter, but thank you for promising to send my letters on to Daddy–wherever he is–and to write me longer letters. Mrs. B says I should write longer letters back to you because you probably miss me as much as I miss you.
Mrs. B says she will take good care of me during the holidays and Mr. B is going to show me how to make things grow in the kitchen garden as soon as the weather is suitable.
With love from your lonely daughter,
Patricia

I screwed the top back on my blue fountain pen and put it down with a sigh. No one came to see me in the sick room and, although there were plenty of books to read and toys to play with, I was lonely. I wished Ann-the-Bank would come back–I would even put up with her sniffing. I climbed up on the window-seat and looked out–it was raining stair-rods and the wind rattled the windows. Mrs. B had told me I couldn't go out until the weather was suitable. I'd asked her what suitable weather was like, and she'd said when it's warm enough for me to go out without getting relapsed. When Mr. B came in to see to the fire, I asked him when there would be suitable weather.

"It should be soon, Pat-a-cake. The robins are busy building nests in the plum trees and two house martins have already set up a home in the stables."

Mr. B also told me the stable cat had kittens and that was another good sign; a sign of what I wondered? Tristan and Iseult never had kittens because they were house cats and slept on my bed. Sometimes, I told them stories. I thought of telling them their own story, about the real Tristan and Iseult, but decided they would like a more cheerful one. So I told them all about a mouse family we'd read about in French. They lived in a mouse house with windows and doors, and tables and chairs. But I didn't know whether to read the story to the cats in French or translate it into English the way we had to in class. I wondered if cats understood me, or if I had to learn Cat language? Mr. B had said you can talk to horses and they understand.

"How do horses understood us?" I asked.

"Have you never heard of horse sense?" he replied.

It wouldn't be fair if only some animals could understand what we tell them and others couldn't. Daddy would have known the answer because he told me that when he was in Burma, his ponies understood what he told them to do when they were playing polo. I wondered if he spoke to them in Horse or English; or whatever they spoke in Burma. I decided to ask him in my next letter. Or perhaps Cedric would know.

29th March, 1942
Dear Mummy and Daddy:
Do you have any bits of wool that you don't need? I know there is a war on and you use up all the wool ends for new jumpers but if there are some little bits that are no good for jumpers (can) please may I have them?
I need to know if the cats can understand me when I talk to them, just like the Welsh sheepdogs understand the farmers. Please tell me if I have to learn Cat Language to talk to them.
I hope you will write to me soon,
With love from,
Patricia

P.S. I have drawn you a picture of the mouse family in their home. Mice are lucky because their houses are underground and won't get hit by bombs and so they don't have to be evacuated.

Good Friday, 3rd April, 1942
Dear Mummy;
Thank you for your long letter and for the scraps of wool. It was lucky that I asked you for it just when you and Dilly were unpicking some old woollies to knit up again. It doesn't matter that the wool is wrinkly. Some of the colours are lovely, especially the bright blue. I remember your favourite cardigan is the same colour.
I'm sorry you can't answer my question about Cat language. Thank you for sending my letter on to Daddy. I hope he is not too busy fighting the war to answer my question.
With love from your grateful daughter,
Patricia

Good Friday morning, I was left by myself while everyone else went to church for three hours. Mrs. B didn't want to take me to church as she thought three hours was too long seeing I'd been sick. She said she didn't want to cope with me having a relapse.

"Anyway," she said. "The church will be as cold as charity."

I asked why charity is cold and how cold *was* that. She replied that I shouldn't be so literal. I thought she wanted me to be literal because she encouraged my writing. Anyway, she said that it was a good job the weather was getting warmer and I could be outside and have different things to do. She said that two months of reading, writing and knitting was enough for anyone, leave alone an eight-year-old, and that it was making me too old for my years. I told her I wouldn't be eight until June and she just said "Hrrumph."

I didn't like being in the house by myself–just me in that massive house, and I couldn't find the cats anywhere. There was nobody else there but I could hear noises—quiet noises. Mrs. B had told me to stay in one spot and not move except to go to the loo. So I sat in my special corner by the Aga. I thought about lots of things when I was on my own.

Mrs. B had said that, if the weather was nice on Saturday, I could go to with them to Bridgenorth for the Easter market. After Easter she said she'd turn me over to Mr. B to keep me occupied with "healthy pursuits" in his garden.

It wasn't long before the cats found me. Tristan got himself all tied up in my knitting wool but Iseult just looked at him with her nose in the air as if to say, *"Aren't boys silly!"* The other day, when Mrs. Tommy saw Tristan all tangled in my wool, she said that perhaps he was trying to make a cat's cradle. I thought that was funny and she said that it was good to hear me laugh again and that I must be better.

I jumped when the grandfather clock in the front hall struck eleven. It would still be a long time before everyone came back and I was tired of talking to the cats. I decided to write to Cedric.

Dear Cedric,

This is my first letter to you. I haven't told anyone else about you coming to see me when I was sick, and Mrs. B has forgotten about it, so I think it should be our secret.

I want to know where you are. I know everyone says you're dead but I know you're not. You weren't dead when you came to see me because you spoke to me. And you didn't have a funeral. My grandmother died, and she is buried under a big mound of earth in the churchyard. But your ship was sunk by the Germans and no one ever found you. Are you living at the bottom of the sea with Tom and the Water Babies? I think that would be nice.

I'll leave this letter under my pillow so when you come to visit me in the night, you can read it.

With love from your best friend,

Pat

Chapter 22

Hamlet

Sunshine flooded the sick room when Mrs. B rolled up the blackout blinds on Easter Saturday. "It's your lucky day," she said. "Warm and sunny for your trip to market."

This was the first time I could go out since I'd been measled, so she bundled me up in my warmest clothes, lifted me into the float, and wrapped a wool rug around me. It felt wonderful to be outdoors again and the excitement of going on a trip made me feel warm anyway.

On market day, Bridgnorth High Street is full of bustle and busyness. In the centre–right in the middle of the street–stands the ancient black and white timbered Town Hall. It was built on arched stilts so it looks like someone took away the ground floor. Vendors' stalls were set up underneath it, and along both sides of the wide street.

The float was trundling past the stalls when Mrs. B called out, "Stop!" She jumped down and rushed to a stall. She called Mr. B over to pick up a sack of potatoes.

"Last year's crop," he said as he heaved it into the float. But it will keep us going for a fortnight or so."

Mr. B clicked at Dobbin and we drove away from the Town Hall, up to the North Gate, which looked like the entrance to an old castle. Against the wall, a small girl squatted–a sack wrapped around her thin shoulders. Tins of food were laid out on the ground around her. Mr. B stopped again and Mrs. B went over to see what she had for sale. In a few minutes she returned, her string shopping bag bulging.

"Well, that was a nice haul," she said as she dumped the bag down next to Mr. B. "Some of it will do for the Rabbit Hole."

She looked back at the pale, skinny girl. "I gave her an extra tiddley for herself. They must be in dire straits to be selling the food from their own store-cupboard and for no coupons."

"Where's Dire Straits?"I asked.

"It's not a place. It's a state of desperate hardship."

"You should have made that threepence a sixpence." Mr. B took a handful of pennies from his pocket. "Here. Give the kiddy this."

While Mrs. B went back to give the pennies to the girl, I looked to see what was in the bag. I found tins of vegetables, beans, two tins of Spam and three of condensed milk. Mr. B took a tin of condensed milk, put it in his pocket, winked at me and whispered, "Mum's the word."

A few stalls away from the girl in Dire Straits, Mrs. B found a rack of second-hand clothes that she didn't need coupons for, and it wasn't long before she had an armful. Some other ladies came and started pushing her away, trying to take some of the clothes she'd picked. They were yelling at her for taking so many. I thought they were very rude. I asked Mr. B why he didn't help her. He shook his head and said, "Edwina Baker can take care of herself–and them–well enough on her own."

And she did! She stuck her elbows out and trod on their toes. "I have forty growing children to look after," she yelled at them. The other women quickly hopped out of her way, muttering rude words. She paid the stall lady and then threw the clothes in the float. She was very red in the face, just like our cook used to look at home, before the war, when she said I was under her feet.

"I wonder where Cookie is now. I really miss her treacle tart and apple dumplings, and she made the best custard in the whole wide world."

Mrs. B fanned herself with her gloves. I waited until she didn't look quite so hot, and when she gave a big sigh and smiled at me I asked, "Please may I get out and come with you next time we stop?"

She looked surprised, but said, "Of course. It will do you good to stretch your legs."

Mr. Baker fished in his pocket and gave her a shilling. "There's a café just by the *Swan*. Why don't you get us a hot drink and a couple of buns. Pat-a-cake can go with you and choose something sticky and chocolaty."

I jumped down. Mrs. B grabbed my hand and we were off, winding our way through the market stalls. Stray dogs nosed under the tables, dirty children chased each other around the stalls, and a man with an eye patch was playing an accordion; a cap, to catch a few pennies, between his feet.

A gypsy woman, held up a willow basket full of clothes-pegs. "Buy some pegs, missus? Buy some pegs and you'll have good luck." She looked down at me. "Tell your fortune, little missee? Cross the gypsy's palm with siller and have your fortune telled."

I was surprised when Mrs. B stopped and took some wooden clothes-pegs from the gypsy. She gave me a silver threepenny-bit to pay for them and told me I'd better cross the gypsy's palm with silver "Just to be on the safe side as you've been sick," she said. The gypsy smiled at me. She looked at my hand and called me "little darlin'" and said I would grow up to be a famous writer. She also said that I would cross water many times. She gave my hand a squeeze, called me "darlin'" again, then turned to another customer.

"How'd she know I'm going to be a famous writer when I grow up?"

"She probably saw the ink on your fingers."

We never went to the café. Something caught Mrs. B's eye and she walked quickly back to where we had left Mr. B.

"Aren't we going to get the buns?" I was disappointed and had to trot to keep up with her brisk strides.

"I have a better idea."

When we got back to the place where we'd left Mr. B, he wasn't there. Then we saw him driving Dobbin towards us across the street. "Where's my drink?" he asked.

"There's a good menu at the *Swan*," Mrs. B told him. "Why don't we get some dinner? Give the child a treat."

The thought of going 'out' to dinner was exciting. I crossed my legs and jiggled a bit. "I have to go to the loo."

Mr. B hitched Dobbin to a post, gave a boy a penny to watch the float, and we went off to the *Swan*.

It looked just like the Town Hall. Black and white, half-timbered and very old; just like the ones in my Shakespeare story book. A blackboard was propped outside the door. On it was written: *"MENU"*

Rabbit Pie	6d.
Braised Liver	6d.
Bangers & Mash	6d.
All Plus Veg.	8d.
Spotted Dick & Custard	2d.
Rice Pudding	2d.
Lentil soup	1d.
Children's meals	4d.

Beside the menu was a wooden box with a money slot in the top. A notice was glued to the front—*"Spitfire Fund"*.

"You should have liver, it's good for you," said Mrs. B.

I liked liver, but not today. I looked at Mr. B and wrinkled my nose. He smiled. "Let the child choose for herself. It's all good food here."

I didn't waste any time. "Please may I have Rabbit Pie?" I loved my Aunt Laura's rabbit pie and I remembered my mother saying, "Laura does not excel in the kitchen, but she does make a delicious rabbit pie."

So rabbit pie it was, with a slice of spotted dick and custard for afters.

By the time we got back to the float, the vendors were packing up their stalls, and hitching up their wagons. The gypsy lady had gone.

"I have one more stop," said Mr. B as we climbed in.

He nodded to the boy and tossed him another penny. "I bought something while you were shopping and I have to pick it up."

A few streets away we stopped at a livestock market. Mr. B jumped down and disappeared inside. He came back carrying a crate full of squawking and fluttering chickens. He said they were hens on point of lay.

"What's point of lay?" I asked.

"It means they'll soon be laying brown eggs for all our breakfasts," Mr. B replied. He went back inside and...Oh my! He brought out a PIG. It was the squealiest, animal I'd ever seen, and it wouldn't keep still. Mrs. B said she couldn't think what possessed Mr. B to buy the creature, but Mr. B said it will eat up all the kitchen scraps and will make some good dinners when it gets fat. "Besides," he added, "it was too small to sell as a yearling so I got it cheap."

Mrs. B grumbled all the way home about it being smelly and noisy and that Mr. B must remember we're a school, not a farm. Mr. B told her that, school or not, we have to be self-sufficient and *she* must remember they have to feed forty little people. When I heard that, I couldn't believe they would make us eat such a darling little pig.

Because the float was so full of chickens and pig, I sat in the driver's seat between Mr and Mrs. B and every time Mrs. B went on about the smelly pig, Mr. B nudged me in the ribs and winked. I asked Mr. B what he was going to call the pig, which set Mrs. B off again. It was so funny seeing Mrs. B cross with Mr. B. When we got back, Mrs. Tommy said I was looking so much better and had some roses in my cheeks.

After tea, I helped Mr. B make a home for the pig in a stone pen by the stables. The front part was open with a stone food-trough and the back was a sleeping house with a pig-sized doorway. We put fresh straw all over the floor in the house part. I kept thinking about what to call the pig. It didn't look much like Christopher Robin's piglet because it didn't stand up or wear a striped jumper. The pig ran around exploring it's new home and squealing.

"I think he likes it," I said.

"Yes...well. I just hope Edwina's not going to get uppity at the noise." He grinned. "Ach, not to worry. Pig'll soon settle down and so will Edwina. C'mon Pat-a-cake, it's getting dark, we'd better go in."

Easter Sunday and I couldn't wait to tell the pig that its name was Hamlet. But first, I had to go to church with the grown-ups. Miss Audrey-Joan gave me a letter from Mummy with an Easter card and a five-shilling postal-order, which Mrs. B put it in my school bank envelope until I'd decided what to buy with it.

"And there are no coupons for sweeties," she said. "There are no toys to be had these days either. All the stuff to make toys has been taken to make guns and the like, for the war."

I said nothing.

"But, you know," she added. "You could get two nice books for five-shillings." She reached over and picked up a frock that was draped over the arm of a chair. "Look what I found amongst that bundle of clothes. I think it will fit you very nicely."

It was a summer frock, white and patterned with bright blue flowers. I jumped up and flung my arms around Mrs. B's neck. "Oh, thank you! It's beautiful. My favourite colour too."

She looked surprised and I wondered if I shouldn't have hugged her. But she smiled, and said, "Off you go now, and get ready for church."

I found Mrs. Tommy and asked her do my hair. She made plaits and put blue ribbons on the ends so they would show below my hat. My hair was so straight and slippery, the ribbons wouldn't stay on, so she put rubber bands on the ends and threaded the ribbon through them. She said she'd never known a child with such difficult hair.

5th April, 1942.
Dear Mummy and Daddy:
Thank you for the postal-order which Mrs. B is keeping until I decide what to buy.
I had a nice Easter. Mrs. Tommy did my hair in little plaits. She says I have difficult hair.
We went to market and bought a pig, just like in the nursery rhyme. His name is Hamlet.
I behaved myself all week-end and remembered my manners.
With love and wishing you a Happy Spring,
your daughter,
Patricia

Dear Cedric,

We went to market and bought a pig and some chickens. I had my fortune told by a gypsy who said I was going to cross water many times. I hope she didn't mean that I would go on a ship and get torpedoed. But if I did, I could come and play with you in Davy Jones's locker.

It's time for bed, so I'll finish this letter and put it under my pillow with the other one for you to read.

We have to go to church tomorrow. Will you be there? And do you get to talk to God?

Your best friend,

Pat

12th April, 1942

Dear Mummy,

I am glad Ann-the-Bank is better and is coming back to school for the summer term and is bringing me a parcel from you. Will you please put in my old tennis shoes, the ones with the red laces, my Flower Fairies book and a pair of jodhpurs for riding? Miss Baker says I'm big enough to ride Dolly.

Your loving daughter,

Patricia

26th April, 1942

Dear Mummy and Daddy,

Thank you for sending my stuff with Ann-the-Bank. I forgot my feet had grown out of my tennis shoes. The new ones are very nice.

The riding breeches are a nice colour but they are much too big. Mrs. Tommy found a piece of rope to tie around my middle to keep them up. She says they'll fit me when I'm twelve. I like riding very much.

With love from your grateful daughter

Patricia.

Chapter 23

Henry VIII

On Easter Monday, Dolly was hitched to the wagonette and Miss Audrey-Joan and Mrs. Tommy took me to the Majestic Cinema in Bridgnorth to see *Fantasia*, a cartoon picture from America. I recognized the music: Tchaikovsky's *Nutcracker Suite*, because we'd listened to it in our music appreciation lessons. We knitted socks for soldiers at the same time as appreciating music.

After *Fantasia*, the Movietone News came on. It showed terrible pictures of the war. Tanks with guns shooting, and bombs dropping on cities. A big ship was torpedoed and we saw it sink; the newsman said, "with all hands."

"Is that the ship Cedric was on?" I whispered to Miss Audrey-Joan.

"No, that was a German battleship, so it's good thing it was sunk."

"I'm glad my Daddy is a soldier and not a sailor," I said.

After the pictures, we went on the cable railway down to Low Town, which was fun. Mrs. Tommy knew the lady who owned the Olde Tea Shoppe who gave us all a big tea for a shilling; Marmite and cress sandwiches, and a piece of sponge cake each. The lady gave me a doughnut covered in sugar. It had jam inside which squished out over my fingers when I took a bite. I licked my fingers. It was very good jam.

Back up in High Town, a boy helped harness Dolly up and Mrs. Tommy gave him a threepenny bit. Miss Audrey-Joan let me hold the reins as we drove back home. Mrs. Tommy said it was nice that I was beginning to think of Normanhurst as home.

Tuesday was another happy, sunny day. Spring had arrived at last, and Mrs. B told me to get out from under her feet and make myself useful in the kitchen garden. Mr. B said he could find plenty to keep me occupied but, if I was too much of a nuisance, he would plant me along with the King Edward potatoes and watch me grow. Mrs. B wrapped a piece of bread and dripping and some dried apple rings in an old tea towel for my elevenses.

The kitchen garden was full of exciting things. It stretched all the way from the path between the stable–yard and the orchard down to the Bridgnorth Road. The tall brick wall surrounding it had been built hundreds of years ago, and kept the garden warm and sheltered from the wind. Blossoming fruit trees grew flat against the walls. Mr. B called them espaliered trees and pointed out quince, apple and plum; and a black pear tree which, he said, was as old as the walls themselves. A giant mulberry tree in the middle of the garden, towered over every-thing. Mr. B said it produced enough leaves to feed an army of silk-worms for the duration–whatever that meant.

The vegetable patches were separated by boxwood hedges that only came up to my knees. Our first job was to clear away all the winter rubbish and turn over the soil ready to plant the vegetables that were already sprouting in the greenhouse and cold frames. I told Mr. B that I thought there was an awful lot for us to do and it would take all summer to dig over the garden.

"Not to worry," he replied. "I've already dug the potato patch. In the next day or two, I'm going to muster all the troops from the house to dig the rest."

"What troops?" I asked

"Why Audrey-Joan of course and Mrs. Tommy."

"And Mrs. B?" I asked.

"Oh, she'll be out here with anyone else who's willing to turn a hand for the war effort. It's their patriotic duty." He picked up a sack with *"Seed Potatoes"* written on the label. "But today, Pat-a-cake my girl, we have our trenches already dug for the potatoes and lined with horse manure. All we have to do is lay these potatoes in the trench."

"In HORSE MANURE? You put the potatoes in HORSE MANURE?"

"Well of course, lass. Nothing grows King Edwards better than fresh horse manure mixed with a good measure of straw."

"And we have to EAT potatoes that were grown in HORSE MANURE?"

"The manure will be long gone by the time we get to eat the potatoes. We don't eat the seed potatoes that we plant. Every one of their little pink sprouts will grow into a big strong plant and, when the time is right, you'll find lots of new potatoes on the bottom."

"No wonder Rowley Smythe stuffs potatoes into his pocket. Perhaps he knows they were planted in horse manure. Ick."

We planted four rows of potatoes and I managed to plant all mine without touching the horse manure with my fingers. I discovered that if I held the potato right at the very top and then carefully plopped it in the trench, I kept my fingers out of the disgusting stuff. I only had to use one hand to do this, so I could hold my nose with the other. I didn't mind the smell of horsey-do in the stables, but in a garden trench? And just a few inches away from my nose? And for something we were going to *eat*? That was definitely not nice.

When it started to rain, Mr. B suggested we break for elevenses.

There were two greenhouses and two garden sheds. One of the sheds was used for storing tools, the wheelbarrows, a lawnmower, and the little thing on wheels Miss Audrey-Joan used to mark out the tennis court. Stacked against the walls were bundles of bamboo canes for beans to climb up, dozens of clay plant pots, piles of sacks and a big bundle of old net curtains to cover the soft fruit bushes to keep the birds from stealing the berries. Mr. B said there were probably mouse nests under the sacks and he was thinking of shutting a couple of the stable cats in there for a night or two. He said that would put paid to the mice's little games for a while.

The other shed was a lot nicer. It had a big window covered with old spider's webs and a piece of ancient lace curtain; I couldn't tell where the lace ended and the webs began. Hundreds of dead flies were caught in both the webs and the curtains.

On the wall next to the window, hung an old calendar from the year I was born—1934—with a picture of a prize racehorse on it called Hyperion. Mr. B said he'd won a pretty penny by backing Hyperion to win the Derby the year before, which is why he kept the picture. On the calendar, were lots of little circles and scribblings around different dates. Picture postcards from foreign places, were pinned on the wall around the calendar.

Piles of seed catalogues mixed in with magazines like *Punch* and *The Tatler* were stacked up on the floor below, and on another shelf to the right–just level with my nose–was a pack of playing cards and some old books that Mr. B said he liked to read when it rained. I read out the titles: *The Countryman, The Farmer's Weekly*, and *The Daily Telegraph Crossword Puzzle Book*. Mummy liked that book too, she was very clever at crosswords.

Opposite the window, a high bench ran the whole length of the shed. It was so full of stuff that it dipped in the middle and Mr. B had wedged an old barrel underneath to keep it from collapsing. I wasn't tall enough to see what was up there, so he turned a box upside down for me to stand on. It was chockablock-full of interesting things. Jam-jars and old tins stuffed with a million treasures: dried beans and peas for planting, and seeds collected from special flowers that Mr. B. used to grow before the war. Old Players Navy Cut tobacco tins were filled with nails and screws and round brass rings. Hundreds of packets of seeds, all with coloured pictures of flowers or vegetables on the front, were lined up in old shoe boxes.

In one corner of the bench I found an old cigar box. On it was a picture of some black men using wickedly long knives to hack at big green leaves and stack them in baskets slung on their backs. Inside the box were spanners and screwdrivers, old spoons and knives, even some horseshoe nails. Another wooden box held balls of string–thick white string and green garden string–some fishing line and a bundle of empty cotton reels. There were secateurs for cutting flowers and scissors for cutting string, old pencils for writing on the wooden seed markers and a wooden spoon with *A Present from Blackpool'* painted along the handle and a picture of Blackpool Tower on the bowl. I found a pencil sharpener, so I picked out one of the crayons–a blue one–sharpened it, and climbed back over the bench to put a big circle around June 20 on the 1934 calendar; it was the day I was born.

There were all sorts of things under the bench too. Welly boots, soldier boots and some long rubber trousers that Mr. B called waders. And so many baskets: gypsy baskets made of willow, some with handles over the top and some with handles at both ends. Wooden trugs for collecting flowers and even a dog basket. Old paint cans were piled up on each other, all with different coloured paint drips on the outside. It all smelled of old rubber wellies, creosote, wet leaves and garden soil. I discovered a hole in the corner by a pile of leaves which must have been where the mice came in. I moved the pile of leaves to take a look. There was something hard underneath. I touched it and...IT MOVED. I screeched for Mr. B and as I jumped back, I banged my head and began to yell.

"What on earth is all the fuss and commotion about?" Mr. B picked me up and rubbed my head.

"There's something alive down there!"

"Probably one of the cats."

"No, it isn't a cat. It's HARD...and...COLD."

Mr. B crawled to the corner and shuffled his hands around in the pile of leaves. "It's only old Torty. I wondered where he'd got too. I couldn't find him all winter and I worried he would freeze."

"Torty? Who's Torty?"

"This is Torty." Mr. B backed out from under the bench, puffing and red in the face. In his hand he clutched a big tortoise. I could only see the shell, because the tortoise had pulled its head and legs back inside. "He's probably a little miffed at being woken up," Mr. B explained. "We'll put him out by the door and see if he'll come out of his shell. Looks like he needs a good clean after sleeping in those muddy leaves all winter. I can't imagine how he got into the shed."

"Torty is a silly name for a tortoise."

"All the tortoises we've ever had have been called Torty."

"How many have you had?"

"Well, now. Let me think." Mr. B sat down on the upturned box. I noticed there was a cobweb in his hair. "At least six or seven."

"And they've all been called Torty?"

"Well, yes. As one got away or got lost, we replaced it and just used the same name."

"Why d'you get more?"

"Because they're useful in the garden. And they don't need much looking after." Mr. B glared at me, but his eyes were twinkling. "And they don't ask a lot of questions. In fact, they don't talk at all. They just mind their own business."

I didn't say anything for a while. Mr. B ran his fingers through his hair, found the cobweb and wiped his hand on his trousers.

"I've never had a tortoise," I said at last. "Actually, I've never had a pet like a cat or a dog, that I could play with and talk to. Except Tristan, and he's not really mine. When I was little, I had a canary in a cage. The cage hung in the window in my nursery and he would sing for me, but I wasn't allowed to touch him."

"Well, tortoises are not what you'd call playful. But they need feeding occasionally and their shells need polishing. In fact, that one," Mr. B pointed to Torty, "needs a bath *and* a polish."

"May I bath him and polish him?"

"I don't see why not. If I gave you Torty to look after, would you care for him?"

"Oh, yes. But I wouldn't call him Torty."

"What would *you* call him?"

I thought for a while. "If you've had six or seven, then this is number eight. And he's kind of round and portly with skinny legs and neck."

The tortoise had finally popped his head out.

"And he has nubbles on his head, like little jewels."

"Well, missee, and what does that have to do with a name for the beast?"

"I think he looks like Henry VIII. I saw a picture of him once, and he was round and portly and had skinny legs, and jewels around his neck and head."

"Henry VIII, eh? Kind of high falutin' if you ask me, but it'll go with all the other animals around here with fancy names."

I think Mr. B meant Tristan and Iseult, and Hamlet.

"I like fancy names. I don't see why a tortoise shouldn't have a fancy name. He leads such a dull life, it might make him feel better."

"All right, Henry VIII it is. But you'll have to clean him up and polish his shell."

"Will he get lost again?" I asked.

"Well, we could paint a red spot, or a white cross on his back."

"All right. May bath him now."

It had stopped raining so I went outside and scrubbed Henry VIII with water from the rain barrel, and dried him with a clean rag. Mr. B gave me another rag and some sort of oil which I rubbed into Henry VIII's shell until it shone and glistened in the sun. Henry VIII seemed to like being clean and shining and sat in the patch of sunlight munching on an old cabbage leaf I'd found.

"Perhaps I'll drill a hole in his shell tomorrow and put a string in him," said Mr. B.

"I don't want you to hurt him."

"Bless you, it won't hurt. His shell is like your fingernails and they don't hurt when they are cut do they? A horse never feels his hooves being trimmed or shoes nailed on. There's no feeling in Henry VIII's shell."

"Alright, but I think he should have a red blob too, so I can find him."

So we settled on a very long string and a red blob, and left Henry VIII eating cabbage.

"Now, Pat-a-cake," said Mr. B. "After all that work it's time for elevenses."

There was a leather armchair in the shed. It was old and cracked, and leaking its horsehair stuffing. Above it, was a shelf stacked with cups and plates. Mr. B opened a cupboard, with a picture of Loch Lomond stuck on it. Inside was a tea caddy and a tin of condensed milk (I think it was the one he took out of Mrs. B's bag when we went to the market). There was also an old Huntley and Palmers biscuit tin and, right at the back, a bottle labelled "Brandy".

"That's for medicinal purposes only," Mr. B told me. " Don't you be thinking you can add it to your tea now. It's only old bones like mine that have aches and pains."

On an old metal table, Mr. B set up a small primus stove, that worked on methylated spirits. He primed, pumped and lit it and put a tin kettle on top to boil the water for our tea. I ate my bread and dripping and drank tea out of an old mug with a picture of the Tower of London on the front. The tea tasted so good made with the condensed milk. Mr. B put some Medicinal Purposes in his cup and told me again, that it wasn't for little girls, only grown-ups. He let me sniff the bottle, but I didn't like the smell. Condensed milk smelled much better.

Then Mr. B cleared away the tea-making stuff and we went outside to plant the rest of the potatoes. "For the Lord knows," he said. "We've wasted enough time playing about with yon tortoise instead of seeing to garden matters." Mr. B grumbled a lot about me holding him up, but I reminded him that it was his idea to bath and clean Henry VIII.

"Well, so long as we get these spuds in today, we'll stay on the right side of Edwina B."

I giggled at the thought of Mr. B having to stay on the right side of Mrs. B. He glared at me so I got on with the potato planting; taking care not to touch any horse manure.

I wished I could plant flowers like Cedric had in his garden, so I asked Mr. B if I could plant some flowers and he said that he was giving all the children Victory plots to plant vegetables, but that we could sow flower seeds around the borders provided we complied with War Effort regulations.

When all the potatoes were planted, Mr. B showed me where we would plant our Victory plots. It was a big space outside the south wall of the kitchen garden, between the stable-yard and the orchard, and opposite the rubbish heap. There was one nice sandy spot, with no weeds. It was next to an archway into the big garden, and close to the water tap. I pointed to it. "I'll take that plot. It looks nice and clean."

"Bad choice, Pat-a-cake." Mr. B shook his head.

"Why? I think it's a good choice. The others all have weeds. Look at the one by the orchard fence. The weeds come up to my middle."

"And that's the one you should choose," Mr. B replied.

"Why?"

"Those weeds are growing tall and strong, which means they are growing in good soil. The sandy spots don't even have a blade of grass growing on them, so you would have to dig in manure and compost to get a good crop."

"Then I'll have the plot by the orchard fence," I said. "And give the sandy one to Arabella Bosworthy."

"That's up to her whether she chooses it or not," Mr. B said. "But if you take the other patch, pull the weeds out after a good rain and they'll come out as if they were growing in butter."

"It was raining earlier. I'll try now?" I pulled at a weed, and it came out easily–just as Mr. B said it would. "Can I bag that spot now?"

"Who are you going to share it with?" he asked.

"Ann-the-Bank. She'll be back from Wales soon."

"All right, but mind you get out here right smart for the first Victory gardening lesson. I'll not be handing out favours to you."

I'd already planned what I would do. When the gardening lesson came up, I would go to the outside lavvy and wait for the lesson bell. Then I would run up here before everyone else. But I didn't tell Mr. B that. And I didn't tell him my plan to make Bossy Bella choose the sandy plot where nothing would grow. Which I did, by saying in a loud voice so she could overhear, that I was going to bag it. And she took the bait. So for the whole war my Victory Garden grew the best and biggest vegetables, and Bossy Bella had to shovel manure.

Every year, I grew flowers around the edge. Just for Cedric. Like his garden in Heaven.

Sunday, 12th April, 1942
Dear Mummy and Daddy,
On Easter Monday, we went to the pictures and saw "Fantasia." This was a special "after-measle" treat for me. The other children had a picnic.
I helped Mr. B plant potatoes last Tuesday. He told me potatoes should always be planted on Good Friday but he's not sure who made that rule. He says it couldn't have been a

God-fearing person because good Christians spend most of Good Friday on their knees in church and eating fish. That's a church rule. Mr. B said the weekend was far too busy anyway and that Tuesday was close enough for him. So we made it a Good Tuesday and planted the King Edwards and said a prayer that they will be abundant.

With abundant love
from your daughter
Patricia

Chapter 24

Ophelia

During those unsettled years of World War II, Miss Audrey-Joan, her family and a couple of her permanent staff, stayed with us for the duration. There was also a continuous procession of casual teachers who came to Normanhurst, taught us for a few weeks or months and then, as suddenly as they had appeared, they went away. Where they went, we never discovered, but we knew it was the war that had taken them away.

Spring, 1942 was just turning into summer when one of the all time best and most unusual teachers arrived on our doorstep.

Her name was Miss Primrose Pendleton.

We were having dinner–shepherd's pie, and elephant's ear with treacle for pudding–when the front door bell rang. As Miss Audrey-Joan went to answer it, some of us crept from the dining room and sneaked around to the entrance hall to see who had come to visit.

Miss Audrey-Joan opened the door, and the most frantic looking person imaginable stood on the porch. She had bright red hair piled on the top of her head but—glory be!—the very top-most curls were bright yellow. She wore a purple and yellow striped frock that came down to her ankles, with a long black feather boa–like my grandmother Alice used to wear–twisted around her neck and floating down her back. She wore so much jewellery, she sparkled like the Christmas tree we'd had in Wales. Rings glittered on every finger and long twinkly balls dangled from her ears. Best of all, she was carrying the darlingest spaniel puppy I'd ever seen. It was the colour of toffee, and had long loppy ears and big brown eyes. The lady's eyes were brown too, but they were all coloured up with bright blue, and her eyelashes stuck out like hedgehog spikes.

Miss Audrey-Joan glared when she caught sight of us peeking so we all scurried back into the dining hall and talked about the amazing lady and her spaniel puppy.

When we'd finished dinner, Miss Audrey-Joan introduced Miss Primrose Pendleton who told us her puppy's name was Gatsby, and that his ears had to be tied up when he ate so they didn't flop in his food.

Miss Primrose Pendleton floated everywhere. As she moved, her dresses drifted out behind her, and her feather boa caught on door knobs and clung to corners. Her hair floated too when she let it loose–red at the top with a tumble of blonde curls on her shoulders. Sometimes she packed it all into a black net snood, decorated with shiny jet beads and black velvet bows. She had long red fingernails and her slim white hands were constantly fluttering, making the bangles on her arms tinkle. We always knew when she was near as we could hear the jangle of her bracelets and smell her perfume long before she appeared. She told us it was a French perfume called *Arpège* and that she only dabbed a smidgen behind her ears because, as Paris was all torn up with the war, she didn't know when she would ever go shopping in the *Champs Elysees* again. Miss Primrose Pendleton was absolutely, smashingly, super incredible and she was there to teach us elocution, drama and classical dance.

Oh bliss! It had been two weeks since Miss Primrose arrived and we had one lesson with her every day. We called her Miss Primrose because she said that 'Miss Primrose Pendleton' was too much of a mouthful and Miss Pendelton sounded too Jane Austin—and *that* was *definitely* not her cup of tea; she could never be the crinoline and corset type. She preferred to think of herself as being closer to Mr Noel Coward's Blithe Spirit. Perhaps that's why she floated so much.

"Not," she said, "that I am an afficionado of Mr Coward's way of life. Just a tincy-wincy bit Bohemian perhaps. As a matter of fact, when I was at a party once with the Prince of Wales..." She stopped abruptly because we were all staring at her, longing to hear one of her stories. "My, how I do ramble on. You are all far too young and precious to be hearing about the Prince of Wales and all *those* goings on."

I was disappointed that Miss Primrose didn't ramble on some more, but we were supposed to be learning about Shakespeare and not the Prince of Wales–whoever *he* was.

Her lessons were fabulous and exciting. We read Lamb's *Tales from Shakespeare* because Miss Primrose said it would make it much easier to understand the 'real thing' if we knew the stories first. In another lesson we learned about the Greek Gods and the adventures of Odysseus. The best lessons were when acted the stories and plays we'd read.

The first two weeks we read and acted Macbeth because Miss Primrose said it was the easiest to understand. It was full of stabbings and murders, and witches with cauldrons that bubbled. I wanted to be Lady Macbeth, but had to be one of the witches instead.

Then we went on to do Hamlet and I didn't even get a part in that one. Ann-the-Bank was Ophelia, because Miss Primrose said she looked pale and ethereal. I didn't think she looked at all ethereal, and she kept stumbling over her words. When she was supposed to be floating down the river, she just lay on a bench with her arms folded across her chest, and looking more like a picture I'd seen of one of those stone Plantagenet queens on top of a tomb in Worcester Cathedral. When I told her that, she stuck her tongue out at me and said I couldn't be Ophelia anyway because Ophelia was blonde and I had dark hair. So I slapped her and went to the kitchen garden to talk to Mr. B about it.

Mr. B wasn't there so I looked for Henry VIII but couldn't find him either. There were so many red bean flowers and strawberries in the garden, Henry VIII's red spot was impossible to find. Then, as it felt about tea time, I decided to see what there was to eat in Mr. B's shed. I found the biscuit tin and a half-empty cup of tea on the bench. Mr. B must have left it to go on an urgent mission for Mrs. B.

"When Edwina Baker calls, you have to fall in and stand to attention! And no dilly-dallying." But he would grin as he said it.

The tea was still warm and it tasted quite different. Mr. B must have put some Medicinal Purposes into it. I decided to finish it up, then he could make some more hot tea when he came back. He was probably unblocking the boys' outside lavvy again.

As I sat and drank the tea, I thought about being Ophelia and how Ann-the-Bank couldn't act for toffee. Maybe I should act it, outside. It would be much better out of doors because after all, Ophelia was out of doors when she floated down the stream. Besides, it was getting very hot in the shed–especially after drinking all the tea so quickly.

I needed some Ophelia dress-up, so I took one of the old lace curtains Mr. B had draped over the blackcurrent bushes to keep the birds out. I made two wild-flower chains, one for my head and one to put around my waist. As I walked, Ophelia's old lace curtain robe floated out way behind me, just like Miss Primrose's. Now I was ready to get into my barge and act at being mad while drifting down the river. But there was no stream in the kitchen garden. One ran across the top of the orchard but I didn't want to go that far in my lace curtain dress. Besides, the tea had made me a little tired.

Then I had an absolutely splendid idea. An old bathtub had been planted at the top of the kitchen garden, to collect rainwater. Now wouldn't *that* make a perfect barge? And I could float beautifully in it. Floating on a bed of wild-flowers. How perfectly Ophelia. And I certainly wouldn't look like a stone Plantagenet queen.

Leaves covered the water in the bath tub. I scattered the flowers on top of them, then laid down, crossed my hands over my chest, and gazed up through the leaves of the old quince tree. The sun was warm on my face; little clouds–like pieces of cauliflower–floated across a blue sky. I could still taste Mr. B's Medicinal Purposes tea on my tongue. How perfectly Ophelia. I felt the water soak through the back of my old lace curtain robe. It soaked through my jumper and my kilt, right through to my knickers. I felt it swirl around my tummy when I moved. I decided to lie very still and pretend Ophelia had drowned; I could just go to sleep and be a dead Ophelia.

Oh, my gosh! All of a sudden I was swooped out of the water and shaken hard from side to side. Then I found myself held tight and hugged against Mr. B's chest. "Saints alive, Pat-a-cake, what are you doing?"

"I'm a drowned Ophelia."

"Glory be, you're alive and speaking. You silly sausage, what on earth possessed you?" He put his nose close to my mouth and sniffed, "And what on earth have you been drinking?"

"Your tea. It was going to be wasted. It was getting cold."

"Oh, Lordy, lordy! What a pickle you've got us both into now." Mr. B carried me to the shed and picked up his bottle of Medicinal Purposes, took out the cork and rubbed it on my mouth. It stung my lips and I struggled and twisted away from him.

"Don't like it. No. Please don't," I cried.

"Pat-a-cake, it's for your own good." I didn't understand what he meant, but I stopped wriggling when he put the cork back in the bottle.

"Now, Pat-a-cake, listen to me. Don't you say one solitary word, young lady, about drinking my tea. Not one word, do you hear? Let me do the talking. My, oh my! Edwina-Jane is going to be in a twist about this."

Mr. B ran with me in his arms, through the kitchen garden. My flower crown fell apart and dropped its blossoms on the path as I was bounced along in his tight hold, my cheek pressed against his prickly chin. He smelled of tweed coat, mixed in with garden. My old lace curtain robe trailed out behind us both, flapping in the wind and tugging at my shoulders. My cold, damp knickers stuck to my bottom.

Mr. B arrived breathless at the back kitchen door, bent forward and, crushing me between him and the door, grabbed the handle and flung it open. "Edwina," he called. "Edwina. Audrey-Joan. Come quick!"

They both ran into the back kitchen.

"Oh, land-sakes," said Miss Audrey-Joan. "What on earth is the matter?"

"Lord a' mercy," cried Mrs. B. "What's happened to the child now? Is she hurt?" She grabbed me from Mr. B. and held me to her bosom. She was wearing her second best navy blue polka-dot dress but she didn't seem to care about that as she clutched me, wet leaves, wet flowers, wet knickers, dripping old lace curtain and all, to her bosom. "And just what's been going on, may I ask?" demanded Mrs. B "This child reeks of brandy."

At that moment, I realized that Mr. B was a true friend.

"She fell into the old bathtub in the kitchen garden," he explained. "She was so cold and wet, I was feared she would be sick again, so I gave her a drop of brandy to bring her round."

I shut my eyes tight, rolled my head away from Mrs. B's bosom and let it hang over her arm. Just as I imagined Ophelia would have done.

"Oh, poor child," she said. "But what is she doing in this getup? All this old netting and flowers."

"Playing dress-up is my guess," he said. "That fancy Primrose filling her head with tom-foolery I wouldn't wonder." Not once did the name Ophelia cross his lips.

"Hrrummph," snorted Mrs. B. She always snorted and "Hrrummph'ed" when she didn't know what to say.

"Get her upstairs and out of those wet things," said Miss Audrey-Joan.

Mrs. Tommy who had come by to see what all the commotion was about, ran on ahead to fill up the big bathtub with hot water–and she didn't even measure five inches. When all was done, and I was tucked up in bed with hot milk to drink, and the curtains drawn to make the room dark, Mrs. B stood over me. "Now then, young lady," she was in her 'let-us-have-no-more-of-this-nonsense' mood. "Get you to sleep. Not that you'll take much rocking with Arthur B's Medicinal inside you. I'm not too sure what went on out there, but it'd better not happen again. Do you understand?"

I squinted one eye open—just a crack, but didn't answer her. After all, Mr. B had said not to say one word. For evermore I would do what Mr. B said. I felt a bit guilty about Mrs. B's second best navy blue polka-dot dress; it still had some mud stains on it, and a leaf was caught in the Brussels lace on her bosom. I turned my mouth down, preparing to wail.

"Now, now! Don't start to cry. There's no need for that. Things could have turned out a lot differently, and it appears you're none the worse for wear. Go to sleep. No more to be said."

With that remark, Mrs. B left the room. The sun still shone through the cracks around the curtains, making gold streaks on the wall. I could hear the birds singing outside and the thunk-thunk of an old tennis ball bouncing off the stable-yard door. I didn't like being put to bed when all the other children were still playing outside.

Dear Cedric,
Did you see me all dressed up and floating on my bathtub barge? Didn't I make the most perfectly beautiful Ophelia? Not like that pale and sickly Plantagenet, Ann-the-Bank.
Cedric, why do you never answer me?
Your very best friend,
Pat

Sunday, 31st May, 1942
Dear Mummy and Daddy,
Thank you for your letters, it was nice to hear from Daddy too. When I grow up I am going to be a famous Shakespearean actress. Yesterday I was Ophelia. Tomorrow, I am going to be Lady Macbeth.
With love from your soon-to-be-famous daughter,
Patricia.

Chapter 25

Now I am Eight

I didn't really expect my mother to visit me on my birthday. The other boarders never saw their parents and anyway, it was the middle of term. A parcel arrived with presents of books, two of Rachel's outgrown summer frocks from last year, and some sweets. The greatest treat of all, was that my birthday happened on a Saturday. A whole day with no lessons and everyone being nice to me. It was a hot, sunny midsummer day, and Miss Audrey-Joan organised games of rounders for the girls and cricket for the boys. The tennis net was up and she brought out the little contraption that painted the white lines. Her feet straddling the lines, she pushed the whitewash encrusted metal box on wheels slowly along the string she'd placed for a guideline. I skipped along beside her, occasionally jumping over the lines, but mostly right in front of her, to make sure she could hear me above the squeaking wheels.

"Pat, if you keep bouncing around like Tigger, you're going to make me either spill the stuff, or make a wiggly line."

I went back to skipping beside her. "When may I learn to play tennis?"

"Well I don't see why you shouldn't start now. Do you have a tennis racquet?"

"No, Miss Baker."

"Well, I have a few tucked away. I'm sure can find one for you."

"Thank you very much, Miss Baker."

Miss Audrey-Joan was good at everything. Not just lessons, like Latin, English and History, but the fun things like tennis, playing ghosts and picnics. That afternoon, after the rounders game, she found me a tennis racquet and taught me how to hold it, and how to watch the ball. It wasn't long before I could hit a ball over the net, although some of them went right over the wall and into the kitchen garden. When that happened, Mr. B shouted "Siiiix" and we knew the ball had landed in one of his vegetable patches; even Miss Audrey-Joan giggled at that.

Tea was fun. When I blew out eight candles on the cake that Mrs. Tommy had made, everyone sang *"Happy Birthday."* After the tea dishes had been cleared away, Miss Audrey-Joan called me into her study. "I have another surprise for you, Pat."

I said nothing. Just hopped from one foot to another and waited. She looked up from her desk and smiled. "Your music didn't get off to a very good start this winter. You spent too much time having measles! Your mother asked how it was coming along, so I promised to give you extra piano lessons."

Miss Audrey-Joan knew this would make me happy. I desperately wanted to play the piano like my mother. So far, I could find middle-C and do a couple of scales.

"For a birthday gift, your next six lessons will be on the grand piano in the drawing room."

That was stupendous news. Usually we had to play on the upright in the dining hall. I'd only ever been in the drawing room once—when my mother came after I'd run away. It was a beautiful room. All pale greens and golds, with a soft carpet and tall vases of flowers. The grand piano was set near a window, and its top was covered with photos of Miss Audrey-Joan and her family.

"Thank you, Miss Baker. Thank you very much."

Miss Baker smiled. "You also asked if you could all play ghosts at dusk. It'll be pretty late, but as it's a Saturday, *and* your birthday, I think we can make an exception–just this once."

I went out and told the other children. They all cheered.

I went to bed happy that night. I was eight, and the most popular child in the school. For a day, anyway.

Sunday, 21st June, 1942.
Dear Mummy and Daddy,
Thank you for the birthday presents. I had an excellent birth-
day and we all stayed up late and played ghosts.
I am learning music on the grand piano. I need a
tennis racquet.
Love from your eight year old daughter,
Patricia

About a month after my birthday, Miss Audrey-Joan called me into her study. "Sit down, Patricia. I have something to tell you."

I sat and waited while she looked through some papers on her desk. When she picked up a letter, I recognised my mother's handwriting–even though it was upside down.

Miss Audrey-Joan leaned back in her chair and looked at me. She didn't have on her "you're in trouble look" but a different look–as if she were trying to think what to say.

"Patricia...Pat. You do understand that one of the reasons you are here with us at Normanhurst is because of the war, right?"

I nodded.

"Well, it seems the war is going on a lot longer than anyone antici-pated. That means we all have to make some serious adjustments to our lives."

I nodded again, but didn't understand what she was talking about.

"Pat...your mother has asked me if you can stay with us–perma-nently–until the war is over. That means," Miss Audrey-Joan paused, then leaned forward. "It means that this is your home for the duration of the war. It means that you stay with us—just like a lot of the other children do—not just for the school terms but for the holidays as well."

I stared at her. I felt a knot grow in my stomach. "D-does that mean I d-don't go home to Wales for the Summer?"

Miss Audrey-Joan took my hand, drew me around her desk, and took me on her lap. "I'm afraid it does, my dear. You'll have to stay here for the summer holidays."

"But that means I won't see Mummy, or Dilly...or...or Daddy?"

"Not this summer."

That started the familiar prickles in the back of my nose and throat. Tears filled my eyes, then overflowed and ran down my cheeks. "Nooo," I bawled. "I want to go home to Wales."

"I'm sorry, Pat. That's not possible now. Your mother is even thinking of leaving Wales and going to live with your Aunt in the Lake District. Now, please Pat, don't cry so hard. We *all* have to make sacrifices while the war is on. And this is one *you* have to make. You really have to be brave about it."

I nodded. I'd learned by now it wasn't any use crying in wartime. It didn't change anything.

Miss Audrey-Joan pulled out a clean handkerchief. I wiped my eyes and blew my nose. Then she hugged me close. "You're better off than a lot of other children. Some have lost their homes in the blitz, and some of them have lost their parents for ever." Miss Audrey-Joan paused and looked out of the window. The bright summer sun streamed in the window and dazzled my tear-filled eyes. When she spoke again, it was in a very low, sort of sad voice. "There are many–too many—children in Europe dying of starvation. And some are shut up in labour camps, behind barbed wire."

We were both silent for a moment and I tried to imagine Normanhurst surrounded by barbed wire, and all of us children with no food to eat.

Miss Audrey-Joan sighed and shook her head–as though she were coming back from faraway thoughts. "You know, the holidays will be fun. There won't be any lessons and we'll go swimming, have picnics and go on field trips to the Clee Hills, or Bredon. Now *that* would be fun, wouldn't it?"

I nodded. Then I had a brilliant thought. "Will I be able to start real riding lessons?" Until now, I'd only been walking around the stable-yard on Dolly.

"What a grand idea. We'll have you riding by the end of the summer."

That night in bed, after I knew everyone was asleep, I cried again. It was a whole year since I'd seen my father and Dilly, and I'd only seen my mother when she was sent for after I ran away. And how long would it be before I saw my family again?

"I hate the war. Why does there have to be a war? Why are children starving to death behind barbed wire, and ships sinking, and friends getting drowned? Why won't it all stop?"

When I awoke in the morning, my pillow was still wet.

5th July, 1942
Dear Mummy and Daddy,
I am very sad that I can't come home for the summer holidays. But I think I understand. Miss Baker says she will teach me to be a good horsewoman, and tennis player. Please may I have a tennis racquet?
With love from your saddest daughter,
Patricia

19th July, 1942
Dear Mummy and Daddy,
Thank you for the tennis racquet and for Rachel's old bathing-costume.
Mrs. Baker cut the toes out of my sandals and my plimsolls as they are too small and hurt my toes. I am enclosing an outline of my foot that Mrs. B drew on a piece of paper. She says to say I'm growing very fast.
I lost another two teeth this summer.
With love from your tall toothless daughter
Patricia

It was September 1942, and summer holidays were almost over. A summer of picnics and long sunny days spent playing in the garden, riding my bicycle around the grounds, or riding Dolly in the orchard, and swimming in the stream that ran though Thatcher's Woods. On very hot days, Mr. B turned on the fountain on top of the rockery in the sunken garden that Cedric had called Camelot and, wearing our bathing-costumes, we clambered over the rocks and through the cold cascades of sparkling water. No one told us off if we sat on a few plants, or squashed the flowers. We played Leapfrog and had three-legged races on the front lawn, and there was always someone willing to hit a tennis ball back and forth over the net, or join in a game of rounders or cricket. On rainy days, we played Shipwreck, Sardines, or Hide-and-Seek; racing all over the house, screaming and yelling. The grown ups didn't seem to mind how much noise and clatter we made. They would often join in and show us good places to hide, like the linen cupboards and storage rooms. Mr. B suspended swings from the ancient beams in the barn and raked in enormous piles of hay. Then he would catch us as we took flying leaps from the rafters into the sweet-smelling, soft mounds.

That summer I had my first proper riding lessons and learned to play tennis. It was fun, but it wasn't the same as being in Wales with Daddy and Mummy and Dilly. I kept all their letters in an old shoe box. At night, hunched under the bedclothes with my torch, I would read them over and over again. All I could think of was how far away they were; I didn't even know where Daddy was. Sometimes I would cry, but no-one heard me because they were all asleep. The next morning, Miss Audrey-Joan would look at my puffy eyes and give me a hug.

One sunny day, Miss Audrey-Joan packed as many of us that would fit into her little grey Morris Cowley, and the rest into Mr. B's old Daimler, and she and Mrs. Tommy drove us to the Clee Hills. We climbed the heather slopes to the top where we found little tarns, all different colours. In some the water was red, in others it was turquoise blue, or green. We played Ducks and Drakes, and paddled in the warm water. After a picnic, we played Tag, which frightened a herd of wild ponies. All the way home, we sang songs and giggled–our mouths and hands stained purple from eating wild bilberries.

The next day, everything changed. After breakfast and bed-making we clustered around the kitchen door to find out what adventures were planned for the day. It took only moments for us to realise something very serious was happening. Our excited chatter melted into silence as we tried to understand why the grownups looked so grim. They were sitting around the kitchen table–silent–their heads bent towards the wireless. None of us dared say a word. One by one, we sat down on the floor, our ears straining to hear what the thin, tinny voice was saying. I remember some of the words...Allies...Dieppe...casualties...battle.... Apart from the announcer, the only sound was the jangling of Miss Primrose's bracelets as she dabbed at her eyes with her hanky. After a while, we crept away and found quiet things to do; reading, knitting, or drawing. I went outside and pulled a few weeds from my Victory Garden plot. And when the dinner bell rang, we tiptoed into the dining hall and ate our food in silence. No-one dared to talk.

At bedtime I asked Mrs. B what had happened, and she told me there had been a terrible battle in a place called Dieppe, which was only a few miles across the English Channel and "a little too close for comfort," she added. She told us many soldiers had been killed or wounded. As I climbed the stairs to go to bed, she called after me. "I think this is a night when you should remember to say your prayers; thankful that you're in a safe place, with enough to eat."

I said some extra prayers, for the wounded soldiers, and for the starving children, and for the children in the barbed wire camps. And, although I didn't know where it was, I prayed for a place called Dieppe.

I wondered if Daddy had been there.

"I must ask Mummy in my letter."

Even though the Germans didn't come, we all knew the war still raged in Europe and North Africa. We were resigned to the fact that it separated us from our families. We got used to making the best of it and, for five- to ten-year-olds, two months of continuous play and no lessons made it easier. As there were only a dozen or so permanent evacuee boarders, we were like a large and gregarious family and, as an only child, that was something I had always secretly prayed for. There was a spirit of comradeship that was nourished by the common denomina-tor of being separated from our families; through no fault of theirs–or ours for that matter. Hitler was the bogey-man, and his bombing raids generated in our immature minds a hatred that, although we may not have understood, nevertheless, festered in dark and unreachable corners of our souls. Conversely, the physical turmoil of war was so far removed, that I even nurtured a belief that Cedric was not really dead, but one day the big wrought-iron gates would swing open, a car would drive through the tall stone pillars, and deliver him back into my life.

A week before the start of a new term and a new school year Miss Audrey-Joan announced at breakfast that we were going on an expedition to Thatcher's Woods to pick blackberries and hazel nuts. We would take a picnic lunch and spend all day there. And tomorrow, if we'd picked enough blackberries, there would be blackberry and apple pie for tea.

I enjoyed outings to Thatcher's Woods. An old cart track, that Miss Audrey-Joan told us had been used by our ancestors for hundreds of years, wound through the trees. Somewhere in the middle of the ancient road, where it met the stream that ran through the woods and down the hill to empty into the River Severn, were the familiar ford and stepping-stones. In the spring, the stream became a rushing torrent but after a long, hot summer it was a gentle and friendly playground. Down-stream, below the ford, the shallow water danced and trickled its way around boulders and little sand bars. Here we would paddle and search for the perfect hopscotch stone–a small, ancient river pebble–flat, round and smoothed by centuries of running water to the perfect size and weight. Up-stream was the old weathered wooden footbridge, where Cedric and I had played Pooh Sticks and he'd run from the deep, dark water. There, the stream ran slow and was deep enough for a swimming hole. If you looked hard, you could see grey shadowy shapes of trout or pike darting back and forth between dark fronds of river grass. It also reminded me of the river in Wales, and the last time I saw my father. Wearing an old pair of khaki shorts he'd carried me under his arm as he waded up the river, skimming my toes into the shining water, pretending to drop me where it ran in a fast, creaming foam over the rocks.

Another time, another river. I was eight now, and too old to be carried under my father's arm. Too old to be afraid of a few inches of rushing white water.

Mummy wrote and told me Ann-the-Bank was bringing a parcel of my cousin Rachel's outgrown clothes and shoes for me. She said nothing about going to live in Westmorland with my Aunt Addie. But she did say that Daddy was safe in England, and not fighting in some foreign field.

I'd lost another tooth, and when Mrs. B measured me against the tape measure glued to the bathroom doorpost, I had grown another two inches. She made a mark on the wall beside it, with my name and the date.

I had just turned eight years old, and it would be another three years before I would be reunited with my parents.

Sunday, 23rd August, 1942.
Dear Mummy and Daddy,
I can ride a horse now, and play tennis. We also play leapfrog and croquet.
I have grown two inches.
I'm glad you are still in Wales.
With love from your tall daughter,
Patricia

Chapter 26

Murder Most Foul

1

On that particular day–at the end of the summer holiday–I wasn't sure I wanted to go to Thatcher's Woods to pick blackberries. Last night, I'd woken up to go to the loo. As I crept down the stairs, the tiny oil night-lamps lighting the way, I heard voices. Tiptoeing round the corner, I saw Mr. B and Miss Audrey-Joan outside the little sick room, talking. I ducked out of sight into a small alcove, to listen.

"Take them on an expedition, or a picnic." Mr. B was saying. "Keep them well out of the way all day, then by the time you get back all traces of the dirty deed will have been cleared away."

"I'll take them blackberrying. It's going to be warm and sunny, so they can paddle in the river afterwards. We'll take a picnic lunch too. That should give you plenty of time to get everything cleaned up."

"Good."

"What time is Ransom coming?"

"Between nine and ten. He usually likes to get at the job earlier, but he understands we have to get the children breakfasted and out of the way first."

"He'll bring his own knives with him, won't he?"

"Oh yes. He never does a job without his own equipment."

"Well, we'd better get to bed then. I'll get up early to make sandwiches and get the children's breakfast. I'll wake them up half an hour earlier."

"Good night then, Joanie."

"Good night, Dad. Sleep well."

I waited until they had gone to their rooms, then I went to the loo and dashed back to bed. But I couldn't get to sleep for thinking about what I'd heard.

"Dirty deed? Ransom? Knives? What was going on? Something terrible is going to happen tomorrow. Is it to do with the war? Is there a prisoner being held for ransom? And knives? Is someone going to be tortured? An enemy spy? A GERMAN SPY?"

Determined to find out what was going to happen tomorrow, I made my plans before finally falling asleep.

Miss Audrey-Joan packed the picnic baskets into the float and backed old Dobbin into the shafts. Dolly was pulling the wagonette. The younger children piled into the float with Miss Audrey-Joan at the reins. Mrs. Tommy drove the wagonette and Mrs Riley climbed in behind, lifting up little Elaine who had a withered foot and was a slow walker. She then helped Alex Gilbert up–he'd fallen off his bike the day before and had a big bandage on his knee. Mrs. B walked behind, a child on each hand. I walked close to them at the side of the lane, waiting for the right moment to carry out my plan. I lagged behind, stopping to pick wildflowers.

"What do you want those for, Pat?" Mrs. B was puffing because the lane ran uphill.

"I want to make a pressed flower picture for my mother's birthday."

"What a lovely idea, but you'd do better to wait and get them on the way back. Pick them now, and they'll be wilted by the end of the day."

So *that* plan wasn't going to work.

About a quarter-mile farther on, there was a copse and the duck pond where Miss Audrey-Joan had skated, and where the hedge at the end of Farmer Bourne's meadow met the lane. As we neared the copse, something happened that gave me the opportunity I needed. A brace of pheasants, disturbed by our little procession, burst from the ditch in a flurry of dust and squawks and half ran, half flew down past the horses and cut right in front of Mrs. B. The children hanging on to her screamed and jumped out of the way. One of the pheasants panicked and took off, flying inches from Mrs. B's head. Seizing the opportunity, I ducked under the five-barred gate leading into the meadow and hid behind the hedge.

To this day, I don't know how Mrs. B didn't miss me. Everyone complained she had eyes in the back of her head, but she must have been so hot and flustered that she forgot about me. Peeking out, I saw her scrambling up into the float which had stopped for her. Squeezing amongst the little ones, she sat against the wooden back support, took out her hanky and fanned her red and perspiring face.

I waited until the expedition was out of sight before I slipped out from my hiding place and ran back down the lane to Normanhurst. The stable-yard gates were shut, and I wasn't tall enough to see through the upright iron rungs at the top, so I tried the arched wooden door that opened from the shrubbery path into the lane. It wasn't locked. Peeking through a crack, I made sure no-one was around before opening it just wide enough to squeeze through. Seconds later, I was across the garden, up the steps and through the side door leading to the cloakroom. I hid on the wooden shoe lockers under the back stairs, until I was sure I was alone. There wasn't a sound. The place was deserted. I sat for a few minutes, to catch my breath and decide what to do next. Where would they keep a prisoner? Definitely not in the house, it was too quiet.

I was trying hard to think of suitable places to hide a prisoner, when a terrible and earsplitting noise made me tremble all over. Screams that went on and on and on. I jammed my hands over my ears but I could still hear them. It was a shrieking like I'd never heard before. Then I had to tear my hands from my ears and tuck them between my legs. I was going to wet my knickers. The lavatory was only a few steps away, across the cloakroom. I *had* to go.

The awful squealing stopped as suddenly as it had begun. Now the only sound I could hear was my heart thumping in my ears. Nothing else. I took a deep breath and dashed across the small space and locked myself in the loo. Whatever it was, it couldn't get me through a locked lavvy door.

While I was going, I thought about the noise and realised it had come from the yard. They'd got the prisoner in the barn, or the stables, or one of the outhouses. He was being tortured. Or maybe murdered already, now that the screaming had stopped. Finished, I put the seat cover down and climbed up to look out of the little window facing the yard. But the glass was all nobbly and frosted so although I saw shapes of people moving around out there, I couldn't see what they were doing. *"So now what?"*

Careful not to make a sound, I unlocked the door and poked my head out. Silence. Still no-one in the house. Then I had an idea. The window on the landing where the back stairs turned, overlooked the yard. From there, I would be able to see what was going on, and no-one outside would see me hiding behind the lace curtain.

I was wearing my cousin Rachel's cast-off Startrite summer sandals with sorbo soles so even if there *was* anyone in the house, they wouldn't hear me. Stair by stair, I crept up to the small landing. Through the lace curtain, I would be able to see everything that was happening in the yard below. They were not hiding in the barn. Whatever they were doing, it was out in the open in the middle of the yard. Not really wanting to look, but knowing that I must, I lifted aside a couple of inches of lace curtain. I looked straight out onto a nightmare. I froze, transfixed by what I saw.

Blood was streaming over the cobblestones and lying in puddles everywhere. Mr. B in Wellington boots and an old Mackintosh was hosing it away. Another man, a stranger, wearing a pair of white overalls that looked as though they had been spattered with red paint, held a huge and ugly-looking knife. My stomach heaved with horror as I realized the red paint was more blood. Then I saw and understood the savagery of the crime.

Lying on his back, his stiff legs pointing straight up, was Hamlet—a huge gash in his throat. In front of the terrible, gaping red hole, was a white bucket full of more blood. Bits of flesh dangled from the slash and every few seconds, one of the stiff legs twitched. Then the blood-spattered stranger and Mr. B each grabbed hold of one of Hamlet's back legs and started to drag him across the scarlet tinted puddles of water that lay in the hollows and dips of the cobblestone yard. They were heading towards the barn. I had seen enough.

I screamed and banged on the window. Mr. B looked up and a horri-fied expression spread over his face as he realised what I had seen. He called out to me. He dropped Hamlet's leg and said something to the bloody man. I turned and ran down the stairs and out the side door. Where to go? I could hear Mr. B's heavy footsteps running towards the wooden door between the stable-yard and the side garden. I dashed through the side garden and took a flying leap into the yew tree. I'd climbed that tree so many times and knew exactly where the footholds were. Holding my breath, I crouched on the branch that hung out over the wall. By the time Mr. B crashed open the yard door, I was invisible. He never stopped calling me, "Pat-a-cake, Pat-a-cake. Where are you? Pat-a-cake, Pat-a-cake!" Echoes were everywhere.

He looked around, ran to the side gate—where I'd come in—opened it and looked out. He looked up and down the lane while I watched from above. Then he turned back towards the house, tearing off his wet, bloodstained Macintosh as he ran. He hopped first on one leg and then the other as he pulled off each boot, then leaped the steps and through the side door. That was my chance. I dropped down onto a brick support buttress about a foot from the top of the wall. It was shaped like a triangle with the sloping side leading down to the grass verge below. In my non-slip Startrites, it was easy to run down its full length and into the lane. I turned left, past the gated entrance way and out to the main road. I could still hear Mr. B calling my name. I hesitated only for an instant, before I turned in the direction of Bridgnorth and ran—and ran—and ran.

I was going home to Wales.

11

I dared not stop. I raced past the thick holly hedge behind the Kindergarten room. Past the high sandstone brick wall at the end of the kitchen garden, where the big black board with gold lettering hung; proudly proclaiming the merits of Normanhurst Preparatory School. Past the hawthorn hedge—still trailing streamers of honeysuckle and wild roses—that bordered the orchard. Finally, when I was beyond the school boundaries, and amongst the cottages of Eardington village, I had to stop running. Not only did I think I was far enough away from Mr. B to feel safe, but I had a stitch in my side and was out of breath. Besides, two boys on bicycles looked at me rather strangely as they passed. Now ahead of me, their bicycles wobbled as they looked back over their shoulders. Then their attention was caught by a tractor that drove out of a lane beside them, and I took the opportunity to slip into the next driveway. A tall tree against the hedge formed a little nook that hid me from the road and from anyone who might be looking out from the house it belonged to. I rubbed my side to ease the stitch and wished I had a drink.

My rest didn't last long. A lady came out of the house and, although she wouldn't have seen me, a dog came running out after her. Pattering this way and that, with its nose to the ground, I knew it would soon sniff me out and start barking; just the way Gatsby always sniffed us out when we played Hide-and-Seek and gave us away. Not taking any chances, I ducked out of the hiding place and back onto the road. The tractor and the boys on bicycles were nowhere in sight, so I felt safe. I decided to walk as though I was supposed to be there, and not running away from school.

I knew the way to Bridgnorth. And I knew how far it was. We'd walked to church many times and I'd been taken there in the wagonette or the float on special outings. Without warning, memories of the trip to the market with Mr. and Mrs. B flooded back. That was the time we brought Hamlet home as a snuffling, squawking live pig. A lump choked the back of my throat and the tears started streaming down my cheeks.

Now I was walking down the hill where the road had been cut through the sandstone cliffs high above the river. Rough steps had been cut in the rock leading up to an old stone 'squeeze-me' stile. I climbed up, squeezed through it and dropped down into a ditch full of long grass and tall fronds of cow-parsley. I sat for a while and thought of the awful things I'd seen. The bucket of blood, the man with the long cruel knife, and Hamlet with the long, gaping slash in his neck, his staring eyes and his poor twitching legs. And Mr.....

"How could he? How could he **do** *that to Hamlet?"*

By now I couldn't stop the tears. I lay and sobbed until the flattened grass under my cheek was sodden with tears and criss-crossed with trails of snot. How long I lay there crying I don't know but, without warning, I started to heave. I scrambled to my knees and emptied the contents of my tummy into the ditch.

Eventually it was over; the heaving and the crying. I moved away from the stink of my sick and groped for my hanky. Luckily I had a clean one in my blazer pocket, and an almost clean one up my knicker leg. I wiped my eyes, blew my nose and scrubbed at my face. I hadn't sicked-up on my clothes, but I had a sour taste in my mouth and I longed for a drink. There was no water, but clusters of blackberries hung on the bramble hedge above me, so I clambered up and picked some. They were sweet and juicy and, as my tummy welcomed them, I knew I wouldn't sick them up. After eating a handful, there were enough left to fill my clean hanky. I knotted the corners together to form a little sack, remembering how Dilly had always done this when we'd collected treasures during our walks in Wales.

"I wish Dilly could be here with me now. It's difficult looking after myself."

But she wasn't, and I had to get on with my journey. I'd gone too far to turn back. Besides, I would never, ever return to that terrible place of death again. And I never wanted to see Mr. B again as long as I lived. I used the ditch as a loo before squeezing back through the stile.

Back on the road again, and swinging my parcel of blackberries, I walked the last mile into the Low Town area of Bridgnorth on the banks of the River Severn and where, Miss Audrey-Joan had once told us, people had lived since before the Romans came.

Now I had to find the station. I remembered what it looked like, but couldn't remember how to get to it. I wandered around, trying to recognise something from when I was there last summer. But then it had been so different. Mr. B had taken Ann-the-Bank and me straight to the station and put us on the train. I knew I had to go up into High Town and that the cable railway would take me there, but I couldn't find that either. Besides, I would need money for that. As I wandered up and down the streets, people stared at me. I wondered if it was because I was dirty, but I saw other children who were dirty too.

Round the next corner, I saw a little cobblestone square between two rows of shops. Wooden benches were set around it, and in the middle was a horse-trough fed by an old hand pump. Two boys were swinging on the pump handle, then ducking their heads to drink from the stream of water that gushed out. Water!

Two years at Normanhurst had taught me pretty well how to fend for myself, so I didn't think twice about going up to the pump. The boys stopped pumping and stood back, looking me up and down and grinning.

I put down my hanky bag of blackberries and grabbed the pump handle. I pulled but it was stiff and hardly moved an inch. I swung on it trying to drag it down.

The boys watched me as I struggled. Their grins got bigger. The older boy nudged the smaller one and they came towards me.

"Want some water then, do you?"

"Yes, please."

"Oh. Yes, please is it, then?"

"Yes, please."

He stuck his hands in his pockets and started whistling–still staring at me.

"I have some blackberries. I'll swap." I opened my hanky. It worked. They took three each, yanked on the pump handle and a stream of sparkling cold water flooded over my face and into my mouth. I gulped it down. Wiping my mouth on the knot of my blackberry bag, I asked, "Where's the station?"

They pointed towards the hill that wound up behind the square. I thanked them, gave them another blackberry each and set off in the direction they'd shown me. As soon as I found the station, I remembered it, and knew what to do. There was a train already at the platform. I asked a porter if it was going to Wales.

"No Missee. Not this 'un. This 'un be going to Birmingham."

I didn't want to go to Birmingham, that's where the Germans were bombing people.

"There's a train leavin' at four o'clock that'll take you to Wales. But you'll have to change at Craven Arms."

I thanked him and wandered up and down the platform, looking in carriage windows and at the piles of interesting boxes and luggage, ready to be loaded onto the train. The big double doors to the luggage van were open and the guard was talking to a tall, and very elegant lady, and a very short man dressed in old riding breeches and a tweed jacket. They were searching for something. At least, the short man was searching while the lady was pointing her black walking cane at a pile of stuff and giving orders. I went closer to see what she was looking for. She saw me, but went on giving orders. Then she spun around to face me, so abruptly, it made me jump back. "And where are you off to young lady?"

"I'm going to Wales."

"Wales, eh. My, my. Well, this train doesn't go to Wales. It goes to Birmingham."

"I know, the porter told me that. So I'm waiting for one that goes to Wales. It goes at four o'clock and I have to change at Craven Arms." I added this information so she would think I was very well organized.

The Tall Lady didn't say anything for a while. She turned back to see whether the guard and the little man had found her parcel. Then, without warning, she pounced on me again.

"And whereabouts in Wales would you be going?"

"Llanwyrted Wells."

"And what's in Llanwyrted Wells that you have to go there?"

"My mother. And Dilly...and...my mother...." I looked down at my shoes.

"And where have you come from?" asked the Tall Lady.

"F-from..." I didn't know what to say. I didn't want to say anything, but the Tall Lady was staring at me, her head on one side, waiting for an answer.

"From where? Come on, gel. Surely, you can tell me where you've come from. You know where you're going, so you must be intelligent enough to know where you've come from." She looked at me up and down. "Even if you are a little small to be travelling on your own."

"I've done it before. Twice. The first time was when I went home for Christmas. And last summer I went...to Wales, t-to my mother...and my father was there too...for a week. When he was on leave from the war."

"Ah, I see."

She broke off and turned back to the short man as he picked up two big parcels the guard had pulled from the back of the van. "Are those the ones Roagey?"

"That they are, Ma'am."

"Good. Get them loaded up if you please. And where are you off to young lady? Wales?" She had her back to me so I don't know how she saw me tiptoeing away.

"Y-yes."

"Well, before you go, is there any message for Miss Baker?"

I froze. How could she possibly know? And how did she know Miss Baker?

"Well, I take it you're from Normanhurst." She turned and poked her cane at my blazer pocket. "You should have worn something other than your school uniform if you were going to run away, Missee."

I'd dressed for the picnic in a pair of old grey pleated shorts and a white Aertex shirt, but had worn my school blazer over the top. I didn't know what to say. Or do. I couldn't run. There was no train to jump on except one going to Birmingham, and I didn't want to go there. I sniffed and scuffed my foot at a tiny clover growing through the paving.

The Tall Lady sighed. "Come," she commanded and pointed her cane at a platform bench underneath a sign where the name 'Bridgnorth' had been blacked out. The flowerbed behind it was full of cabbages but, here and there, a bright marigold shone through the crinkly sea of green. She poked her stick at the bench again, indicating that I should sit beside her. The short man had obviously stowed his parcels and was coming towards us.

"Roagey. See if you can find a drink from somewhere and take..." She fumbled in an oversized black handbag and produced a large man's handkerchief, perfectly folded and ironed.

"...take this and get it dampened down."

The short man looked at me and nodded, "Roagey-Mac at your service, Miss."

"Yes, yes, Roagey. That's enough, thank you. Please get that hanky nice and damp. And perhaps a drink of water."

"On the double, Ma'am. On the double." He trotted off in the direction of the station booking hall.

The Tall Lady planted her cane between her black-booted feet, her hands on the handle. Resting her chin on her hands, she sucked in her breath then blew it out slowly. Turning her head so her cheek now rested where her chin had been, she looked at me. She grinned.

"Now, first of all I have to know to whom I am speaking. What is your name?"

"Patricia."

"So, Miss Patricia, what happened that forced you to make this sudden decision to go home to Wales?"

She didn't say 'run away' and for that I was grateful. I didn't answer her at first but, encouraged by her friendly grin and her willingness to listen, I thought she might understand. So I told her what had happened. Slowly at first, afraid she might laugh at me when I told her about the midnight conversation I'd overheard, the funny feeling that something terrible was going to happen, and how I had to go back and find out. She looked very serious when I told her of my suspicions that they might be holding, perhaps torturing or, worse, murdering, a German spy. But she just nodded. When I got to the bit about seeing Hamlet with that great gash in his throat, his poor twitching legs, the rivers of bloody water, and that awful white bucket full of blood, I felt the hot stinging tears in my eyes. My throat closed up and I couldn't say any more. I just sat there and sobbed.

She let me cry for a while. When I stopped crying and looked at her, I could see by the look on her face that she understood.

"Good grief, child. And this was your pet pig?"

"Well, not exactly mine, but I was with Mr. B when he bought Hamlet at the market, and he told me I could name it and be its friend. Hamlet liked me to scratch his back. And I used to feed him sometimes. And... and...I think he liked me because he always came to greet me when I went to his sty."

"Good grief. No wonder you ran. You've never seen an animal butchered before?"

"Noooo," I started crying again and this time I couldn't stop.

"Hey, hey, now. Hold up, child. Hold up here. You have to stop blubbering or people will think I'm pinching you. Anyway, here's Roagey. Let me clean you up and have a drink."

I turned to her and tried to stop crying. She wiped my face with the big wet hanky and gave me the glass of water Roagey-Mac had brought." Is this all you could find Roagey? "I think what we need is a good strong cuppa."

"Yes Ma'am. Well there's a wee caff of sorts and I'm sure they 'ave tea but you know what station tea's like Ma'am. Strong enough to stand the spoon up in, so 'tis."

"Maybe that's just what we all need."

I leaned towards the Tall Lady's ear. "I have to go to the loo."

"I'll bet you do. Come child we will find the loo and a good cup of tea. That should put the ginger back into you. Roagey, please organise tea for all of us. You must join us and give us your views on the little problem we have here."

The Tall Lady produced a penny for the loo. Inside she cleaned up more of me, using the red Lifebuoy soap from the station wash-basin. Not only did she wash my hands and face, but scrubbed my knees that were stained with grass and blackberry juice. She produced a comb from her big black handbag, and combed my hair. She also found two Kirby Grips which she criss-crossed in my hair to hold it off my face. When I was cleaned up to her satisfaction, we went back to the waiting room where, on an oilcloth covered table, Roagey-Mac had laid out three steaming cups of tea, and a plate of sticky buns.

In spite of the sterilised milk, the tea tasted so good, especially as it was sweetened with real sugar instead of saccharine. The sticky bun was stodgy but fresh, and I counted six currants in it. No one spoke until I had finished the whole thing, tea and all. I licked my fingers and the Tall Lady didn't say a word. Neither did Roagey-Mac, but he winked at me.

The Tall Lady finally spoke. "So tell me. Do you have your train ticket to Wales?"

I wriggled in my chair and looked down at my plate. There were still a few crumbs of sticky bun left and I started pressing them onto my finger. I didn't know what to say.

The Tall Lady sighed. "Well, let's try another question then. Do you have enough money to purchase a ticket to Wales?"

I shook my head.

"Then how in the world did you propose to get there?"

"I don't know." I looked up at her–she was obviously waiting for an answer. Roagey-Mac gave me another encouraging wink.

"When I ran out, all I could think of was Hamlet."

"Hamlet?" Roagey asked.

"That was his name. My pig's name. Hamlet. All I could see was the blood and Hamlet lying there with his legs stuck straight up in the air, and that great hole in his throat was all quivery. And the blood. There was blood everywhere. I just ran and ran and it wasn't until I was here in Bridgnorth, that I decided to go home. I really want to see my mother."

"Hmm. I see."

The Tall Lady and Roagey-Mac were looking at each other. I could see they were thinking what to do with me.

"Are you going to take me back to school?"

"Well, young lady, Wales is a very long way away and you don't have any money for the ticket. Of course, I could buy you a ticket and put you on a train, but suppose your mother isn't there? What would you do the other end? After all, she's not expecting you, is she?"

"No. But..."

"But what?"

"I don't know. I suppose I'll have to go back. But Miss Baker will punish me dreadfully and I'll be sent to Coventry. Or maybe expelled," I added hopefully. "Then I'd go home to my mother anyway."

The Tall Lady sighed again. Her finger under my chin, she turned my head so I had nowhere to look but straight into her eyes. They were the brightest blue eyes I'd ever seen. "You know, Patricia, your parents sent you away to Normanhurst because they wanted you to be somewhere safe during the war, and where you would learn your lessons. And *I* think, if you went home, they would probably just send you right back."

I turned my head away to avoid her gaze. But I knew she was right.

"Besides, your Daddy must be away fighting."

"Yes, ma'am."

"Well, don't you think he wants to believe that you are being a good girl and learning your lessons? Wouldn't he be very disappointed to find out you'd run away?"

I wriggled uncomfortably. I didn't want the Tall Lady to know I'd run away before. "Yes ma'am."

"Now this is also what I'm thinking. I don't think you really planned to run away from school. I think you just ran from what you saw had happened to your pig...er...to Hamlet. The sight of a murder most foul shocked you, and you had to get away from that dreadful spectacle. I am quite convinced that, had I seen such a sight when I was just...what are you? Nine years old?"

"Eight, ma'am. I was eight in June."

"Eight, eh? Well, I think that experience was more than enough to send an eight-year-old flying. What do you say Roagey? Don't you think that was a lot for someone to stomach who was eight in June?"

"Yes indeedy, ma'am. I can't imagine anyone I know that's just eight, 'aving to come across such a murderous and grisly sight. Murder it was, ma'am. Murder of a pet too. Shame if you asks me."

"Yes, yes, Roagey. But you know, we have to explain to this young gel here, perhaps why Hamlet was, er...shall we say, sacrificed?"

I pricked up my ears. Sacrificed! Now that was something I hadn't thought of. Perhaps Mr. B and that other man were Druids and they were making a sacrifice. But why Hamlet? "Sacrifice? To what?" I was whispering now.

The Tall Lady nodded at Roagey. He leaned towards me across the table.

"It's like this, little missee. There's not a doubt that this 'ere war is a wicked enough thing, so it is. People are sent away from 'ome. Dads have to go away and fight. An' lotsa folk are bombed out, so they are.

And it's very difficult to find enough food for everybody. That's why we 'ave Victory gardens, and grow cabbages, like on the platform here. We have to raise all our own food. An' 'specially at a school like yours where there's lots o' nippers to feed. That's why they probably 'ave hens and ducks, and a big kitchen garden. Am I right, missee?"

I nodded. "We have hens, so we get lots of eggs. But no ducks. There is a huge walled garden where Mr. B grows vegetables to feed us. And we have our own Victory gardens and grow lettuce and radishes so that we all eat our own too. And we share what we grow."

"Right you are. And do you ever 'ave chicken to eat?"

"Sometimes."

"So sometimes p'raps one of them 'ens is sacrificed so you can 'ave a Sunday dinner?"

I hadn't thought of that, but I remembered that once I saw a lot of feathers in a big sack in the back kitchen. Mrs. B said she was going to stuff pillows with them.

"S'right missee. Now then..." Roagey stopped talking and looked up at the Tall Lady, who nodded. "Well, now missee. As for those eggs the 'ens lay. Don't you sometimes 'ave bacon with your eggs?"

I nodded. "Once. At Christmas."

"Well, when they bought the little pig wot was your friend, they... um...they acksherly bought it to fatten up for bacon. And p'raps some nice joints of pork for the winter."

I slumped back in my chair. I didn't know what to think. Hamlet? We were going to be eating Hamlet in the winter time? *Oh, no!* I felt like crying again.

The Tall Lady sat up in her chair and took my hand in hers. "Now come on, little gel. Patricia. You know by now, we all have to make sacrifices for the war effort. I'm quite sure that if Hamlet knew he was sacrificed to feed hungry children, he would be quite happy about it."

"Do you think so?"

"I'm sure of it. Now come along. It's getting late and the train for Wales is long gone. Roagey and I will take you back to Normanhurst in my barouche before they send out the Home Guard to look for you. They must be worried sick, wondering where you've got to. Come, child.

Everything is going to be fine. And I'm sure Miss Baker will understand once I've explained it all to her.

The Tall Lady's barouche turned out to be an old fashioned landau in spanking condition. Black, with a coat of arms painted in gold and green on the door panel, and red leather upholstery. The drive back in this wonderful old-fashioned carriage, with the short man called Roagey at the reins, was much better than walking all the way on my own. However, my tummy sank again when the familiar walls came into sight. And when we stopped at the front door, the red-framed glass eyes stared at me; a warning of what was to come.

Roagey was lifting me down from the carriage when the doors were flung open and Miss Audrey-Joan leaped out onto the front porch. "Where on earth have you been child? Patricia what on earth possessed you to...?" Then, seeing the Tall Lady, she stopped. "Why this is a surprise Lady H. What...?"

"May we go inside for a few minutes and I'll explain?" The Tall Lady asked calmly.

"Of course. Patricia, get inside and sit on the chair outside my study. I'll deal with you later."

Miss Audrey-Joan showed the Tall Lady into her study and the door closed behind them. I could hear them talking, so I slipped off the chair and put my ear to the keyhole. I couldn't hear much–just a few words like, "shock", "blood", and "pet." And then, "only eight years old"...and "she was on her way to her mother in Wales." There was more quiet talking and then I heard the Tall Lady say, quite loudly, "But she's only eight for God's sake. And away from her parents for so long..." And Miss Audrey-Joan's voice, "I know, but she's been here two years now... it's not the first time...and we do have younger...she went home last summer...they all miss their parents." Then there was silence and I skipped back to the chair, just in time. The door opened and they both came out.

"Good bye Patricia. I'm sure everything will be just fine." The Tall Lady smiled at me.

"Good bye ma'am. And thank you for the tea and the sticky bun."

When she had gone, there was just Miss Audrey-Joan and me left in the hallway. I slid off the chair and stood in front of her. Neither of us spoke. She pointed, indicating I should go into her study. She sat behind her desk–I stood in front of her. There was a long silence; then: "What am I going to do with you Patricia? Do you know, I very nearly sent for your mother again?"

"Oh. Gosh. Then if I'd gone to Wales, she wouldn't have been there."

"That's right. What on earth possessed you to leave the picnic party in Thatcher's Woods. When I found you missing, we searched the woods for hours thinking you'd had an accident."

I hadn't thought of that.

"I-I don't know. I just had a feeling that I had to come back. That...I don't know. I just wanted to come back." I didn't want to tell her I'd eavesdropped on her midnight conversation with Mr. B.

Miss Audrey-Joan shook her head. "What am I going to do with you?"

"Give me the cane?" I suggested. "But not Coventry. Oh, please don't send me to Coventry."

"I could give you a caning but..." She paused and seemed to be considering what to do with me. "Sending you to Coventry during holidays is not the answer either."

She sighed and sat back in her chair, all the while looking at me and tapping first one end of her fountain pen and then the other, against the blotter. Finally she leaned forward.

"Oh gosh. What has she decided to do to me?"

"Well, seeing that you like writing, you can give up your riding time tomorrow and write an essay on why you should obey the rules and not run away from picnics. Or from school. And you can describe how much trouble and worry you have caused all of us; and especially Mr. Baker. All of the staff were worried and spent the day searching for you. We were at our wits end wondering what had happened to you. Now you'd better go and find Mrs. Baker and tell her you need a bath, some tea and then straight to bed."

"Yes Miss Baker."

I turned and walked down the hallway, past where the wooden floor turned into flagstones by the kitchen door, to the back stairs. Then I stopped. Not for the world could I go up those stairs and pass the window looking out on to the stable-yard. I turned back. Miss Audrey-Joan stood in the hall, watching me.

"Please. Please, Miss Baker. I can't." Tears, once more, came running down my cheeks. I couldn't talk for sobbing.

Miss Audrey-Joan strode down the hall. She sat on the stairs and turned me round to face her, wiped my eyes with her hanky and took my hand. "It's all right now. There's nothing to see. I'll come with you."

Slowly we went up the stairs together. When we got to the half-way landing, I shut my eyes tight. We stopped.

"Open your eyes. And look outside. I promise there is nothing there"

I opened my eyes just a slit, and looked through my lashes. Sun glinted on the cobblestones. There was no blood. I opened my eyes a little wider. Everything looked normal. Except...except, lying in the hollows and dips of the cobbles, were a few puddles of water. Just water puddles. No blood. No Hamlet. Just a few puddles.

But it hadn't rained all day.

I swallowed hard and looked up at Miss Audrey-Joan.

"Where's Hamlet?"

"He's gone. He's not here."

"He was a sacrifice?" I whispered.

"Yes, I suppose he was." Miss Audrey-Joan sounded surprised. "Yes, in a way, I suppose he was."

I awoke screaming. In the darkness of the blackout I could see rivers of bright red blood. They were flowing towards me and I couldn't get away. Blood lapped around my shoes, staining my white socks. I screamed and screamed.

There was a rush of feet and strong arms picked me out of bed. They carried me from the attic dormitory and down the stairs to the first floor. I could see the night-lamps flickering, sending leaping shadows onto the walls as we passed. More scurrying feet, low voices, questions and answers.

"What's the matter?"

"It's all right. It's all right."

Then I was in this huge comfy bed and snuggled in amongst soft feather pillows that smelled of lavender. Someone snuggled down beside me and held me close. I sobbed and sobbed. "Shhh. It's all right.

You're quite safe now. Go to sleep, little one." Miss Audrey-Joan stroked my hair and rocked me in her arms until I fell asleep.

The last thing I heard before I fell asleep was, "I'm so sorry you saw that. So very sorry."

When the getting-up bell woke me I was in my own dormitory bed and sunbeams were peeking around the blackout. I could feel the familiar warmth of a cat stretched across my feet. I knew that as soon as I got up I would have to answer a million questions from the other children as to where I had been. But it didn't matter for I knew what I was going to tell them. That it was just another adventure. And it was secret. Of course I had an essay to write for Miss Audrey-Joan. But somehow that didn't matter either.

An hour later, the essay almost finished, an odd thought struck me. The Tall Lady had never told me her name. And Miss Audrey-Joan never mentioned it either. It would have been nice to write and thank her, but she's gone now. And I would probably never see her again.

But it would be a long, long time before those rivers of blood were lost in the mists of my memory.

Chapter 27

The New Boy

There were a few new children on the first day of the Autumn Term, 1942. Only one of them was in our form and he was the most incredible, amazing and excellent person; and his name was Antony. I stood next to him in the sweet queue and while we were getting our sweets out, he was putting his in. He showed me his tin—inside were millions of chocolate drops.

"How did you get all those? They're rationed."

"My daddy works at Cadbury's and he brings home the chocolate that doesn't turn out right. They've all got little dents or holes in them. Take a look."

Antony shoved the tin under my nose and I could see what he meant. Some of the chocolate drops had bumps, or tiny holes and some were not quite round. The smell of chocolate made me feel giddy.

"Do you want some?" Antony asked when I'd dragged my head out of chocolate heaven.

"Oh, yes. Um…oh, please. And thank you very much."

"Have you got something to put them in?"

I was standing in line and my little bluebird toffee tin–with half a Mars Bar and two humbugs in it–was sitting on the top shelf of the sweet cupboard.

"My pocket?"

"They'll melt. Have you got a hanky?"

I pulled a handkerchief from my sleeve. It was very dirty as the day before I'd used it to clean Henry VIII after he'd crawled through a mud puddle.

Antony looked at it and wrinkled his nose. "Don't you have a clean one?"

"Oh, gosh, yes. I forgot. I've a clean one in my knickers pocket." I hitched up my skirt and pulled out the handkerchief, still ironed into a neat square.

"Open it up," Antony instructed..

We squatted down and I laid the hanky on the floor between the other children in the queue. Antony tipped up his tin and poured a pile of chocolate drops on to it. I folded the corners in over the pile.

"Where are you going to put it?" Antony asked.

"Back in my knickers pocket of course. No one will see it there."

I stood up and searched the queue for Ann-the-Bank. She'd come back from Wales in a bossy mood and I knew that if she'd seen Antony give me the chocolate, she would tell on us. Luckily she was further down the line and had her back to me. I ducked down to Antony again.

"They'll melt there too, silly," said Antony. "Here, I'll make it into a bag for you."

He quickly tied the corners together, then, with the ends, made a tiny handle which he slipped over my finger.

"There. Now if you hold your hand—so . . ." He adjusted my fingers over the precious parcel. "Then they'll think you're just holding your hanky." He smiled at me again.

"Will you be my friend?" he asked. "I'm new and I don't know anybody here."

"Of course I'll be your friend. And I will never-never-ever tell on you when you're bad. Never-ever. Cross-my-heart-and-hope-to-die." I licked my finger, made an 'X' over my chest and held out my hand.

Antony looked up to see if anyone was watching, but they were too eager to get to their sweet tins to take any notice of us squatting on the floor. He touched my hand quickly then jumped to his feet. I followed.

"But you don't have to give me chocolate to be your friend," I said. "I like you, even without the chocolate."

Antony smiled, "I'd have given you the chocolate anyway. I can always get more. By the way," he went on. "All my friends call me Ant so if you're my friend you should too."

"All right. Ant it is, then."

It was our turn next in the sweet queue.

"Why isn't your daddy fighting in the war?" I asked.

Ant and I were searching for Henry VIII–I'd forgotten to tie him up and he'd wandered. I knew pretty well where to find him. There was a patch of ground at the back of the stables that nobody ever bothered with, wild spinach and sorrel grew there and an elderberry tree hung over a crumbling stone wall. Henry liked that little patch. He would lose himself in it for days and do nothing but munch on juicy wild salads, and sleep. Ant was turning a pile of last year's leaves with his foot and I was poking around in the long grasses and stinging nettles with a stick.

"'Cause he fought in the Great War and now he's doing an important job making sure that the soldiers, sailors and airmen get enough food to eat. And chocolate."

"So why are you here and not at home with your parents?"

"Because the Cadbury factory is in Bournville, a part of Birmingham, and the Jerries keep bombing it. So they sent me here, and my sister to Cheltenham Ladies College. She's older."

"My Daddy's entered me for the Alice Ottley School in Worcester when the war is over."

"I'll be going to Bromsgrove."

"Bromsgrove?" I squeaked.

"Yes," he answered. "It's a family tradition."

"My daddy teaches at Bromsgrove when he isn't being a soldier," I said.

"Whizzo. So we can go on being friends forever."

I thought about that. I really liked the idea but couldn't think of anything to say. Finally I said, "So we can go on doing things together then?"

"Of course. Forever. Hey, here's Henry. My, but he's dirty. C'mon, let's bath him in the rainwater barrel."

Dear Cedric,

I have a new best friend called Antony but I call him Ant. Ann-the-Bank is still my friend and you were my best friend when you were here all the time. Ant is very good at thinking up games and he wants to be my best friend forever. So now you will be my very best friend.

I told him about you and he said your ship was probably sunk by a German torpedo. He knows all about those things, especially aeroplanes.

Do you mind if I share Merlin's lair with him? It's lonely in there without you, although I thought I saw you there once when I fell asleep under the tree. I told Ant it was a special place and he promised not to tell. Maybe his arm is long enough to find your Allie.

With love from your very best friend,

Pat.

Chapter 28

Off with Her Head

About a month after Hamlet's sacrifice, I woke up with a horrible tooth-ache. I was still on my very best behaviour and paying careful attention to my lessons and my manners; I knew that Miss Audrey-Joan, Mrs. B and Mrs. Tommy were watching me.

Ann-the-Bank tugged at my bed covers. "Come ON. Get out of bed. We can't be late for breakfast, I can smell the porridge burning all the way up here."

Mrs. B was a jolly good cook, but at breakfast she was too busy doing other things, such as cutting the bread or making the tea, and kept for-getting to watch the porridge. She burnt it at least twice a week and if we weren't one of the first down and got a ladle-full off the top, we got the bitter burned stuff from the bottom.

"I can't," I wailed. "I've got terrible toothache."

"Don't be daft. You can't have toothache."

"Well I *do*." I wriggled up from my warm tent of bedclothes and glared at her.

"Oooh. Your face is all swollen up. Like you've a plum stuck in your cheek."

Now that *did* get me out of bed. Ignoring the cold floor under my bare feet, I dashed to the bathroom across the landing and looked at my face in the mirror. Sure enough, there was a lump on the side of my face exactly like Ann said; I had a plum stuck in my cheek.

Ann had followed me. "Does it hurt?"

"Of course it hurts, silly." I shot her a dirty look. "Owww," I wailed again. It hurt even more when I yelled.

"I'll go and get Mrs. B." And off she sped.

A thick fog outside made the house dismal and damp. I shivered and climbed back into bed. I didn't feel like breakfast anyway and if Mrs. B was coming to see me, then the porridge would be burned beyond hope. It wasn't long before I heard the heavy slow footsteps as Mrs. B landed on the top floor. She always started off up the stairs at a run, but by the time she got to the third floor she slowed down. I could hear her breathing hard as she stumped along the corridor.

"So what's our excuse for lying in bed today, Miss Patricia?"

The bed gave mightily as Mrs. B sat on it. She pulled my covers back. "Miss Ann said you have a poorly tooth."

I turned my head and looked at her full in the face, saying nothing.

"Humph. I can see that you do. How poorly is it?"

"*Very* poorly," I mumbled. "It hurts a lot."

I knew it was no use piling on the agony. Mrs. B had an uncanny knack for recognising malingerers and try-ons from the real thing. We both knew this was the real thing. She was quite gentle as she opened my mouth and inspected my top teeth. She lifted the corner of my upper lip with her little finger to get a better look. I winced. She let my face go and humphed again. "Come down to the bathroom, and I'll give you an Aspirin. That may ease it a little."

Considering that I was still in a lot of trouble and disgrace for running away, Mrs. B was quite friendly and kind about the whole thing. I followed her downstairs to the second floor bathroom, where she unlocked the medicine cabinet and gave me an Aspirin. I gulped it down with water from the bathroom tap.

"You'd better go and climb back into bed," she said. "Let the Aspirin do its job. After breakfast I'll make arrangements to take you to the dentist in Bridgnorth. Mind you, with all the trouble you've caused, maybe we'll just get your head chopped off. That would solve the tooth problem." She returned to her breakfast duties, leaving me to go back upstairs and into bed. I didn't mind. Tristan was curled up in the middle of my eiderdown and I had the new Arthur Ransome book under my pillow. At least I would miss Mrs. Riley's Algebra lesson.

Mrs. B's suggestion about getting my head chopped off echoed in my mind. We'd been learning in History lessons that a lot of people had their heads chopped off, sometimes for very silly reasons. Henry VIII chopped Ann Boleyn's head off just because he didn't want her. Now she's supposed to walk the Bloody Tower with her head tucked underneath her arm–or so the song goes. Besides, they would have to ask my mother and father first—and *they* certainly wouldn't let anyone chop off my head. I was sure of that. I heard the bell go for prayers and the start of lessons. I snuggled down under my covers and thought about the others doing Algebra, which made me feel a little better. I hated Algebra.

The mid-morning break bell had gone and everyone was outside playing when Mrs. B climbed the stairs again. "Well, missy. Get dressed and come down to the kitchen where it's warm. We have to get the one o'clock bus into Bridgnorth in time for your appointment at two."

"Yes, Mrs. Baker."

"And wear your warm jumper. It's still quite cold and damp outside."

I did as I was told. In the kitchen Mrs. B and the daily help, Mrs Evans, were preparing the midday dinner. It smelled good—like onions cooking. Miss Audrey-Joan sat at the table having her elevenses. "What you will do to miss Algebra," she smiled as she said it, but her face became serious when she saw my swollen jaw. "My, but that *does* look painful. Must be an abscess."

"What's that?" I asked.

"It's like the boils you children sometimes get on your legs and arms. But it's inside your gum, right by the root of your tooth. That's why they're called gumboils."

"I told her that maybe we should cure it by chopping off her head," said Mrs. B. "That way she won't have to worry about gumboils, or Algebra, ever again. It would cure her of running away too."

"Now that's an idea," Miss Audrey-Joan smiled. "Perhaps we should arrange it."

I said nothing. Why all this talk about chopping off my head? I put my hand around the back of my neck. My hair was straggling; I hadn't pushed in enough Kirby Grips to hold it."

Miss Audrey-Joan pulled me towards her. "Come here, Pat. Let me plait your hair for you. Have you got ribbons?"

"No, Miss Baker."

"But you did have some. Pretty green and white check that your mother sent."

"I lost them. My hair is so slippery they slide off. I may have one somewhere upstairs."

"There's some coloured binding tape in that top drawer." Mrs. B. nodded her head towards the Welsh dresser. "I'm sure there's some dark green that will do."

There was a comb in the drawer too, so Miss Audrey-Joan combed and plaited my hair. She twisted rubber bands around the ends and covered them with flat bows of green tape. "Now, you look really neat and clean." Her eyes crinkled up at the corners as she gave me a big smile.

Mrs. Baker set a plate of toast and Marmite, and a cup of tea in front of me.

"I can't eat anything. My mouth hurts too much."

Mrs. B nodded and moved the plate aside. "Try the tea," she suggested. One sip was all I could manage.

The bell went for the end of break and Miss Audrey-Joan tipped her chair back, stretched and yawned. "I'd better be getting back to class. You were happy to miss Algebra Pat, but the next lesson is History. William the Conqueror and the Norman invasion this week. You'd enjoy that. You'll have to catch up when your tooth is taken care of."

"When they've chopped off her head, you mean." Mrs. B was laughing; she thought it a huge joke. "Only way to cure it. Off with her head." She mimicked the Red Queen from *Alice in Wonderland*, "Off with her head!"

She went into the back kitchen to help Mrs Evans peel potatoes and carrots. I left my seat at the kitchen table, and settled into the rocking chair in the corner. It was covered with an old patchwork quilt. Mrs. B liked to sit in there while she was waiting for a cake to bake. The fog had lifted and an autumn sun streamed in the large window above the sink. On the opposite wall, the big round clock tick-tocked, its black second hand jerking with each tick and tock.

There was a clatter and a slither in the corridor, and Antony slid to a stop at the kitchen door. "What are you doing here?" he demanded.

I looked up and he gasped as he saw my face. "Coo-er. That's a whopper. What've you got in there?"

"A bad tooth. I have to go to the dentitht." Now I was finding it difficult to talk properly.

"I hear they're going to chop your head off. To get rid of your toothache AND you!" He grinned.

I threw a piece of my uneaten toast at him, "You're a bit uppity for a new boy."

Thanks," he grinned again, picked up the toast and disappeared back up the stone flagged corridor.

"Who was that?" Mrs. B bustled back into the kitchen carrying a massive black saucepan full of peeled and cut potatoes.

"Just one of the boys. He ran past."

"And just where did he think he was going, I wonder."

"I don't know. I didn't see."

"Humph." Mrs. B opened one of the heavy Aga covers and slammed the saucepan down. The stove hissed as water slopped over onto the hot surface. "Well," she said. "You'd better go and get your coat and outdoor shoes on. It's nearly time to go."

"Yes, Mrs. Baker."

"And wear your scarf and gloves. You will have to have your face wrapped up to come back. I don't want you catching a cold."

"What if they chop off my head? I won't need it then. And I won't get a cold."

Mrs. B clamped her lips together and glared at me. "All right, Miss Smart-Knickers. Suppose we have to use the scarf to *tie* your head back on. What then? Eh?"

I knew Mrs. B well enough to know when to stop. I jumped off the rocking chair, and headed towards the cloakroom. There was no sign of Ant, but Ann-the-Bank came creeping down the back stairs. "Haven't you gone yet?" she whispered.

"What are you doing out of class?"

"Going to the loo."

"Well I'm going to Bridgnorth soon. Mithith B ith taking me on the busth."

Ann sniffed. "You always get the fun. How do you manage it?"

"It'sth not fun having a toothache. It really hurtsth. And I can't eat or drink."

Now dressed in my outdoor clothes, I slid the striped woolly scarf I'd finally finished knitting, off my coat peg and pulled a pair of gloves from my locker. Then, turning my back on Ann, I returned to the warm kitchen. I could hear her sniffing as she went back up the stairs.

Mrs. B and I landed at the kitchen door at the same time. She marched in, and I trailed behind her. Almost immediately, the back kitchen door opened and I could hear the familiar sound of Mr. B stamping his welly-boots on the mat. He came through to the front kitchen. I turned away. I still couldn't bring myself to talk to him; not after what he did to Hamlet.

"Well hello there, Pat-a-cake. What are we all dressed up for?"

Mrs. B answered for me, so I was spared the agony of having to speak to him. "We're just about to catch the mid-day bus. Your Miss Pat-a-cake here, has a raging toothache so I'm taking her to the dentist."

"I have to go into town, Edwina. My big rake has broken and I want to see if Joe the Blacksmith can mend it for me. If he can't, I'll have to get a new one."

"That would help and save a lot of time. We're ready, so hitch Dolly up to the wagonette and we can get going."

Ten minutes later, we were all tucked up in the wagonette on our way to Bridgnorth, our gas masks over our shoulders; Mrs. B balancing her big black handbag on her lap.

"That's a big bulge you have in your jaw, Pat-a-cake." Mr. B looked over his shoulder at me. "So what d'you think they are going to do to you?"

"Chop off her head," Mrs. B answered for me again. "That will put an end to her running away and fix her toothache at the same time."

"Oh dear. Drastic measures indeed." Mr. B clicked his tongue and Dolly kept up a sharp trot through Eardington village and along the Bridgnorth road.

I recognised all the places I'd passed only a few short weeks ago. We drove through the deep cut in the sandstone rock, below which the River Severn swirled muddied waters from last night's rain. When we came to the rough cut steps in the rock leading to the 'squeeze-me' stile, I glanced up; blackberries still hung there, black and luscious, and glinting in the sunlight.

Then it was all downhill into the Low Town. We turned sharp left, past the pump where I had swapped the blackberries for a drink of water, and Dolly climbed the now familiar hill into High Town. When we reached the black and white half-timbered Town Hall, Mr. B pulled Dolly to a stop.

"Take her to the dentist," he said. "I'll go to the blacksmith and meet you back up here in, say, an hour?"

"That should be time enough to fix her Ladyship." Mrs. B got out of the wagonette and held my hand as I jumped down. I still hadn't spoken to Mr. B, but I looked back, and he turned and waved before urging Dolly into the traffic.

We went down a narrow street opposite St. Leonard's church. Half way down, Mrs. B stopped on the pavement and waited for traffic to pass so we could cross to the other side. "There it is," she said, pointing. "There's the dentist's office, right opposite."

I looked across the street. There was a small flower shop. Above it, was a big window on which was printed, in large flowing gold script,

*'Headly and Sharpe,
Barristers, Solicitors and Executors of . . .'*

I didn't read any further. I just opened my mouth and screamed. *"THEY REALLY WERE GOING TO CUT MY HEAD OFF."*

I wrenched my hand out of Mrs. B's grasp and started running back down the street. I hadn't gone a dozen steps before I ran slap bang into Mr. B. He caught me and held me. "Hey! Steady on! What's all this? Whatever is the matter now?"

I was screaming and trembling from head to toe and pain shot all up one side of my face, right into my head. "D-don't let them d-do it. Pleasth don't let them ch-chop my head off." I was begging now.

Mrs. Baker came running up to us. "Whatever is the fuss about?"

"I don't know," said Mr. B. "For the life of me I can't fathom this child out. She's talking about having her head chopped off."

"What are you doing here anyway? You said you were going to Joe the Blacksmith's."

"You left your handbag in the wagonette. I turned right around to get it to you before you went into the dentist's office."

Now I was shaking. I was really and truly frightened. Passers by were staring at me. Staring at all of us.

Close by, was a small stone bench set into an alcove in the church wall. Mr. B went over, sat down and took me on his lap. Mrs. B sat beside us. She mopped her forehead with her hanky and heaved a big sigh, she was obviously vexed with me. "Now once and for all, Patricia, stop this ridiculous display and tell us what is wrong. It's no good being afraid of going to the dentist, and it won't get better on its own. You have to have it seen to."

"I...I d-don't want to have my head chopped off. I promith I won't be bad any more. Croth-my-heart-and-hope-to...d-die."

"Chopped off? What on earth...?"

Mr. B looked over my head at Mrs. B. She shrugged her shoulders. "What gave you that idea? Was it because I said that we should chop off your head?"

I nodded.

"Surely, you have more sense than that? You couldn't possibly think..." Her voice trailed off helplessly.

I sniffed and swallowed. "But it sayth *executors* over there on the window. Where you were taking me. Pleasth don't have them do it. I'm not that bad. Truthfully."

"Well, I'll be..." Mr. B coughed and his shoulders shook. "You can't possibly believe we'd have your head chopped off, now do you?"

I could only shake my head.

Mr. B went on. "You know that word is *exec*utors, not exec*utors*. Besides, you're thinking of *executioners*. Executors are people that see to settling estates and wills and things when people.... when people need them done. For their families. Besides," he added, "that's not the dentist's office. It's a solicitor's office. The dentist is next to the flower shop. The one with the blue curtains. Come, let me show you."

I walked across the street between Mr. and Mrs. B, one hand in each of theirs, and up to a porch recess. On the white painted pillar was a brass plate which read:

Dr. Hugh Welborn
Dental Surgeon

The recess led to a big oak door with a brass knocker and latched handle. Mrs. B lifted the latch and we walked in. I hung back, and slid behind Mr. B. He turned and squatted down on his heels until his face was level with mine.

"Pat-a-cake. I know you find it hard to forgive me for taking Hamlet away from you and we will have to talk about it some time. But for now, believe me, you have to be a brave girl and let the dentist mend your tooth. It will probably hurt a little, that's to be expected. But I know you are a brave little girl and will make us all proud of you. And I promise, cross-my-heart-and-hope-to-die, that no one is going to chop off your head. Ever. I won't let them. All right?"

Mr. B licked his finger and made an 'X' over his chest.

I nodded. Mrs. B took me by the hand and led me to a desk where an older lady sat knitting. "Young Miss Mashiter to see Dr. Welborn."

The lady put down her knitting and smiled at me. "My you have got a lump, haven't you? The doctor will soon put that right. Now let's see. What treatment should we suggest do you think? Pull out the tooth, or chop off your head?"

My knees felt weak. Mr. B slapped his hand to his forehead and Mrs. B gave the biggest hurumph I'd ever heard.

I stuck my chin in the air.

"No oneth going to chop MY head off." I glared at her, "Mithter B wouldn't allow it."

When it was all over, Mr. B carried me out to the wagonette and laid me across Mrs. B's lap where she wrapped me in a blanket. The dentist had given me something called laughing-gas, but it didn't make me laugh, just put me to sleep. When I awoke, I still had a lump in my cheek but it was from a wad of gauze that was jammed into a hole where my tooth had been. I held another piece of gauze in my hand in which Dr. Welborn had wrapped the tooth. My legs felt wobbly and I couldn't stand up, but I couldn't feel any pain in my face either. Mr. B climbed up into the driver's seat and clicked Dolly into a trot.

"Home now, Pat-a-cake. Home we go."

The September sun was warm on my face, as Mrs. B wrapped my scarf around my neck and over my mouth. Snuggled in the blanket on Mrs. B's lap, my last thought before I fell asleep was that it wasn't holding my head back on. And I wouldn't have to walk around with it tucked under my arm like Ann Boleyn, after all.

Sunday, 20th September, 1942.
Dear Mummy and Daddy,
I had to have a tooth out as I had a nabsess and my face swelled up. It hurt a lot and I couldn't talk properly. I had to miss Algebra.
Mrs. Baker made some jelly and junket just for me.
Please will you send me some more hair ribbon as I'm not getting my head chopped off.
With love from
your daughter Patricia, who is glad her name isn't Ann Boleyn.

Chapter 29

Letters from Home

8th October, 1942
My dearest Pooh!
What a dreadful thing to have an abscessed tooth. They are
so painful. I'm sure you were a brave little girl at the dentist.
I have decided to stay with your Aunt Addie in Westmorland.
Daddy is now in command of the Castle in Carlisle, which is
quite close and so when he has a twenty-four hour leave, he
can be here in an hour. We are packing up in Wales and I will
be gone next week.
Dilys has decided to stay in Wales. She is going into the Land
Army and will be working on a farm close by that is owned by
John-the-Post's family. She is looking forward to it.
I am enclosing a packet of stamped envelopes, already
addressed to me in Westmorland, but be sure to put the new
address in your address book and perhaps you could include
a note to your Aunt occasionally. She loves to hear from you.
With lots of love,
Mummy

10th October, 1942

My Dear Patty,

Your mummy will have told you that I am staying in Wales and so I won't be with her when you see her again.

I will miss you lots but I am sure that after the war, we will all spend some holidays together. You will always be family to me. As you know, I was an orphan and as I have been with you since you were a baby, I regard you as my special family.

I have left that red glass vase you always liked so much, as a gift for you to remember me by.

With fondest love and memories,

Yrs. Respectfully

Dilly.

P.S. If you want to write to me, send it c/o the Post Office, Llanwyrted Wells, Breconshire and John-the-Post will see I get it. I don't know my new address yet.

I could hear the letters crackle in my overall pocked as I squeezed onto the three-legged stool beside the Aga. Tristan rubbed his soft head against my shins, then looked up at me—his whiskers tickling my knees. I had told Ann-the-Bank, Ant and the others I was going to look for a book. I took the letters out of my pocket, unfolded them and smoothed them out on my lap. I had read them both so many times.

"Where was everybody going? The war was taking everyone away from me."

The familiar prickling started in my nose, and my throat closed. I didn't want to cry, but the tears were gathering. They spilled over and Tristan flicked his head as one dropped on his furry face. That was how Miss Audrey-Joan found me a few minutes later.

"Oh my goodness gracious, Pat." She squatted down on the floor beside me. "Whatever is the matter now?"

I didn't answer. I didn't know what to say. She got up, pulled one of the wooden kitchen chairs closer to me, and sat down. I handed her the letters to read. She read them quickly and in silence. Then she folded them and handed them back to me.

"How far is Westmorland?" I asked.

Miss Audrey-Joan sighed. "Quite a long way, I'm afraid. But it's very safe up there and your mother will be happier living nearer to your father. Wales was very isolated, you know."

"I liked Wales. But that's not why I'm sad." The tears had started to fall again, and I was sobbing now. "It's D-Dilly. Sh-she's gone into the L-land Army. She's l-left me."

Miss Audrey-Joan leaned forward, picked me up and set me on her lap. She took a hanky out of her skirt pocket and wiped my eyes. "I know it's hard for you to understand. But I expect Dilly got called up and she chose the Land Army. She has to do that, you know. Everyone has a part to play in our effort to win this war."

I tried to stop crying, but it was difficult. Everything just seemed *so* sad. "It's not only Dilly, and Mummy, but...but..." I started wailing again. "I d-don't have a home any more. I can't even remember what my real home looked like. I want to go hoooome."

Miss Audrey-Joan hugged me close, and rocked me back and forth while I cried. She said nothing—just let me cry.

Finally, when I felt as though my throat was on fire and my head was aching, I just laid my head against her and she mopped my face with her hanky. "You have to think of Normanhurst as your home now," she said gently. "And all the children as your family. And Mr. and Mrs. Baker, Miss Primrose, Mrs. Tommy and, and.... well, we're all your family for the duration of the war. And when the war is over, your mummy and daddy will take you back with them. You'll see. You will have a lovely home again, with your own family."

I nodded, but it didn't seem the same. She went on, talking softly and rocking me. "The other children, who are full boarders here, also have to think of Normanhurst as their home."

"Ann-the-Bank can go back home to Wales," I said. "And now I can't."

"True. But Antony can't go to Birmingham either. Although it's closer than Wales, there are still too many raids there. And the City of Coventry, which is close to Birmingham, was completely demolished. Coventry was one of the first cities to be bombed in 1940."

"Who by?"

"By the German Luftwaffe with their big bombers. Even Coventry Cathedral was reduced to rubble. That's why Nathan and Natalie Robbins stay here. They lived in Coventry and their home has completely disappeared. Bombed. Nothing left. So you are lucky in one way. You will have a home to go back to."

She pushed my hair back from my wet cheeks. "So, Pat. Try and think that your home is *here* until the war's over. We've grown to love all our children here, and we think we are lucky having such a large and lovely family." She smiled, and her eyes crinkled at the corners. "Besides, there's one good thing about your mother leaving Wales."

"What's that?"

"You won't be getting into trouble for running away to Wales any more, will you?" She grinned and hugged me tight.

But, instead of smiling, I hung my head and whispered, "No, Miss Baker. I promise I won't run away again. Ever."

"That's good news." Miss Audrey-Joan plopped me back on my stool and walked over to the pantry. She came back with a jug of milk and the biscuit tin.

"Here, let's have a little something to make us feel better." She poured two glasses of milk and opened the biscuit tin. "Oh, look, Pat, we have a treat in here—Mrs. Tommy's special cocoa oat cakes. Miss Audrey-Joan took out four, gave me two, and started munching on hers. The smell of chocolate made me feel a little better.

I could hear running along the grey flagstone hallway outside the kitchen; Ant slithered to a stop when he saw me. "Hey. Where've you.... what're you eating?" His words faded to silence when he saw Miss Audrey-Joan come out of the pantry, after putting the milk jug back.

"Come on in Antony," said Miss Audrey-Joan. "You're just in time, before I put the biscuit tin back." She gave him two of the cocoa cakes, then turned to leave us. "Stay here, until you've finished your cakes. I don't want the whole school chasing me for Mrs. Tommy's treats. Then go back to the dining-hall and play with the others. It's nearly time for bed anyway."

Ant sat, pushing against a table leg with his foot so he could tip his chair back and forth. He stopped, leaned forward and peered at me. His left eyebrow, shot up to disappear under a fall of black hair. "You been blubbing? You have! What happened to make you blub?"

I told him about the letters, and that I didn't have a home in Wales any more. Or in Bromsgrove, for that matter.

"You silly sausage. Lots of people don't have homes any more. They've been bombed out."

I told him about Dilly going into the Land Army and my mother going to Westmorland. "I don't even have a family any more." I could feel the tears start to prick my nose again.

"Silly sausage," he said again. "This is our home, for a while anyway. And it can be quite fun. Besides," he added. "You can always come home with me and be my sister. I don't like the one I've got—she's too old." He grinned. I brushed at the unshed tears and grinned back.

I picked up his empty glass. "I think we should wash these."

We went into the back kitchen and carefully washed them and left them upside down on the draining board.

"After all, this was my home now, and I had to help keep it neat and tidy."

18th October, 1942
Dear Mummy and Daddy,
Thank you for your letters and the parcel. I hope you like it in Westmorland. I am sad that Dilly is going into the Land Army. Miss Baker says that Normanhurst can be my home until the War is over. So now I have some brothers and sisters. But they are not all nice.
With love from your almost homeless daughter,
Patricia

25th October, 1942
Dear Dilly,
Thank you for giving me the red vase. I will keep it forever. I am sorry you are leaving our family, but I hope you enjoy the Land Army. Do you have to wear that uniform with the green jumper?

Please say 'Bura da' to John-the-Post, he is very nice.
With love from
Patty XXX

Chapter 30

Rowley Smythe

It started off as just another autumn day. I remember because it was a Friday, the day before Hallowe'en, 1942. The sun was shining and we scuffed up the dry, dead leaves, looking for conkers. Apart from hopscotch, the most popular outdoor game at that moment, was a conker contest.

"You know, it's not fair." Ant was scrabbling through the leaves at the base of one of the giant chestnuts down by the entrance gates.

"What isn't?" I was hunkered down with my back against the tree, watching and waiting to point if I saw a big one.

"The dailies get their mothers to boil their conkers in vinegar. That way they're harder and always smash ours to smithereens."

"Maybe if we find a couple of really good ones, I could ask Mr. B to harden them."

Ant's left eyebrow arched upwards, as he looked at me. "Really? He would do that?"

"Well, he might. He's got lots of stuff in the shed that would make conkers hard. Stuff like varnish, or paint."

"You can't paint conkers. The others would notice and you'd be banned from playing."

"Well, p'raps he could boil them for you. I'll ask him. I wonder if we'll go to Thatcher's Woods this weekend. We'd find some super conkers there."

Any more searching was stopped by the bell for lessons. We all traipsed in, changed our shoes and went up the back stairs to our classroom.

Miss Audrey-Joan wasn't there. Usually, she was hurrying us into our seats. So we sat at our desks and waited. Ant read a *Beano* comic he'd hidden in his desk, and I started to draw a sketch of a horse; I liked drawing horses, they were my favourite things right now. Arabella Bosworthy pulled a copy of *Film Star* out of her satchel that had a photo of Margaret Lockwood on the front. Ann-the-Bank had her desk lid up and was doing something secret. And Giles Farmer was busy making paper pellets to flick at us from the end of his ruler. It was then that I noticed Rowley Smythe's desk was empty. "Where's Rowley?" I asked.

Everyone turned to look.

"Prob'ly emptying his pockets in the boys' lavvy," said Giles.

"Well he's getting into trouble wherever he is," said Arabella. "Let's send him to Coventry again." Rowley was always getting sent to Coventry, just because nobody wanted to get near him and his smelly pockets.

"Ouch," said Ant. Giles had managed to hit him in the back of the neck with one of his pellets. "Fains you do that again." Ant lurched out of his seat and was just about to fling himself on Giles, when Miss Audrey-Joan came in the room.

"That will do, children. Seat please, Antony."

"She stood with her back to us for a while, gazing into the small fireplace where a wet log sizzled and popped as the flames tried to catch it alight. Then she hunched up her shoulders and let out a big sigh before straightening up and turning to face us. "Children, I want you to sit very quietly and listen to what I have to say. It's important, and very sad."

At the word "sad," we sat up very straight in our seats. All eyes and ears were on her.

"Children, the sad news came today that Rowley Smythe's father... er...Rowley's daddy, has been killed whilst fighting in the war. He was serving in North Africa, in the desert, and...and, tragically, he was killed. Right now, Rowley's mummy is here to tell him."

It was hard to understand. I hadn't even thought about Rowley having a daddy, and certainly not a daddy who was fighting the war in North Africa. No-one made a sound. I dropped my head; in my lap my fingers traced the square patterns on my green and white check overall.

"Poor skinny, red-haired, red-nosed Rowley. Rowley, who hated to eat anything white. I remembered the first day I was at Normanhurst, and I saw him stuffing his porridge into his pockets. Poor Rowley, who never told us he had a Daddy who was fighting in the war.'

Miss Audrey-Joan broke the silence. She said, "Do you all know where North Africa is?" She walked over to the world map hanging from the picture rail. She pointed to the top part of Africa. "There are some places in North Africa where fighting has been going on for many months. Places like Alexandria, Tobruk..." The tip of her yellow wooden ruler touched tiny black dots. Then it swept in little circles all over the top of Africa. "It's called the Middle East," she went on. "And here is a place called Alamein where there is..." She paused and looked around at us. "Where there's some very heavy fighting going on right now. Rowley's daddy fought with The Eighth Army there. He was with a unit called 'The Desert Rats.'"

Giles Farmer snickered through his nose, and Miss Audrey-Joan threw him a look that should have turned him to stone.

"Rowley will go home with his mother for a few days, but when he comes back, I want you to be much nicer to him than you usually are. He will be a very sad little boy for a while, and we must all do what we can to help him through this."

Rowley came back the following Monday. He looked even smaller and paler than ever. He hardly spoke to anyone; just kept to himself. In break times, he would go into a corner—whether it was outdoors or indoors—and sit all alone. We tried to be nice to him and asked him to join in our games, but he just shook his head and sniffed. He went home every weekend now; his mother lived only an hour away, in Kidderminster, and she'd decided that Rowley would be a weekly.

Rowley went on stuffing his food into his pockets, but nobody said anything to him. And when Mrs. B caught him doing it, she just sighed and shook her head. "What's the use of saying anything to him," I heard her say. "He's never going to change."

After his daddy was killed, I never saw Rowley smile again–well, just once. And that was when Giles Farmer fell out of a tree and broke his arm.

1st November, 1942.

Dear Mummy and Daddy,

I hope you are well. I'm glad Daddy is in Carlisle and not North Africa.

I got a gold star for my music lesson this week. Mrs. B says I play very nicely. I will play better when my feet can reach the pedals.

With love from your musical daughter,

Patricia

Chapter 31

Just Another Christmas

There were twelve of us who had to stay at school for Christmas. The weeks leading up to the holiday were mostly the same as the year before. Rehearsing the Nativity play, collecting acorns, oak-apples and beech masts from Thatcher's woods, and turning them into gifts for our families and our special friends at school. On the last day before the holiday, there was a Christmas party feast for which chocolate and sugar, hoarded by Mrs. B and Mrs. Tommy, had been turned into treats—the like of which we never saw again during the coming year. Under the tall Christmas tree—topped with it's star of Bethlehem—little packages mysteriously appeared; the pile getting higher as Christmas came closer. Even though the dailies and weeklies took their presents home the day before Christmas Eve, there was still a big pile left.

Ant went home for Christmas. He'd asked his mother if I could go to his house for Christmas but when I wrote to ask my mother's permission, she had replied that she didn't really want me to spend time in Birmingham because of the air raids. Another disappointment; but I was used to disappointments by now. After all, I was eight-and-a-half years old.

We had fun. At half-term, all those who couldn't go home, had helped Mrs. Tommy and Mrs. B stir up the Christmas puddings. Odd-shaped packages from Mrs. B's pantry appeared; in them we found raisins, figs, currants, and dried orange peel. We helped by taking the stones out of prunes and cutting them up, measuring and weighing the ingredients on the heavy kitchen scales with its pile of big round weights and—when we thought the grown-ups weren't looking—we dipped our fingers in the brown sugar and the black treacle, and slipped a few raisins into our overall pockets. Where Mrs. B got all the stuff from, she wouldn't tell. Even Miss Audrey-Joan was surprised at her hoard of baking supplies. But one day, just after I'd had my tooth taken out, I was sitting in my corner by the Aga, when there was a knock at the back door. I peeked out to see who it was and I recognized the little man called Roagey-Mac belonging to the Tall Lady who brought me back from the station the day I'd run away. He had a large willow basket covered with a red and white chequered tea towel, which he handed to Mrs. B. He also gave her four dead rabbits hanging from a string. After she'd put everything away in the cold, red-tiled pantry, she caught me watching her. She put her fingers to her lips and said, "Shhh. Hear no evil, see no evil and definitely speak no evil, Miss Patricia."

I nodded and grinned. It was the first time Mrs. B had shared a secret with me, so when she smiled back at me and winked, a happy feeling came over me. I then understood what Mr. B meant when he'd said that, "Edwina B's bark is worse than her bite."...even though I'd seen the bite part when she spanked someone, or put them in the corner, for being naughty. She could be a fearsome person at times.

With Christmas came the cold winds and sharp frosts. We huddled down in our beds, all of which now crackled with newspapers layered between the thin blankets. On Christmas Eve, Mr. B hauled in piles of logs and in every fireplace, cheery fires burned that evening and the whole of Christmas day. We went to the village church on Christmas Day so we didn't have to walk far. Dinner was delicious, we even had a turkey—which I'm sure came in another willow basket covered with a red and white chequered tea towel. Stuffed with bread, onions and the sweet chestnuts we'd gathered from Thatcher's woods, and smothered in gravy, it was a feast. The plum puddings were slathered in thick custard and there was even a mince pie each to finish off.

At three o'clock in the afternoon, we listened to the King speak. He told us that the War would not be over for a while, but that he was proud of every British man, woman and child who were all helping with the war effort. After that, Miss Audrey-Joan read us *A Christmas*

Carol by Charles Dickens and when evening came, we played games. Miss Audrey-Joan and Mrs. Tommy did some magic poker writing and showed us a game, called The Spirit Moves—which was another magic trick. Mrs. Tommy went out of the room and had to shout out the name of the person on whom Miss Audrey-Joan had made the Christmas Spirit rest. And she got it right every time.

We all had parcels from home. Book-tokens and postal-orders from my aunts and uncles and a new knitted jumper from my mother. All of us received a gift from the staff. I had ribbons and slides for my hair from Mrs. B, a new music book of Chopin preludes from Miss Audrey-Joan, and a tiny brooch in the shape of a butterfly from Miss Primrose. Mrs. Tommy gave me a silver bangle she'd got when she was in India before the war. Under the tree, there was a very lumpy parcel from Ant. Inside was a *papier maché* cat, painted black and white to look like Tristan; he must have made it in the boys' handwork class with Mr. B.

Snow fell on Boxing Day and we spent the rest of the holidays playing in it, making snowmen and sledding. New Year's Day, 1943 passed, and lessons started again. The winter dragged on, either very cold, or very wet; it seemed never-ending, especially during Lent. The only bright thing that happened was that a new girl came after Christmas. She was a weely and her name was Janet Kennedy. She took private dancing lessons on the weekends, not ballet, but tap and jazz. We thought that was absolutely stupendous. She said she was going to be a film star when she grew up. She sang the latest songs that we never got to hear at school. She taught us all Vera Lynn's songs, and some American ones too, like *Mairsydoats and Doeseydoats*. So we spent the long winter weekends dressing up and performing "jazz" concerts—just the way Janet showed us. All us girls were totally stage struck and would bribe the dailies to bring us film magazines.

And so another dark winter passed, and it was Easter again, with the promise of another summer. There was more to do in the summer, and more trouble to get into.

14th March, 1943.
Dear Mummy and Daddy,

Thank you for your letters and the parcel. It was nice of Auntie Addie to make me some flapjacks.
Please will you send me some Drene Shampoo, and a pair of tap-dancing shoes
With love from
Patricia

4th April, 1943.
Dear Mummy and Daddy,
Thank you for the shampoo and the dancing shoes. It doesn't matter that they were Aunty Addie's when she was a little girl. They fit me and look very nice. Miss Primrose calls them flapper shoes.
I have enclosed a letter to Aunty Addie to thank her.
With love from your dancing daughter,
Patricia

Chapter 32

The Black Death

Miss Audrey-Joan Baker, B.A. (Hons.) was a Classicist. From that description one might deduce that she was a highly intelligent and learned person. She was. One might also deduce she was a dedicated and proficient teacher.

Correct.

And, all things considered, one might deduce that her class of six- to ten-year-olds, would fidget, fret, look out the window and do anything to avoid learning by rote, long passages of Latin prose or the dates of the Kings and Queens of England.

Incorrect.

Miss Audrey-Joan's History and Classics lessons were a joy. Everyone— well almost everyone—loved them. After reading out loud all the facts and figures of a particular period in History, and drawing the inevitable diagrams, pictures and strategic battle patterns on the blackboard, her next question was always, "Now who wants to be the king?" (Or the queen? Or the archbishop? Or the princes in the tower?)

In the Classics, it was who wants to be Odysseus, or Helen of Troy, or Caesar, or Cleopatra? Out would come the dressing-up trunks. We would don robes of velvet and satin, or white togas and sandals, or crowns of stiff gold paper stuck all over with 'gems,' then pick up our swords and go into battle. It was usually a battle although occasionally, there was a more dramatic event to portray; such as the arrest and trial of Guy Fawkes, or the beheading of Mary Queen of Scots. I can remember distinctly, being mounted on Dolly—sidesaddle of course—dressed overall in gigantic hoop, ruff, and velvet cape; a pearl looped on my forehead below a ferocious red wig, and yelling across the tennis court at assorted Elizabethan sailors leaning against a cardboard man'o war,

"I know I have the body of a weak and feeble woman, but I have the heart and stomach of a king. And a king of England too."

And that was a story in itself.

Before I went to bed, I studied the pictures of Queen Elizabeth in my History book. She looked magnificent in her jewelled gowns, and huge ruffs. It was the picture of her riding to Tilbury to give the famous speech that we were to enact the next day, that really caught my eye. There was something so different about the picture and about how I was going to portray the Virgin Queen. *She* was riding a white palfrey, and *I* was riding black old Dolly. Something needed to be done about that. I put on my thinking cap.

I sat up in bed, "Alana, are you still awake?"

A sleepy, "Yes. What do you want?" came from Alana.

"I'll do your stable chores in the morning."

"Why?"

"'Cause I have to get Dolly ready for the play about Queen Elizabeth."

"What d'you have to do?"

"Just see she's properly groomed, and I want to decorate her bridle."

"I'll help."

That didn't really fit in with my plans. "It's alright. I can manage."

"No," Alana was insistent. She loved Dolly as much as I did. "Please let me help. I really want to."

"Alright, but you must do everything I tell you."

"I will. I promise."

Ann-the-Bank was stirring. "Who's talking?" She grumbled sleepily? "I'll fetch Mrs. B."

"No, you won't," I snapped back. "Shut up and go to sleep."

Mrs. B tiptoed in and woke Alana at six o'clock to get up for her stable chores. Alana woke me. We dressed and scooted out to the stable; we had a lot of work to do.

While Alana mucked out the stalls and fed the horses, I went hunting through the shed next to the barn. There was a myriad of exciting and unusual things in there, including just what I needed; a tub of white-wash powder that Mr. B used to whitewash the inside walls of the stables. I dumped some in a bucket, mixed it with water, found two big brushes, and took it all back to the stables. Alana had just finished putting down fresh straw for the horses; Dolly was happily munching on her breakfast.

"Here," I instructed Alana. "Take a brush and get going."

Alana picked up a brush. "Doing what?"

"I'll show you." I took the other brush and dipped it in the bucket. With careful strokes, I daubed the whitewash on Dolly's hind-quarters.

"See," I said, "It's easy. But you can only go one way—downwards. Otherwise her coat'll stick up, and that won't do. She has to look like a virgin queen's palfrey."

"You can't do that," Alana protested. "We'll get into awful trouble."

"Don't worry. I won't say you helped. It was my idea. And I'll give you a whole chocolate bar if you do it and don't tell. Well, they'll see it anyway, but I want it to be a surprise when we do the play this afternoon. You'll see—it'll be quite dry by then."

Alana grumbled a bit, but she dipped her brush in the bucket of whitewash and started painting Dolly's black coat. Dolly didn't seem to mind at all. She went on munching her breakfast as if having her coat painted happened every day.

With the two of us working at it, it didn't take long. Her tail had to be done really carefully so, while Alana held the bucket up, I dipped her whole tail into it. I just hoped she wouldn't flick it around too much before it dried. When Mrs. B shouted to us, " Girls! Five minutes to breakfast," we barely had time to get cleaned up in the girls' outside lavvy and change into our uniforms before the bell rang.

Alana didn't say a word. But she grinned at me all through morning lessons. I think she rather enjoyed the whole thing.

Before afternoon lessons, we all dressed up in our finery for the pageant. Everyone had their allotted tasks: putting up the scenery, sorting out acting positions and those who had speaking parts, having a last look over their lines. I wanted to make a fine entrance, so I picked up my hooped skirts and walked regally into the stable-yard. Mr. B was fixing Dolly up with the side-saddle, and the decorated bridle. He had his back to me. His head was down and his shoulders were shaking.

"Mr. B? What's the matter?"

He turned to face me. He was laughing so much, that tears were rolling down his cheeks. "What will you get up to next, Pat-a-cake?"

"Will I get into trouble?"

"Oh, no doubt about it. But I don't think it'll be the end of the world!"

Ant, who was all dressed up as Lord Robert Cecil, came up behind me. "Coo-er. What did you do?"

I didn't answer him. After all, Queen Elizabeth shouldn't be questioned like that by her secretary. All he was supposed to do, was carry her speech on a purple velvet cushion in case she forgot what to say. Still laughing, Mr. B hoisted me up into the saddle. I sat up very straight and queen-like, and gathered up the reins.

Ant looked up at me. "Actually, you look rather spiffing up there. And Dolly looks pretty spiffing too."

I gave him a regal smile, and rode my white palfrey out into the garden, towards the end of the tennis court where a royal canopy had been erected. As I expected, there were gasps from everyone. I ignored them. I manoeuvred Dolly into the right position, and delivered my rousing speech to my loyal British sailors. The sailors cheered and clambered around the man o' war, preparing to meet the Spanish Armada. The Spanish were hiding out under the weeping ash at the bottom of the garden waiting for the signal to sail out, and the battle to commence. It was only then, I dared to glance at Miss Audrey-Joan. She had her back to me, but her shoulders were shaking, just like Mr. B's. Miss Primrose, who was laughing fit to burst, called out, "Bravo!"

I didn't get into too much trouble. Just a talking-to by Miss Audrey-Joan about thinking before I did things. And, of course, I had to give Dolly a bath to get her coat black again.

It took two hours to clean all the whitewash off Dolly. Mr. B showed me how to do it and Alana helped—which I thought was nice of her. It didn't all come off and Dolly looked a bit stripy–rather like a faded zebra—for a few days. But she didn't seem to mind, and every time it rained she got a little cleaner.

With Miss Audrey-Joan's teaching, we became immersed in History from all times—British History of course, and the Ancient History of the Greeks and the Romans. And then there was Mythology too, Norse mythology with Woden and Thor, along with other battles fought against the Vikings. We were forever fighting glorious battles, and usually emerging triumphant. I think the only one that really bored me was the Wars of the Roses; they went on far too long—almost a whole winter term. We acted out important historical events with gusto and a dedication that, as Miss Primrose said, would have rivalled Olivier and Gielgud, although, undoubtedly, our talent needed a little polish. But not everything was so nice. I especially didn't like The Black Death and The Plague–they seemed to go on for centuries.

It was a hot summer day, when Miss Baker announced, "We are going to learn about the Plague and then the Fire of London. It all happened in a few short months, one very hot summer back in 1665."

So we all trooped out into the stable-yard for another history lesson.

"Now," said Miss Audrey-Joan. "We will all divide up into a families— a boy and a girl, and two children each. Then you will decide what trade you represent."

So spinners, bakers, butchers and candlestick-makers set up their little lean-to homes amongst the outhouses and barn, and the empty pig-sty. Those who didn't have a trade, pushed wheelbarrows around and called to the little families, "Bring out your dead!"

I didn't enjoy that nearly so much as being Queen Elizabeth. I didn't like looking at the empty pig-sty.

Besides, the whole thing reminded me that Cedric was dead, and that made me sad.

Sunday, 9th May, 1943
Dear Mummy and Daddy,
Thank you for your letters.
History is really interesting now. This week we learned all about the Plague, and the Black Death. In 1348 it started with black spots under the arms and spread up to London.
With love from,
Patricia

Chapter 33

Down the Rabbit Hole

We were half-way through a Geometry lesson when the air raid siren sounded. Geometry was only marginally worse than Algebra, and the whole class was bored, bored, bored. Giles Farmer was picking his piggy-nose and lining up the grubbies on the edge of his desk. I was drawing a horse in my scribbling book, hoping that Mrs. Riley—who was about as boring as Geometry—would think I was taking notes. At the same time, I was finding it difficult not to laugh at Antony's efforts to stick the end of one of Arabella Bosworthy's long blonde plaits into his ink well. Mrs. Riley was drawing an Isosceles triangle on the blackboard, and droning on and on about how important it was for us to get neat angles and straight, fine lines.

The loud wailing of the village siren, perched on a flat roof next to the Dog and Cock pub, made us all jump. Of course, we were used to Air Raid practices which were held once a month, but we were usually told when they were going to happen. The Chief Air Raid Warden for Eardington village, his ARP helmet perched on top of his head, would ride his rickety black bicycle up the gravel driveway, lean it against one of the tall porch pillars, and yank on the iron handle of front doorbell.

Whoever answered the door, was informed that there would be a practice air raid drill that day. It was really a test to make sure the siren still worked properly in case it was ever needed. At the same time, it reminded the villagers to make a quick check of where to find their gas masks, and to put fresh water jugs in their Anderson shelters or their cellars.

We were usually on break when he came, so when we saw him we would calculate which lesson would be interrupted that afternoon. It was never the same day, so the teachers couldn't change the timetable around and make us miss games instead of Mathematics. Besides, when it was a practice, the siren only wailed up and down three times. This time, it was different; Wailing Winnie went on and never stopped. This was a real Air Raid. This was the REAL THING.

Our gas masks were supposed to be with us at all times, but in the two-and-a-half years I'd been at Normanhurst, there had never, ever been a real air raid. We had, therefore, become a little careless and didn't carry our gas masks everywhere, all the time. We had them within reach, but not slung from our shoulders. When we went for break, we threw them in a heap close to where we were playing. When we had meals or were in class, they served as footstools. At night, we dangled them from the bed rails, or dropped them beside our shoes. And I never took mine with me when I went riding. I left it hanging on a nail in the stables and picked it up when I got back.

Chattering with excitement, we picked up our footstools, slung them across our shoulders and lined up, as we'd practised so many times. Ant, too busy peering out the window trying to catch a glimpse of an enemy aircraft, was last to get into line. If he'd had his way, he would have been up on the barn roof; the telescope his daddy gave him for his birthday sweeping the sky to catch the first glimpse of a Messerschmitt, or some other enemy plane. He could identify them all.

"Mister Antony. If you please. In line NOW. This is *not* a game."

"Yes, Mrs. Riley." Ant slipped into line behind me.

"Now children, all gas masks on. Quickly, quickly. Everyone put their gas masks on immediately. IMMEDIATELY."

Mrs. Riley pulled the black rubber straps of her gas mask down over the back of her head, then went up and down the line adjusting our giant insect-like face masks. Orderly and quietly, but totally unafraid (after all, were we not in the country and safe from all enemy bombing?) we marched down the back stairs, along the hallway to the kitchen and the door to the cellar known as Rabbit Hole Number One.

Rabbit Hole Number Two was the Anderson shelter built into a huge pit sunk beside the rubbish heap between the barn and the orchard.

We were just about to go down Rabbit Hole Number One, when Miss Audrey-Joan came rushing up. "Take these older ones to Rabbit Hole Number Two," she ordered, her voice strangely muffled through her gas mask. "I want Number One for the little ones. They're coming in from the Kindergarten room and the Anderson is too far."

So our straggly line, insect heads wagging, about turned and marched out across the back yard. Joining up with more straggly lines of children, coming from other lesson rooms, we headed towards the Anderson.

Ant was right behind me. "Whizzo," he said. Through the little window of his gas mask, I could see the excited gleam in his eyes. "We can hear more from this one."

It was Ant's dream to witness the downfall of the Jerrys, especially their Luftwaffe. He kept a scrap-book of newspaper pictures showing downed enemy aircraft, or aerial dogfights. He studied the illustrations of enemy aircraft printed on the backs of the comics his Daddy sent him every week, and could identify them all. A dog-eared copy of *Aircraft Recognition*—the Penguin Economy Series version—lived in his pocket. He spent Saturday mornings scanning the sky through his telescope or, if the sky was overcast, racing around with a toy Spitfire in one hand, and a German Me110 in the other; waging dogfights between the two. The enemy aircraft always ended up on the ground, its wheels in the air or its nose in a flowerbed, while a happy little Spitfire zoomed off to notch up another victory. Then, with the aid of a toy army lorry, some string and wind-up pulleys, he would salvage the enemy plane so it could be cleaned up to lose another battle.

Because Rabbit Hole Number Two, was mostly underground, it was a bit damp and smelly. In the winter, even with a couple of paraffin stoves, it was freezing cold. It was furnished with old wooden chairs and a couple of dilapidated Put-U-Up's, heaped with brown woollen government issue blankets. There was a tin trunk overflowing with books, jigsaw puzzles, and games of Ludo, Snakes and Ladders, and Tiddlywinks. In fact, anything that got too old and battered for use in the house, was relegated to one or other of the rabbit holes. Lined up on shelves were emergency supplies of tinned food, sweets and giant water-jugs.

This was a real air raid. Mrs. B looked worried and Mr. B, who had hurried from the kitchen garden to join us in the shelter, hustled us down the steps before clanging the metal door shut. He set about lighting the hurricane lamps, and handing out bright-beamed battery lamps and torches. Mrs. Riley set the chairs in an orderly circle and Miss Primrose, with Gatsby under her arm, directed her Upper-Two class to sit down at the far end of the long narrow room. Ant and I pushed past the others and he bagged two places on a Put-U-Up, while I grabbed two *Beano* comics, a film magazine with a picture of Vivien Leigh on the cover, and a bag of Jacks. Once we were settled, Mrs. B—who still looked a bit worried—told us we could take off our gas masks, but that we should be ready to put them back on in double-quick time if told to do so. Then she passed out some boiled sweets before pulling her knitting out of the huge carpet bag she always carried; wherever she was, it was never far away. She never sat idle, but was always busy, darning our socks, unpicking jumpers, or knitting socks for soldiers, sailors or airmen.

Miss Primrose wrapped her floor-length fox fur coat over her purple summer silk, and settled herself in an old armchair that looked as though it had been salvaged from the bonfire pile. When Gatsby had turned around three times on her lap before settling down to sleep, she held up her arms and shook them—her bangles jangling; we recognised the familiar request for quiet. Everyone stopped talking. "Now children, settle yourselves down and I will read to you. Who shall it be? Mr Dickens or Mr Ransome?"

"Arthur Ransome, Arthur Ransome." Everyone was shouting at once.

The bracelets tinkled again. "Tsk tsk," she tutted. "Oh, my children, where are your discerning tastes? Lack-a-day, lack-a-day." Miss Primrose, who always went on like that, placed a slender white hand to her brow and swept back her head in a dramatic disclaimer.

Everybody laughed. We were so used to Miss Primrose's dramatics and her teasing. We loved her dearly.

"Well, Mr Ransome it will have to be then. I suppose Mr Dickens is a little too..." She paused and looked at us. The smaller children were wide eyed, and some looked frightened. I saw Mr. B catch her glance and give a small nod. Miss Primrose leaned forward and stretched out her arms as if she would gather us all into her protective clasp. "Well then. Arthur Ransome does spin an exciting yarn, and I'm sure the little ones will enjoy him just as much as the older ones do."

Miss Primrose adjusted her butterfly-shaped spectacles and opened *Swallows and Amazons*. While we sat huddled in blankets, our faces strangely shadowed in the thin, flickering light of the emergency lamps, she made–with her own special dramatic flair—the adventures of John, Susan, Roger and Titty come alive. Miss Primrose read on through the first three chapters, and all the while, as a menacing accompaniment, we could hear the monotonous wailing of the air raid siren.

Suddenly, a new noise filtered through the air vents from above-ground. Ant dug a sharp elbow into my ribs. "Listen. A dog fight." He wriggled in excitement and cocked an ear towards the steps. "No wait. There's just one plane." He raised his voice, "That sounds like a Messerschmitt and it's coming closer."

"How do you know it's a Jerry plane?" Giles Farmer challenged. "It just sounds like an engine or something outside."

"I can tell by the engine noise," replied Ant. "It's an Me110. I know it. And it's coming closer." He paused, listening intently. "And it's coming lower."

I saw Mr. B glance over to Mrs. B. She raised her eyebrows in a silent question and he replied with another, very slight nod.

Miss Primrose had stopped reading the moment we heard the plane. Mrs. B stopped knitting. Everyone stopped what they were doing and listened. Twenty pairs of eyes stared at the domed, corrugated iron ceiling. I gripped Ant's hand. The excitement in his face had faded, and he licked his lips. He turned to me and I could see he felt the same as I did. Frightened. Ann-the-Bank was curled up in a tight ball, her chin on her knees; I'd never seen her face so white, or her eyes so tightly shut. I held my breath. I could hear my heart thumping.

The muffled whine of the plane came closer. I gulped and swallowed. The noise was coming right at us. Even though we were underground, the roar became deafening. Louder and louder. Closer and closer. It was overhead. It kept going. We knew then, it had passed right over the shelter. I heard so many gasps—we'd all been holding our breath. But it was not over. Only seconds later, there was an almighty thud and the earth around us shook and shuddered. Inside the Anderson, little bits of dust and rock rained down on us. Things fell off the shelves. There was a tinkling of broken glass, and water splashed from the big earthenware emergency jugs. We braced ourselves for what might happen next.

A bang. Then another. Then total, total silence. Little crippled Elaine started crying; she'd fallen off her chair. Mr. B picked her up and sat her on his lap. Her crying softened into muffled sobs and sniffs. Still no one moved. It seemed forever before anyone spoke.

"Hurrmmph," said Mrs. B. It broke the spell. Everyone spoke at once.

"Was that a bomb?"

"Where did it drop?"

"It sounded close."

"Did it hit the house?"

"Did it land in the orchard?"

"Is it over?"

"Are we safe now?"

"I'm thirsty."

"Do you think it killed anyone?"

"I have to go to the loo."

"I've lost my hanky."

"I want to go to the loo, too."

"I'm hungry."

"I feel sick."

Mrs. B stood up. "Quiet, quiet, children. Now, let's have some order here. We are all fine and right end up! No casualties. Sit down, and we'll have a drink and something to eat."

Mr. B headed towards Ant and me. "Move up Pat-a-cake and take care of Little Elaine." He settled her beside me and I put my arm around her. I liked Little Elaine. She'd had polio when she was only two, and she wore a boot fitted with heavy iron struts up each side of her left leg. This helped her to hobble from place to place. I'd never heard her complain when she couldn't join in games and dancing, and she was always cheerful.

"Why were you crying?" I asked her.

"I was frightened. The bomb shook me off my chair and I couldn't get up."

"If there's another one, I'll hold on to you," I promised.

Mrs. B handed out biscuits and tipped a bottle of Government issue bright orange concentrate into one of the water jugs. Then, glory be, she dived into a box under her old arm chair and counted out twenty Fry's Chocolate Creme bars. One for each of us.

Just as Miss Primrose jangled her bangles and announced she would read another chapter, the air raid siren stopped. It had been wailing the whole time we'd been down the Rabbit Hole. We stopped chewing and listened. Then, out of the silence, came the long high-pitched screech of the 'All Clear.'

"It's over, it's over. They've gone."

Mr. B bade us all to stay sitting, while he checked outside to see if it was safe. He went to the door, hesitated, then came back and pulled on his gas mask. "Just in case," he explained, nodding at Mrs. B who said, "Put your gas masks on again, children. Let's be on the safe side and obey the rules."

Mr. B pulled open the door and a shower of earth and compost fell down the steps. A blast of fresh air raised goose bumps on our arms, the All Clear still screeching in our ears.

Mr. B shouted down from the top of the steps. "You can all take off your gas masks. I'll be back in a few minutes after I've checked with the wardens."

Fifteen minutes later he came stumping back down the steps. "Well, there was no bomb," he announced cheerfully. "But you must all go straight into the house. No playing outside. Straight into the house."

As we scrambled to get out of Rabbit Hole Number Two, Mr. B edged past us to talk to Mrs. B. Ant and I hung back, straining our ears to hear what he was saying.

"Odd, thing," he was saying. "That wasn't a bomb. It was a rogue Jerry plane. Crashed in the field beyond the orchard. Fire Brigade and Dad's Army are there right now. Don't know if the pilot baled out or what, but we should keep the children indoors. Just in case."

I glanced at Ant. His face was alight with excitement. Grabbing my hand, he pulled me behind him as he shoved his way up the steps into the fresh air. I couldn't guess how long we'd been down there, but it was a light, bright afternoon; the sun playing peek-a-boo with small, fast moving clouds. As we reached the top step, we both looked towards the orchard. A thick column of black smoke spiralled up from beyond the far hedge, then eddied and streamed away on the wind to join the clouds; grey-black wisps mingling with white. "It must have crashed in Farmer Bourne's field," Ant said.

Reluctantly, he kept in line as we headed for the house—but he walked backwards, craning his head to see as much as possible. Later, at tea time, Ant nudged me then, leaning over, whispered in my ear, "We have to see it."

"See what?"

"Shh." He glanced around to see if anyone was listening. "The Jerry plane. We've got to go and see it."

He had my attention. "How can we? We can't go out. Anyway, it's out of bounds. We'll get caught and that'll be the cane. Or worse." We were both acquainted with 'worse,' and it was not pleasant.

"I'll think of something," he muttered and went back to his Woolton pie, jabbing at it with his fork. "I hate this stuff. Good mind to stow it in my pocket like Rowley's doing."

"Give it to Giles Farmer. He'll eat it."

So he did.

Chapter 34

Night Ops

As we'd missed most of the afternoon lessons, there wasn't much home-work. Miss Audrey-Joan gave us the evening off, but we had to play in the house. There was to be no going outside; it was too dangerous.

The minute we were dismissed, Ant and I dashed to the third floor to look out the small boys' dormitory window. From there we could see right across the orchard to Farmer Bourne's fields. Ant was squinting through his telescope. and muttering things under his breath like, "Coo-er. Coo-ER," which he was allowed to say, and "blimey," which he was not. I got really impatient.

"C'mon Ant. What can you see? What's happening? Tell me, tell me."

"It's an Me-110 all right. I guessed as much when I heard the engine."

I didn't argue with him. Ant knew all about planes, both Allied and enemy; after all, a copy of *Aircraft Recognition* lived in his pocket. "Ant. C'mon. Let me look."

Finally he handed me the telescope."Here, take a shufti. But be quick."

Adjusting the lens, I peered through the long spyglass. "Gosh!" I said. "Oh golly-gosh!" I could hardly believe what I saw. Lying in Farmer Bourne's field was a tangled mess of metal. All around it, his crop of green oats had been burnt black. Dark wisps of smoke still curled up into the sky. The village fire engine was there, and a dozen uniformed people, mostly Home Guard, were running about the field and looking in the hedge bottoms. Two people were standing by the wreckage; one looked like Constable Penny, the local Bobby.

"That's enough. Give it back." Ant took the telescope and put it to his eye. "You've messed up the focus," he grumbled. Then he said something totally shocking, "We could go there after dark."

"Whaaat?"

"Had Ant gone crackers?"

So I said, "Don't be silly. Anyway, how could we get out?"

"Easy." He sounded as though he had done it before.

I looked over my shoulder to make sure no one was around to hear us. "All right. Then tell me how, Mr Clever-Dick."

"Back kitchen window. It's always open 'cos the catch is broken. So if you go out and someone shuts the window, you can still open it from the outside."

He *must* have done it before.

"And the blackout blinds are easy there. They roll up half way."

He *had* done it before. I felt a bit cross about that and challenged him. "You did it without me? That's not fair."

"Silly sausage. How am I supposed to tell you when I go, without waking your whole dormy? Besides, I don't always know I'm going. Sort of a spur-of-the-moment thing."

I stared at him. "What d'you mean you don't always know you're going?"

He put down the telescope. "Sometimes, I just want to go out. My daddy and I used to go for walks after dark. To pick out the stars and stuff. I've only done it twice here. The first time I wanted to get my planes that I'd left in the sunken garden and I came right back. The other time I took my telescope to look at the stars from the barn roof. It was too cloudy to see much." He grinned, "But I saw a badger. It was rummaging in the rubbish heap." Ant snapped the telescope shut. "Let's go somewhere safe and plan our secret mission."

"What mission?"

"Salvage operations."

"Oh. Right."

We crept into the empty sick room, closing the door behind us. Settling on the big cushioned window-seat, Ant outlined his mission plans. "It has to be midnight. All secret missions are carried out at midnight That's why they're called Night Ops."

The mission *sounded* easy. Once out of the house, we would go through the orchard to Farmer Bourne's field. We would inspect the wreckage and bring bits of it back.

"Shrapnel," Ant explained, "is very valuable. You can swap it for almost anything."

"What if there's someone there?" I asked. "Guarding the wreckage?"

"Hmm. You're right. There probably will be. We'll have to be extra careful and recon the unknown territory before every move."

"Recon?"

"It's an army term for checking the way's clear. And we'll wear camouflage of course."

"What camouflage?"

"Wear dark clothes and blacken our faces."

"With what?" This 'secret mission' was beginning to get complicated.

"With dirt, silly. C'mon Pat. Fains you back out. Fains you have to come with me."

I sighed. 'Fains' was a code that could never be broken. Whether I wanted to or not, I had to do it. Anyone who broke a fains was an outcast—forever and ever, Amen.

"How will you tell me when it's time to go?"

"We'll have a secret signal."

"What signal? And from where?"

"Let me think." Ant assumed his 'thinking' position. Forehead on his knees, arms dangling. I sat, silent. I'd learned not to interrupt when Ant was thinking.

His head shot up. "I've got it."

"What?"

"Dangle something out of your window and, when it's time, I'll tug on it and you come down."

"You must be barmy. For one thing, what would I dangle and for another what would I dangle it on? It's a long way down from the second floor."

Ant glared at me. "All you need is a ball of string and something tied to the end of it. Tie the other end around your wrist and, when I tug, you'll feel it." He grinned, pleased with his clever idea. "Then if you've gone to sleep, it'll wake you up."

"All right. But where will I find the string?"

"Ask Mr. B. He'll give you some."

I knew he was right. I nodded. "I can get that."

"We'd better go down to the common-room, before we're missed."

I found Mr. B setting out the tiny oil night-lamps, ready for black-out time.

"Mr. B?"

"Well, hello there, Pat-a-cake. What can I do for you?"

"I need some string. To tie up something. May I get some from the back kitchen? Please, Mr. B." Luckily he didn't ask me what I wanted to tie up.

"Of course," he replied. "There's a ball of garden twine in the second drawer from the left. Just inside the yard door."

"Thanks, Mr. B. You're a brick." I sped off down the back stairs, before he could ask me what I wanted it for. The back kitchen was empty. I found the twine, then slipped into the cloakroom, and hid it in my shoe-bag.

Ant had already arrived in the common-room, and was busy playing convoys with toy army jeeps, lorries and dozens of soldiers. I whispered in his ear, "I've got the string."

"Ripping!" He grinned. "Go play with Ann-the-Bank. She's been asking for you. See you at midnight."

I joined Ann who was working on a jigsaw of the Tower of London. Her face didn't look so white as it had during the air raid. "Where've you been?" She looked at me suspiciously. "And what've you been doing?"

"Reading."

"Hmph. Well, now you're here, help me with all this sky. I hate sky."

"I don't want to do sky. I like the other stuff too. Look, here's almost a whole raven." I waggled the piece under her nose. She snatched it out of my hand.

"I know. I have all the raven pieces in one place. Do the sky."

I sighed and leaned over to pick up a piece of sky, just as Mrs. B came in.

"Time to start putting toys away. Bedtime in fifteen minutes."

I jumped up and headed for the door.

"Not so fast, young lady. What about putting your things away. And why the hurry to go to bed?" She squinted at me through her glasses. "We're not sick again, are we?"

"Oh no, Mrs. B. I just want to read in bed before lights out. I've come to a good part. Besides, I didn't get any toys out. I was helping Ann with a jigsaw." I gave her my best smile.

"Hmph," she said, but she let me pass.

I collected the ball of string from my shoe-bag, and made it to the dormitory before anyone else. I had to find some way of letting the string out of the window with something attached to it. While I was thinking, I took my old green corduroy riding breeches, a navy-blue jumper and a pair of black plimsolls from the wardrobe, and shoved them all down my bed.

My bed was by the window and the top sash was down about three inches. Although it was still light, the blackout blind was down to save Mrs. B coming around later. I let the blind up a little and pushed the bottom sash up, then pulled the blind back down. There was a small rip in the bottom corner which Mrs. B had covered with a piece of Elastoplast. I eased the plaster up, and made the tear bigger; when I replaced it at the outer edge, it was impossible to see the bigger tear. I shoved the ball of string under my pillow and looked around for something to use for the signal. It had to be something that wouldn't break, or wouldn't make a noise.

Edward Bear's boot-button eyes stared up at me from my pillow.

Six of us shared the dormitory. After 'Lights Out' we would all hunch down under the bedclothes and read by torchlight. After about half-an-hour, most of us would feel sleepy enough to turn off our torches and settle down. Besides, there would be some long, dark nights if we let our torch batteries run out; they were hard to come by in wartime. I tried to read a chapter from Enid Blyton's *The Adventurous Five*, but all I could think of was our night-ops. Ann-the-Bank whispered, "Good night, Pat. Don't forget it's my turn to be first in the bathroom in the morning."

"All right. Good night, Annie."

Ann muttered grumpily, "Don't call me that." She hated me calling her Annie. She huffled and snuffled for a few seconds and then shot up in bed again. "Shhhhhhh."

Alana and Emma Simon who had been whispering ever since lights out, ignored her and went on talking.

Ann was furious. She was dormitory prefect and took her duties very seriously. "I said shhhh. Or I'll tell–right now." She stuck one threatening foot out of bed and the whispering stopped. They knew if Ann told on them, Mrs. B would haul them out onto the landing and make them stand there for half-an-hour.

Hilary and Lucy, who were scared of Ann, quickly pulled the covers over their heads and pretended to be asleep. I grinned to myself. Just what I needed; everyone tucked into bed and sleeping. I lay on my back, listening. It wasn't long before I was the only one still awake. I was wearing my vest and knickers under my pyjamas, which I quickly pulled off and tucked under my pillow. I wriggled into the riding breeches and jumper and then went to work on the window. I carefully removed the Elastoplast and lifted the corner of the blackout. It was a warm night. I stared out at the last rays of sunset turning the red sandstone walls into a fiery gold. Ducks flew in a V across the clear evening sky, and the boundary trees were black silhouettes against the sun's fading glow. I decided it was a very good night for an adventure.

I tied the string around Edward Bear's tummy, gave him a quick hug and carefully slid him through the tear in the blackout and out the window. I watched the ball of string unwind as I lowered him. It was a long way down, but at last I felt the string go slack and knew he was sitting in a flowerbed. I wrapped my end of the string around my wrist several times, and slid back under the covers to wait. No chink of light came through the blackout and I stared up into the darkness, determined not to fall asleep. I did everything I could think of to keep my brain awake while I waited for Ant's signal. I recited my times-tables, conjugated French and Latin verbs, and tried to remember the poems I'd learned by heart.

What if he never came? I tested the string with my thumb and first finger. I could feel a light bouncing on the other end. Edward was still there.

"Oh, hurry up Ant. What are you waiting for? I'm ready."

The string around my wrist jerked violently. Instantly, I was wide awake. I pulled Edward up a little and jerked the string several times. It rasped on the window sill; I stopped. After a pause, one almighty jerk almost pulled my wrist from my arm. Ant was definitely on the other end. Hand over hand, I hauled Edward up the side of the house. Fathoms of string lay tumbled on the floor beside my bed before I heard Edward bump against the window; I wriggled my hand through the gap and pulled him in. Five seconds later, Edward and his string were tucked under my pillow. Exactly as I had learned from adventure books, I rolled up my eiderdown, stuffed it lengthways down the bed and smoothed the blanket over the top. Picking up my plimsolls, I crept silently towards the door and the dim flickering of the night-lamps on the landing. It was not the first time I'd roamed around the house in the middle of the night. If anyone heard me, the excuse that I had to go to the loo was perfectly acceptable, but I didn't want to be caught dressed in old riding breeches and jumper, with my plimsolls in my hand; now *that* would be a calamity. As quickly and as silently as I could, I crept down the two flights of stairs. The bottom stairs ended in the hall right by the back kitchen. I crossed the stone floor to the window above the sink, pushed up the blackout a few inches, and peered out. No one there. Where was Ant? I'd been very quick.

Then I saw him, and he was acting so strangely that I nearly giggled out loud. From the shadow of the barn, a dark figure darted across the yard to the doorway of the girls' outside loo. Then it flitted from shadow to shadow, zig zagging towards the window, where it crouched down under a rhododendron right below me.

"Pssst," hissed the shadow.

"Pssst yourself. You know I'm here."

"Shh. Open the window and climb down beside me."

I did as I was told; it was a short and easy drop. As I landed, Ant pulled me down onto my knees. He put his finger to his lips and looked furtively around.

"What are you doing?"

"Sshhh." He had a small tin in his hand. He scooped something out of it with his fingers and smeared it on my face. It smelled dirty.

"What are you doing? Stop it."

"Shhh. Don't say a word. Follow me." He stood up and sniffed the air; for all the world like Gatsby. Bending almost double, he sped back to the barn door shadow where I'd first seen him. I ran after him. "Keep down," he commanded. "Keep low to the ground."

"Whatever for?"

"Cos that's the way good commandos on secret missions move around at night."

"Oh. I see. Well, c'mon, let's go."

"Wait! See if the coast is clear first."

"Of course it's clear, silly."

It was dark but just by the way he held his head, I knew he was glaring at me. "You have to wait 'til the moon goes behind a cloud before you move."

I looked up at the sky. It was a warm, clear summer night. "There aren't any clouds," I hissed.

"I know that, silly. That's why you have to use the shadows."

Ant grabbed my hand and we darted towards the yard gate. Keeping in every shadow, he led me up the path, past the compost heap, past Rabbit Hole Number Two and the rubbish heap, and past our Victory gardens, to the orchard gate. There he pulled me down to ground level, "There's a moon, so we have to be careful. *Really, really careful.*"

I knew he was right. We had to cross the orchard to get to Farmer Bourne's field, so we had to be on the lookout for the Home Guard; they would be on the alert for anyone who shouldn't be there. I thought for a minute, figuring out the best way to go. I knew my orchard, better than Ant did. I rode there almost every day. "We'll go over the gate and follow the fence to the left corner, and then up the hedge to the cut where the field joins the orchard," I said.

"All right. You go over the gate first. But duck down and wait for me."

"Why?"

"'Cos then, if anyone saw you, we'll hear the shouts. But if the coast is clear, we can go on."

He was right–again.

No one saw us. With our heads down, we skirted the orchard under cover of the high summer growth of alders and hazel, until we came to within a few yards of where the hedges dipped. There, a wooden stile was cut into the corner, marking the boundary where the school property met Farmer Bourne's fields. Beyond this point was out of bounds to all. Not that there was anything to go over for; only cows in winter and crops in summer.

"Down," ordered the Chief Commando.

I ducked down.

"On your tummy."

"What?"

"On–your–tummy."

I obeyed and wriggled, snake-like, until I was lying beside him— about four feet short of the stile. Ant's mouth was very close to my ear. He barely breathed his next orders, "Wriggle to the stile 'til we can see into the field."

He must have felt my head nod. He said nothing but started to wriggle slowly and silently forward. I kept up with him, pulling myself along on my elbows. We almost gave ourselves away when we saw, through the bottom rung of the stile, what was lying in the field.

Ant's gasp was loud. So was mine.

"Cooo-errrrrr."

"Gosh."

"How absolutely ripping."

It was my turn to say, "*Shhhh.*"

This year, Farmer Bourne had planted this particular field with oats. We'd hung over the stile and watched while his Land Army girls ploughed the field and sowed the seed. Yesterday, it had been about a foot tall and a really pretty green. Now, almost as far as we could see, instead of shimmering and waving in the moonlight, it was low stubble, burned to a dark blue-black. It smelled like one of Mr. B's rubbish bonfires.

About twenty yards away was a jumbled mass of wreckage. The plane lay tilted to one side. The right wing had snapped in half and lay away from the rest, its tip pointing straight at us. The dented tail fin was cocked up in the air. The fuselage was a burnt out mess and we could see dark lumps of stuff scattered all around. The Messerschmitt—for we found out later Ant was right—had burned up and set Farmer Bourne's oat crop ablaze. On the wing tip, untouched by the fire and gleaming in the moonlight, we saw the menacing symbol of the enemy–a Swastika.

"Cor blimey," breathed Ant in my ear. "What a rippingly awful thing." He pointed through the stile. "Look over there."

Beyond the wreckage we could just see, outlined in the bright moonlight, a couple of bicycles leaning against the field gate. Sentries. Everything was deadly quiet. Not a sound.

Ant was wearing one of his prized possessions–a miniature army camouflage jacket. Undoing a couple of buttons, he fished his telescope out of an inside pocket.

"What use is that?" I whispered. "It's dark."

"The moon is bright enough to see a few things. Be quiet," he hissed. He put the telescope to his eye and twisted the focus. Minutes passed and still he fiddled. I could hear him muttering under his breath. I moved closer.

"Coo-er. Cor-Blimey!"

I wriggled with impatience. He dug me in the ribs with his elbow. His mouth was at my ear again, "I can see two people. Prob'ly Dad's Army blokes."

"Where?" I breathed back.

"By the bicycles."

My heart sank. We'd come all this way for nothing. I'd risked getting the cane, getting expelled—everything—by coming out here. And now we had to go back. "We have to go back," I whispered.

"Not on your Nellie," came the muffled reply. "There's some shrapnel close by. Look. By the wing."

It *was* very close and the Home Guard men *were* far beyond the other side of the plane. "All right," I said. I knew that, now we'd come so far, we had to do it. I remembered a saying of Dilly's, "In for a penny, in for a pound." *Now* I knew what it meant.

Ant whispered instructions into my ear. I nodded, knowing I had to remember them and obey them to the letter. Do something wrong, and we would both be caught. Besides, he was Commander in Chief of Covert Operations.

With Ant leading the way, we inched forward and squeezed through the bottom rung of the stile. Snake-like wriggles brought us out into the open field. A couple of feet of wing-tip and dozens of pieces of shrapnel were about a tennis-court's length away. We wormed our way towards the burnt-out plane. All of a sudden, there was a scraping noise and a small flame flared. We froze. We stared, horrified, as we saw a man's face illuminated as he cupped his hands around a match and lit a cigarette.

"Put that out, mate." The voice was so loud it made us jump. "Put the bloody thing out."

"Wotcher worried about? There's no one here for miles. And the only Jerries here are dead ones." The man with the cigarette laughed and blew out the match.

"Go back to sleep, Joe. I'll keep watch another hour then I'll wake you."

I gasped. I'd been holding my breath. I put my forehead down on the charred grain stubble; my heart thumping in my ears.

Ant was panting for breath too. We lay like fallen statues, afraid to move.

Minutes passed. Then Ant nudged me, "C'mon. We're nearly there."

And we were. A few more seconds of wriggling and we were amongst the scattered pieces of shrapnel. Ant fumbled in a pocket and pulled out his blue shoe-bag. He shoved it into my hands, "Here, take this. Fill it up with the bits lying around." His voice was a hoarse whisper but I could hear the excitement in it, "Mind you don't cut your fingers. Shrapnel is sharp stuff."

I picked up three or four pieces of the dark metal and put them in the bag. As I groped around, I saw something glinting in the moonlight. I squinted at it, then picked it up. It was round and shiny. I didn't put it in the bag, but stuffed it into my breeches pocket.

We squirmed around on our stomachs, picking up the smaller pieces of twisted metal. The full moon was excellent in one way, but risky in another. While it lit up the field and the wreckage with a ghostly but bright light, it greatly increased the danger of being seen. Now that we had left the comparative safety of the orchard and were in the open field, there was very little cover. Everything was outlined in a silvery light–including us. Ant's idea of wearing dark clothing was good, but we needn't have bothered to streak our faces with dirt. After scrabbling through the burnt-out stalks of Farmer Bourne's oat crop, I could see in the moon-glow that Ant looked like a chimney sweep; I must have looked the same. The ground was soggy where the firemen had doused the flames and as I crawled around, the acrid smell of wet ash got up my nose and made my eyes water.

Ant came closer to me. "The bag's full now. We'd better get back."

I nodded. The back of my throat felt raw and scratchy from breathing in the bitter tang left by the burning plane. I choked on the sour taste and wanted to cough.

Ant gripped my wrist. Tight. "Shhh. Shut up."

I tried to stifle the rising tickle in my throat. I buried my head into the smelly, dirty ground and nearly choked.

Ant's mouth was against my ear again. "C'mon. We have to get back to the orchard. Now."

I raised my head, trying to control the urge to cough. Ant was already up and, making a dash for the stile. To heck with wriggling I thought, as I came to my knees. Monkey-like, I ran on all fours. I was halfway to the stile when I heard a shout:

"Hey. Who's there?"

Beyond the plane, the two men started calling and rushing around. Just as I reached the stile and scrambled through, the challenge came.

"Halt. Who goes there?"

"Oh God! Now I'm going to be shot."

The other voice said, "Whatcher all panicky about? There's no one there."

Now we were crouched down, peering back through the stile. In the soft night air, the voices were clear and we could hear every word.

"I thought I heard someone...something."

"Nah. I don't see anyone. Didn't hear anyone neither."

"Well, you were asleep. I definitely heard something. Over beyond the plane. By the stile."

The other man laughed, "Jerry's ghost prob'ly. Come ter haunt ya. Anyway, if it makes you feel better, we'll go and take a gander."

We didn't have to see or hear anyone coming towards us. We knew they were. Ant turned and took a flying leap into the ditch under the boundary hedge. I jumped in immediately behind him. He dragged me further down, pushing my head down amongst the midsummer grass and ragged robins. I put my hand on a nettle. The sharp sting made me gasp, "Ouch." I started to cough again.

A filthy, smelly hand latched onto my nose and mouth. "Pat, please!" I could hear Ant panting and gasping. I tried to swallow some spit to calm my throat. It seemed to work. I tried to make more spit, but it wouldn't come. I sucked my tongue and swallowed again.

There was a sudden scrape as a boot caught the first rung of the stile, only a few feet from where we lay. We both jumped a little way out of our skins.

A light flicked on and swept across the ground in front of us. We cowered down in the ditch bottom.

"Dowse that light, mate."

"There's no Jerry's around here. No live ones anyway!"

"I just want ter see what's going on."

The light swept around to the other side of the stile. Ant and I lay like stones. I could hear his breathing—or was it mine?

Then a rustle in the grass and a small white scut bounced in the moonlight.

"Look mate, there goes your Jerry. A bloody bunny."

"Well, I'll be...I could have sworn I saw two shadows move."

"Well you know what bunnies are, mate. Where there's one, there's usually two. And then, before you know it, there's a round dozen!"

"All right, all right. It must've been bunnies then. Let's get back. I could use that Thermos of tea."

As they walked back to their bicycles, we could hear their boots scratching through the burnt-out stubble. The sounds became fainter. Then silence. We lay like rocks in the bottom of the ditch, straining our ears for the slightest sound. All I could hear was the thud, thud, thud of my own heartbeat until a small rustle in the grass beside us broke the silence. I jumped.

"What was that?" I dared to whisper.

"Mouse. C'mon, the coast is clear now. Let's get back quick."

Ant wasn't so particular now about crouching down, wriggling on tummies, or darting from shadow to shadow. He leaped out of the ditch and ran as fast as he could across the orchard, to the five-barred gate. I was only two steps behind him. The gate was a familiar obstacle and we both knew where to place our feet. Up right, up left, up right to the top bar, both feet together, crouch, and leap to the ground; in all of three seconds. Then on down the path towards the yard. Half way down, where our Victory Gardens lay in tidy little patches against the outer wall of the kitchen garden, Antony came to a full stop. I almost bumped into the back of him.

"What?"

He peered at me in the bright moonlight, then reached out and rubbed my cheek with his thumb.

"What?" I asked again.

He held up his hands, palms facing me and spread his fingers. "Look. We're filthy."

That was the first time I'd ever known Ant worry about being dirty. His hands were black. I looked down at mine. The black soot I'd picked up in the burnt-out field, glistened under the full moon. "We have to wash," I said.

"And we can't take these clothes back in the house," said Ant. What'll we do?"

"I have an idea. Come on." It was my turn to lead, and I knew exactly what to do and where to do it.

I led Ant through the archway, into the walled kitchen garden, and up the path to the back corner and Mr. B's garden sheds. As the leader of his gardening gang, I spent a lot of time in the big shed helping Mr. B sort seeds, pot little plants and making tea when it rained. The smaller shed behind it was used to store tools and old garden junk. I stopped at the old bathtub that had once been Ophelia's barge; now used to wash garden tools. It was almost always full of rainwater, leaves and little water bugs; once I'd even found tadpoles in it. I sat on the old curved wooden garden seat beside it and outlined my plan. "We'll take off our dirty clothes and wash our hands and faces in the bathtub. I'll hide our stuff in the little shed and we can get it another time."

"What about our shrapnel?" Ant held up his blue shoe-bag.

"We'll put that in there too and get it tomorrow. You've got to think of a place to hide it."

"I'd planned to leave it in Merlin's lair but it was too risky to go there tonight."

"There's a good hiding place in the shed. It's unlocked and I've hidden stuff in there before and Mr. B's never found it."

"Oh yes?" said Ant. "And what did you hide?"

"Just stuff. I'll tell you another time. Now we have to get cleaned up and get back in the house. It must be nearly morning."

Ant looked at the sky. The moon was dipping towards the horizon. Dawn came early in June. "No. We've still plenty of time." He laid his telescope on the bench. "I'm not leaving *that* in your old shed."

I was already out of my breeches. Soon our filthy outside clothes were lying in a heap on the bench and we were in our underclothes. I laughed at Ant, he looked so funny. White legs and arms, hands and face as black as coal. We scrubbed ourselves clean, using leaves and rainwater from the bathtub. I rolled our dirty clothes into a bundle and led the way to the tool shed; it was never locked. Inside, I clambered up onto the workbench, stuffed the bundle into an old gypsy basket, and shoved it on the highest shelf. Ant handed me his bag of shrapnel and, standing on tiptoe, I placed it on top of the clothes. "No one will find it there. Mr. B never uses that basket 'cos the handle is broken."

With Ant clutching his telescope, we kept to the shadows and made our way back to the yard. The back kitchen window was still open. A streak of pale pink stretched along the eastern sky as we climbed back inside and replaced the blackout. We stood for a moment, listening.

Ant touched my arm. "We made it."

Although I couldn't see his face, I knew he was grinning.

"Mission accomplished," he whispered. "That was a cracking good time we had. And you did really well on your first Night Ops assignment, Private Patricia. See you at breakfast!"

He couldn't see my nod, but we both knew it had been a most amazing adventure.

We crept, like tip-toeing mice, up the stairs and into our dorms. I knew everyone was still asleep because no bedclothes rustled as I quietly removed the eiderdown from down my bed, wriggled my pyjamas over my underclothes and snuggled down under the covers. I picked up Edward Bear, settled him on my chest and imprisoned him in my arms.

"Gosh. What an absolutely rippingly-super, scathingly-brilliant adventure.

"And wouldn't Cedric have loved it. I must write and tell him all about it."

Sunday, 13th June, 1943.
Dear Mummy and Daddy,
There was an air raid on Friday and we had to go down the Rabbit Hole. A German plane crashed in Farmer Bourne's fields. It burned all his oats.
Will you be coming to see me on my birthday next Sunday? I am going to be nine. I haven't seen you for two years now.
Please may I have a soldier's camouflage jacket for my birthday.
Your devoted daughter,
Patricia

My Birthday, 20th June, 1943.
Dear Mummy and Daddy,
I'm sorry you couldn't come for my birthday, but I'm getting used to school birthday parties now. Thank you for all the

nice presents, I needed new clothes as Mr. B says I'm growing like one of his weeds in the kitchen garden.

I am enjoying the summer. I ride a lot and play tennis. Antony is my tennis partner in doubles tournaments and we usually win.

I am doing well at my lessons but we have exams soon, which I don't like.

With love from your nine-year-old daughter,

Patricia

Chapter 35

Blooded

Saturday was always my favourite day. There was so much that *didn't* happen on a Saturday. And there was so much that *could* happen on a Saturday. There were no lessons and most of the children were gone; only the full borders were left. Best of all, we got to do more or less what we liked, so long as we didn't get into trouble. On this particular Saturday, Mrs. B gave me permission to ride Dolly, "It will keep you out from under my feet for the morning."

I went to the stables early. Dolly was happy to see me and ate the apple cores I'd brought for her breakfast. The other children were very good about giving me their apple cores; even though they'd been picked so clean there was hardly any apple left on them, Dolly enjoyed them.

Mr. B was a long time coming to saddle Dolly so I decided to do it myself. He'd placed an old wooden ladder against the wall so I could reach Dolly's bridle and saddle that hung from big wooden pegs—as thick as my arm—driven into the whitewashed stone wall. The bridle was easy to get down, but the saddle was high up above my head and very heavy. Hanging on to the top of the ladder with one hand, I used the other to push and poke, easing the saddle, little by little, away from the wall. I tried to balance and use both hands, but the weight of the saddle almost tipped me backwards. Grabbing the top rung of the ladder with both hands, I steadied myself just in time, then went on inching the saddle forward on its perch. Finally, it tipped from the huge rope-wrapped peg and fell in a tangle of leather and canvas straps. The loud clank-clank of the heavy iron stirrups on stone cobbles made Dolly, Paddy and Bondy snort and stamp—their hooves clattering and scraping on the floor.

"It's all very well for you, Dolly," I muttered. A black ear twitched in my direction so I knew she was listening. "All you have to do is stand still, while I do all the work to get you dressed."

Standing on a tree-stump stool, made me tall enough to get the saddle onto Dolly's back. That done, I ducked under her belly, grabbed the two canvas girth straps and tried to fasten them under the stirrup leathers. Dolly took a deep breath and puffed out her sides. I punched her in the side with my fist. "Stop that, Dolly. Don't you want to go out and have some fun with me? Let it out! Let me tighten the girth."

Dolly grinned—at least that's what it looked like to me. By that time, my hands were so dirty and sticky with sweat, that they slipped off the straps as I tried to pull them tighter. Oh where was Mr. B? He knew how to deal with Dolly when she puffed herself up. I sat down on a bale of straw to think.

I loved being alone in the stable away from the other children. It was quiet and smelled of horse, old apples and leather. To me, it was a place where time didn't count and the war was shut out. Looking around, it was easy to believe that the big black iron rings and hooks on the old stone walls had been used for hitching and hanging tack for hundreds of years. An old-fashioned side-saddle, high on a wooden peg, dripped cobwebs and could have been there for centuries. Did a beautiful Georgian lady dressed in long flowing velvet, sit elegantly on that saddle, mounted on a pure white palfrey? Had she too, taken a shrivelled apple from the barrel and given it to her pony? Dolly scraped her iron-shod hoof on the cobbled floor and my daydream was broken. So much for silk and velvet as I wiped my hands on my new jodhpurs, leaving dark smudges and streaks. They really were a mess; I'd collected grime and cobwebs when I climbed the ladder. I picked up some straw and scrubbed at the dirt, trying to clean it off. My mother had sent me the jodhpurs last week in a parcel with two bars of Fry's Chocolate Cream and letters from both her and my father. The letter from my father was a great surprise as he is usually too busy with the war to write.

"I am very pleased that your riding is coming along so well," he wrote. *"And as I have a few extra clothing coupons, I asked Mummy to get you a smart pair of jodhpurs as a reward. However, I must insist that you pay as much attention to your Mathematics and Latin as you do to English and History and, of course, riding and gardening are only pleasure subjects and will not get you into big school. By all means enjoy them as recreation on your weekends but I have asked Miss Audrey-Joan to ensure that all your homework is completed before you are allowed recreation time.*

I miss my little girl very much and cannot wait until the end of this wretched war and I can return home to my precious family. With lots of love, my treasure, from Daddy."

The jodhpurs were very smart, the colour of porridge when they were clean. The very first day I wore them, I got a big dirty smudge on the seat. When Ant saw it he said they should have been black and then I could have worn them for the duration and no one would have seen the dirt.

A nicker from Paddy's stall and I realized that he'd seen me give the apple cores to Dolly. I went over to him.

"I'm sorry Paddy. I forgot you were there." Luckily there was a pail of shrivelled old root vegetables that were no use for the kitchen. I found a withered old bendy carrot, climbed on the gate of Paddy's stall and gave it to him. It was then I noticed that Paddy had been saddled and bridled ready to go out. But why would Mr. B get Paddy ready for me instead of Dolly?

I didn't really like riding Paddy. He was taller than Dolly, and thinner. He had longer legs and pranced around showing them off. Usually, only the older boys who were good riders were allowed to ride Paddy. I had ridden him once around the yard, but Mr. B had told me to get off.

"You'd better stick to riding Dolly until you've grown another couple of inches," he'd said.

I thought about that for a while. When I was in the bath with Ann-the-Bank last week, Mrs. Tommy was surprised that we weren't same height any more. "Well I don't know," she said. "The Lady Patricia here seems to have grown somewhat. Unless little Miss Ann has shrunk. There's about two inches difference between you now."

Ann-the-Bank sniffed and said that she didn't really care anyway as her mother was known as "petite" and she definitely would rather be petite like her mam, than lanky like a bean pole. I don't think she liked Mrs. Tommy calling her a 'miss' and me a 'lady.'

So perhaps I *was* tall enough to ride Paddy. *That's* why Mr. B had saddled him for me. Leading Paddy out into the cobble-stone yard, I stuck my tongue out at Dolly. "After all the trouble you put me through, now you can stay behind. All dressed up and nowhere to go. So there."

"So where?" Ant's voice came from somewhere high up in the old yew tree that grew against one end of the barn. Mr. B had told us the yew tree was so huge and so old, that it was probably the only thing holding the barn up. Some of it's branches had grown right into the stonework and inside, the brick floor was bumpy and uneven where its roots had spread; or so Mr. B said, and he was usually right. And he'd said they would never cut it down because to fell a yew tree would bring bad luck.

"Dolly wouldn't let me tighten her girth straps and so I'm going to ride Paddy instead. That's where."

The yew tree shook as Ant wriggled his way out from the second highest branch. He liked it up there. He would sit against the old chimney stack for hours, watching for planes. He said it was like being on watch on an aircraft carrier.

At the sudden movement in the tree, Paddy shied and rattled the bit with his teeth. He skittered sideways as Ant landed beside us. "You can't ride Paddy. You haven't been given permission."

"It's my riding morning and Mr. B must have got him ready for me instead of Dolly. Besides I've grown two inches."

"What's that got to do with it?"

"Mr. B said I could ride Paddy when I'd grown a couple of inches."

"Whizzo. But you'll have to be careful. Paddy's difficult to handle and he's skittish."

"What's skittish?"

"Don't know but I heard Mr Jeffrey tell Mr. B that Paddy was really skittish one day when he took him cross-country and was hard to handle. Look at him. He's jumpy right now."

"That's because you jumped out of the tree and scared him. If you'd keep still he'd be all right. Anyway, Paddy likes me. I gave him a carrot and he winked at me."

"Okay. But I'll watch you from the roof. I can see right across the orchard from the roof."

"You're not allowed to say okay. It's slang."

"It's American. And the Americans are helping us win the war now. They're called allies. So I don't see why we shouldn't say it."

"Well I'm not saying it. It's not ladylike." By now Paddy was prancing sideways again, eager to be off. "I have to go, Paddy's getting restless."

"Want me to come and open the orchard gate for you?" Ant hopped from one foot to another ready to dart ahead and race us to the gate. "The loop is on the gatepost."

"If you like." Actually, having to unhook the leather strap that hitched the five-barred gate shut, was always a nuisance and, with Paddy so fidgety, could prove difficult.

Ant galloped ahead, his hand slapping at his trousers, his imaginary horse leaping make-believe obstacles, and shying at fanciful shadows. I let him beat us.

Jumping on the gate as it opened, he turned and grinned, "I'll shut it too, if you like."

"Of course I like. Anyway, you want to swing on it."

A huge iron weight bearing the raised inscription "**3 stone**" hung from a heavy chain and made the gate swing shut. Mr. B had invented that too. He said he was fed up with having to chase the chickens out of the orchard because 'Mr Nobody' had left the gate open.

As soon as he was through the gate, Paddy kicked up his heels and threw me forward in the saddle. His head came up and I almost lost a stirrup. "Damn you Paddy," I yelled. "Damn you! Behave!"

Ant heard me. "Coo-er. You swore. You said damn."

"So did you then," I shouted back over my shoulder. I hauled on the reins to keep Paddy down to a trot.

Damn is a swear word, and it's not ladylike to swear. But before the war, I'd often heard my Daddy swear at the polo ponies when they didn't do what he wanted. And I'd once heard Mr. B say "damn woman" under his breath when Mrs. B had been giving him orders.

So I swore at Paddy again, "Damn you, Paddy. Behave."

And Paddy behaved. For a while.

Paddy ran faster than Dolly who was a bit of a lazybones. He had longer legs, skinny shoulders, and a long thin neck that arched prettily when I pulled on the reins. We stopped by the fallen apple tree because I knew Ant would be back up in his crow's-nest on the aircraft carrier, watching. I stood up in the stirrups and waved in that direction. Paddy snorted and tossed his head, impatient to be off again.

Another circuit of the orchard and I decided that, as Paddy was enjoying himself, he wouldn't be so difficult to handle after all. I set him at one of the jumps on the gymkhana strip Mr. B had constructed earlier that summer. He sailed over it. And the next. And the next.

"He's certainly a very good jumper," I thought. Loosening my grip on the reins, I leaned forward to pat Paddy's neck and at the same moment, he jerked his head back so suddenly that he caught me right on my nose. "Ouch," I yelled. "What did you do that for? Damn horse!"

Dropping the reins, I cupped my hands over my nose. I felt a warm and sticky trickle edging down towards my mouth; the tip of my tongue identified the tell-tale metallic taste. "Damn you Paddy, you've made my nose bleed. You've broken my nose. Damn you..."

But Paddy wasn't listening to me. He was listening to something else. His head was up, his ears were twitching. He skittered back and forth, turning first one way and then another. I wiped my nose on my sleeve and grabbed the reins again. I saw my riding crop sticking out of a bunch of nettles—I must have dropped it when Paddy hit me. Well, it would have to stay there for now. Paddy was being most unmanageable and I wasn't sure what the matter was. Perhaps he'd been stung by a wasp. He tossed his head up again, but this time I kept my nose well out of the way. It still throbbed, but it wasn't bleeding as much. Holding the reins in one hand, I used the other to grab the hanky from my jumper sleeve and wipe my face.

Then I heard what had caught Paddy's attention. He hadn't been startled or stung. He'd heard something. Now I could hear it too–away in the distance. The baying of fox hounds, the blast of a hunting horn. A fox hunt. The familiar sounds were getting closer and louder; they must be coming this way. Paddy was getting more and more excited. Head up, ears alert, his front legs dancing—he was obviously getting himself in a real twist. I quickly stuffed my hanky back; I needed both hands to try and control Paddy.

"Let the horse know who is master," my father had instructed, so high up on his black horse and I so small on my Shetland pony, Tinker Bell. "And always keep your heels DOWN."

"Heels down," I echoed from the memory.

Then I saw them. Beyond the fallen apple tree and the hedge marking the border between the school property and Farmer Bourne's fields, were flashes of scarlet hunting jackets and bobbing black velvet hats. I could see the waving tails of the hounds flickering through the tall undergrowth as, with their noses to the ground, they followed the scent of the fox. I stood up in my stirrups to get a better look. "Here they come!" I shouted to Paddy. "Here they come!"

Paddy didn't need telling. He saw, as did I, the mounted huntsmen come leaping over fences, hedges and gates, and the hounds wriggling and nosing their way through the ditches. We both heard the constant *View-halloo* urging on every horse, rider and hound.

What I didn't remember was that when Mr Jeffrey–a friend of Miss Audrey-Joan's sister, Miss Margaret–came for the weekend, he often took Paddy foxhunting and he would say afterwards how Paddy loved a good chase and was a natural born hunter.

As the hunt came into the next field beyond the orchard, I realised—too late—that I was not paying enough attention to Paddy. Drawing his weight onto his back legs, he hunched into a "ready-steady-go" position, then hurled himself forward into an instant gallop, racing towards the hedge and the hunt.

The reins were too slack in my hands and, as Paddy took the bit between his teeth, I knew I was in serious trouble. Luckily, I hadn't lost my stirrups but I *had* lost my riding crop, and I was being bounced around in the saddle like a sack of Mr. B's King Edward potatoes.

"Paddy, whoa! Whoa! Paddeeee!" I was screaming now, and tugging as hard as I could on the reins. All the lessons we'd learned on how to handle a horse, had flown right out of my memory. All I wanted to do was STOP THE DAMN HORSE.

"Paddy, stop. Please. Stop!"

Paddy was not sticking to the usual orchard trails. He struck out through the rough patches and I could feel tall grasses and weeds whipping at my legs. Then, out of nowhere came the blur of a tree branch; I ducked my head just in time. The boundary hedge of the orchard loomed ahead and Paddy raced straight for it, and for the hunt that was noisily galloping up the other side. Surely Paddy would stop at the hedge? A flash of memory and more of my father's words, "Never let the horse know that you are afraid."

"Well it doesn't happen like that. I AM afraid."

"Stop. Paddy, please stop."

But Paddy didn't stop. When we were right up against the hedge, I thought he was going to crash through it. I shut my eyes and screamed. Then he veered sharply to the left and almost unseated me. Long switches of hazel whipped against me, stinging my shoulders right through my jacket. One lashed my cheek and I yelped at the pain.

"PADDEEE. STOP...STOP!"

But Paddy was enjoying himself. Stretching his gallop, he kept up with the horses on the other side of the hedge. We were coming up fast to the corner of the orchard where Normanhurst's and Farmer Bourne's boundary hedges dipped and joined. My heart sank as I realised what Paddy was going to do. And I knew I *had* to go along with him. Clenching the reins even tighter, I grabbed a chunk of Paddy's mane and twisted my fingers into the coarse hair. I leaned forward and hung on, my cheek bouncing off his narrow neck. And just in time, as I could feel Paddy gathering himself for the leap.

"I'm going to die!" For a split-second I saw myself, pale and cold, being carried on a five-barred gate back down the orchard and into the stable yard. And everyone crowding around. And Ant saying, "Coo-er."

"Oh, gosh. I can't die yet. I"m too young." I hung on for dear life. Literally.

Paddy landed. I could feel the jolt right through my legs, up my back to my shoulders, where my arms felt as if they'd been wrenched from their sockets. I lost my grip and the reins slipped from my hands. The thick coarse mane was all I had to hold on to. I slithered and bounced as I tried to regain a lost stirrup.

"How cross my father will be that I didn't keep my heels down."

The clank of iron on my ankle and another shot of pain. My foot fumbled, my toes groped. Somehow, I managed to hook my foot back into the stirrup. Now to disentangle my hands from the thick mane. I managed to free one hand, and frantically searched for the thin length of leather lying against Paddy's neck. Tales of runaway horses breaking their legs by tripping on lost reins, raced across my mind.

"Oh God, Paddy. Don't trip."

I tried to talk to him, but I couldn't breathe properly and words wouldn't come. I was now in the middle of the hunt, surrounded by huge horses, their hooves thudding, and kicking up clods of earth that stung my face. Paddy breathed in great snorting gasps and the smells of bruised grass, churned earth and horse sweat, made my eyes water. The hounds, baying and yelping, were darting every which way; noses to the ground. I now had a good grip of the reins again with one hand, and was trying to untwist the other hand from the thick, scratchy hair, cutting into my fingers. Pull. Twist. Uncurl my fingers.

"Oh, damn, damn. DAMN!"

Then–it was free. I felt for the cold leather; grabbed at it, caught it and held on to it. With both hands on the pommel of my saddle, I managed to pull myself upright. I had the reins. Long black hairs from Paddy's mane, were still wrapped around my fingers.

"I'm not dead. Oh! Thank you God."

The reins back in my hands, it felt as though Paddy had slackened his speed. But he was still on his own. With the bit between his teeth, there was nothing I could do to control him. He wanted to go with the hunt; I had no choice but to go with him.

I became aware that I was not alone. A lady, mounted on a colossal black hunter, came up beside me. She was riding side-saddle, her long black riding habit trailing across the horse's back and belly. "I say, are you all right little gel? Did you get separated from your party?"

"N-no just from my stirrup. B-but I'm all right, thank you. M-my party's just ahead."

"Jolly good! But it looks like your horse has grabbed his bit. Here. Let me deal with him."

Keeping pace with Paddy, she edged in until she could lean over and grasp Paddy's reins just under his chin. She jerked his head up and I heard the bit clatter against his teeth. "Tidy your reins, little gel. Tidy your reins. Jolly good. You've got him now. Let him know who's master. But where's your crop? And what on earth have you done to your nose?"

"I-I...d-dropped it Ma'am. The...the crop. I dropped it in some nettles. And I-I b-bumped my nose. But I'm all right. And...and anyway, he get's edgy when I use the crop. Thank you. I-I've got him now."

"Good gel. Been huntin' often?"

"N-no. This is my first."

"Good grief! And you're not on a leading rein? Well, go and catch up with your party. You're doing super. Super little rider. But do you always stammer? Tell your mother to get you some speech therapy, little gel. Can't grow up stammering y'know. 'Bye now."

With that she loped off on her black hunter, long flimsy black streamers flying from her elegant black riding bowler. Everything about her was black.

"You heard that Paddy? I'm a super little rider. Not that you were much help. Anyway, I've got you now. We're having a foxhunting day. You've got your way, so start behaving."

As the hunt had slowed down, we were now cantering along at a fairly easy pace. The hounds were nosing around in a small copse in the middle of Farmer Bourne's turnip field. The horses were gathering around, snorting and breathing hard–flecks of white sweat-foam dappling their necks and chests. I guided Paddy around to the other side of the copse, well away from Lady Side-saddle, who was watching me. A fat man with very red cheeks, and riding a huge bay, was leading a small boy on a dapple-grey pony. The boy turned his head away as I rode up, so I passed him and went further around the copse. The sun shone and I felt warm and sweaty. Every time I wrinkled my nose I could feel the dried blood, stiff and crackly. I pulled out my hanky, spat on it, and scrubbed at the blood. It hurt a lot, but I hoped it looked clean. I adjusted my riding hat which had slipped—unfashionably for a hunt—onto the back of my head. My plaits had come undone and my hair was trailing in lanky wisps around my face. How I hated having difficult hair. By now, I was enjoying myself and reckoned that everybody considered me to be an official part of the foxhunt, instead of recovering from a severe case of runaway horse. I sat up straight in the saddle and Paddy played the part by prancing and showing off.

"Oh, gosh! Oh, golly! Oh...damn!"

Straight ahead of me, sitting on a pony several sizes too small for him, was that red-haired, snivelling Rowley Smythe. His nose was running as usual, right into his mouth which opened a little wider when he saw me. His mother, who was also riding a small horse that could have used a good grooming, had him on a leading rein. And, horrors of horrors, she was talking to Arabella Bosworthy's mother. If Rowley Smythe told his mother I was at the foxhunt, then Arabella Bosworthy's mother would tell Arabella, and 'Bossy Bella' would tell Miss Audrey-Joan and then...then I would be in terrible trouble. My mother would be sent for. I could be expelled. Oh gosh, what could I do? Rowley Smythe was already tugging at his mother's sleeve, trying to get her attention.

"I'm a dead duck. A very dead duck."

What happened next, was so unexpected that it took everyone by surprise. And it saved my life. The fox saved my life. There was a flash of russet fur, and the fox broke cover, appearing from under the end of a fallen tree and darted for the open field. The hounds were in a frenzy at the other end of the tree, their noses rootling through the long grass where they thought the fox had gone to ground. Most of the huntsmen were gathered in the same spot. The fallen tree had turned out to be hollow and the wily old fox had wriggled through its length, then seized his opportunity to make a dash for freedom; leaving the hounds bunched together in an opening far too small for them. The fox passed close to Paddy and me. He looked straight at us, his bright eyes darting this way and that. He was panting, his long pink tongue lolling out the side of his mouth; I could see his wicked teeth. Bits of twig and grass had caught in his coat and a bundle of burrs was clinging to his brush.

The commotion upset Rowley's horse, and his mother had a hard time controlling it with the leading rein. Rowley lost both stirrups as the pony bucked and backed away from the fox. I decided to seize the opportunity and get away from Rowley and his mother—and Arabella Bosworthy's mother. So as the *'tally-ho'* rang out and the huntsmen crashed through the copse, and the hounds rushed after the scent of the fox, I joined them and was soon in the middle of a pack of running hounds and galloping horses. Paddy was now behaving, as this was what he enjoyed doing most, chasing foxes. All I had to do was to concentrate on good riding. As we cantered away, I could hear Rowley's mother shouting, "Heels down, Row. Heels DOWN!"

I giggled when I heard her call him Row. We would have some fun, teasing him about that. Row! Row! Wait until I tell Ant about little Row.

"Oh gosh – Ant." I wondered if he was still in his look-out and if he could see me now. *"What if he's told someone?"* But Ant would never tell on me. Perhaps he was still watching me from his lookout point, high on the stable roof.

I'd been hunting once before with my father who'd borrowed a little pony for me. He'd kept a tight hold on my leading rein and only let me trot along beside him. He'd also kept me well away from the fast, galloping hunters, and took me home long before the kill. I'd never seen the end of a fox hunt, and as this one had sort of saved my life, I was not sure I wanted to see him caught. Besides, he'd looked like a nice old fox.

Paddy and I were well along with the leading riders, right behind the hounds. The call of the hunting horn, the hard breathing snorts of the foam-drenched horses, the yells of the riders to each other, and the wet leaves and dirt kicked up by the horses' hooves, were all part of the excitement I felt. I smelled the sweat of both horse and rider as I passed them, and heard the creak and squeak of leather boots and saddles as the chase got faster. And closer. And all the while, the continual tinny call of the hunting horn. *'Tally-ho! Tally-ho!'*

"He's tiring," someone shouted. "The hounds'll soon get him."

"Oh dear," I remembered the flash of red fur and the darting, frightened eyes. *"Oh dear. Please God, help the fox get away."*

Then it came. The call, *'Gone to Earth.'* Tired and beaten, the fox had found a hidey-hole and the hounds were scrabbling and digging in the earth to get at him. I was rushed along within the mass of riders all jostling to get near. I couldn't see Rowley and his mother—thank goodness—but I was close to my side-saddle lady. She saw me and smiled, "Great going, little gel. Exciting, eh? We've got the little bugger beat now. We've got old Reynard."

The chase was over, and everybody reined in to watch the hounds do their work. The horses were still prancing and snorting and I had quite a job keeping Paddy under control. He wanted to go on running.

Then, without warning, a bunch of hounds came rushing towards us, their jaws clamped tightly on what looked like a bit of old red fur coat. It dangled limply and the hounds were shaking it and worrying it, each trying to tear off little bits. Their faces were soaked in blood, and I realized that the piece of old fur coat was the poor fox. I felt a bit sick.

The Master of the Hounds, and a couple of other men in their coats of hunting pink, dismounted and waded into the excited, bouncing pack of hounds, their riding whips lashing out at the frenzied animals. Yelps of pain rang out in the midday air and, one by one, the hounds were dragged away from their prize—pink tongues licking the warm blood from their faces.

"*Oh, God. Please don't let me be sick.*" Then I very nearly was, because I heard someone in the crowd behind me, being sick. I half turned my head, then turned it back again. It was Rowley. If I saw him sicking-up, I would too; hearing him was bad enough.

The Master held up, high above his head, the limp and bloodied body of the fox. Some of the hounds were leaping up, trying to grab it. Whips cracked and they slunk off yelping.

"Who gets the trophies?" He called to the crowd. "Who gets the mask?"

"Sir Gerald gets it," someone shouted. "It's his fiftieth anniversary as a member of the hunt."

The Master of the Hounds was hacking away at the horrible bloody mess with a large and very nasty looking hunting knife. The head came off. I turned away. "*I will NOT be sick.*"

"Who gets the brush?" He held up the long and beautiful bushy tail. There was no blood on it at all, just the burrs still tangled in the fur.

"I had my dibs in for that." My side-saddle lady rode forward and claimed the brush.

"Now, what about the pads? Who gets a pad today? Anyone's first hunt?"

The boy on the pony was led forward by the fat, red-faced man. The Master, holding one of the fox's paws he'd cut off at the joint half-way up its leg, leaned over to the boy; who almost fell off his horse as he tried to back away. He smeared some of the blood from the cut-off end on the boy's cheek, before presenting it to him. As the red-faced man led him away, I saw the boy was crying. The man was angry—telling him off for blubbing. I could hear him muttering something about "being a man not a mouse." And, "he was behaving like a little girl."

"Who's next?"

A lady walked forward leading a tiny girl riding a Shetland pony, took the pad from the Master, and hurriedly led the child away. No blood smear. Just a big smile from the little girl, whose golden curls were clustered under her new hunting bowler, and who looked as though she hadn't even ridden with the hunt. Her hands in spotless white gloves held the reins very daintily, and her riding jacket and jodh-purs were neat and very clean. I glanced down at my own dirty and muddied jodhpurs, and at my filthy hands. My sleeve was smeared with the blood from my nose and my hair dangled in my eyes. *"How could anyone possibly keep* **that** *clean?"*

"And the third pad? Who gets the third pad?"

To my surprise, it was Rowley Smythe. His mother led him forward. He looked awful. His sick was all down his riding jacket and he'd been crying. When the Master leaned down and put the pad near his cheek to bloody him, Rowley threw up again. I looked away, and saw that my side-saddle lady had ridden up beside me.

"And the last pad?" The Master shouted. "Who gets the last pad?"

Side-saddle lady's arm shot up. She was still holding the brush. "Right here. This little gel. Super rider and her first hunt."

Which it wasn't, but I said nothing.

She motioned me to follow her, so Paddy and I rode up to the Master of the Hounds. Lady Side-saddle looked very important and—as my father would have said—cut a fine figure on her black hunter; whose coat gleamed in the midday sunlight. I felt important too, even if I *was* grubby and blood-stained, and my hair was straggling around my face.

"Congratulations, young lady. I officially blood you and present you with this fox's pad." He held out four inches of russet fur. At one end, dirtied and broken with bits of grass and earth still caught and held in them, were the fox's long claws. At he other end, a very white round piece of bone with little strings hanging it from it oozing blood. He held the bloody bit to my cheek.

"This is important. I will not *be sick. I will* not *be sick."*

I felt the hard bone graze my cheek. Then something warm and wet. I felt the cool breeze turn the warm-wet to ice-cold. I stared into the Master's eyes and tried to look sacrificial. This was a sacrifice but I wasn't sure whether it was me or the fox that was being offered up. Then I felt the same on the other cheek. Warm and wet turned to cold and stiff. The Master held out the pad.

"Take it little gel. Take it." Lady Side-saddle nudged me.

I grasped the pad in my right hand. "Thank you," I whispered.

"Well done, well done." The master and Lady Side-saddle both spoke at once. A few people clapped, and I heard Rowley's voice whining about something. Now if only his mother would keep away from Bossy Bella's mother. The riders parted and made a sort of path for Lady Side-saddle and me to ride between them. She appeared be an important person. I felt like a victorious gladiator riding in triumph out of a Roman Coliseum. Bloody, messed up, but victorious. *"So boo snubs to Rowley Smythe."* People were clapping. Clapping *me*.

Outside the gathering of hunters, Lady Side-saddle turned to me. "Come and get a drink, little gel. I have my groom here with lunch."

I followed her to where a five-barred gate led into the lane that ran from Normanhurst to Thatcher Woods. Just inside the gate, was the most unusual and colourful thing I'd ever seen. It was a real Romany caravan, gaily painted blue with green trim, and with yellow wheels. The door was divided, and the top half stood open; along the outside were wee shuttered windows framing the chintz curtains hanging inside. I knew it was a Romany caravan because a long time ago, my mother had shown me pictures of them in a book. "Gosh. Is that yours?" I asked.

"It jolly well is," Lady Side-saddle cackled. "And believe me, I wouldn't be without it. Had to give up the Rolls, y'know, because of the war. No petrol to speak of, at least not enough to run a Rolls. So I got me this. Old Ned pulls it for me, and Roagey-Mac here, drives it."

"Roagey-Mac?" I'd heard that name before somewhere.

Roagey-Mac poked his head out over the bottom half of the door. Wearing a bright yellow jockey cap and a yellow and green muffler wound around his neck, he matched the caravan. As soon as he saw Lady Side-saddle, he opened the rest of the door, jumped down to help her dismount. Thankfully, I slid off Paddy's back. My bottom was sore from the long ride and my legs were aching and wobbly. Standing beside him, Roagey-Mac wasn't much taller than me.

"Oh! Gosh! Was it? Could it be? The very same Roagey-Mac that..."

"Come inside, gel. Roagey-Mac will take care of your horse." Lady Side-saddle led the way into the caravan, while Roagey-Mac disappeared with both horses.

"And Lady Side-saddle? Was it? But she didn't look a bit like..."

"He used to be a jockey, y'know. Rode for my grandfather's stable when I was a young gel. Rode a lot of winners too. But he had a bad fall and that was the end of his racing. Grandpapa gave him a job as a groom and a flat in our coach house, and he's been with us ever since. Don't know what we'd do without him and what he doesn't know about horses you could get under a postage stamp. Now, sit ye there at the table and I'll get us a drink. What'll it be? Lemonade?"

"Y-yes please, and thank you very much f-for...rescuing me. And thank you for getting me the fox's pad."

"You deserved it. You rode jolly well, and without a leading rein. But, young lady, I'm inclined to think that you were on your own, eh? No-one with you today? Care to tell me about it? Come on gel. I won't bite and I won't tell on ye either. What happened?"

I was fishing in my jumper for my hanky as my nose had started to run and I didn't know whether it was blood or snot. Lady Side-saddle understood my needs and opened a drawer. She found a face flannel and wetted it with warm water from a thermos. "Here. Try this. It might make you feel better. But don't wipe Reynard's blood from your cheeks yet. You have to wear it all day, don't y'know. Out of respect, of course."

I didn't know, but I wasn't quite sure about wearing it to go back to school. *"BACK TO SCHOOL."* I had forgotten. "Oh, dear," I wailed.

"Hey. Don't fold on me now, gel. Chin up and tell me what happened. You're in a scrape I s'pose. Well, don't worry. I was always in scrapes when I was your age. Suppose you start by telling me your name, and where you live."

That did it. I managed to get out, "M-my name is Patricia . . ." and then it all came tumbling out. How I'd taken Paddy from the stable because I couldn't get Dolly saddled properly. How Paddy had bolted when he heard the hunt because he loved hunting. How I didn't mean to go on the hunt, but Paddy wanted to and I was going to be in so much trouble when I get back because nobody, absolutely nobody EVER rides outside the school. Never, ever, ever. And how I was sure they would send for my mother and I would get expelled and...and.... By that time, I could feel the tears rolling down my cheeks.

"Hey there. Don't blubber now, you'll wash the blood off. That must stay on your cheeks out of respect to Mr Reynard the Red, who came to an untimely end. And, yes, I know you wanted him to get away. All of us feel like that sometimes. But some do and some don't. And this one didn't. So dry your eyes, and don't fret."

Abruptly, Lady Side-saddle stopped talking. She was looking at me hard; her bright blue eyes fixed on my face. "Patricia, eh. Well now, let me think. I have an odd feeling we've met before somewhere. What say you, Roagey-Mac?"

Roagey-Mac was back inside the caravan by now, and fiddling with a wicker picnic basket. Unwinding his muffler, he came over and peered at me.

"Oh my Gosh. I had seen him before. And the Lady was..."

"Why yes, M'Lady. I believe we 'ave come across this nipper afore. Summat to do wiv a pet pig if I remember rightly. A pet pig wot got sacrificed in the name of bacon, if I'm not mistaken." Then he winked at me. Oh gosh, I remembered that wink. But Lady Side-saddle looked so different with her hair all bundled up in a snood, and her long black riding habit.

"Hmmm." She stared at me for a long, long time. "In trouble again, are we?"

"Yes. Well, no...not really...I-I didn't do it on purpose."

"Often in trouble are we Patricia?"

"Yes...well no. I'm not *bad* like some of the others are. And this was an accident. I was riding in the orchard when the hunt came by. And Paddy took off with me."

"Did he now? Well, we'll think about what to do later. Come, I have a picnic lunch here and I don't know about you, but I'm starving. Let's eat."

Lady Side-saddle and Roagey-Mac opened the wicker picnic basket and brought out packages wrapped in greaseproof paper. Glory be! Inside the packages was food, I'd only seen in my dreams. Sandwiches with real butter on the bread and filled with ham, chicken, or salmon. There were scones, with cream and real strawberry jam in little glass pots. And fruit I'd never seen or had forgotten about. I recognized an orange. "But what is that long yellow thing?" I asked.

"Why it's a banana. Ye don't know what a banana is?"

"I've seen pictures. I must have eaten them before the war, but I don't remember. What do they taste like?"

"Like a banana! Go ahead. Have one. Here, let me show you how to take the skin off."

I held the banana, the strips of skin dangling over my hand. I sniffed. It smelled...exotic. Lady Side-saddle was still talking. "I don't know where they came from. Roagey-Mac gets them, and I don't ask from where. But I believe he has connections, as they say."

"Fell of the back of a lorry, that one did, M'lady. Right into me 'ands, like."

Lost in a banana heaven, I didn't answer. It was almost as good as chocolate. Besides, it's rude to talk with your mouth full.

Lady Side-saddle let me eat as much as I wanted. When I finally stopped, she said, "Now young lady, it's time to go. But before we do, I have something for you."

She left the caravan, but was soon back. She was carrying the brush belonging to the late Mr Reynard. "Whether you were breaking school bounds or not, I want you to have this." She plunked it down in my lap.

"I have more than enough hunting trophies. Besides you earned your blooding by good riding, which is more than can be said for those other namby-pambies there. Who was that dreadful fella who kept up-chucking? He certainly didn't deserve his pad. And as for that golden haired mummy's darling. She never even rode with us. Mummy brought her in right at the end, just in time to get her prize. Pshaw. I dread to think what they'll grow up into; chinless wonders and spoiled brats. There I go, ramblin' on again. Anyway, this is yours."

"Th-thank you very much." I stroked the long red fur. There was still a tangled mess of burrs caught in it. I started to pick them out. "But what do I do with it? It's all raw at the end, like the pad."

"Ah yes, you're at school of course. Well, Roagey here, will take them to the taxidermist and have them cured and mounted for you. D'you think you'd like that?"

"Oh yes, ma'am. Very much. Thank you."

"Good, then that's settled. Now I suppose the next order of business is for me to intercede for you once more with Miss Audrey-Joan Baker." She saw me wince. "Oh yes, I know her well so let's be off. Come along, we'll drive the caravan and Roagey-Mac will bring the horses."

Old Ned was encouraged to stop munching Farmer Bourne's grass and haul us out into the lane. Roagey-Mac was riding Lady Side-saddle's hunter and leading Paddy. Now I was in for it. The time had come to face the music—as my father would have said.

But strangely enough, I didn't get into much trouble.

The caravan rumbled up the Normanhurst driveway and stopped in front of the columned porch. I could see children at the windows, staring at us in amazemenet. The front door opened and Miss Audrey-Joan Baker, B.A. (Hons.) stood on the porch. She wasn't smiling. I shrunk down on the driver's bench, trying to make myself invisible. Lady Side-saddle turned to me. "You stay there gel, while I chat with Miss Baker."

Gathering up her long skirts, she allowed Roagey-Mac to assist her down from the caravan. When she joined Miss Audrey-Joan on the porch, I heard her say, "May we talk inside?"

"Why Lady Harriet. What a nice surprise. Yes, please come in." As Miss Audrey-Joan escorted Lady Side-saddle indoors, I caught her looking over her shoulder at me. Her eyebrows were high on her fore-head. The doors banged shut, and the glass eyes glared at me.

I slid along the driver's bench to where Roagey-Mac stood beside the caravan; he'd tethered Paddy and Lady Side-saddle's hunter behind it. Old Ned was stretching his neck and shaking his head. The heavy harness collar rattled and tinkled.

"Is that her name? Lady Harriet."

Roagey-Mac turned to me. "That's right miss. Lady 'Arriet from the 'All."

"You mean from the Manor House? She's the Lady of the Manor?"

"That's right Miss. Lady 'Arriet of Heardington Manor."

"Oh gosh. B-but, this is Eardington Manor. Why isn't she living here? And how can she possibly keep me out of trouble with Miss Baker?"

"Don't worry Miss. She 'as a bit of a say about wot goes on in the village. And 'specially in your little school. Hafter 'all, it's 'er 'ouse. Or was 'er 'ouse...til . . .."

"Till when Roagey-Mac?"

"Never mind Missee. That's none of our beeswax. I said too much already. Just remember, she's got a lot o' clout with yer teacher."

"Oh Roagey-Mac," I pleaded. "Please tell me. Pleeeese. I have to know. And I won't tell. Cross-my-heart-and-hope-to-die." I licked my finger and made the sign of an X over my chest. I could still taste the banana on my finger; I licked the other fingers.

Roagey-Mac looked at me for a considerable spell, then shrugged his shoulders and started. "Well it's on account of the war see. She loaned this 'ouse for what they call an evacuation school. A school like, that couldn't stay where it was 'cos of the bombing. Came from near Brummigam as I recall."

"But where does Lady Harriet live?"

"Why bless you, she lives in a nice big 'ouse t'other side of the village. Though 'er Ladyship calls it the little 'ouse. She hinerited a lot of property you see, and she can't live in it all at once. 'Roagey-Mac,' she sez to me. 'Roagey-Mac, we'll all go to the little house'—as she calls the 'All—'and let the manor go to someone who needs it. It'll be part of our war effort,' she sez. 'We'll let children live here an' learn. And I 'ope the children will have a happy war here.'"

"A happy war? Can war be happy?"

"Well now, young lady. 'Appy is what you make it I s'pose. Well, maybe 'appy is not eggsactly the right word. More like cheerful. Or making the best of things. But I tell you, 'tis strange how some folks find 'appiness in tough times. Take me f'rinstance. It was a sad day when I had to give up wearing the silks and I sometimes I long for the feel of a winner beneath my saddle as t'were, but I'm very 'appy doing what I'm doing. And I wouldn't change a thing."

"Oh." I began to feel a little bit better.

When I saw Ant sneaking around the corner of the house, I felt even better. He slipped around the back of the caravan to the other side where he couldn't be seen. Roagey-Mac moved away to check on the horses; Old Ned, his reins tied in a huge knot, stood with his head down, shaking it occasionally when a fly buzzed too close to his ears.

Ant slipped around to where I was sitting on the driver's bench. "Pssst!" he hissed. "What have you been up to? You're in terrible trouble. You're going to get the cane for sure."

"Do you think I'll get expelled?"

"Dunno. Maybe."

"Hey. Did you see me with the foxhunt?"

"You bet I did. It was ripping. I watched you all the way. I could see right up as far as the dingle copse in Farmer Bourne's turnip field. I can see everything for miles from my lookout."

"What else did you see?"

"A lot of horses and people and hounds. But I saw you take the hedge and I saw you galloping with the hunt. And then I couldn't see you any more 'cos you got too far away."

"Did you tell on me?"

"Of course not. But they knew. I didn't tell anyone. Cross-my-heart -and-hope-to-die."

"Somebody told on me. 'Cos they knew."

"Well I dunno who told on you. Didn't even see anybody come in through the gates. Tell you what, though. Maybe Mr. Jeffrey was going to ride Paddy to the hunt."

I hadn't thought of that. "Did you see Mr. Jeffrey?

"I wasn't looking for anyone coming up the drive. I was trying to see you and the hunt. I say, you did take that jump pretty well."

I didn't tell Ant that I nearly didn't make the jump at all. And that I'd lost a stirrup. I noticed he was staring at me in a peculiar way. "What's all that brown stuff on your face? It looks like blood."

"It *is* blood. I got blooded by the Master of the Hounds 'cos it was my first hunt. And I got a pad and Lady Side-saddle gave me the brush."

"Lady Who?"

"Lady Side-saddle. That's what I called her. She rode side-saddle in those long black skirts. Now Roagey-Mac tells me she's really Lady Harriet from the Hall."

"Holy cow! You *are* going up in the world. And she's gone in to see Miss Audrey-Joan about you? Gosh!" Ant was silent for a while. I could see he was considering something. Ant was always considering things. "I wonder what she'll tell her," he said.

"I dunno. But what's worse is that Rowley Smythe was there with his mother and *she* was talking to Bossy Bella's mother. And Rowley was sick all over the place. He even threw up on the Master of the Hounds when he got blooded. And his mother called him Row. Isn't that a scream. Wait 'til he comes back on Monday morning."

"Don't be mean to him," said Ant. "His Daddy was killed fighting for us, y'know."

"Atten-shun," Roagey-Mac called from the back of the caravan." Straighten up you two. It seems your medicine is on its way, Missee."

"Quick," I said to Ant. "I've got something for you. Take it." I took the banana I'd hidden under my riding jacket and shoved it into Ant's hand. His eyes widened in surprise and the eyebrow shot up as he rolled it up under the hem of his jumper.

The front doors opened and Lady Side-saddle came out. Miss Audrey-Joan was right behind her. "Patricia, you may come in now," Miss Audrey-Joan looked sternly at me, but then smiled as she shook hands with Lady Side-saddle. "Thank you so much for bringing Patricia back, and for your interesting account of her foxhunting adventures."

"Oh Lawks. I'm in so much trouble. I'll probably die. I'll be shut up in a little room with only bread and water; and I'll die."

As I climbed the porch steps, Lady Side-saddle turned from Miss Audrey-Joan, took my hands and squeezed them. I looked up at her and she winked at me. Then the moment was over and she straightened up and dropped my hands, "It was very nice to meet you again, child. And I hope we shall see more of you. Work hard at your lessons, m'dear and try to overcome that stammer. I've told Miss Baker to give you some special voice exercises that will help. And let me know when your mother comes up to visit, I would like to meet her. Good-bye now, and try and keep out of trouble for a few days, eh?"

With that, she sailed down the steps and up onto the front seat of the caravan. Roagey-Mack was already mounted on the hunter. He must have taken Paddy back to his stable while I was talking to Ant.

"C'mon Neddy, old thing. Time to go home for tea." At Lady Harriet's encouragement, Ned turned on the big gravel circle and set off down the drive at a brisk trot. The brightly coloured caravan was watched by 20 pairs of eyes in 20 heads as they jostled for the best view from the school windows.

I looked up at Miss Audrey-Joan.

"Come," she boomed and led the way through the hall and into her study. A small fire that had been hurriedly lit, struggled in the grate and the remains of the tea that had been served to Lady Side-saddle cluttered the small, round fireside table. It looked as though Miss Audrey-Joan had been interrupted from a Saturday afternoon rest. A book was open on a side table and a newspaper lay on the floor at the end of the brown leather chesterfield. The room smelled of wood smoke. Tristan and Iseult lay curled up on the window seat and Mrs. B sat in the armchair beside of the fireplace, her feet resting on a tapestry-covered footstool. She was busy unpicking an old jumper of Mr. B's. As she pulled each row apart, she wound the wool onto a ball.

"You may sit, Patricia." Now *that* was a good sign. "On the stool over by the table." *Not* such a good sign.

Miss Audrey-Joan went over to the window that faced the drive. She stood for a long time, staring at the sycamore tree across the lawn. Her back was towards me but I could hear her sucking at her teeth. I knew she was thinking of what to do with me. I risked a glance at Mrs. B who went on unpicking and winding. A half-burnt log fell from the fire onto the hearth and Tristan opened his eyes. He looked at me and stretched, kicking Iseult with his back paws. He licked a front paw, looked at me again and wriggled back into a round mound of fur, the tip of his tail across his nose, and went back to sleep.

And still Miss Audrey-Joan stood, staring out of the window. It seemed I waited for ever. I sniffed. Twice.

"Handkerchief please," Mrs. B said, without looking up from her jumper-unpicking.

"It...it's a bit dirty." I pulled out my disgustingly blood-stained hanky.

Mrs. B looked up. "And where did all that blood come from young lady? From what I've been hearing, I gather that is fox's blood?"

"Oh, no. That's still on my cheeks and I have to keep it there all day. The blood on my hanky is from my nose. I knocked my nose wh-when P-Paddy bolted and jumped the hedge." It was a small lie, but it served it's purpose.

At that, Miss Audrey-Joan spun around on her heels so fast that I jumped off the stool and stood to attention. "And is that what really happened? Paddy bolted with you?"

"Yes, Miss Baker. He was all right until he heard the hunt and then he seemed to want to go with the hunt.... I couldn't hold him. I tried. I really did."

"And just what were you thinking of? Riding Paddy? You're supposed to ride Dolly."

"I-I thought that Mr. B had saddled Paddy for me, 'cause Dolly wasn't saddled and it was my turn to ride early. And as Mrs. Tommy had said I'd grown a couple of inches, I thought he meant me to ride Paddy. He said I could if I grew two inches. Please Miss Baker, I thought I was supposed to ride Paddy."

"That will do," Miss Audrey-Joan thundered. "THAT WILL DO."

She moved to her desk that had been carefully placed between the two windows, so that she could see what us children were up to outside. She sat down in her chair. Her uncapped fountain pen lay on an open exercise book covered with her writing. She picked up the black and grey mottled Swan pen—turning it around and around in her hands. I knew she was thinking of what punishment I should get. Then she picked up the fountain pen cap and screwed it on. She looked up at me. "Come here and let me look at your nose."

I moved forward.

"No. Around here."

I stepped around behind the desk and stood by her chair. The top of my head was level with her shoulder. She put a finger under my chin and tilted my head up. Then she turned it from side to side. "Well it doesn't seem to be broken, although it must have bled a lot. But you are a very grubby little girl. And your face is filthy. What am I going to do with you Pat?"

"Expel me?"

Her eyebrows shot up behind the fringe of floppy brown curls. "No. No, I don't think you broke any rules deliberately, did you?"

Hope began to flicker. "No, Miss Baker. I just wanted my Saturday morning ride in the orchard."

"Lady Harriet seems to have taken a liking to you. Anyway she said that you put up a good show at the hunt and once you'd got control of your horse, you rode well. She recommended you for a blooding. That was an honour, you know."

"Yes, Miss Baker."

"Lady Harriet asked me to make sure you'd come to no harm and she would prefer that you don't get punished for your adventure. She thinks the experience you went through was—to use her word– 'exacting'. Exacting enough for one day. Or a weekend for that matter."

"Yes, Miss Baker. Thank you, Miss Baker."

"Thank Lady Harriet, not me. She interceded for you. And it's not the first time, she has pleaded with me on your behalf, is it? She appears to have taken a shine to you and asked that you go up to the Hall one Saturday morning and ride with her."

I look at Miss Audrey-Joan. I tried to say something, but the words wouldn't come. I felt a familiar tingling at the back of my nose. I felt a tear roll down my cheek.

"Oh no. I can't cry. It'll wash off Mr Reynard's blood."

I jabbed my knuckles across my eyes, hoping to catch my tears before they did any damage. Then my nose started to run.

Miss Audrey-Joan sighed and offered me a clean handkerchief, but I shook my head and grabbed the filthy one from my sleeve. I could probably find one corner that would do and I couldn't possibly dirty Miss Audrey-Joan's hanky. It was so very white and clean.

She peered at my face for a long minute without speaking. Then turned to Mrs. B, "A little delayed reaction here, I think. We should get this child cleaned up. Perhaps some camomile tea?"

"Very well." Mrs. B sighed, put down the old jumper and heaved herself out of her comfy old chair. "Come with me, child." She took my hand to lead me from the study.

Miss Audrey-Joan said, "You realise this doesn't happen again, Pat?"

"Yes, Miss Baker."

"And you realise that I will have to write to your mother and tell her what happened?"

"Yes, Miss Baker I'm going to write to her tomorrow and tell her myself." Sunday letter-writing was mandatory.

"Very well, see that you do. And for goodness sake, child, stop stammering. You never stammer."

"Yes Miss Baker. No Miss Baker."

Later, cleaned and out of my muddied and bloodied clothes, and with a smear of special ointment on my nose, I was allowed to join the rest of the children for tea. I'd thought I would be sent to bed without any, but I'd heard Mr. B rumbling at Mrs. B when I was in the bathtub. What he said to her I don't know, but I do know that for reasons known only to herself, she left the tiniest smear of Mr Reynard's blood on each cheek.

"Well," she said. "We mustn't break with tradition, I suppose. Or we'll have her Ladyship marching up our front drive again."

I slipped in to the space that Ant had saved for me at the tea table. There was complete silence in the room.

"Oh gosh, they've sent me to Coventry."

Then, "Tally ho! Tally ho!" Titters and giggles followed the high squeaky voice from another table. It had to be little Monty Marsh. He always squeaked.

Ant turned and smiled at me. "Don't take any notice," he advised. "They're just jealous, that's all. Actually you're a heroine right now and they all want to be your friend."

"Why?"

"So that the next time you go in the caravan, you'll take them with you."

"All of them?" I hissed.

"No. That's why they're being nice to you. They want to be picked." A sharp elbow nudged me in my side. "And they'll give you some of their sweet ration," Ant was whispering close to my ear now. "But I didn't tell them about what you gave me. It was whizzo, super-bang-on. Thanks." His breath was warm on my cheek and smelled of banana.

"Tally ho! Tally ho!" The room was filled with tally ho's, children calling my name, giggling. And there are smiles everywhere. Friendly smiles.

Ann-the-Bank sniffed, but said nothing.

I bent my head and got on with my tea. Cheese and potato pie with bits of hard-boiled egg in it, and two pieces of bread each. One of my favourite teas. I smiled at my plate. Today had been exciting. An adventure. A scathingly-brilliant adventure. And tomorrow I would write and tell my parents all about it.

And Cedric too. I'd tell him everything.

Sunday, 19th September, 1943
Dear Mummy and Daddy,
Yesterday I went foxhunting with Lady Harriet from the Hall.
I got blooded and was given a pad and Lady Harriet gave me
the brush. She is getting them taxi-somethinged for me. Lady
Harriet said I rode well. I'm sorry but my jodhpurs got a bit
grubby. I have grown two inches.
Love from
Your tall and blooded daughter,
Patricia

Chapter 36

Lady Harriet

"You have a visitor, Pat. Come, wash your hands and I'll try and do something with your hair to make you look a little more presentable."

Mrs. B bustled me out of the stables, where I'd been grooming Dolly. Although it was Saturday, the ban on my riding was still in effect. Mucking out the stables, cleaning tack, and grooming Dolly for four whole Saturdays—AND NO RIDING—was penance for my foxhunting adventure. But this was the last one—next Saturday I would be back to normal.

"Who is it? Is it my mother?"

"Now why on earth would your mother traipse all the way down from Westmorland to see you? Travel is hard these days—and dangerous as a lot of the railway lines have been bombed. No, it's not your mother. It's Lady Harriet."

"Lady Harriet?"

"Yes, little Miss Echo. It's Lady Harriet. And don't forget to mind your manners."

A few minutes later, hands and face scrubbed, and my hair brushed and tied in two bunches, Mrs. B led me by the hand to Miss Audrey-Joan's study.

In the two armchairs either side of the fireplace, sat Miss Audrey-Joan and Lady Harriet; my Lady Side-saddle from the fox hunt. Mrs. B poked me in the middle of my back. I moved forward and held out my hand.

"How do you do, Lady Harriet. Did you bring your caravan?"

"Well, how do *you* do, Patricia? No, I didn't bring my caravan, I rode my bicycle."

Miss Audrey-Joan patted a leather patchwork pouffe at the side of her chair, "Come and sit here by me. Lady Harriet has brought you a gift."

"A gift? For me?" I calculated quickly. *"It wasn't my birthday and it certainly wasn't Christmas."*

"Oh. Thank you." I couldn't think of anything else to say.

Lady Harriet smiled and dug in a huge khaki haversack which was propped against the side of the armchair. She pulled out a long, thin, brown paper parcel tied up with string. Smiling, she handed me the parcel. "Take a look. I think you'll like it."

Moving from the pouffe, I knelt down on the hearth-rug. The parcel was soft and light. I glanced up at Mrs. B and Miss Audrey-Joan—just to make sure I was doing the right thing. Miss Audrey-Joan smiled and Mrs. B nodded. So far so good. But what on earth could it be?

"Did ye find your riding crop, gel?" boomed Lady Harriet.

"Oh, yes. Thank you Ma'am. It was where I thought it would be. In a bunch of stinging nettles. But I wore my gloves to get it out." By now I'd untied the string and was winding it around my fingers. We'd been taught to save string, so I handed it to Mrs. B who put it in her apron pocket. I removed the wrapping paper, and laid the gift on the pouffe. I couldn't believe my eyes. I put out a hand and stroked it.

"Oh, my," said Miss Audrey-Joan. "Oh, my. What a beautiful thing."

"Hurrumph," said Mrs. B.

I held in my hands, the souvenirs of my foxhunting adventure. The fox's brush–reddish brown, black tipped, sleek and clean. It wasn't soft and silky like Tristan's fur, or even Gatsby's; more like rough-haired dog fur. At the top, where it had been attached to the fox, was a little silver mount–and fitted neatly into its top was Mr. Reynard's pad. Close-furred and softer than the brush. I turned it over; the little black cushions under the paw were hard and two of the claws, although they had been cleaned, were broken and rough. I didn't know what to say. I felt Mrs. B's finger in my back again.

"Thank you. Thank you very much, Lady Harriet. It's beautiful. I shall keep it for ever."

Lady Harriet pointed to the mount. "There's a tiny hole at the back, so you can thread a string and hang it up."

"It's...it's brilliant. I've never had a treasure like this before. My Daddy has an elephant's foot that he brought back from Burma. We used to keep umbrellas and walking sticks in it–that was when we had a proper home. And in my grandfather's house, there are some deer heads and glass cabinets full of stuffed birds. But no one has a fox's brush and pad."

"It's very special y'know, gel," said Lady Harriet. "After all, it was your first foxhunt and you were blooded with that pad. Keep it safe and one day you'll tell your grandchildren the whole exciting story."

I got up and shook her hand again. I would liked to have kissed her cheek, as I would have done if my mother had given me such a gift, but I didn't think I should. So I just said, "Thank you again, Lady Harriet. I shall keep it for ever and ever."

I folded up the brown paper and handed it to Mrs. B. "Where shall I keep it?"

Miss Audrey-Joan reached out and stroked the long silky brush. "I think, for now, you'd better keep it in a drawer in your bedroom. We'll think about where to put it later on."

"Shall I go and do it now?"

"Wait a moment." Miss Audrey-Joan indicated that I should sit down on the pouffe again. "I think Lady Harriet wants to ask you something."

"Well, little gel...er...Patricia. You haven't been riding outside the school property yet, have you."

I wasn't sure if the fox hunt counted, but I decided not to mention *that*. "No, Ma'am."

"Well, you've been riding for a year or so now, and you sit a horse very well. But you have to have some knowledge of riding outside the school property. The rules of riding on the roads and lanes for example. And how to open gates and watch for traffic. I have asked Miss Baker if you may come to my house and ride out with me next Saturday. I understand your detention will be ended by then. So what about it? D'ye think ye'd like that?"

"Oh...Lady Harriet. I'd love to come. I promise I'll be very good and on my best behaviour," I added quickly before Mrs. B had a chance to poke me again.

"That's settled then. Roagey-Mac will come and collect you at—say, nine o'clock."

"What...who...shall I ride?"

"Why Dolly of course. You are used to her. Roagey-Mac will ride with you."

"Oh, thank you."

"That's settled then. And I must say, Miss Baker's done a good job of curing the stammering. Excellent job."

I glanced at Miss Audrey-Joan. I recognised her look that meant, *"Careful, Patricia."* So I just said, "Thank you, Lady Harriet. Thank you very much."

The interview ended and I was dismissed. When the study door closed behind me, I ran and skipped down the hallway. I leaped up the back stairs two at a time–Ant had taught me how to do that–and flung myself on my bed, just missing Tristan who was dozing in a patch of sun. I tickled him awake with the end of Mr. Reynard's tail. He sniffed at it, patted it with his paw, sneezed, then settled down to sleep again. Very carefully, I laid the brush and pad at the back of the bottom drawer in the chest I shared with Ann-the-Bank. It just fitted.

Back downstairs, I went outside to look for Ant to tell him my good news. I reached the little side garden just as Lady Harriet was leaving. She was perched on what my mother called 'a-sit-up-and-beg' bicycle. She wobbled a bit as she steered it down the gravel driveway and through the open wrought-iron gates. She rode a horse far better than she rode a bicycle.

Later, while I was sharing a bathtub with Ann-the-Bank, and Mrs. B was washing our hair ready for church the next day, Mrs. B said, "You're a very lucky young lady, you know. Very lucky. I don't know why Lady H has taken a shine to you, but she has. You'd better not let Normanhurst's good name down by getting into more trouble."

"Oh Mrs. B. You know me better than that. I'm really very good. It's just that, sometimes...*unfortunate* things happen to me."

"Humph. Well, I don't know. So far this term, you've had an 'unfortunate' report. That whole episode of the fox hunt was..."

"Was an accident Mrs. B. An accident. I didn't mean to go, Paddy bolted." I sighed. *"How many more times did I have to go over this?"*

Ann-the-Bank said nothing, but I knew she would say something later. She was like that. Always quiet in front of the teachers and scathingly wordy when we were on our own. She flicked her long soapy hair back and it stung my cheek.

"You...you..." But I didn't go any further. She was only trying to get me into trouble with Mrs. B again. She was my best friend—well, my best girl friend. Ant was my best friend of all, and she was jealous. When I sometimes got favours, or what *she* thought were favours, she always got spiteful. But when she liked me, she couldn't do enough for me. She was like the girl in the nursery rhyme: '*When she was good, she was very, very good; And when she was bad, she was horrid.*'

Later, when we were going to bed, I said to her, "Don't worry Annie. I'll get you an invitation to Lady Harriet's place sometime. Just wait 'til I've been there a few times."

"But I don't like riding." Ann still played with dolls.

"Well maybe she'll have a picnic or something."

Ann sniffed. "Well I hope you aren't going to wear those filthy jodhpurs. They're disgusting. Lady Harriet won't want you all dirty."

She was right. My beautiful new fawn jodhpurs were covered in grass stains, splotches of mud and horse manure; even blood.

When Mrs. B came to put the lights out and make sure we hadn't touched the blackout, I asked her about washing my jodhpurs. "Look," I said, spreading them out on my bed. "I have to get these clean. They're too dirty to go riding with Lady Harriet."

Mrs. B heaved a big sigh and sat down on my bed. "As if we didn't have enough laundry to do, we now have to wash riding breeches and play clothes as well?" Mrs. B held them up, turned them over and hrmmphed. "Well, Miss Patricia. I think *you* can wash these. Monday is wash day, but by the time school is finished, it should all be done and drying. I'll save some soapy water from the wash boiler and show you how to scrub them clean. They'll be done in plenty of time for next Saturday. Now you go to sleep, young lady. You too, Miss Annie. By-the-way, where did you put your trophy?"

"It's in my jumper drawer."

"Did you see Pat's trophy, Ann?"

Ann-the-Bank wrinkled her nose. "Yes, I did. And I think it's disgusting. DIS-GUS-TING."

"Humph. Well, each unto his own, I suppose." With that, Mrs. B turned out the lights and stumped off down the corridor.

I couldn't get to sleep, wondering what Lady Harriet's house would be like. I didn't really care about getting an invitation for Ann, but I had to work on getting one for Ant. Then we *could* have some fun!

Sunday, 3rd October, 1943
Dear Mummy and Daddy,
Lady Harriet brought me my foxhunting trophy today. It is mounted on real silver.
Lady Harriet has invited me to go riding with her next Saturday. Miss Baker says I may go.
How is the war going?
Lots of love from
Patricia.

Although there had been thick fog the day before, and I worried it would stop me going to Lady Harriet's, Saturday was a bright and sunny day. I didn't really like Autumn because there was no more summer, just short days full of rain and fog, followed by winter snow and bitter cold. I hated the cold.

I had woken before the getting-up bell, and dressed quickly in my clean jodhpurs and the dark green polo-necked jumper that Mummy had knitted. She always knitted me one or two jumpers for the winter; even though wool was rationed. She and my aunts shared wool and patterns and sometimes they got old jumpers at jumble sales, unpicked them and knitted them up again. But Mummy had knitted this one from brand new Welsh wool that she had bought from the weaving factory before she left Wales. She'd had a kilt made up for me in matching green tweed, and the outfit was my Sunday best. It was a bit big, but that was so it would last the whole year.

My jodhpurs were clean again. Mrs. B had saved some of Monday's soapy wash water and shown me how to scrub them. Earlier in the day, she had put wet salt on the blood stains and so, apart from a few shadows, I'd managed to get them clean. All day Tuesday they hung outside on the washing line in the sun. When we brought them in, they had dried bright and clean and Mrs. Tommy ironed them as she didn't want me to burn myself. They looked almost as good as new.

On the way downstairs, I gave a double bang with my fist on the door of the boys' dormitory. Before I got down the corridor leading to the kitchen, I could hear Ant leaping down the stairs two at a time; he slid down the bannister on the last flight of stairs and caught me up.

We got the first two ladles of porridge, and the first pour from the milk jug, which meant it was almost cream. Mrs. B was bustling about sorting out the bread and the tea. Miss Audrey-Joan was munching on a piece of toast while she ladled out the porridge. Ant didn't say a word until we were sitting in the dining hall. Just the two of us; everyone else was still upstairs. "So this is the day you're going to that Lady Whatsername?"

"Harriet."

"Hmm. How long will you be gone?"

"I don't know. Most of the day, I hope."

"Hmph." He sounded a bit like Mrs. B.

I could see that Ant wasn't very smiley and I felt sorry for him. After all, we mostly did things together on a Saturday. In the mornings while I was riding, he was on the barn or stable roof, scanning for enemy planes, or he was playing with his war toys: aeroplanes, army lorries, and model soldiers; the rest of the day we did stuff together. So I tried to cheer him up. "I'll explore and see what's at Lady Harriet's place. And if there's something for you to do, I'll ask her if you can come next time."

"How d'you know there'll be a next time?"

"There will be. I just know."

"All right. I just thought I might be able to do something in that super caravan."

"I'll look around and find out what's there."

Then I had to stop talking about it. Ann-the-Bank thumped her porridge bowl down on the table and sat down beside me. I could tell she was in a miff because she must have sniffed at least six times. I knew she was upset I was going to Lady Harriet's and I was sorry about that.

But I wasn't going to let her spoil my day.

By ten minutes to nine, I was sitting on the front porch, waiting for Roagey-Mac. After breakfast, it had taken me all of five minutes to do my bathroom chores and make my bed, before I raced out to the stables to get Dolly ready for the day. But Mr. B had beaten me to it and I found Dolly saddled up and ready to go. "Go and wait out at the front, Pat-a-cake. When Roagey-Mac arrives, show him the way around to the yard gates and then we'll get you mounted up."

As I leaned against the tall pillar, I glanced over my shoulder at the round glass 'eyes' in the front door that had frightened me three years ago. Sometimes I still believed they were looking at me disapprovingly but on this bright sunny morning, they sparkled and smiled.

Ant, hands in pockets, was pacing up and down, kicking at the gravel and whistling. "So when's Roagey-Mac coming then?"

"Any minute now. Lady Harriet said he would be here at nine o'clock."

Ant said nothing, just went on kicking the gravel, but he didn't whistle any more. I wondered why he was so quiet and I was just about to ask him, when Roagey-Mac rode in through the school gates. "Glory be, here he comes," I yelled.

"Coo-er." Ant stopped kicking the gravel. "That's a big horse he's riding."

It *was* a big horse. A bay hunter and Roagey-Mac looked so small sitting way up above me. I went to him and my head hardly reached the stirrup.

"Good morning, Mr Mac."

"Roagey, Miss. Call me Roagey. Ev'ryone else does."

"All right, Roagey. Would you please go round to the stable-yard. Outside the big gates, turn right and follow the wall."

As Ant and I ran through the little side garden, we could hear the rhythmic clippety-clop of the big horse's shoes as Roagey rode up the lane. The double gates were open and he rode into the stable-yard just as Mr. B swung me up into the saddle. Of course, I could mount Dolly by myself from the old tree stump we used as a mounting block, but it was nice to be helped up by Mr. B. He would put one hand under my armpit and one under my bottom and the next moment I was flying through the air, as he flipped me up and over to land neatly into the saddle. After adjusting my stirrups, he attached a leading rein to Dolly's bridle and, as he handed it to Roagey, he said, "Miss Baker's compliments, but please start her off on a leading rein. At least until she's got used riding in the roads."

I opened my mouth to protest, but then I saw Roagey-Mac wink at me. "To be sure, Mr. Baker, Sir. I'll keep her safe. Not to worry."

As we rode out, I heard the dull scrape and thunk as Mr. B closed the gates and pushed the iron bolt down into the cobbles. I looked back and saw Ant watching through the vertical metal bars. With his hands clinging to a bar either side of his face, he looked like a Medieval prisoner begging to be released. I waved to make him feel better.

The leading rein was slack as I rode beside Roagey-Mac. Dolly and I seemed so small beside the big bay, who didn't seem to mind that we were riding so close. At the end of the lane, just past the big front gates and their lion-topped pillars, Roagey-Mac turned right. We rode through the village, past the Dog and Cock pub, past the church and the post office, and out along the main road. The sun was warm on my face, I could smell woodsmoke in the air and, for once, I was riding somewhere other than the orchard at Normanhurst. And as Roagey-Mac grinned down at me, I knew it was going to be a very good day.

"How far is it to Lady Harriet's?" We'd been riding for about ten minutes and I didn't even know where she lived. "Where are we going?"

"Why to the Hall of course, Miss. It's not far down the road now and we turn into another lane. Then we're on the property as t'were."

I could see the railway line to the left and the deep winding cut of the River Severn beyond. Standing high on the opposite bank, was the tall spire of Quatt church.

"I don't know why I have to be on a leading rein, Roagey. There's hardly any traffic." So far we'd passed two ladies on bicycles, and four boys on bicycles had passed us. We'd met a tractor coming down the other side of the road driven by a Land Army girl in her green and fawn uniform, and the Bridgnorth bus taking the village housewives to the Saturday market.

"Well now, Missee. I suppose you're right, but your Miss Audrey-Joan would have my guts for garters if I let you off the leading rein. So would Lady 'Arriet." The last bit was muttered more to himself than to me. "Any road up, here's the laneway. We'll get you across the road, and then let you go free."

We crossed over and into the lane leading to the Hall. Dry dusty wheel tracks that would turn to mud after a morning's rain, ran both sides of a central path lined with cutch grass, clover and chamomile. Hawthorn and brambles–a few late blackberries still clinging to them–grew tall either side of us. The ditches were full of teasels, bulrushes, and the umbrella-shaped seed heads of the cow-parsley and ladies' lace. With Roagey leading, we trotted up the middle, the sharp tangy scent of the bruised camomile blossoms tickling my nose.

I had never really thought much about the way houses were built, but as soon as I saw Lady Harriet's home, it reminded me so much of my grandfather's house in the Lake District that it made me notice it. It stood four square, built of red brick, and was covered on one side with Virginia creeper that framed square-paned windows. The white front door was set back in a porch, its pointed roof held up by a column on both sides. It looked for all the world like the house from Beatrix Potter's *The Tailor of Gloucester*. Long brick walls stuck out either side of the house, a wide archway set in each; through them I could see a hotchpotch of buildings. I stood up in my stirrups and craned my neck to see more.

Roagey-Mac was riding beside me now. "There's a stable-yard at the back," he told me."With a barn, stables and the coach house. Back of it are cowsheds and pigsties. The kitchen garden is behind them on the right."

The wrought-iron gates were open. Tall chestnut and silver birch lined a wide drive-way, leading to the house, where it branched off on both sides and disappeared. Each side of the drive, wide lawns stretched back to flower beds, bright with a brilliant autumn mass of chrysanthemums, dahlias and Michaelmas daisies. Of course, cabbages had been planted all along the edges. We rode around to the right side of the house and through the archway into a cobblestoned yard. I could see horses' heads peering over the top half of the stable doors on the left. Opposite, big double doors were open–just far enough for me to catch a glimpse of Lady Harriet's gay little caravan. We were met by so many barking dogs that I thought Dolly would take fright. But she stood there calmly, only side-stepping when one came too close.

"QUIET," roared a voice from inside one of the buildings. "Down, boys and girls. BEHAVE."

Immediately the dogs quietened down and moved away to sit panting in the shade of an old horse-trough. There were several hounds, two golden retrievers and a wire-haired terrier bunched together, while a Welsh corgi and a spaniel–the spitting image of Gatsby–sat apart.

Lady Harriet came out of what looked like a tack room. She was wiping her hands on a bit of old towel. A big smile lit up her face when she saw us. Dressed in an old pair of baggy green corduroy trousers— which had definitely seen better days—and a torn woolly jumper, and with a few curls of her greying hair flopping around her ears where they had escaped from her bun, she didn't look a bit like my elegant Lady Side-saddle.

"Here you are at last. Suppose you dismount and let Roagey-Mac look after Dolly while we go and have some hot chocolate and decide where we are going to ride."

"Hot chocolate! Oh gosh! This was going to be a really good day!"

I dismounted in a flash and, after handing the reins to Roagey-Mac, followed Lady Harriet through the back door. The dogs jumped up and came running behind us. A golden retriever shoved its nose into my hand.

"No, girls and boys. Back you go. Stay outside. STAY." The dogs turned and slunk back to the horse-trough, except the corgi and the little spaniel. "Oh, all right. You two can come in." Lady Harriet shook her head, "These two are spoilt babies."

As she led the way through to a big kitchen, complete with Welsh dresser, rocking chairs and a huge Aga, she called over her shoulder, "The corgi is Taffy and the spaniel is Precious."

Five minutes later I was sitting at the kitchen table with my nose buried in a big mug of chocolate heaven. In between gulps of the miraculous stuff, I made friends with two cats who were occupying the rocking chairs. Actually, I made friends with only one of them, a fat fluffy marmalade called Marmaduke. The other one was strange. Her fur was a mottled, muddy brown, and she had blue eyes. When I went to touch her, she arched her back and hissed at me. She kept on hissing. Every time I spoke to her, she hissed more.

"Her name is Annie," said Lady Harriet.

"She's not a bit like an Annie. She hisses too much. She should be called Hissy Cat." I went back to my hot chocolate and was about to tilt my head back and poke my tongue up the mug to lick the last little drop, when I remembered my manners. I put the mug down on the table and wiped my mouth on my hanky.

Lady Harried grinned, "So you enjoyed your hot chocolate then?"

"Oh yes, Ma'am. Very much thank you. I can't remember having hot chocolate like this since I was at home, before the war when I was a very little girl. Where did it come from?"

"Well now. Our good and faithful Roagey-Mac does most of my shopping. He seems to know where to find the best treats. But, I don't ask where he shops." Lady Harriet leaned across the table and said in a loud whisper, "I think he has 'connections.' It's best not to ask who they are. But shhh, that's our little secret."

"All right," I replied. "Cross-my-heart-and-hope-to-die. I promise I won't tell a soul, not even Ant."

"And who, pray, is Ant? Sounds like an insect."

"Ant–his real name is Antony–is my best friend."

"And do you call him Ant because he is full of formic acid and scurries all over the place?" Lady Harriet threw her head back and burst into cackles of laughter.

Not having the remotest idea of what she meant, or what formic acid was, I didn't answer. But I grinned anyway.

She looked at me, smiled and patted my hand. "I'm sorry. You'll have to get used to my little jokes. But, seriously, I thought that little fair haired whats-her-name? Little Miss Bank? is your best friend."

"Oh, Ann-the-Bank? Well she's my best *girl* friend. But I have more fun with Ant. He's a jolly good sport. But...please Lady Harriet, when are we going riding?"

"If you've finished your chocolate, we can go right now. Put the mugs into the sink m'dear while I quickly change into my riding togs. Then we'll get mounted up."

The horses and Roagey-Mac were waiting for us. Lady Harriet's magnificent black hunter, Roagey-Mac's bay, and Dolly. Lady Harriet, now dressed in a pair of old brown riding breeches, high leather boots, and a thick fisherman's knit jumper rode proper English saddle; I felt quite smart in my clean jodhpurs, green jumper and tweed jacket. I made a clean mount from the mounting block, which pleased me (once, at Normanhurst, I'd leaped from the mounting block and gone right over Dolly and landed on the cobblestones the other side).

We had a scathingly-brilliant morning ride. Down lanes, across meadows and through woods. I was taught how to open and close gates without dismounting. After we'd ridden for some miles, we came to open moorland spattered with outcroppings of rock and golden-flowered gorse bushes. We reined in our horses.

"Now, my gel. Want a gallop?"

"Oh yes, please."

"Well, there's two miles of solid turf here that's just made for a good run. Keep up if you can, but don't push Dolly. If she tires, slow down. We won't be far ahead."

"So off we went. Dolly loved it and kept up a good pace only a few yards behind the bigger horses. With the feel of a horse beneath me, the warm Autumn wind flying in my face and the whole of Shropshire around me, I couldn't have been happier. It was so clear, I could even see the purple-shadowed Welsh mountains far away in the distance. I wanted this to last for ever.

"Oh Cedric, if you could see me now."

Then the thought came to me. He probably could see me. And it felt as though I was not alone after all. On this wonderful day of freedom, Cedric was riding right along with me. I could almost see him.

An hour or so later, we were leisurely making our way back to the Hall. We'd had a great gallop, and the horses had white flecks of foam on their chests and rumps. When we got to a big paddock behind the hall, Lady Harriet turned to Roagey and me. "I have a wonderful idea," she said. "We ought to put up a few gymkhana jumps here. You know, my gel, you were very lucky when you went over that hedge at the fox hunt. Very lucky. I thought for sure you were going to fall and break your neck. It was a miracle you not only cleared the jump, but you stayed on. Mind you, it was terrible style, but you had the determination. I liked that. So I think we should teach you to jump properly."

"What? Now?"

"Good gracious, no. We've all had enough for today, and so have the horses. No, we'll do it next time you come."

"Next time? So there was going to be a next time! I was coming again. Did you hear that, Cedric? We're coming again."

"Yes," said Lady Harriet. "You've kept up well today. Of course, you must come again. Not much doing once winter sets in, but next summer we will have some fun."

"Next summer. Why wait til next summer?"

"Don't you ride in the winter?"

"Of course we do. But it's not much fun, having jumping competitions in the rain. Besides it's mostly hunting on Saturdays. And I doubt very much if the remarkable Miss Baker would let you do *that* again."

She grinned and I grinned back. "I don't suppose she would," I agreed.

Back in the yard we unsaddled the horses, rubbed them down and fed them. There was a spare stall for Dolly and she looked right at home in it.

"Let's go and see what cook has drummed up for dinner. You can explore the house this afternoon and then ride back to Normanhurst in time for tea."

After dinner, (Toad-in-the-Hole with mashed potatoes, peas and thick brown gravy), Lady Harriet took me on a tour of the Hall. There were so many rooms; most were very grand and looked as though they were never used. One of the rooms I remember the most and which I liked best, was a den that was the most cluttered and untidy room I'd ever seen. There were dogs, books, magazines, papers and knitting all over the place, and a large desk—open and spilling over with more papers. A log fire crackled in the grate above which the wide mantle-piece was crammed with photographs; mostly of Lady Harriet either on a horse or surrounded by dogs. The other room I liked was a very big room lined with books, which Lady Harriet referred to as 'The Heirloom Library.' "So when it's too wet to ride, you can find a book to read. Or there's an attic full of toys and games which I'm sure you will want to explore."

I had serious doubts. "But will Miss Baker let me come?"

"Well, perhaps not every week, but I am sure we can come to some arrangement. Perhaps once a month or so."

"Once a month? That would be very much all right."

"Oh yes, Lady Harriet. Once a month would be just perfect."

"That's settled then. And now we had better be thinking of getting you booted and spurred and way off back to school. It's later than I thought. We don't want to blot our copybook by getting you back late on the first day, now do we?"

"Oh, gosh, no. That would be awful."

Back in the yard, Roagey-Mac and Dolly were ready to take me back to Normanhurst. I turned to Lady Harriet, "Thank you for a scathingly-brilliant day."

"Thank you, my dear for coming. We'll see you again."

To Roagey-Mac she said, "Lead on MacDuff. Lead on."

As we went out under the arch and into the driveway, I turned and waved. Lady Harriet waved back then cupped her hands to her mouth and shouted at me, "Maybe you should bring that insect friend next time."

I shouted back, "Oh yes. Thank you." I turned to Roagey-Mac, "Lead on MacDuff. Lead on."

"Cheeky nipper," he said. But he smiled. "So did you enjoy your day?"

"Oh yes, Roagey, thank you. But there's one thing I would like to know."

"And what's that, Missee?"

"Where do you do your shopping? Where did you get that heavenly hot chocolate?"

"Ahem." Roagey's ears went slightly pink. "Well, Missee, it's like this. I was riding along on my bike, right behind a lorry. And this 'ere tin of chocolate...well, it just fell off the lorry. Bounced right into me bicycle basket it did too. Quite a miracle, that was."

"Oh." I couldn't think of anything to say about that.

"Mind you, Missee. We don't talk about it much. No-one would believe us, would they?"

"I s'pose not."

"But it's s'prising wot falls off lorries y'know. As I said, miraculous!"

"But nobody would believe us if we said it was a miracle."

"Right. You've got it, Missee. No one would believe us."

"Right, Roagey."

And we grinned at each other.

Sunday 10th October, 1943
Dear Mummy and Daddy,
Yesterday I spent the day riding with Lady Harriet. I enjoyed it very much and we had Toad-in-the-Hole for dinner.
I remembered all my manners and didn't disgrace you or Normanhurst.
I got a 18 out of 20 for Algebra, which Mrs. Riley said was somewhat of a miracle. I hope Daddy will be pleased.
With love from your miraculous daughter,
Patricia

Dear Cedric,

Did you enjoy yesterday? I KNOW you were there. I felt you riding along beside me. You were probably riding a white horse or was it a magical winged unicorn?

I saw some model ships at Lady Harriet's, but I suppose you don't like to think about ships much, seeing that yours sank. Did the Germans really torpedo your ship? I HATE the Germans for making a war and I wish it would end so I can see my Mummy and Daddy again.

Is your Daddy with you yet?

I hope you will come riding with me again. Did God teach you to ride?

With love from your very best friend,

Pat

P.S. I've grown two inches but I still can't reach your Allie.

Chapter 37

The Pirate Ship, Spring 1943

It was a Friday afternoon. Lessons always finished early on Fridays as Mrs. B always needed time to clean up the weeklies and get them ready for their mothers. The rest of us who lived at Normanhurst were allowed to do–more or less–what we wanted. It was April and there were no showers, just big white cauliflower clouds sailing along in a bright blue sky. So I thought it was a good idea when Antony said, "C'mon, let's play in the orchard."

"That's not a tree. That's a pirate ship foundered on a coral reef, with all hands drowned."

"Couldn't they have got ashore? Onto a desert island or something. Or maybe another pirate ship—a friendly one—rescued them. But they didn't drown. Only Cedric drowned."

Ant climbed up onto the trunk of the fallen apple tree and stared down at me. His left eyebrow disappeared under the thick fringe of blue-black hair that fell over his forehead. Standing, feet apart, hands on hips, he announced, "I'm a pirate captain!"

The eyebrow came down and he leaned forward, this time looking at me, his grey eyes half-closed. He just looked at me. "All right then. They swam ashore after their ship foundered. But they were eaten by cannibals. So they didn't have to be drowned. Just eaten."

With outstretched arms for balance, he ran the length of the fallen trunk, turned and came back. I was standing by the giant roots that had been torn out of the ground during that terrible storm years ago, when a bolt of lightning had hit the old Bramley apple tree. Even if I spread both my arms out wide, I still couldn't reach either side of the twisted tangle of roots, and they were so tall, even Mr. B couldn't see over the top of them.

"Why don't you come aboard?" Ant pulled out his handkerchief and wrapped it around his head. It made him look very piratey.

"Can I be a pirate too?"

"Yes. You can be First Mate. That means you have to do what I say. On a ship the captain gives the orders. And the crew have to obey."

"What happens if they don't?"

The eyebrow disappeared into the hair again. *"How did he DO that?"*

"They get hung from the yardarm. Or keelhauled. Or made to walk the plank."

"Fains you hang me from the yardarm," I yelled. "Fains I get keel-hauled. Fains I walk the plank."

"You can't fains all that."

"Yes I can. I can say fains anything and *you* have to obey—even on a Pirate Ship. It's a rule. Like the cross-your-heart-and-hope-to-die rule. Or the being sent to Coventry rule."

"I won't hang *you* from the yard arm, silly. You're First Mate and first mates don't get hanged unless they mutiny. And you're not going to mutiny because I'm a good pirate ship captain and treat my men well. Prisoners are different. They'll get keelhauled and made to walk the plank. But not hanged." He grinned, "You silly sausage, I wouldn't hang anybody." He thought for a minute, then added cheerfully, "Unless of course, it's a Jerry!" He looked over the side of the tree. "Keelhauling would be good though. There's lots of nettles growing in the ocean."

"And walking the plank too–there are some good prickly thistles in the ocean too. Do you think we could make Jerries walk the plank?" I asked.

Ant looked around. Since the German plane had crashed in the next field, we were all rather frightened of Jerries turning up in our orchard. "No, I don't think I want to take Jerry prisoners." For a moment he looked serious. He shook his head and grinned, his face full of fun again. "But we could capture that big bully Giles Farmer, and make him walk the plank."

"And Arabella Bosworthy." I started to make a mental list of potential plank walkers and keelhaul candidates.

Ant jumped up, "Shiver me Timbers!" he called over his shoulder. " C'mon, We've got to reccy this and get her ship-shape. Jump to it me hearties. Yo-ho-ho and a bottle of rum!"

"Yo-ho-ho and a bottle of rum," I echoed and jumped up to follow the Pirate Captain to inspect our vessel.

It certainly made a very fine ship, this tumbled apple tree. Lightning had struck it right down the middle–but not all the way through–killing it instantly. When it fell, its enormous roots had been wrenched out of the earth with such force, that a deep hole had been left in the ground. The tree lay amongst the tall grass and stinging nettles, and over the years, had become greyed and weatherbeaten. In winter the gaping cleft clean along its centre filled up with snow and rain which froze solid, and by spring it all would be a little smoother, a little wider and a little greyer.

"See," said Antony. "It's hollowed out perfectly all the way from stem to stern."

"From what to where?"

"Front to back, silly. If you are going to be First Mate of a pirate ship, you've got to learn the correct naval terms."

"Oh. Stem to stern. Which is the stem? Front or back?"

"Stem is the bow, which is the front. Stern is–well, the other end. And this..." Ant ran lightly along the smooth edge of the hollowed out trunk, scrambled up the towering root system and perched on top of it. "this is the poop deck."

"The poop deck?"

"The poop deck is the captain's deck of course. From here, he can watch everything that's happening on the main deck. You steer the ship from the poop deck." He pointed at me, "And *you*, Mister First Mate, me hearty. *You* have to start reading the 'Mr Midshipman Easy' books if you want to learn about ships. Much better to read adventure books than all those silly old Shakespeare plays you do with Miss Primrose."

"They're not silly and I like them."

"I'd seen the Mr Midshipman books in the library. Perhaps I'll read one when I've finished Arthur Ransome's "We Didn't Mean to Go to Sea" that Mummy sent me last Christmas. Anyway, that's all about sailing too, so I know a lot more than you think, Mister Smarty-Pants Pirate Captain."

Ant was staring at me, waiting for an answer. "All right. I'll read one," I promised.

"That's good. If you want to be a good first mate to a pirate captain, you've got to know how to sail a ship." He looked around as if searching for something important. "We have to get a ship's wheel from somewhere. We need a wheel to steer the ship."

"There's an old cartwheel in the stables. That would make a good ship's wheel."

"Whizzo," Antony beamed. He leaped down from the poop deck onto the hollowed-out trunk. C'mon, let's get it."

"Get what? What are you going to get? Can I come?" The squeaky voice came from behind the poop deck.

We both looked around the great poop deck and downwards. Monty Marsh, better known as Squeak, was squatting in the sandy hole where the roots had been. Warm and sheltered, the littler children liked to use it as a sand pit. "What are you doing down there, Squeak? You'll drown."

"Soppy-date," he squeaked, "you can't drown in sand. Anyway, you're not sailing now, so this is the beach where you're tied up."

"Well, as soon as we set sail, this is a pirate ship. Ant's the Captain and I'm First Mate, and we're going to hunt down Spanish Galleons and relieve them of their pieces of eight."

"Coo-er. Can I come? And...and Bubble of course?"

Bubble, whose real name was Martin, and who hardly ever spoke at all, was Monty's twin. Bubble was poking a twig into the sand, trying to make it stand up straight. They did everything together and were never seen apart. They even slept together. Every night, Bubble would creep into Squeak's bed, where both would be found the next morning, curled up like two little puppies.

"What could you do?" Antony asked. "You'd have to be part of the ship's crew. You'd have to be a pirate. You'd have to DO something."

"We could be lookouts," Squeak squeaked.

Bubble looked up, grinning and nodding his head.

"Weeell. I dunno." Ant looked at me, "What about it Mister First Mate? Should we let these two come aboard and be lookouts?"

I thought about all the other children in the school we could have in our pirate crew. Certainly not Arabella Bosworthy–nor her sissy brother, D'arcy. None of the other boys. It was a pity Cedric wasn't here, he'd have made a good pirate. As for the girls. There was Ann-the-Bank—but she didn't like climbing trees. Or Alana. But when she wasn't riding, she was doing ballet with Miss Primrose. Anyway, Bubble and Squeak were nice and certainly not tell-tales. "All right," I agreed. "They can be members of our pirate crew."

"Come aboard you two," Captain Blackbeard Antony commanded.

Bubble and Squeak scrambled up out of the sandy pit and climbed up into the hollowed-out deck.

"You'll have to be more nimble than that," said their captain. "You have to be quick when dealing with Spanish Galleon sailors. The lookout post is up there." He pointed to one of the highest perches among the dead boughs of the fallen tree. "You can go up and keep a lookout while we go and get the ship's wheel."

"What wheel? Where?"

"Stop squeaking, Squeak. And only squeak when you are asked a question. That's the first rule for pirate crew members. Do as your captain says, and *don't* question him. Grrrrr." Ant made threatening pirate-captain noises.

Bubble retreated a step or two. Squeak stood his ground, opened his mouth to say something, then thought better of it. He started towards the lookout branch. Then he turned back and looked up at Ant, who was much taller than the tiny Squeak. "Can I wear an eye patch?"

"I wear the eye patch." Ant was thundering now, "*I'm* the Pirate Captain. *I* wear the eye patch."

Squeak looked disappointed as he climbed up to the lookout branch. Bubble was already astride it and picking off bits of dead bark to see what was underneath.

"But you can wear a handkerchief on your head, like mine," Ant called after him. "And you can both wear gold earrings." He tugged at my arm, "C'mon. Let's go and find the wheel."

Taking care not to land in any nettles, we jumped down from the Tree-that-was-Really-a-Pirate-Ship, and headed out across the orchard on our mission to find a ship's wheel.

"Hey," I panted for it was hard to keep up with Ant's long legs. "Hey, we're in the water. We can't run in the ocean?"

"We're not running. We're swimming." Ant started swinging his arms wildly over his head, imitating a swimmer's crawl. So, arms circling, we set off for the stables, looking more like windmills than swimmers. I felt good today and we were having fun. Spring had finally arrived, trees were blossoming, I could hear a cuckoo calling–and the whole summer was before us. Best of all, I was First Mate on a pirate ship.

The stables were cool and quiet. The whitewashed walls glowed golden from sunbeams that pierced the cobweb-curtained windows. Nickers from the horses welcomed us and we gave them a few withered apples from the bucket. I showed Ant the old cartwheel–dusty and covered in cobwebs.

"C'mon, let's get it." He jumped down from the low stone wall that separated the horses' stalls from the rest of the building.

"Do you think we ought?" I was a little nervous about taking it. After all, it had been there ever since I could remember.

"Ought to what?" We nearly jumped out of our skins at Mr. B's deep booming voice. He had come out of nowhere and was standing right behind us.

"Saw that you two were on some sort of a mission. Scurrying pretty fast into here weren't you. Now what is it you think you ought—or ought not—to do?"

Antony's nudge sent a clear message. I had to persuade Mr. B to let us have the wheel. It was much easier than I thought.

"What do you want it for, Pat-a-cake? Tell me what you're going to do with it."

"We need it for a ship's wheel. A pirate ship's wheel."

"Oh you do, eh? And pray, where would this pirate ship be sailing right at this moment? Or is it anchored in the kitchen garden perhaps?"

I knew he was thinking of the old bathtub which had got me into trouble more than once. "Oh no. It's in the orchard. It's a huge pirate ship and it's in the orchard." I beckoned in the direction of Mr. B's head and he leaned down so I could whisper in his ear, "It's the old apple tree that got struck by lightning a long time ago. It's our pirate ship."

"Ah. Now that *would* make a good pirate ship. And, come to think of it, you can't sail her out on the high seas without a ship's wheel. So get along with you and take it. It's no use for anything now, except firewood."

"Coo-er," said Antony.

"Thank you very much Mr. B," I said. "You really are a brick. A super brick."

"Hrummph." Mr. B sounded a bit like Mrs. B when she couldn't think of anything to say.

"You know," Ant said as we were rolling the wheel back to the orchard. "To be a proper pirate, I've got to have that eye patch. Where am I going to get an eye patch. And an earring. All pirates wear gold earrings."

"Don't worry. I know where I can get you an eye patch. And earrings."

"Really? Whizzo. You're going to make a ripping First Mate."

I didn't answer, but I could still hear the cuckoo in the distance. The sun felt warm on my back. I knew it was going to be a very good summer.

It was easier to carry the wheel between us across the orchard than roll it. We both agreed that it was an orchard again, and not an ocean. Getting it onto the Tree-that-was-Really-a-Pirate-Ship was more difficult. Ant and I lay full length on the edge of the split trunk facing each other and, while Bubble and Squeak pushed the wheel from the bottom, we hauled from the top. With a lot of slithering and bumping we finally got it on board.

"But it's got to be up on the poop deck," Antony protested. "It must be on the poop deck."

I looked at the broad steep slope that led up to the top edge of the roots. "Once we get it up there, how do we make it stand up?"

Ant glared at me. I was being practical and he didn't like it when I was practical. He liked to be the practical one. And he hated it when he knew I was right *and* practical.

"I'm working it out," he snapped. With forehead on hunched up knees, and arms dangling, his fingers drummed a little tattoo on the rough old bark. He always sat that way when working things out, so nobody could see his face while he was thinking.

Movement by the orchard gate caught my eye. "Mr. B's coming."

Antony shot back into his pirate-captain role. "And where are the lookouts? Why aren't they looking out? Do you want to be keelhauled you lazy-bones lookouts?"

Bubble and Squeak leaped into action and scrambled up to their lookout branch. "It's Mr. B," Squeak squeaked. Bubble nodded vigorously.

"I know it's Mr. B, silly. Patty saw him. Where's he going?"

"He's coming here. He's carrying a jug."

I shaded my eyes against the bright afternoon sun. "That's the lemonade jug."

"Permission to come aboard, Cap'n Pirate, Sir?"

"Permission granted Mr. B."

"When I told Mrs. B you were keeping out of mischief and playing nicely in the orchard, she said I should bring you some lemonade."

Mrs. B's lemonade was very good and a rare treat. Lady Harriet sent all sorts of treats that were rare in wartime. Roagey-Mac would deliver them riding a rickety old bicycle; a basket strapped to the handlebars and another on the carrier behind him. Mrs. B would meet him at the back kitchen door and invite him in for a cup of tea. By this time, Ant and I would have snuck down the hall, to say hello to Roagey and to see what he had brought.

Sometimes it would be fruit—oranges or lemons, occasionally packages of sugar and tea, or tins of baked beans or (my favourite) pilchards. He would always tell Mrs. B that the stuff fell off the back of a lorry and he'd happened to find it. So this day, it must have been lemons that had fallen off the back of a lorry, and Mrs. B had made lemonade. Even though it was sweetened with saccharine, it tasted delicious.

"Now then," said Mr. B when we'd all finished drinking and the big white enamel jug and mugs had been carefully placed in the grass where he wouldn't forget them. "Now then. Where's your ship's wheel going to be housed?"

"Housed?"

"Where are you going to put it?"

"Well," said Antony. "It's supposed to be up on the poop deck. Up there." He pointed to the mess of tangled roots above us.

"My, my." Mr. B clambered up the curved face of the poop deck and looked at the top. "You're going to have quite a job fixing that up." He turned and looked along the length of the ship and at the two lookouts who had returned to their perch after their lemonade.

"You've got your lookouts in the crow's-nest I see."

"Is that what it's called?" I asked.

"That's what it is, my lady. A crow's-nest."

"I'm not a lady today. I'm a pirate ship's First Mate."

"Sorry Mister Mate, Sir."

Mr. B's face twitched as he turned back to Ant. "Well Cap'n, Sir. I think I can help you with this. Let me go back to my shed and see what I can find. That is, Cap'n Sir, if you'll sign me on as the ship's Chippy."

"Chippy?"

"Navy term for ship's carpenter."

"That would be perfectly acceptable Mr. B." For a fierce pirate captain, Ant was very gracious.

About an hour later, a rough ladder—made from some dead branches Mr. B had sawn off and nailed together, became what he called a companionway leading from the main deck to the poop deck. Another tall branch, stripped of its twigs, stood upright and well secured on the main deck; rising above the poop deck by almost three feet. At the top, Mr. B had driven an iron spike through the centre of the wheel and right through the upright branch. He'd hammered a wooden cover over the sharp end of the spike so we wouldn't hurt ourselves and–lo and behold!–we had a ship's wheel on the poop deck. A couple of old wooden boards formed the poop deck floor, room enough for two of us to stand. The gnarled roots curving up behind prevented us from falling over backwards into the ocean-sand-pit.

"Mr. B," said Antony. "You're an Honourable Ship's Chippy. And we will never, ever have you keelhauled or make you walk the plank."

"Well that's a relief!" Mr. B gathered up his tools. "Have fun now and may the wind always fill your sails. But please remember. You may be pirates, but don't be cruel pirates. Be merciful to your victims and only plunder enemy ships. Now, you've got about an hour before the tea bell, so weigh anchor me hearties, and God Speed on your maiden voyage."

As Mr. B trudged back across the orchard, his tool bag in one hand and lemonade jug in the other, Ant said quietly, "He said, 'may the wind always fill your sails.' SAILS! We've no SAILS. A pirate ship has to have sails."

"I got sails," a tiny voice said behind us.

Bubble had come down from the crow's-nest and was looking up at Ant.

"You...Bubble." I gasped in surprise, "Bubble you actually talked."

Bubble grinned, "I can talk when I want to. Mostly I choose not to."

Squeak shrugged, "He's only been like that since our Daddy was killed in the war."

"Oh, Bubble. Oh, Squeak. That's so sad."

"S'alright," Squeak replied. "We're used to it now. Bubble doesn't like talking to people 'cos they always say we're poor little things to have lost our Daddy. But Bubble says we haven't lost him 'cos he talks to him all the time. And then...and then he tells me what Daddy says." Squeak hung his head, "I can't hear Daddy talk. Only Bubble can. B-but, please. Don't tell."

"Of course we won't," said Ant.

I knew Squeak was telling the truth when he said Bubble talked to his daddy, because I'd talked to Cedric when he came to visit me.

There wasn't much else we could say after that, except Ant promised he would never have them keelhauled. And that made them both smile.

"Sails tomorrow," said Bubble just as the tea bell rang.

((

The next morning there were still no April showers, only bright sunshine. We were having breakfast and talking about spending a day pirating and sailing the seven seas.

"But I usually ride on Saturdays," I protested. "I don't want to miss my riding."

"Then I'll just have to get another First Mate."

"You wouldn't."

"I would too."

I thought for a moment. This wasn't a Lady Harriet Saturday and, anyway, I'd only get about half an hour's riding. I was sure Miss Audrey-Joan would let me ride for a whole evening, if I gave up my half-hour to someone else; Alana perhaps.

"All right then. I won't ride this morning. But I fains you get another First Mate. Ever."

Ant grinned. "Silly sausage," he said. "Who d'you think I'd get? Bossy Bella?" He was sitting opposite me, so I kicked his shin under the table, then quickly curled my legs underneath my chair so he couldn't reach to kick me back. I could see him slide further and further down in his chair, trying to find my legs.

"I've got you an eye patch," I whispered across the table.

He pulled himself back up in his chair. An eyebrow cocked.

"And some gold earrings. Enough for everyone."

The other eyebrow went up. "How d'you find those?" he asked.

"Never mind," I replied. "I think they fell off the back of a lorry. And will you *stop* doing that thing with your eyebrows."

Just before bedtime the previous night, I drank as much water as I could get into my tummy so I would wake up to go to the loo. When I awoke, it was dark and the little oil night-lamps were making scary shadows on the walls. I crept downstairs to the next floor because I wanted to get to the biggest bathroom–the one with the medicine cabinet.

Everyone was asleep and I could hear some really loud snores–two lots of loud snores, coming from Mr. and Mrs. B's room. I tiptoed towards their bedroom. Their door was always open, just a little, so they could hear when anyone was sick or crying in the night. I squeezed through the small space and stood for a moment, listening. Mrs. B snored the loudest, snorting in through her nose and sort of whistling out through her mouth. I stuffed the end of my nightie into my mouth to stop myself giggling out loud. Mr. B's snoring was just as loud, but more like I thought an old bear would sound–deep and snuffly. Every now and then he would make loud grunts.

"Oh, Lordy, Lordy," I thought. "If ever they woke up and saw me, I'd be a dead duck. Oh well, if they did I'd just have to start wailing and pretend I'm sick."

A small night-light stood on a table by their bed, so I could see them both. Mrs. B was lying on her back, her hands clasped across her huge bosom which was heaving up and down as she snored. Her mouth was wide open and, glory be! she had no teeth. A bright pink hairnet covered her head, right down to her eyebrows. I almost choked on my nightie, trying not to giggle. Mr. B was lying on his side and looked quite normal. His mouth was closed, and he seemed to be smiling.

Suddenly, Mr. B flung out his arm and yelled, "Yo-ho-ho, me heart-ies. Yo-ho-ho."

That made me jump, and I almost fell back into the door. I thought for sure they'd hear me. I got out–quickly. I ran down the long landing and around the corner where I crouched on the floor in between the lavvy door and the bathroom. My heart was thudding in my ears and I felt sure I would be caught. I crept into the loo and shut the door very, very quietly.

When I came out, all was still and quiet. No one had woken. I was safe. I slipped into the bathroom, the night-lamp giving enough light for me to see what I was doing. The medicine cabinet was locked but the drawers underneath were not and I knew where to find the eye patches. They were pink with a white elastic band that fitted around our heads when we had a stye or something in our eye. I picked one out, shut the drawer and tiptoed back around the corner to the sick room. No one was sick that night, so I was lucky again. I'd spent so much time in that room after the measles–*and* the whooping cough, *and* the mumps–I knew it well.

This time I did shut the door; there was no night-light, but I knew where to find a torch. I balanced it on the table where we kept the paper and craft materials, including a box for scissors, pencils, rulers and pairs of compasses for making circle patterns. It didn't take me long to cut a shape out of black crepe paper to match the eye patch, and stick it over the pink with paper glue. I knew there was a box of brass curtain rings in the sewing drawer, which would make perfect pirate earrings. I took a reel of cotton–I thought red would be a good colour for pirates—and a handful of the rings. Quietly, I shut the drawer, put the torch back and opened the door. As I stepped onto the landing, one of the shadows in front of me moved. I jumped back in fright and dropped the cotton reel. It was Tristan. He ran after the cotton reel and pounced on it.

"Oh gosh. More noise. Now I'm done for."

I felt my heart thumping again. I snatched up the cotton reel and dashed for the stairs. The painted wood was cold on my bare feet and the shadows of the night-lamps jumped and danced in the breeze as I ran past and into my dormitory. With one leap, I was back into bed. I shoved my pirate loot under my pillow and pulled the blankets over my head. A moment later I felt a familiar plop as Tristan landed. He padded up and settled down on my pillow, nuzzling the back of my neck. His whiskers tickled my ear as he purred.

Well, it was done. I'd got what we needed and I hadn't been caught. My feet were frozen, but the last thing I remembered before I fell asleep was Mrs. B's dreadful pink hairnet.

"Whatcher smiling at?" I had let my legs down from the chair and now Ant was nudging with his foot; but not kicking.

"Oh nothing much." I looked at him. "I was just thinking that the eye-patch is big enough to cover your eye *and* your eyebrow."

Ant sniffed.

Breakfast was over and I was on the washing-up gang, so by the time I got out to the orchard, everyone else was there. And what a sight. There was Ant, standing stiffly on the poop deck steering his pirate ship into uncharted and dangerous waters. Bubble and Squeak were aloft in the crow's-nest branch and...what on earth...?

Sails were billowing out from the branches of the Tree-that-was-Really-a-Pirate-Ship. Two square sails caught by the April breeze. Oh gosh! And a flag! A real skull and crossbones, fluttering proudly above the sails. On this bright spring morning, the Tree-that-was-Really-a-Pirate-Ship was in full sail and bound for the Spanish Main under the command of her fearless captain.

But the sails. They were PINK? Two pink sails?

"You'd better come on board, Mister Mate, before you drown in the nettles."

I scrambled up onto the deck.

"You're late, Mister Mate. We sailed with the tide y'know."

"Sorry Captain, Sir. Duties ashore."

"Victualling I hope Mister Mate. Did you get our victuals?"

"Yes sir, Captain Sir. Here's your eye patch. And pirate earrings for every member of the crew.

With red cotton loops over our ears, our earrings dangled pirate-like just above our shoulders. The boys had handkerchiefs around their heads, but I had gone one better by winding my blue scarf–a present from that long-ago-but-never-forgotten Christmas in Wales–around my head and knotting it so that one end dangled down over my shoulder. I also had a pigtail; my plait reached below my shoulders now. I was wearing my jodhpurs and a black leather belt complete with the sword and scabbard I'd used when I played Macbeth last winter. I noticed Ant had also raided the dressing up chest for the perfect pirate outfit, including a vicious looking dagger stuck in his belt. Bubble and Squeak were happy with their earrings and kerchiefs.

"Where did you get the flag?" I asked

Our fearless Captain grinned. "Mr. B. gave it to me after breakfast. He said that, if we were going to be proper pirates, we had to show our true colours and fly the Skull and Crossbones from the masthead. He said that it would be a good thing because, if any Jerry ships saw us they would turn tail and retreat under full sail. He said that no Jerry would want to walk the plank or get keelhauled. Then he muttered something about yellow-something-so-and-so's that I couldn't hear properly."

"How did we get sails?" I asked. "And why are they pink? A ship full of fearless pirates can't have PINK sails."

"That was Bubble," Squeak was squeaking again. "Our mummy gave him pink sheets 'cos she didn't have any other colour and I had the blue. Anyway, he never sleeps in his bed so he said we could have his sheets for sails. Is...is it all right if they're pink? I s'pose I could get my blue."

"Pink's fine," said the Pirate Captain. "They're pink because we dipped them in the blood of our enemies before we sailed. They used to be blood red but we've sailed the seven seas so many times that most of the blood has blown out of them. So now they're pink." He glared at me, warning me not to argue with the Pirate Captain.

"Pink's fine," I repeated. "Thank you, Bubble for the sails. Pink's super."

And Bubble beamed; his smile as bright as the April sun under which we sailed our pirate ship.

I think Bubble was almost happy that day.

Chapter 38

Bubble

1

About two Saturdays before my ninth birthday, I realised I was getting old. Mr. B told me the older you get, the more responsibilities you have to take on.

"What sort of responsibilities?"

We were in the kitchen garden, sowing lettuce. I was helping because Henry VIII had stolen some juicy little seedlings for his elevenses. I'd forgotten to tie him up and give him one of the bolted lettuces.

"Well..." Mr. B scratched his head, leaving a little trail of soil in his thick silver hair. "Well, now. You're responsible for feeding Henry VIII. Because you didn't, he helped himself to the food which goes to feed you children. So now you're accountable for the dinner table going short on lettuce. You have to take the responsibility for Henry VIII's unacceptable behaviour."

I had to think about that for a minute. "But I didn't eat the lettuce. Henry did," I grumbled.

"Ah, but would he have done so, if you'd fed him the lettuce we put by for the animals?"

"He might've." I wasn't at all sure I wanted to be responsible for other people's or—for that matter—animals' doings.

"Well, he might have, yes," Mr. B conceded. "But we can't take that for granted, now, can we? You have to be prepared if someone or something you're in charge of, doesn't follow the rules. And you know what happens when you don't follow rules."

I knew only too well. Many times, my hands and bottom had been smacked with a ruler. The only difference between which of the two parts of my anatomy got the punishment, depended upon the gravity of the crime.

"If you want special privileges, you have to learn the rules of responsibility that go along with those privileges." Mr. B was not going to let this alone, so I settled down for a lecture while I dropped the tiny black seeds into the shallow drill that ran the whole width of the weeded and raked nursery bed.

"You like to ride," he went on. "So you're responsible for seeing that Dolly is rubbed down, and given water and feed when she comes back. You help groom her and generally take care of her. That's part of your responsibility towards Dolly." Mr. B went on rambling about responsibilities and how, now that I was nearly nine, I also had to be responsible for helping out with the little ones. Like making sure they were not bullied by the older children and, if I found one of them crying somewhere, or had wet themselves, I should take them inside and find Mrs. B or Mrs. Tommy.

The June sun was hot on my back and the rich, dark soil was warm and smelled good. A centipede wriggled out of the mound in front of me and I picked him up. I started to count his legs to see if there really were a hundred, but he wouldn't keep still. He wriggled and curled around my fingers and thrashed his tail around. I threw him away and he landed, still squirming, on the ferny frond of a carrot top. My little packet of seeds was almost empty, and I thought about the excellent adventure we'd planned for the pirate ship that afternoon. Captain Blackbeard Antony had charted an expedition to a desert island. We were going to bury some of our treasure and make a map so we could find it again once we'd vanquished all our enemies. Sailing on the Spanish Main, we wouldn't have to worry about sowing tiny black specks of lettuce seeds, or how many carrots were enough to feed forty children, or whether the little ones wet their knickers. And I wouldn't have to listen to Mr. B droning on about responsibilities.

"I've finished all the seeds."

Mr. B had already begun to flick the fine soil over the little seed drill. "You've done a real nice job there, Pat-a-Cake. The dinner bell will be going soon so why don't you find that greedy tortoise of yours and tie him up before he gets into any more trouble?"

Henry VIII wasn't hard to find. The big red blob of paint on his shell was easy to see amongst the cabbages. A long line of thick string knotted to a rusty old hook at the back of Mr. B's garden shed was threaded through the hole drilled in back end of his shell. This gave the tortoise enough room to roam amongst the current bushes and the potatoes, all the way up to the cabbage patch. Sometimes I would find him at the very end of his string, neck stretched out, gazing at the young salad shoots that he liked so much. I fed him a good supply of lettuce that had gone to seed and should keep him munching for hours.

Captain Blackbeard Antony and his crew of cutthroat pirates had agreed to meet at the Tree-that-was-Really-a-Pirate-Ship after dinner. As I was passing our Victory gardens on the way to the orchard, I saw Bubble sitting on the little pebble path that separated his garden from Squeak's; hands dragging on the ground, yellow head on his knees, he seemed to be sleeping.

"Bubble," I called. "It's time to set sail if we want to catch the tide. You should be in the crow's-nest."

He didn't move. I went over and crouched down beside him. "What's the matter, Bubble?"

He didn't answer.

"Bubble? Where's Squeak?" It was odd that he was here alone. We never saw the twins apart. They were inseparable.

He raised his head and looked at me. I could see he'd been crying; grubby tear-streaks ran down his cheeks which were bright red, as though he had been lying in the sun. "Squeak's gone to get Mrs. B," he whispered.

"Why?"

"I don't feel well. I can't stand up properly." He laid his head back down on his knees. Then his knees parted and he fell forward until his head almost touched the ground.

"Here, Bubble. Let me get in behind you."

I straddled his back and slid down the wall. I felt my shirt slide up, and my back smarted as the rough bricks grazed my skin. When I was sitting on the ground behind him, I folded both my arms around his waist easing him back to lie against my chest, his head under my chin. He lay there—still and silent.

"Bubble?" I was whispering now. "Bubble, what's wrong?"

"My daddy is talking to me."

"What's he saying? Can you see him?"

"Oh yes. He's standing right in front of us."

Gooseflesh crept down my arms and legs. I tightened my arms around Bubble.

"My daddy says there's nothing to be frightened of. He's smiling. They're all smiling."

"They? All? Who?"

"There are lots of people with my daddy. He says I can go with him very soon."

"With him? Where?"

"Wherever he is. With all those smiling people. And children too."

"Children? Is...is...can you see Cedric?"

"Of course."

"Oh God! Bubble."

I looked down at his head resting on my chest. The golden curls, that all the other boys teased him about, were damp and dark against his forehead. His long eyelashes were wet with tears. He shivered. And so did I.

"Cedric," I whispered. "Cedric, are you here?"

"He's here, and he knows you're with me. But you can't see him. My daddy's waiting for me. I'm going with him very soon."

"But what about Squeak. Is he going too?"

"No. I don't think so. 'Cos he never sees my Daddy. Only I do."

Somehow, I didn't feel frightened, but I was frightened for Bubble. I could feel his back against my tummy and his head against my chest; they were both burning hot.

"Oh where was Squeak with Mrs. B and Mrs. Tommy?"

Bubble's eyes were closed now. He was smiling and whispering something I couldn't hear.

The sun seemed to shine brighter. It hurt my eyes. I closed them against the dazzling light. Someone came, I heard them panting.

"What's up?" It was Ant's voice. I opened my eyes, he was standing between me and the bright sun.

"Bubble's very sick. Go and get somebody. Quick, please."

"He looks asleep to me." Ant was looking down at Bubble.

"Then get someone to put him to bed," I yelled.

"All right, all right." Antony ran off in the direction of the house.

The light was even brighter now. Bubble was whispering again. I bent my head as close as I could to his mouth, but I still couldn't hear what he was saying. And all the time he was smiling. I shut my eyes against the blazing light around me. Like a sunbeam striking a window pane; it blinded me–until all I could see was black.

I don't know how long it was before anyone came. All I remember was feeling a cold breeze when someone lifted Bubble off me. My shirt and shorts were soaked with his sweat. I was wide awake now.

Mr. B was already halfway to the house, carrying Bubble in his strong arms. He was running. Mrs. Tommy was running beside him, trying to keep up and Mrs. B was following, waddling as fast as she could. Miss Audrey-Joan had lifted me up and was brushing me down. Ant stood by her side, shifting from one foot to another. "Are you all right Pat?"

"Yes, Miss Baker. Is Bubble all right? He was crying so I helped him."

"He'll be all right. Are you sure *you* feel all right?"

"Yes, Miss Baker."

"Very good. Then I will go and see to Bubble. Don't stray too far from the house this afternoon. The sun is really hot."

"I don't feel like sailing the pirate ship this afternoon," I told Ant. "Besides, half our crew are missing. Bubble and Squeak."

"Right-oh." Captain Blackbeard Antony kicked at a stone on the pathway, his black hair falling over his eyes. He blew upwards to get it out of the way. "So what *is* wrong with Bubble?" Now he was looking me straight in the eyes. He expected me to tell him.

"I-I couldn't hear what he was saying. He was whispering."

Ant came very close, almost pushing his face into mine. "You know, but you're not going to tell me." Now he was accusing, and angry.

I backed away. Away from that wide grey stare. "I'll tell you later."

Antony just shrugged. After glaring at me for a long moment, he turned away and walked towards the house. I knew he was hurt and upset. He didn't turn back, but walked on down the path, scuffing his feet and kicking at loose stones.

"So this is what it feels like to be nearly nine. I feel so old now, I wonder what it will feel like when I am nearly ten."

((

"They're leaving."

Ant and I were standing on the window sill in the top-floor boys' dormitory. If we pressed our foreheads against the window, we could see straight down onto the big pillared porch below. Bubble and Squeak's mother was standing by a black car. She was holding Squeak's hand and talking to Miss Baker.

"So where's Bubble?" Ant pulled his head back and rubbed the glass with his sleeve where his breath had huffed it up.

"I dunno. P'raps they're waiting for him now."

"I don't think he's here. I think he went to the hospital."

"Don't be daft. Anyway, why d'you think that?"

"I was still awake last night when I heard a car come. I got up and looked out the window. It was an ambulance."

"If you were up here, how could you see it was an ambulance? They can't show any lights 'cos of the blackout."

"I lifted the blackout up. The moon was out and I could see a big red cross on the roof. It was an army ambulance."

"So why would an army ambulance come and take Bubble to the hospital? He's not in the army."

"I know, but they take us to that Air Force Base hospital when there's something really wrong. Remember? You went there to have your tonsils out."

"I didn't go by ambulance."

"No because you weren't sick enough. Mrs. B took you in the wagon-ette. But they brought you back after you'd had them out."

"So they did. I don't remember much about the ride back from the hospital. But I remember Mrs. B gave me lots of ice cream and jelly to eat until my throat was better."

"Judith Roberts went by ambulance when she had that lump behind her ear. And she didn't come back for a whole term."

"P'raps that's where Bubble is, and his mummy and Squeak are going there to see him."

"Prob'ly. Hey. Squeak's looking up. Wave. D'you think he can see us?"

We waved but Squeak didn't wave back.

"He looks very sad," I said. "Like he really doesn't want to go with his mummy."

"She looks sad too. And she's all dressed in black."

I'd never seen Bubble and Squeak's mummy before. She was wearing a black overcoat with a black fur collar, even though it was a hot day. A little black hat was perched on her golden curls. *"Like Bubble's."* Even the hanky she was holding up against her cheek, was black. Miss Baker put her arm around her and helped her into the back of the black car.

Abruptly, Squeak turned to run back into the house, but he tripped on the steps. Miss Audrey-Joan went after him. She knelt down on one knee and took both of his hands in one of her own. She talked to him and ran the fingers of her other hand through his yellow curls. Squeak was nodding his head as she spoke to him. Then she took out her own white hanky and wiped his eyes.

"He's crying. He really doesn't want to go with his mummy, does he?"

"Maybe he just wants to stay and sail on the pirate ship," Ant replied.

Miss Audrey-Joan led Squeak to the car and lifted him into the back by his Mother. Then she closed the car door and stood back as it moved slowly down the gravel driveway. All we could see was Squeak's face in the back window as he stared back at the house.

"He's looking up at us," I whispered.

Miss Audrey-Joan stood on the steps, gazing at the swirling dust on the driveway long after the car had disappeared. Then, shaking her head, she walked slowly up the wide stone steps and disappeared under the porch roof.

The dinner bell sounded.

"C'mon." Ant jumped down from the window sill, "I'll race you to the dinner queue."

I followed, my shoes skittering on the wooden floor as I tried to outrun him to the dormitory door. We squeezed through together and raced down the long landing to the grey-painted stairs. I decided that after dinner I would go and find Mr. B in the kitchen garden and ask him if Bubble was in the Air Force hospital.

Somehow I didn't think he was.

And somehow I didn't feel hungry.

///

"Did Bubble go with his Daddy?"

"Goodness no child. His daddy was killed in the war." Mr. B was thinning carrots and I was crouched down beside him, collecting the tiny pink roots and laying them side by side in a wooden trug.

"I know his Daddy's dead. B-but Bubble could . . ." I didn't say any more as I wasn't sure if Mr. B would understand about Bubble talking to his Daddy. But he knew about Cedric.

"But what Pat-a-Cake? What could Bubble do?"

"Well, you know how Cedric came and talked to me? When I was sick?"

"Yes. I remember. And you used to write him letters. But that was a long time ago and you know it was only a dream now, don't you."

"Surely Mr. B didn't think I DREAMED that Cedric talked to me?" I wanted to shout at him, *"It wasn't a dream."* Instead, I whispered, "It wasn't a dream. He really did talk to me."

Mr. B was silent for a very long time. I could tell he was thinking hard so I went on putting the thinnings into the trug; the little feather tops up one end and the cotton-thread roots the other. "Well, now, Pat-a-Cake, have you seen Cedric since you were sick?"

"No. But Bubble saw him."

"Did he now? When was that?" He turned towards me.

"When I was holding him yesterday. And . . ." I took a deep breath and looked Mr. B straight in the eyes. "He saw his Daddy too. His Daddy was talking to him. His Daddy often talked to him. Squeak couldn't see him, only Bubble, and then he would tell Squeak what his Daddy had said."

"I see. But Bubble had trouble talking didn't he?"

"He could talk when he wanted to. He talked to us. He talked on the pirate ship."

"Now I come to think of it, I did hear him speak that day I put up your ship's wheel."

"He didn't like talking to people. He just wanted to listen to his Daddy talk."

"Ah, I see."

We went on thinning the carrots and soon the wooden trug was full of tiny green feathers and little pink threads. "So, Mr. B, did Bubble go with his Daddy?"

Mr. B sighed. He stood up and straightened, his two hands rubbing the arch of his back.

"Did he?" I had to have an answer.

Mr. B looked at me very hard. Then he bent down and put his two hands on my shoulders and his eyes held mine. They looked kind, but watery. "I don't know, Pat-a-Cake. I honestly don't know, and that's the truth. But if you think he's with his Daddy then that's all right by me. If that's what you want to believe m'dear, that's all right too."

So now I knew for sure. A dark cloud passed over the sun and I shivered. The warmth had gone out of that bright June day.

IV

After tea, Ant and I went out to the orchard, to the Tree-that-was-Really-a-Pirate-Ship. The wind had dropped and the pink sails were twisted and caught in the grey skeleton branches.

"We should take Bubble's sails down," said Ant. "He might need them when he comes back from the hospital."

"He's not coming back." There was such a lump in my throat, I could only whisper.

"Why not?"

"He's dead."

"He can't be. How do you know?"

"I know he is. When I was holding him yesterday–when he was sick– he told me he was going to be with his Daddy."

"Is that what you wouldn't tell me yesterday?"

I nodded.

Ant jumped up and ran around to the other side of the tree. "I don't believe you. No. No. No." Now he was yelling, "You're lying. I don't believe you."

I went after him. He was crouching down the way he always did when he didn't want me to see his face. His forehead was pressed to his knees, his hands clasped at the back of his head, his arms covered his ears. Shutting out the world.

"Go away. GO AWAY."

I went away, back to the other side of the tree. I, too, put my head down on my knees. I could feel the hot tears trickling down the insides of my legs and soaking into my socks. After what seemed like hours, I heard Ant coming back. I lifted my head and he knelt down beside me. He shoved a hanky into my hand; it was wet.

"Here. Wipe your eyes."

Neither of us spoke for a long time.

Then, "I think it's time we dropped anchor and furled in the sails," he said. "They're torn to shreds anyway."

I nodded. So we climbed up into the Tree-that-was-Really-a-Pirate-Ship—far out to where the sails were knotted in a tangled mess around the old dead branches. It took a long time to untwist and gather in the faded pink cotton tatters still fluttering in the evening breeze. We climbed back to the crow's-nest.

"Look what's here." Ant was groping around in a gnarled old hole where two branches joined.

"What?"

He held out a gold pirate earring, its red thread knotted several times where it had broken while Bubble was doing battle with Spanish galleons. I took it from him.

"There's more." He pulled out a purple and green striped jumper.

"That was Bubble's favourite. Look." I pointed to a few strands of yellow hair caught in the shoulder button.

"He never undid his buttons before he took it off," Ant said. "Just pulled it over his head."

"What shall we do with it? Put it back where we found it?"

Ant stared at the jumper which I was smoothing and trying to fold neatly. I knew he was thinking, so I kept quiet. "If we put it back, someone else'll find it and they won't know it was Bubble's. They won't care either," he added.

"Maybe we should bury it," I suggested.

"That's a good idea. But where?"

I tried to remember what Bubble liked to do, when he wasn't being a pirate. "When we first made him a pirate, he'd been digging in the sand behind the poop deck"

"Right," agreed Ant. "Let's look."

We jumped down onto the circle of soft, sandy soil, under the tall twisting roots of the fallen Tree-that-was-Really-a-Pirate-Ship. Warmed by the summer sun, it was a good place to sit.

"Look." I pointed to some small twigs sticking into a small mound of sand. "Those are Bubble's twigs. I think this is a good place to bury his jumper." I opened my other hand which had been tightly closed up to now. "And his pirate earring."

"Right," said Ant again. "Let's get the spades."

From the small, unused animal stall where the children's garden tools were kept, we shouldered two spades and marched back to the orchard, where we dug a small square hole in the sandy patch behind the poop deck, taking turns at scooping out a spadeful of the red-gold sand, and heaping it carefully around the edge. When we couldn't reach in any further, I stood in the hole. It came up to my knees. "I think that's deep enough. It feels cold at the bottom."

"We'll put everything in a box," said Ant.

"So where do we get a box?"

"Wait here," he replied.

I sat down by the hole and watched him gallop across the orchard towards the gate, his long brown legs leaping over the tall wild flowers and rich green grasses. While he was away, I untwisted the threads of golden hair from the jumper button, wound them around my finger, and carefully knotted them in a dry corner of my hanky.

Ant was soon back. He was carrying a small cardboard shoe box.

"Where d'you find that?" I asked.

He grinned. "Fell off the back of a lorry."

"Did not. You got it from the Rabbit Hole. You know you're not allowed down there unless there's an air raid."

"Poof. As if you never go down there to pinch a barley sugar," he accused.

He was right, as usual. The Anderson shelter buried beside the rubbish heap, was out of bounds and everything inside was only to be used during an air raid. But the door was often left open, and sometimes, in bad weather, we would creep in out of the rain.

"Anyway," he went on. "There were only a few old pencils and crayons in it. I just dumped them in one of the toy boxes."

We folded Bubble's tattered and bedraggled pink sheets and placed them in the hole, with the box between them. Inside the box went the jumper, the pirate earring and a bunch of yellow buttercups, and tiny blue speedwells the same colour as Bubble's eyes. Then we shovelled all the sand back into the hole. Ant took the two small twigs Bubble had left and placed them on top to make an 'X'.

"'X' marks the spot," he explained. "The spot where the treasure is buried. We'll make a treasure map and tear it in half. You keep one half and I'll keep the other. Then nobody will be able to find the treasure except us."

"What treasure?"

"Pirate's gold of course, silly. Pirate's gold." He paused, then whispered, "Bubble's gold."

We were quiet for a long time. We didn't know what to say.

"Ant, why do children have to die in the war?"

"Bubble didn't die in the war. He died 'cos he was very sick."

"Cedric died in the war. His evacuee ship was torpedoed by the Germans. And he drowned."

"I know." Ant's big grey eyes stared into mine, as if he was seeing into my head, and hearing what I was thinking. "I know, Patty. And I'm sorry. Really I am."

"Do you think we'll die in the war, Ant?"

"No, silly. Of course we won't. That's why we're here. So we won't die in the war."

"That's all right then."

We never sailed on the Tree-that-was-Really-a-Pirate-Ship again.

And on my ninth birthday, I had two visitors. My mother and Cedric.

Chapter 39

My Ninth Birthday

I loved having a midsummer birthday. Not only was it a convenient time for presents—halfway between Christmas and Christmas—it also meant it could be an outdoors birthday. I had vague, misty memories of a birthday before the war. A visit to Dudley Zoo with all my aunts and cousins, followed by a picnic in the Randan Woods. I remembered the woods, because my Aunt Laura saw a snake and wouldn't stop scream-ing. I remembered strawberries and cream, and chocolate cake.

In 1943, my ninth birthday was on a Sunday. This meant no lessons and, although we were supposed to follow quiet and useful pursuits on Sundays, if it was someone's birthday the rules were forgotten and we had a party.

The Saturday before my birthday, I was in the stables grooming Dolly when Ann-the-Bank came marching importantly across the yard towards me. With her chin in the air, and the quick click-clack of her button shoes on the cobbles, I knew she was bursting to tell me some-thing, "You've got to go to Miss Audrey-Joan's study. RIGHT NOW. She wants to see you."

My heart sank as I wondered what I'd done wrong. I looked at Ann. As usual, she was enjoying telling me what to do.

"RIGHT NOW," she repeated. "You have to go there immediately, if not sooner."

I sighed and put down the curry comb.

Miss Audrey-Joan met me at the door of her study. Her face didn't look too grim, so perhaps I wasn't in deep trouble. "Come in, Pat. I have a surprise for you. Someone is here to see you."

She stood aside as I entered the room. A familiar lady wearing an unfamiliar dress rose from the armchair by the fireplace. "Hello, my darling!"

For an instant, I hesitated, uncertain what I should do, or say. Then she held out her arms.

"Mummy!" I flew across the room.

The rest of the day was so special. My mother followed me around as I showed her everything. My own little corner in the dormitory, where Edward Bear lay with Tristan on the old eiderdown that leaked feathers. In the classroom, my mother sat at my desk while I proudly showed her my neat exercise books; pointing out the gold stars, highlighting work well done. In the kitchen, Mrs. B made tea while I told Mummy about the garden, and riding and showed her the three-legged stool in my corner by the Aga.

I heard the familiar run-slide-run up the stone flagged hall, and Ant poked his head around the door looking for me. I introduced him to my mother and he shook her hand very properly and said, "How do you do." Mrs. B hrumpph'd and gave him a cup of tea and a biscuit. He politely answered all my mother's questions and remembered not to talk with his mouth full. When we'd finished, he shook her hand again and held the door for her–which was open anyway.

"What a nice mannered little boy," Mummy said when Ant had left. I knew he would go straight up onto the stable roof to watch us through his telescope; I was glad he hadn't heard her call him "a little boy."

I showed Mummy the gardens, and she met Dolly and Mr. B. We walked around the orchard, but I didn't show her Merlin's lair, or tell her about the Tree-that-was-Really-a-Pirate-Ship. Then she told me to change out of my dirty riding breeches into something more fitting to go out.

"OUT?"

She took my hand and we walked through the big wrought-iron gates, into the lane. At the corner of the Bridgnorth Road, we caught the bus and went into town, where she shopped for me, and we had dinner at the Castle Café. Then she took me to the Majestic Cinema to see a real picture from Hollywood. Called *Reap The Wild Wind*, it was the very first grown-up picture I'd ever seen. Mummy worried a bit that I would have nightmares after seeing the giant octopus, and she "tsk-tsk'd" when the handsome man kissed the beautiful lady on the lips. Afterwards, we had tea at another café before catching the bus back to Eardington.

"I'm staying at a B and B in the village," Mummy said as she kissed me goodnight. "So I'll go to church with you tomorrow, then we can celebrate your birthday together."

I fell asleep quickly, but awoke in the night with butterflies in my tummy.

"My mother was here. Really, really here and would come for me in the morning?"

I tossed and turned, and felt sick, and when morning came I couldn't eat the Spam fritters I'd chosen for my birthday breakfast. When everyone wished me 'Happy Birthday' and piled their hand-drawn cards and favours in front of my place, I felt awful. But I thanked them properly. I got ready for church and hung around the front gates, waiting for my mother; then I saw her walking towards me, her face all smiles–just for me.

I'd begged Miss Audrey-Joan to take us to church at Quatt and she'd agreed. It was wonderful to see my mother, so pretty in a blue and white silk flowered dress, and a navy straw hat, sitting gracefully in the long punt amongst all us children. I sat beside her and she held my hand the whole time, and smiled at everyone. During the service, I felt sick again, and I leaned my head against her shoulder. Her arm went around me and I snuggled to her, breathing in the familiar scent of Lavender Water mixed with Pears soap.

We had a picnic lunch on the lawn, under the weeping ash. A small table, laid with a pretty tablecloth, held two plates of cold roast beef and salad from Mr. B's garden, and a jug of Mrs. B's lemonade. Mrs. B said that it was a more suitable lunch for my mother, than the Shepherd's Pie and Treacle tart that I had asked for.

But I still couldn't eat. Mummy tried to persuade me so to please her, I poked at bits of lettuce with my fork. I'd had about two bites when Miss Primrose, Gatsby at her heels, came floating across the lawn. She carried something large, round and brown. When she set it down on the table, I gasped. Mummy had brought a real birthday cake from a real bakery, covered with shiny chocolate icing, and decorated with squirls and squiggles; it had been hidden in the pantry ever since she arrived. Across the centre was written in white icing, '*Happy Birthday Patty*' and a large number '9'.

Gatsby, who'd been greeting everyone, wagging his tail and poking his nose into everything, suddenly leaped up and took a great big lick from the side of the cake.

"Oh no!" cried my mother. I screamed and Miss Primrose grabbed Gatsby before he took another lick. "Naughty doggy," she said, and smacked him on his nose. "Naughty Gatsby."

I was wailing by this time, but Mummy shh'd me, picked up a spoon and carefully carved out the piece of cake that Gatsby had licked. "There," she said, and dropped the piece of cake on the grass where Gatsby, who had wriggled from Miss Primrose's grasp, gobbled it up. With calm efficiency, my mother had put everything right with one stroke of a spoon.

I broke off a tiny piece of cake, but I couldn't eat it. A headache, that had been threatening all day, now pounded behind my eyes. I turned to my mother, "I d-don't feel very well." Tears streamed down my face. Mummy held out her arms. I slipped from my chair and onto her lap.

"Goodness me, child. You're boiling hot. Feverish. And just look at your eyes."

I couldn't see my eyes; I'd been crying but I didn't care.

Miss Primrose's long fingers turned my chin and she looked at my eyes.

"Hmmm," she said. "I think we'd better take her in out of this hot sun."

My mother carried me across the lawn and into the house. Miss Primrose followed, holding the cake high; Gatsby was jumping up to get another lick. Miss Audrey-Joan met us in the hall. By this time I didn't really care what anyone wanted to look at. My eyes, my skin–everyone had something to say about me. My mother undressed me, as though I were five again, and put me to bed in the little sick room. Then she went out on the landing to talk to Mrs. B. I could hear a few words, "Severely jaundiced"..."Send for Dr. Mole immediately"..."high fever."

That's all I remember.

Until Cedric came.

Shadows and voices came and went. Dr Mole, Mrs. B, Miss Audrey-Joan. But, all the while, my mother was there; her voice and her touch, smoothing, stroking, bathing my head, singing to me, holding me and rocking me. I awoke once, and saw her sitting at the end of the bed, her hands clasped beneath her chin, her eyes closed; her lips moved, but I heard no words.

The next time I awoke, I looked for her at the end of the bed and I was surprised to see Cedric there instead. He was leaning against the bedpost, his knees drawn up, his hands clasped around his shins. When he saw me looking at him, he stretched his legs out and grinned. "Hello," he said, and held out his hand, "I brought you these from my garden."

I struggled to sit up, and took the flowers. A sprig of honeysuckle and a wild rose. Their scent filled the whole room. "Thank you," I said. I'd looked for Cedric so many times and now he was here, I didn't know what to say. I laid back down and held the flowers under my nose, breathing in their perfume.

"Want to come out and play?" asked Cedric.

"I can't. I'm sick."

"Course you can. I'll look after you. C'mon. I'll show you the best places to play."

I tucked the flowers under my pillow. "All right. Where are we going?"

Cedric said nothing; just held out his hand. I took it. It felt light and gentle. Now he was hovering just a few inches above me. The tiniest tug from Cedric and I floated up off the bed and joined him. "What about my mother?" I whispered.

"She's sleeping. Look." Mummy was sitting in the rocking chair, her head back against the cushion, fast asleep.

I looked down again at the bed. "Cedric...what's happening?" I could see myself lying in bed, yet I was floating above myself, with Cedric.

"Oh, don't worry about that. You don't need that where we're going. C'mon."

Together we floated down and ran–our feet barely touching the floor–along the landing to the stairs. I ran down the first few stairs to the half-way landing by the big window overlooking the stable-yards. Cedric flew down, without touching a stair.

"How d'you do that?"

"Easy. Just do it. Hold my hand, and point your foot to the bottom of the stairs." I held onto Cedric and launched myself towards the grey flagstones. I felt the breeze pass me as I flew down the stairs, my hair streaming out behind me. At the bottom I looked back up, "Can we do that again?"

Cedric shrugged, "I s'pose so."

Going up was easy too. We ran lightly to the top of the stairs and then flew back down again. At the bottom, we heard footsteps and saw Miss Audrey-Joan walking towards us. I tugged at Cedric's hand to run and hide, but he smiled and said, "She can't see us. Watch."

On silent toes, he ran towards her. As he passed her, his fingers lightly touched her cheek. She put her hand up to the spot and turned her head. Cedric was leaning against the wall, laughing. Miss Audrey-Joan shook her head, wafted her hand as though to brush away a cobweb, and walked on down the hall. As she passed me, I couldn't resist touching her arm. She paused for an instant, looked straight at me, then shook her head again and climbed the stairs. At the landing she turned and looked back down at me; Cedric was at my side again. A puzzled look came over her face. Then she shrugged her shoulders and disappeared around the turn on the landing.

"C'mon," said Cedric. "We're wasting time."

Outside, a full moon lit up the warm midsummer night. Cedric headed for the sunken garden that once was Camelot. We laughed, remembering how he'd played King Arthur and defended the rockery castle against his enemies. Cedric flew up and stood on the very top, dressed in a suit of golden armour; my cotton nightie had become a flowing white gown, girdled with gold, and with sleeves that brushed the silver of the moonlit grass. While I watched, Cedric battled hoards of invading Saxons, his gleaming Excalibur thrashing back and forth. One by one, his enemies melted into thin air.

Then, from the base of the rockery, came a roar and a spurt of flame, and a dragon erupted from depths unknown. Seeing Cedric, it unfurled its wings and spiralled upward towards him; fire gushing from its nostrils, long and vicious claws extended towards him.

I shouted, "Cedric! Run! Fly!"

Cedric stood and laughed at the dragon and waited until it came within striking distance. And when the moment came, that it could have grasped him in its talons, Cedric thrust Excalibur between it's blood-red eyes. The dragon reared up, hovered for a instant, then fell backwards, melting into the darkness.

And Cedric stood alone, one hand on the old fountainhead, the other holding Excalibur aloft. The moonlight caught it and, as I watched, it turned into a fiery cross that flared up, bathing Cedric in a bright, white light. Then it melted away to nothing. Cedric, his armour gone, bounded down the rockery and tugged at my hand.

"Come, there's lots more to see." He took off towards the orchard, his hand never losing its clasp on mine. "Gotta check Merlin's lair."

We flew, like Peter Pan and Wendy, over the five-barred gate and across the orchard. As we passed The Tree-that-was-Really-a-Pirate-Ship, I saw two figures at the ship's wheel. They looked up and waved.

"Look, Cedric. It's Bubble." I could see his golden curls, shining silver in the moonlight. A tall man, stood behind him—his hands covering Bubble's—helping him to steer. They both wore pirate eye patches and were laughing. "Who's with him."

"That's his Daddy," Cedric told me. Bubble always wanted to be the pirate captain and for his Daddy to play with him. Now he can do both. But Ant was his hero, you know."

"No, I never knew that."

As we passed over them, the pink sails billowed in the wind, and it was a real ship, sailing on an ocean of silver grasses that bent and rolled in the breeze. A silver ship on a silver sea.

We flew on, to the corner of the orchard and floated down into Merlin's lair. The moonlight bounced off Cedric, as he stood in a circle of light; illuminating the small glade and blinding me for a moment. When my eyes became accustomed to the brightness, Cedric stood before me dressed in a long brown woollen robe, a rope-belt around his waist.

"Merlin!"

"Are you here to get your Allie?" I asked.

He laughed. "No. That's left for you to find. I don't need it any more. Look." He dug deep into a pocket in his robe, and brought out a shiny glass marble full of coloured threads. He laughed again and threw it up in the air, where it exploded into thousands of tiny round raindrops–or were they bubbles? They danced and spun in the air, showering us with specks of light, all colours of the spectrum—just as the prism in Miss Audrey-Joan's study window would catch the setting sun, and fill the room with dancing light-fairies.

"You don't mind Ant knowing about this place, then?" I asked.

"Course not, silly. Sometimes when you're here, I come too."

"You're *here*? When we are?"

"Yes. And sometimes I come when you're here by yourself—just so's you're not alone. But you know that anyway." Cedric put away his marble, as if he had tired of playing with it. "Let's ride." He grabbed my hand and, magically, we were standing outside Merlin's lair. A pure white horse stood in the moonlight, quietly cropping the grass.

"My white palfrey! Or was it Cedric's?"

"Where . . .?" I began. I didn't ask any more. It seemed that when I was with Cedric, anything was possible. I didn't need to know why, or how.

"It's the quickest way," said Cedric. "Get on." He gave me a gentle shove and, instantly, I was astride the horse's soft silky back. Like a feather touch, Cedric settled in behind me; I felt his arms around my waist. "Just wind your fingers in his mane," he instructed. "I'll tell him where to go." Again, I did as Cedric bade me, and in a trice the great horse leaped forward. To my astonishment, he kept on going–up. Up and up. Over the orchard, over the house. I looked down at sleeping Normanhurst, and wondered if my mother had missed me yet.

"Where are we going?" I shouted to Cedric. "To the moon?"

He laughed. "Not tonight. I want to show you special places."

We flew to everywhere I remembered. The house in Wales, the river in the valley and the bracken-covered little mountain. In a patch of sunlight, someone was walking down the mountainside behind a flock of sheep. Cedric called out, the person looked up and waved. It was Dilly. I shouted and waved back. Then she put her hand to her forehead, shading her eyes, as if searching for something.

"Did she see us?" I asked

"For a moment," replied Cedric. "But maybe it's just a dream for her, too."

"This isn't a dream. This is real...isn't it?"

"Of course," said Cedric.

"Look," I shouted. "There's the sea."

Ahead of us was a sandy beach. Rocky cliffs rising out of white surf and a stretch of blue sea in the sunlight. "It's Cornwall, I recognise it. It's Mummy's home. Can we go?"

Cedric was silent.

"Take the horse to the sea, Cedric. Please, I want to see the sea."

"You go. The horse will take you." Cedric spoke quietly, almost a whisper, "The sea...I still can't...I'll wait for you."

I knew Cedric had left me, I was alone on the horse, but it seemed to know what I wanted and responded to my silent wishes.

"I want to walk on the beach. I want to feel the sand between my toes again."

The horse set down on the sand at the edge of the sea, and I slid from its back. Gentle wavelets swept over my feet, leaving tiny foam bubbles and little shreds of green seaweed caught between my toes. A small girl, about four years old, played in a rock pool; I knew it was me from long ago. I recognised my father who was building a sand castle nearby. He looked up and out to sea, shading his eyes against the glare. Then he picked the little girl up and carried her to the edge of the dying waves.

"Look, my treasure," he said and pointed far out to sea. The child's eyes followed his finger. "A tea clipper, in full rig. Remember it my darling, it won't be long before they've all vanished."

I followed his gaze. In the distance, I saw a ship, her square-rigged sails billowing in the wind as she moved swiftly across the horizon. Caught in the glow of a setting sun, the ship shone like pure gold."

"I see. I see," the child that I knew was me, cried. And I remembered. So long ago.

"Daddy?" I moved towards him. But there was nothing–only a sand castle and a small rock pool. Then, behind me, I heard more children laughing and four small tow-headed, suntanned boys, raced across the sand and into the waves. I didn't recognise them.

The sunlight disappeared and the beach was deserted. The horse nickered, pawing at the sand. I floated onto its back. The thundering of the rolling, white-capped waves got louder and louder and I saw, riding on the crests of the surf, a hundred–or was it a thousand?—foam-white horses racing towards me. My horse reared and snorted, and tossed its head. As the thundering herd came ashore, it turned and joined them and I was flying back across the sand, over the cliffs and towards green fields; just me, riding with a myriad horses in the moonlight. Beyond the fields I could see the blackness of a forest and as the first wave of horses reached it, they disappeared amongst the trees. I was about to follow, when Cedric appeared at the edge of the wood–Thatcher's Woods; we were nearly home. I stopped, the other horses passed and Cedric slid up behind me. "It's time to go back now," he said.

"I want to stay with you. Besides you haven't shown me your garden. Or where you live."

Cedric looked up at the sky. "Well, it'll have to be quick. You have to go back, Pat. You *have* to. You can't stay with us yet."

He turned the horse and I saw below me a small thatched cottage, nestled in a valley. It was sunny again, and the cottage was surrounded by a garden, filled with a rainbow of flowers. A man and a lady and a small girl were walking amongst the flowers. The child was picking flowers and handing them, one by one, to the man.

"You live there?" I asked. Is that your mummy and daddy and your sister?

"Yes, that's my family," replied Cedric. But we don't really *live* there. We can be anywhere, with anyone. Any time." The horse turned.

"Cedric, wait. Tell me who those four little boys were on the beach."

"They're yours," he replied. "They haven't arrived yet. They're waiting."

I wasn't sure I understood what he said, but he didn't give me time for more questions. "Come," said Cedric. "I must take you back."

"No, Cedric," I begged. "Please. I want to see one more place."

"Where?"

"The Fairy Ring. In Thatcher's Woods. I want to dance with you in the Fairy Ring in the moonlight. Please. It's not far."

Cedric hesitated for an instant. "All right. But then you really *must* go back."

Our horse set us down in Thatcher's Woods, right by the fairy ring.

"Cedric, look! It really *is* a fairy ring!"

The little toadstools glowed in the dark. A circle of light in a dark forest. Tiny beings–like the glow-worms that my father used to catch in a jar–flitted and darted amongst the toadstools. Moonbeams bounced off the shiny quartz of the rock. Standing within the ring, were Cedric's father, mother and little sister.

"What are they doing here?" I asked.

"Waiting for us, and to make sure I get you back in time." With a touch of his hand, Cedric wafted me up onto the top of rock. His family joined hands around it.

I felt a strange glow pass through me.

"They're wishing for you, Pat." Cedric explained. "They're wishing you well."

I stood up and spread my arms wide. I could feel warmth and light flow through my whole body; I felt wonderful. I laughed out loud.

"Come," said Cedric. I stepped off the rock. I felt hands touching me, guiding me onto the horse. I turned to wave goodbye. No-one was there.

We flew back, over Thatcher's Woods, to the familiar house that was now my home, and where my mother slept. In the stable-yard, I slipped from the white horse's back and took his head in my hands. I kissed his nose and he nuzzled my cheek. I pushed back his forelock. I felt something hard. He bent his head and I clasped my hand around a tiny horn that gleamed like mother-of-pearl in the moonlight. "Thank you," I whispered. "Thank you." I turned to Cedric. "I have one more question."

"What now?"

"When we were in Thatcher's woods–before, with Miss Audrey-Joan and we all wished for something. What did you wish for?"

Cedric looked at me for a long moment before he answered, "I wished I could be with my Mummy, and my Daddy, and my sister. Forever."

In no time at all, I was floating above my bed, looking down at myself sleeping.

"You're all right now." Cedric put his hand on my forehead. "The fever's gone."

"Will I see you again?" I asked.

"Maybe one day. But I'm never far away. You know that." He pushed me gently onto the bed. "I have to go now." Again, a feather-light touch on my forehead, and he was gone. The flame of the little oil night-lamp dipped and flickered—touched by a passing breeze.

Sunlight flooded the room and pierced my eyelids. I awoke slowly, wondering who was there. I opened my eyes and Mummy was looking down at me, smiling, but with a worried look in her eyes.

"Feeling better, Pooh?"

"I...I think so."

"You had quite a nasty time. But your fever is down and I think you're on the mend."

Mrs. B bustled in. "How's our patient today? My, what some people will do to get out of lessons." But she smiled as she handed my mother a bowl of hot water and a face flannel.

After my mother had washed me and brushed my hair, she took me out of the bed and onto her lap. Mrs. B came back with some clean sheets to remake my bed. She flung back the pillow. "My goodness, what've we got here? Someone brought you flowers, isn't that nice. But I'll throw them out, they're all wilted."

"NO!" I shouted. My mother and Mrs. B jumped as I yelled again, "NO!"

"No what?" asked Miss Audrey-Joan as she came through the door of my room. "She must be better if she's shouting 'no'."

"It's...they...I want to keep them."

"Well," said Miss Audrey-Joan. "If they mean that much to you, I'll take them and press them between some blotting paper for you."

I had a collection of pressed flowers, which I kept between the pages of my Bible. "Thank you, Miss Baker. Yes, please...would you do that?"

"Of course."

I slid off my mother's lap and picked up the flowers–a sprig of honeysuckle and a wild rose–and handed them to Miss Audrey-Joan.

Later, when my mother went to have a cup of tea and I was alone, I pushed back the bedclothes and, very carefully, picked the sand from between my toes and slipped it into the little pocket of my writing case.

It's still there.

Chapter 40

The Very Best Summer of All

"You're as skinny as a beanpole," said Ant. "But at least you're not dead."

It was a Saturday, so Ant was allowed to be in the kitchen with me. I sat on the three-legged stool and he, as usual, was pushing his foot against the table leg to see how far he could tip his chair without falling backwards.

"Did you think I was going to die, then?"

"Everyone said you were. Just like Bubble."

"Well, I didn't."

Ant went on swinging and I went back to reading a new Arthur Ransome Mummy had bought for me. But I couldn't concentrate.

It was July, and would soon be the end of term. Now that I was better, would Mummy go back to Westmorland? At that moment, she was talking to Miss Audrey-Joan in her study; about what, I didn't know. Just thinking about it put me in a gloomy mood. Missing all the sports and tournaments had been bad enough. I had to sit in the shade of the Sycamore tree and watch everyone else have fun. Although it had been funny to watch Ann-the-Bank and Ant in the three-legged race.

She couldn't get the rhythm right and when she fell over, she blamed Ant and kicked him.

I especially hated missing the tennis tournament; I played really well now and Ant and I always won the doubles matches. Of course, when Arabella Bosworthy found out I couldn't play, she just *had* to ask Ant to be her partner. When he said "All right," she shot me such a triumphant look, I could have slapped her. I stuck my tongue out at her, but she didn't seem to care. Anyway, she missed some really good shots and Ant got mad and called her a silly cow. Now that *was* funny. I missed being ball-boy for the teachers' tournament, too. I loved crouching by the net, then dashing to pick up the balls that didn't go over. Miss Audrey-Joan played a cracking good game of tennis; all the teachers were good, but she was the best.

Mrs. B bustled in. "Stop that incessant swinging, Mister Antony, please. One of these days, you'll go too far and fall over backwards and break your neck."

Ant brought his foot down and the front legs of the chair crashed onto the tiled floor. "What's for dinner?" he asked. It was Saturday, and we usually had bangers and mash.

"Sausages and mash," Mrs. B echoed my thoughts. "With stewed tomatoes from Mr. Baker's greenhouse. And rice pudding. We'll get you fattened up again in no time, Miss Patricia."

Ant rolled his eyes at the thought of me being fattened.

There was a flurry in the hallway and Miss Audrey-Joan came into the kitchen, closely followed by my mother and–of all people–Lady Harriet. I jumped up and ran to her. She gave me a big hug and then held me at arm's length and looked me up and down. "Tsk, tsk," she said. "Roagey-Mac will have to work some of his magic on you."

I didn't understand her comment and turned to my mother, who smiled and said, "Lady Harriet has asked that you stay at The Hall for the summer holidays. So that you'll have a real chance to recuperate." She turned to Lady Harriet. "Are you sure she'll be alright on her own? I mean...with the riding, and...such?"

I couldn't believe my ears. What was my mother saying?

Lady Harriet came to my rescue. "The child is nine now," she said. She was five when you last had her under your feet. She's had to fend for herself these past three years and she's tougher than you think."

My mother shook her head, "You're right. I hardly know my daughter now, and I've missed her growing up. I hate how this wretched war has forced families apart for so many years. Who would've thought it would last so long?"

"And it's not over yet," Lady Harriet replied, a grim look on her face. "That's why we have to let the children enjoy what they can, whenever an opportunity comes along. Let her be. The worst she can do is break her neck!"

My mother smiled. "Very well, she may spend the summer at the Hall."

"The whole summer? Mummy, pleeeeeeeeease."

"Yes, darling. The whole summer."

Ant was looking down at the floor, kicking at the tiles with the toe of his Clarks sandal. Lady Harriet was watching him. "And I'm sure we can arrange for you to have friends over to play. Can't we, Miss Baker?"

Miss Audrey-Joan nodded, "With the whole summer holidays ahead, there'll be plenty of time for visits."

Ant's foot stopped it's poking, "Really? I can visit?"

"Of course," said Lady Harriet. "That's settled then. Patricia, when term ends, Roagey-Mac will collect you and your things, and you can spend the summer with us."

The whole summer! And the Hall was the most exciting place on earth to stay. The horses, the toy room in the attic, and Roagey-Mac. And, if I had anything to do with it, Ant would be there a lot. What more could I want? I went to my mother and slipped my hand into hers. "I wish you could stay at the Hall too, because this is going to be the best summer of all."

And it was.

The morning after the summer term ended, Roagey-Mac arrived in a very smart horse and trap to take me to Lady Harriet's. After he'd stowed my luggage, including my bicycle, in the back of the trap, I left

Normanhurst for the whole summer holidays. Ant was perched on one of the stone columns, as we drove through the gateway. "Don't forget I can visit," he called.

"Don't 'ee worry, Master Ant," Roagey-Mac shouted back as we drove past him and out into the lane. "I'll be back along to get 'ee soon enough."

Thus began, the most exciting and fun summer holidays I'd ever had. Although the holiday in Wales with my father had been the best so far, this was even better. Lady Harriet and Roagey-Mac allowed me to do pretty much whatever I wanted. Climb trees, explore the barns and outhouses, follow Roagey-Mac around, or ride my bicycle at breakneck speed around the grounds. And, of course, there were the horses.

Lady Harriet had six horses. Her big black hunter, Midnight. Old Ned who pulled her gypsy caravan, a super bay that was a retired race horse and Roagey's special mount, two smaller ponies which Ant and I rode, and a wee Shetland pony who was more of a pet and mingled with the dogs and followed everyone around. The dogs were fun too: two foxhounds, a sharp little wire-haired terrier called Bobby—who persisted in hunting hedgehogs and would come home with spikes sticking out of his nose. Taffy and Precious, the house dogs, and two wonderful golden retrievers, followed Lady Harriet everywhere and slept on her bed at night. Then there was Hissy Cat, whose real name was Annie, who kept herself to herself, and if anyone tried to pet her, she would arch her back and hiss. Fat Marmaduke slept on my bed; day and night.

It wasn't long before Ant had his own bedroom and stayed at the Hall with us. This was because Miss Audrey-Joan caught him riding his bicycle out of the school gates to come and visit us at the Hall. What she didn't know was that he'd often done it before. Lady Harriet said the solution was obvious. So he got permission from his parents, and now he was staying for the whole summer.

Lady Harriet had Roagey-Mac set up some jumps in the paddock and taught me to jump properly. Although Ant had never ridden a horse, when he saw what fun I was having he decided to try. He learned quickly and we would go out with Lady Harriet, or Roagey–or both– and ride through the lanes, the woods, and up into the hills. We had a glorious summer. We went on picnics, Roagey-Mac took us fishing, we helped with the haymaking, and on rainy days we played in the attic with the toys that long ago, had belonged to Lady Harriet's children.

Two things happened at the end of that perfect summer holiday.

On the last Saturday before we had to go back to school, Lady Harriet organized a gymkhana for us, and for the children belonging to all her hunting friends; there were about twenty competitors. Roagey-Mac was one of the judges and Lady Harriet presided over the whole thing and presented the ribbons. I won two firsts in the girls nine to ten, and Ant won one in the boys. And the youngest child, who was only three and rode a Shetland pony, got a special prize.

Afterwards, long tables were set up under the chestnut tree for tea; all the mothers had brought sandwiches and home-made cakes. The highlight of the tea was when Roagey-Mac appeared on a real *Stop-me-and-buy-one* full of Wall's ice cream bars. While the children clapped their hands, I heard some of their mothers wondering to each other where he had acquired so many. Of course, Ant and I said nothing about lorries and what fell off them.

The other thing that happened was a phone call from my mother.

"Patty, I have some news for you. Dilys is getting married."

"Dilly? Married. To who?"

"To whom," my mother automatically corrected. "She's marrying John-the-Post. And they are going to live on a farm in Wales. You should write to her."

I knew then, I would never see Dilly again. Ever.

And I never did.

Chapter 41

Winter 1943-44

There was nothing memorable about the following winter except the fires threw out less heat and the portions on our plates were smaller. As the war entered its fifth year, there were more cuts in fuel and food rations. Pipes froze, the water in our washbasins froze–we froze. We huddled around the meagre fires to keep warm during the day, and begged, borrowed or stole newspapers to pad our beds and keep the cold out at night. I longed to be in Westmorland with my mother, but when she wrote and told me she went to bed wearing socks and a thick jumper, I realized it would be no better there. She also wrote that now they could only get one fresh egg each every two weeks, and that she'd stood in a queue for two hours to get half-a-pound of sausages. She told me I was lucky to be at school where Mr. B's garden provided us with plenty of vegetables and fruit, and chickens to give us eggs.

But this winter, even the supply of vegetables for the endless stews and soups dwindled. One day, when I was tucked away in my kitchen hidey-hole, a man was talking on the wireless about how the British–thanks to rationing and good food management–were 'lean and fighting fit.' Mrs. B hrumphed at him and said her supply of bottled fruit and salted beans would never last. I was certainly lean, but didn't necessarily feel fighting fit. Epidemics of whooping-cough and mumps broke out in early months of 1944, and for weeks there were empty places in the classrooms and the dining hall.

There was also an epidemic of chilblains. The rotten damp and cold raised red itchy bumps on fingers and toes; some children had them so badly, their hands were bandaged for most of the winter. Although I escaped the chilblains, I made up for it with boils, which broke out on my legs and arms. One on the back of my thigh was so painful I could hardly walk. Every day Mrs. B would take a spoon wrapped in a face-flannel and dipped in boiling water, and cup it against the angry red lump to try and bring it to a head. Finally, one night when I was in the bathtub, she told me to stand up so she could lance it. I screamed as the pain shot up into my belly, and a warm river gushed down the back of my leg. For the first time in my life I fainted. Antony had boils too, and we compared the disgusting eruptions on our skinny limbs. But we agreed that it was almost worth having boils, not to have to go out in the freezing midwinter cold.

Christmas 1943 came and went.There were twelve of us who couldn't go home, including Ann-the-Bank–who sulked for a week when she got the news she had to stay at school. We had our usual party, with Scottish dancing, and played Musical Chairs, Musical Bumps and Pass the Parcel. Roagey-Mac brought us some holiday treats from Lady Harriet; one of which was a large turkey for Christmas Dinner. As Ant said, "Roagey must have been following a lot of lorries for all *that* lot to have fallen off."

Later, that evening, when Ant and I were playing a game of Snakes and Ladders, Mrs. B bustled in. "Come with me, Patricia." I followed her into the hall, where she picked up the telephone and handed it to me, "Your mother will be on the phone in a moment, they're trying to make a connection."

"Why was it always a phone call?"

Not only did I talk to my mother on the phone, but to my father. He told me he had a short leave and was spending it with my mother. I didn't really know what to say. I hadn't spoken to him for so long, I hardly recognised his voice. So I just thanked him for my presents.

I cried myself to sleep that night.

"Was the war ever going to end? Would we ever have a real Christmas in our real home again? Would we ever be a real family again?"

Sunday, 2nd January, 1944.

Dear Mummy and Daddy,

Happy New Year. It was nice to talk to you on the telephone, even though it was crackly.

Thank you for the Christmas presents.

Will the war ever end? And will I spend Christmas with you ever again?

With love from,

Patricia.

Chapter 42

"It's Over!"

The winter did end–finally. On my tenth birthday, my mother phoned and told me she found it difficult to believe I was in "double figures" and nearly as tall as she. Mrs. B had written to tell her I'd grown out of all my clothes, so I was happy when a parcel came with a dress that she'd made from a curtain she'd found at a jumble sale. We had long since stopped wearing school uniform as it took too many clothing coupons, although Mrs. B kept a cupboard full of out-grown garments she'd been hoarding since long before the war. So whenever we went "out" to church, or a special occasion, she would dress us in green blazers with gold piping and the school crest on our pockets. I'd long ago grown out of my beautiful maroon bicycle; my knees bumped the handlebars, but I still rode it–standing on the pedals.

So passed another summer, another autumn, another Christmas and another long, cold winter. Teachers came and teachers left. New children came and some children left; we never knew where they went; perhaps they had just died like Bubble and Cedric.

Then came spring of 1945. Thatcher's woods was carpeted with bluebells, and we picked primroses on our way back from church. Ever since I'd been made head prefect for the girls, Ann-the-Bank hardly spoke to me. She thought *she* should have been head prefect. After all, hadn't she been at Normanhurst a whole six months longer than me?

"What was six months out of nearly five years?"

The previous autumn, I had passed the entrance exam for Alice Ottley School in Worcester, so I would go there when the war was over. But, as no one really thought the war would ever end, the idea of leaving Normanhurst never entered my head. Ant, who was elected head prefect for the boys, said he was going to go on to Bromsgrove School–sometime–probably after the war too.

After Easter we re-planted our Victory gardens, hunted for hop-scotch stones, and practised our tennis strokes. And we learned our lessons. Just as we had done for the past four-and-a-half years.

Then, one day in May 1945, quite unexpectedly, it all came to an end.

Mrs Riley was boring us with trigonometry. Ant was drawing aeroplanes in his scribbling book. I was reading *The Moonstone* which was open on my lap. Ann-the-Bank was flapping a piece of paper at me from under her desk on which she'd written "I'LL TELL" and Alana was drawing a horse. Giles Farmer was picking his piggy snout and, as usual, wrapping the grubbies into paper ammunition. Bossy Bella was sighing over a photo of Clark Gable. Everybody was doing anything but listen to Mrs. Riley.

The shrill squeal of the All Clear cut through the open window.

"The All Clear? When was there an air raid?"

Miss Audrey-Joan burst into the class room. "It's over. It's all over. Come. Come."

Mrs Riley forgot her trigonometry and rushed out of the class room. Mrs. B was ringing the school bell and shouting, "It's all over. At last! It's over."

We all looked at each other. Had everyone gone off their rocker? What's over?

We stood, silent statues, beside our desks for a full minute. Then something clicked, and we all rushed after the teachers, leaping down the stairs, running along the hallways and outside into the bright sunlight.

"WHAT'S OVER?" we all yelled.

"The war. The war. THE WAR IS OVER." The All Clear was still blaring through the village, over the fields, into every home, shop and pub–everywhere.

By now, the whole school had gathered on the front lawn. The teachers were jumping about, laughing, hugging, dancing and generally acting like children. We children just stood and watched them. Not one of us moved. Then, above the shrieking of the All Clear, the laughter and chattering of the grown-ups, we heard something else.

Church bells! Church bells had been silent ever since 1942—after they had rung for victory at Alamein. And now we could hear the village church bells ringing and, a few minutes later–from across the River Severn–came the peal of bells from Quatt. And in the distance, more church bells; from where, we couldn't tell. Gradually, we were aware of other odd sounds. Horns honking, bicycle bells jingling. Hooters, rattles and–cheering. We crept down the driveway and to look through the gates into the village. People were out, dancing in the street, calling, hugging, laughing, kissing – and crying.

"They've gone bonkers," said Ann-the-Bank.

"I think they mean it," said Ant. "I think the war really *is* over."

"Does that mean we can go home?" I asked.

"I don't know," he replied. "We don't even know if we have homes to go to."

"No, I s'pose not."

We were still wondering what all the fuss was about, when Miss Audrey-Joan and the other grown-ups came running down the driveway. "Come, children," she said. "Come on. Let's join in the fun."

We all followed her, as though she was the Pied Piper. Out of the school property, onto the Bridgnorth road, and over to the village square, bordered on one side by the Dog and Cock and the church on the other. People were streaming out of their houses. Talking, laughing, shaking each other's hands. I'd never seen so much hugging and kissing. Housewives were banging pots and pans with spoons, bicycle bells were jangling, and children were clickety-clacking sticks up and down the church railings–anything to make a racket. Someone was blowing a bugle, and I could hear the whine of bagpipes tuning up. Drums were beating.

"Here!" A village child shoved a frying pan in my hands.

I looked at Ant, "What...?"

He picked up a stick and started banging it. We both grinned. We Normanhursters mingled with the village children and started leaping, banging, screaming and shouting along with them. The only thing the village children could do that we couldn't, was whistle piercingly through their teeth. As little ladies and gentlemen, we'd never learned to do THAT.

Roagey-Mac and Lady Harriet arrived in the trap and joined in the celebrations. People kept on coming, until the small square was packed–all of them laughing, cheering and crying. Yes, crying! Such a commotion we'd never seen before. And amongst real people, too. Amongst our village neighbours, whom we'd only seen at church on sundays, but never met during the five years we'd been shut away behind high stone walls and holly hedges.

From somewhere, a gramophone played. Or was it the wireless? Vera Lynn was singing *The White Cliffs of Dover* and *When Johnny comes Marching Home*. Then, accompanied by the assortment of musical instruments people were playing, the crowd started singing: *Land of Hope and Glory, Rule Britannia,* and *Jerusalem.* The whole village was singing. Roagey-Mac swung me up in his arms and on up onto his shoulders. Even though he was not very tall, I sat up there and watched the throng of people cheering and celebrating.

When trays of beer came out from the Dog and Cock to be passed around, Miss Audrey-Joan started rounding us up to go back to Normanhurst. Time had flown by and it was dusk. In straggling groups, we headed back for the big iron gates and The Manor House, which was our home. We walked up the driveway, and gathered in a group on the front lawn. Silent, we stared at the great house, we couldn't believe our eyes. Every single window was lit up and light spilled out over the driveway, over the lawns and onto our faces. Throughout all the years of blackout, not a chink of light had been allowed to escape from the blinds or the huge wooden shutters; closed tight from dusk til dawn.

And now, on this night, every window was ablaze with light. Welcoming us home.

"Gosh," said Ant. "I've never seen anything like that before."

"Neither have I," I replied. "It's so...so *bright*. Even the stars look brighter."

Ant looked up at the sky. "I think the war really *is* over," he said.

The next day, the telephone rang incessantly from parents and friends calling Miss Audrey-Joan. My mother called and I spoke to her. "Am I coming home?" was my first question.

"Of course, darling. At the end of term. We have to make sure we get our house back from the government. Besides, Daddy won't be demobbed for a few weeks yet."

"What's demobbed?"

"Released from the army. There's a lot of red tape to be sorted out first. But I promise he'll be home by the time you get here."

I had to be content with that. But my mother's words disturbed me. *"Make sure we get our house back? Daddy won't be demobbed yet. And what was red tape?"*

Mummy and Daddy had just become names on the letters I'd had to write every Sunday. It was hard to remember what living with them was like, and I'd forgotten most of what my home ever looked like. I had vague recollections of my nursery, and some of my toys, and my Nanny whom I'd hated, and called 'Naughty Nimmy.. And Dilly, whom I loved, was now married to John-the-Post, and living on a farm in Wales.

I would have to leave Miss Audrey-Joan, Mr. and Mrs. B, Mrs. Tommy, Miss Primrose and Gatsby, Lady Harriet and Roagey-Mac, Dolly, and Tristan. Even Bossy Bella, and Ann-the-Bank would be gone. And Ant would be gone; I would be an only child again.

I wouldn't have my little "corner" by the Aga. Or Merlin's Lair. Or... or Ant.

"I don't want to go home. This is my home now. Perhaps it would have been better if the war hadn't ended."

I couldn't get to sleep that night.

After prayers the next morning, Miss Audrey-Joan announced that this day would be a holiday–to celebrate Victory in Europe. After dinner, we would all go to the pictures as a special treat.

None of us minded the long walk into Bridgnorth. We hopped and skipped along the road, not bothering to keep the crocodile neat and straight–only taking care to move to the side of the road when any traffic came along. Every house, cottage, and shop we passed, had Union Jacks flying and big notices saying things like, 'My darling is coming home,' 'Wee Georgie is on his way,' and 'God Save the King.' Pictures of Winston Churchill giving the big "V" for Victory sign were everywhere.

We trudged up the hill to High Town and joined the queue outside the Majestic Cinema. Chattering and laughing, we hopped from one foot to another in excitement. The lady in the ticket booth told Miss Audrey-Joan that we could all get in for thruppence apiece, "Seeing as it's a celebration, like." We filed into the cinema, each one of us remembering to thank the lady.

The picture show was all fun. *The Keystone Cops,* some Charlie Chaplin adventures and a Mickey Mouse cartoon. When the last picture was over, we were all waiting for the lights to go on when the *Movietone News* started up. This was exciting because it showed all the celebrations that were going on in London; people jumping in fountains and climbing all over the statue of Eros in Piccadilly Circus. Then came pictures of soldiers sitting on tanks and lorries, being driven through the bombed cities in Europe. Everyone was waving and throwing flowers at them. We all stood up; cheering and waving too. The picture changed again. The voice of the news reporter changed. There was no more cheering, no more waving. What followed, I will remember vividly for the rest of my life.

Walking skeletons. Naked skeletons. Claw-like hands reaching out to soldiers. Crying skeletons. Crying soldiers. Silent skeletons. Silent soldiers. More skeletons; some half-naked, some in striped shifts. Great black eyes in sunken white skulls.

I reached for Ant's hand and grabbed it. His nails were sharp as they bit into my palm.

Another picture. A more horrifying picture I'd never seen. A mound of skeletons. Not crying, not moving. Silenced for ever. Skeletons piled one on top of another. A heap of dead skeletons. Some tall, some very short–child-size. Cedric's size.

I stared at the screen. Transfixed by the horror, I couldn't move. I wanted to scream, "STOP!"

Then the picture went black. There was no more sound. No more skeletons. Nothing. I felt someone's–a grownup's–hands on my shoulders. The hands turned me and guided me out of the cinema. It was empty. Just Ant and me being led outside.

Outside I blinked, dazzled by the bright sun on that May afternoon. We gathered in silent groups. I stood, dazed and unaware of what was going on around me; except I knew Ant was beside me. Another hand guided me into our crocodile line. No one spoke. Even on the way home, no one spoke, laughed, skipped, or sang. We just walked. I didn't notice where I was walking, or how far it was. All I could think of were those living, moving, silent skeletons. And the mound of dead ones. Particularly the dead ones. Ant walked in silence beside me.

I don't remember much about the rest of the day, until Ant and I went out to Merlin's Lair after tea. We sat under the old crab-apple tree and watched the changing colours of the sky as the sun dipped, until we heard the bell for baths and bed.

I spat out the grass stalk I'd been chewing on. "So where *was* that? What we saw."

"I heard someone say they were camps where Hitler put people he didn't like."

"And children?"

"Yes. And children."

"So that was the war, then?"

"I s'pose so, yes. That was the war."

With sleep came the nightmares. All I could see in my dreams, were skeletons. Mounds of skeletons. Everyone I knew was a skeleton. And Cedric . . .

My screams woke me up. Just like the other time, when Hamlet was sacrificed, Miss Audrey-Joan swept me off to her bed. She held me close. My tears soaked the front of her nightgown. But she didn't seem to mind.

When the getting-up bell woke me, I was back in my own bed, with Tristan curled up on my pillow. I lay there for a few minutes, thinking about the nightmares, and what had happened the day before. I didn't feel like breakfast, but I got dressed and went downstairs anyway. I was heading for the back door, when Miss Audrey-Joan saw me, "No breakfast, Pat?"

"I...I don't feel hungry. I'm going outside. To the orchard...for a walk." I knew this didn't sound convincing, but she seemed to understand.

"Why don't I come with you."

It was a soft, warm morning. I scuffed the dew, making dark trails on the grass. We didn't speak until we reached the five-barred gate.

"Where do you want to walk, Pat?" And she looked straight over at the corner where Merlin's Lair was hiding behind tall brambles and hawthorne.

I nodded towards the Tree-that-was-Really-a-Pirate-Ship. So many things had happened there, especially in the sandy spot, below the great roots. It was there, she and I had talked about where Cedric might be after he drowned. We walked over to it and sat down; and although she never knew it, with Bubble's buried treasure beneath us. I noticed the twigs marking the "X" had been blown away.

She turned to me. "Now, Pat. Tell me what's bothering you?"

"Yesterday...at the cinema...."

She leaned over and smoothed back the hair from my eyes. "You know, I never wanted you children to see those news pictures. I didn't know they would be shown. I'm really sorry."

All I could do was nod. We were both silent for a while. Then she went on, "Remember, we talked about sacrifices for the War. Well, there were some who made much greater sacrifices. And those people in the concentration camps...well...only God knows the sacrifices they made."

I nodded.

"But although, we cannot...and we must *never* forget the awful things that happened in the War, it's over now and you have to look forward. Just think. Soon you'll be leaving us and going home to your parents.

"But I don't want to go home."

"You...don't...? What are you saying, Pat?"

"I don't want to go home. I want to stay here. With you and Mr. and Mrs. B and...and everybody. I've forgotten what my home is like and I don't even know if it's still there."

"Of course it's still there. I had a letter from your mother saying that the government left it in an awful mess, with dozens of black telephones in every room." She grinned. "The government always has a lot of telephones, I hear."

"So my home is still there? And Mummy and Daddy will be there too?"

"Oh, yes. By the end of the term, they will have got it all back to ship-shape fashion."

"But...I won't know anyone. And all my friends are here. Lady Harriet, and Ant."

"Ant will be leaving too, you know."

"He will?"

"Yes. And I believe he's going to Bromsgrove, where your father teaches. So I'm sure you'll see something of him. Besides, you're going to Alice Ottley in Worcester, and that's a very good school."

I sighed. I was so used to being at Normanhurst, and I really didn't want everything to change.

"Besides," Miss Audrey-Joan went on, "don't forget you'll be making lots of new friends at Alice Ottley. And another, very important thing you have to remember."

"What's that?"

"Your parents. They've missed you so very much. And they are longing to have you back. Your mother did mention in her letter to me that they were hoping to be able to open up your summer place in Cornwall again soon."

"Cornwall. The golden sand. The sea. The white horses."

"It's time to move on, Pat. It's time to grow up. You will soon be eleven, and it's all part of growing up. I'm sure you'll never forget the years here, with us at Normanhurst, but there are much, much more exciting times ahead. And adventures too!"

"Growing up? I'd been grown up for years." But I nodded and smiled at Miss Audrey-Joan–my friend.

"Anyway," she said. "You won't be so far away. And you can always write to us."

"Yes, I will. I'll write to you."

"Good girl. And now I think we'd better be getting back. Assembly starts in five minutes."

"Yes, Miss Baker."

She got up and brushed the sand from her skirt. She didn't notice that I'd replaced the twigs in an "X" marking the spot. This time I'd weighted them down with a stone.

Chapter 43

Time to go

The end of the summer term came too soon. Even though we didn't have many lessons that last few weeks, we still had to write our 'end of year' exams. When those were out of the way, we had sports days, tournaments, and cricket and rounders matches; Normans vs. Saxons. Ant and I won the tennis again, both our own singles and the doubles.

Of course, there was the annual Commemoration Day to which all the parents were invited. Not only did we receive awards and prizes, but Miss Primrose had organized a complicated entertainment programme. A demonstration of Greek dancing, a concert, and a dramatic production that included parts of Act II of *A Midsummer Night's Dream*. We used the Sunken Garden as a stage.

"From Camelot to a Shakespearean Theatre–was this really goodbye?"

After that the children started to leave. The dailies and the weeklies went home with their parents. By Friday, there were only four of us left. So many goodbyes. Most were happy to go because they would be seeing each other again in September when the Autumn term began and when Normanhurst became just an ordinary school, instead of an evacuation school. But some of us were leaving for ever.

I'd said goodbye to Ann-the-Bank on Thursday. Her mam and her da came and packed all her stuff—and Ann—into a little old car and took her back to Wales.

"I thought we would be best friends forever. I never saw her again."

The four-bed dormitory that we'd shared the past two years with Alana and Emma Simon was deserted. The mattresses were rolled up into sausages, one at the end of each empty bed. All the pictures, the teddy bears and toys were gone; just a few unwanted clothes-hangers swung on the wardrobe rail. My trunk was on the floor–packed but not closed; I still had one more night. And I still had one last letter to write to Cedric.

"Come on," said Ant, "Let's go to the orchard."

He took off, running down the path between our Victory Garden patches on one side and the Rabbit Hole on the other, towards the five-barred gate. He didn't bother to open the gate. In one leap and a bound he vaulted on to the top bar of the gate and landed in the long grass on the other side. I followed, scrambling up to the top bar and stood looking down at him.

"You could have landed in horse manure," I said disapprovingly. "Mr. B says you should always look before you leap."

"I did."

"You couldn't've, you went too fast."

Ant didn't reply but loped off across the orchard. I knew where he was going so, after carefully choosing my landing spot, I jumped down and followed. We made for the far right hand corner of the orchard, behind the Tree-that-was-Really-a-Pirate-Ship, to Merlin's Lair. Hidden behind a stand of blackberry brambles and a self-seeded holly bush, it was so tangled with long prickly canes that it looked impossible to penetrate. However, at one end, between a rock and an old tree stump, tall grasses concealed a small tunnel. Ant said a witch had passed by and, seeing a good hiding place, had put a spell on it so that she could get in and park her broomstick. But I knew it was Cedric who guarded the secret hideaway. Amazingly, no-one else had found it, and we always made sure no-one ever saw us go there. A hole in a small sandy bank under the old crab-apple tree had always been our secret hiding place. Years ago, I'd taken an old Players Navy Cut tobacco tin from Mr. B's shed to store my treasures in.

"We'd better get all our stuff out," said Antony. "This is the last time we'll be here."

I felt sad about that. This was a magical place and right now honeysuckle and wild roses covered the farmer's hedge, and the bright July sun filled the hollow with warmth. I stuck my hand down the hole to haul out our tins. "There's an extra tin," I said. "There should only be two."

Antony took the third, a blue and gold patterned 'Blackcurrant and Glycerine' cough drop tin from me, and put it down beside him.

"What's in there?" I demanded.

"Just some things."

"What things?"

"I'll show you in a sec."

I opened my tin. It contained all the treasures I'd collected during the past five years. The champion hopscotch stone of all time, perfect weight, size, and shape. A piece of shrapnel from the German plane. My pirate earring. A bright shiny button. And a small twist of golden hair. I held it in the palm of my hand, remembering that awful day.

"Bubble?" asked Ant.

I nodded. "I took it from his jumper button."

We sat in silence for a while. I couldn't believe I would never be in this place again. This safe, private little place where I could go, knowing that I was where no-one could find me.

"Merlin's Lair. Cedric. Cedric, slayer of dragons and my friend forever."

And then I remembered. I pushed my arm as far as I could down the little hole under the old crab-apple tree. The sandy soil was cold. I stretched my fingers out–carefully, cautiously. And then I felt it; round, hard, and cold.

"I've found it," I said.

"Found what?"

"Cedric's Allie." My hand closed around it and I pulled it out. I brushed the dirt away and cleaned it with the hem of my frock. I held it up. The sunlight caught the myriad of ribbon twists inside the little glass ball, then bounced back into my eyes. The light was so bright, that Merlin's Lair glowed, and–for an instant–I thought I saw Cedric; smiling, and reaching out his hand for the Allie. Then the sun went behind a cloud and he was gone. I put the marble in my tin.

"We could stay here for ever and no-one would ever find us. We wouldn't have to go to s- school, or...or s-say goodbye." I was stuttering and I didn't know why.

"We'd get awfully hungry," replied Ant, maddeningly practical. "And we'd get wet when it rained."

I didn't reply. I couldn't think of anything to say.

Ant caught sight of the button in my tin."What's that?"

"Oh that? I found that when we were on Night Ops. It's just a button." I handed it to him.

"It's a button from a Jerry uniform. It must have been the pilot's." His eyes sparkled as he looked at. "I say, what a jolly cracking souvenir."

"Why don't you keep it? It'll remind you of the most scathingly-brilliant adventure we ever had."

"Are you sure?"

I nodded. "It's from me to you. To remember."

"Thank you...thank you very much." Ant turned the button over and over, then laid it in his tin with the shrapnel. "So what have you got to remember the adventure by? Now that you've given me the button."

I thought for a moment, "I've got Edward Bear." I grinned, "Edward's good at keeping secrets, but he'll remind me!"

"Good old Edward Bear," said Ant.

I laid back on the grass, looked up at the sky, and thought how I really didn't want to leave. I wanted to stay here for ever with Mr. and Mrs. B, Miss Audrey-Joan and the cats and Dolly. And Ant. I couldn't even remember what the house, that I hadn't seen since I was five, looked like. And I certainly didn't want to go to a new school where there were four hundred girls I didn't know. And my father was coming home. Trying to recall his face was difficult. I hadn't seen him for so long. How would I talk to him and what would he say to me? Would it be like talking with Mr. B? And I definitely didn't want to be an only child again.

Lost in my own thoughts, I didn't hear Ant move but I realized he was lying very close to me. I turned my head and he was staring at me. His big grey eyes were looking straight into mine and I could feel his breath on my cheek. "I'm going to marry you when I grow up," he said.

"Marry me?" I must have sounded like an echo.

"Yes. We promised to be best friends for ever. That means we'll get married when we're old enough."

This didn't exactly sound like all the romances I had read about. The ones where the handsome prince rode in on a white charger and knelt at the princess's feet and kissed her hand. Ant was handsome all right, but he had dirty smudges on his face and grass stains on his knees. I didn't say anything. His face was very close to mine.

"When two people are going to get married, they kiss each other," he told me.

I still didn't say anything.

"May I kiss you?"

"If you want to." I moved my cheek roughly to the point where his mouth was and waited.

"It's got to be on the lips," he said. "When two people are going to get married, they kiss on the lips."

I knew very well he was right–at least according to all the books I'd read–but I asked, "Who said so?"

"My sister."

"What does she know?"

"Everything. She goes to Cheltenham Ladies College."

"All right," I said. "But you can't see my thing." I remembered time spent behind the Kindergarten room. Besides, when Arabella Bosworthy wanted Martin Stapleton to kiss her, he said he would, but she had to show him her thing.

"I don't want to see your thing," he replied. "I've seen my sister's."

"All right then. But just a little one." I turned my head towards him and closed my eyes.

A feather touch somewhere between my chin and my bottom lip. A tiny moment and it was gone. Somehow, I felt disappointed.

Antony lifted his head. I opened my eyes and stared at his face. Grey eyes, eyelashes that were longer than mine and thick eyebrows. A lock of his black hair had fallen onto the bridge of his nose and one of those incredible eyebrows peaked as he put his head on one side and smiled.

"How *do* you do that?" I asked

"Do what?"

"Lift one eyebrow."

"It's a family thing. My daddy does it and so does my sister."

I tried to do the same, but my efforts only made him laugh. "You're very pretty," he said.

I knew enough to say 'thank you.'

"And you're very handsome. You look just like that picture of Sir Lancelot in Miss Audrey-Joan's book of King Arthur."

Ant didn't reply, but he looked pleased. "I've got a present for you," he said, picking up the blue and gold tin he'd stashed in the roots of the old crab-apple tree. "Actually, I've got two presents for you."

I was mightily curious but I remembered my manners and, saying nothing, sat up and folded my hands in my lap, and waited.

He opened the tin, took out two small objects and closed his fist over them. "I'm trying to decide which one to give you first," he said. He placed one of the objects behind his back on the grass. The other he held out for me to take.

"Thank you," I said primly. "Thank you very much." I studied the small flat stone. It was a sandy colour, and very flat.

"Turn it over, you've got it wrong way up."

I turned the little pebble over and saw, embedded in its surface, the perfect outline of a tiny fish. It was fascinating. I could see the head, one eye and a small ridged body, ending in a perfectly shaped tail. "It's so beautiful," I said.

"It's a fossil," Ant explained. "It's millions of years old. My uncle gave it to me. He said he found it in the wild African wilderness when he was on safari."

"You don't find fish in the wild African wilderness."

"That's why it's so special. That's why I want you to have it."

"I think it is perfectly amazing, and I'll keep it forever."

Ant retrieved the second object from behind him and, taking my hand, and carefully placed it in my hand. "This is to plight thee my troth," he said; his face turning a little pink.

On the palm of my hand lay a small ring. It was a glowing brown colour with flecks of gold and black, like the eye of a cat.

"It's made of tortoiseshell," he said. "I didn't know whether to give it to you because of Henry VIII. But then I thought it would be all right because it isn't exactly Henry, and it would remind you of him when you don't have him any more." That, for Antony, was a very long speech.

I peered closely at the ring, and saw a little pattern had been carved into the surface. Little squirls and squiggles that made it glint in the sunshine. "It is so pretty. I've never seen anything like this before. Thank you very much. Did your uncle give you this too?"

"No I got it out of my sister's sewing box, that Christmas when I went home."

I looked up, horrified. "You took it without her knowing. You stole it."

"Of course not. I said I was looking for a present for somebody and could I have something out of her box. She was busy, and said I could take anything I liked except her silver thimble. So I chose this. She's what my Mummy calls a hoarder anyway. She's always picking up stuff from any-old-where and hoarding it. Mummy says, by the time she's an old lady she'll have so much junk, we won't be able to find her amongst it."

"Am I supposed to wear it on my finger?"

"If you want to."

I tried it. It was far too big, and it fell off. We both laughed.

"I'll keep it in a special place with the fish fossil until my finger gets fatter."

"Here," said Ant, digging in his pocket. He pulled out a piece of green garden string and, taking the ring from me, threaded the string through it and tied it in a knot. Then he slipped it over my head. "There! Now I plight thee my troth."

"I think you'd better kiss me again and then it will be properly plighted." I turned my head back towards him until my nose was almost touching his. He moved his head forward and pressed his lips against my tightly closed and puckered ones. His lips felt soft and warm and the tips of our noses were touching. I closed my eyes, let the pucker out of my lips and took the softness and nearness into my mind and into my heart. I could smell the grass stains, and the sweaty dampness of his hair. I could feel his hands on my shoulders and they were gentle.

Antony kissed me again, and I fell in love forever.

We swung on the five-barred gate. There was a finality about the way it clanged shut. Still standing on the second bar, our forearms draped over the top, we looked out and across the old orchard at Normanhurst Preparatory School. And we knew we would never, ever see it again.

Neither of us spoke; each remembering the adventures and the good times. The Tree-that-was-Really-a-Pirate-Ship, Merlin's Lair, and Farmer Bourne's fields beyond, where Paddy had taken me on the ride of my life, and where the German plane had crashed.

"I still have to write to Cedric," I said. "What shall I tell him?"

"Tell him you found his Allie."

So I did.

The End

CPSIA information can be obtained at www.ICGtesting.com
Printed in the USA
LVOW10s1516061014

407464LV00002B/405/P